THE MUSHROOM-PICKER

THE MUSHROOM-PICKER

A Novel by
Zinovy Zinik

TRANSLATED FROM THE RUSSIAN
BY MICHAEL GLENNY

ST. MARTIN'S PRESS
NEW YORK

For information, address St. Martin's Press, 175 Fifth Avenue, New York, N.Y. 10010.

Library of Congress Cataloging-in-Publication Data

Zinik, Zinovy.
The Mushroom-picker.
Translation of: Russofobka i fungofil.

I. Title.
PG3490.I495R8813 1989 859'.334 88-29844
ISBN 0-312-02616-1

First published in Great Britain by William Heinemann Ltd.

First U.S. Edition

10 9 8 7 6 5 4 3 2 1

THE MUSHROOM-PICKER

1 HEARTBURN

Marriage to a foreigner and consequent emigration *in partes infidelium* do not go unpunished: he felt sick and his guts were churning with heartburn. The acts so rashly committed by his insatiable reason were being repudiated by his squeamish stomach. Bile was rising up his gullet, burning everything in its path like napalm, blurring his vision with the acrid fumes of the fire in his thorax. Everything around him seemed loathsome: the English lawn, trimmed to a military crew-cut; the English garden furniture – those agonisingly uncomfortable iron chairs and a wobbly little table painted hospital white; the English sun, clearly suffering from persecution mania as it glanced out panic-stricken from behind the clouds; and finally those English faces, white and eyeless, like the huge toadstools that grow among the sickeningly green grass of a cemetery – the kind of fungus that one so enjoys kicking in passing with the toe of one's gumboot or slashing with a hazel-switch.

As he belched without bothering to cover his mouth with

his hand, Kostya instantly caught the censorious glance of his wife and mistress of the house, Nuclea. Her name was really Clea, but in his irritated mind she was nicknamed 'Nuclea', since for as long as he could remember the words 'nuclear bomb' had scarcely left her lips.

Nuclea was a militant pacifist. At the moment, however, she was ready to exterminate her Russian husband, to wipe him from the face of the earth by a World-War-Three nuclear explosion, provided the conflict could have been limited to the area occupied by his eructating gut. Unfortunately this nuclear strike would also have obliterated the fruits of her years of peacetime effort – the little four-roomed house behind them and the little four-metre-square patch of lawn on which they were sitting. The house, of course, was hardly a mansion, and when Kostya went to the toilet on the first floor (Clea tried unsuccessfully to insist on him calling the lavatory 'the toilet', instead of using that disgusting pseudo-French Russian word '*sortir*'), the sitting-room door downstairs had to be firmly shut because he emitted such monstrous sounds when discharging his natural functions that a nuclear explosion might well have been taking place inside his body.

But such prolonged sessions of solitary meditation were as nothing compared to those occasions at night upon the connubial couch when Clea was woken up by the rumbling of his stomach – small wonder, when one considered those tons of dressed lamb, beef and pork; all those miles of Italian sausage and salami rammed into twisted lengths of bulls' intestines; those endless kidneys and acres of tripe; those geese's necks and chickens' gizzards. . . Clea would have visions of apocalyptic caravans of decapitated cows, gutted sheep, birds with their necks wrung, all of them bleating, bellowing and squawking until these sounds merged into the single noise of Kostya's rumbling stomach. And now Kostya was sitting in front of her, his hands smeared with blood, and belching.

'Go and drink some bicarbonate,' she said in English, but Konstantin pretended not to hear – or not to understand: his modest command of English would disappear without trace somewhere into his rectum whenever she said anything to him that his mind found indigestible. It was not surprising that he had become terribly rude and unpredictable. The worst was his unpredictability: he was ignoring her advice about bicarbonate of soda and Clea was now trying to guess what trick he might pull in order to settle his stomach in a way consistent with his barbaric propensities. There had, in fact, been a time when he used to insist that during large meals one should follow the precepts of the French and the ancient Romans, namely to vomit after every third course in order to relieve the stomach and consequently the soul, since body and soul are one. This time, thank God, the menu of the lunch to celebrate the first visit of Margot and Anthony to the new house had not exceeded the standard four courses.

For a 'starter' Clea had served boiled globe artichokes with garlic mayonnaise, but Kostya had announced that he couldn't stand boiled vegetables, forgetting his predilection, in his Moscow days, for reading out French recipes from Marcel Proust, which were stuffed with artichokes on every page. He had, however, consumed single-handed almost all the mayonnaise by soaking his bread in it. For his sake bread had had to be served in gigantic quantities, so that there was practically none left for cheese at the end of the meal – and to buy those French baguettes Clea had been obliged to traipse off to a special bakery in Covent Garden, while Konstantin had simply devoured this crusty exotica as though it were ordinary English sliced bread in a plastic wrapper from the supermarket. He invariably ate bread without cease, indeed he could eat nothing without bread; he was never without a slice of it in his hand, as though someone might be planning to take it away from him, so that one of his hands was always occupied – the same hand that is meant to hold a knife when one is eating. Perhaps this was why Konstantin never used a knife while he ate; as a result, he had to tear the uncut morsel with his teeth directly from the fork, and so, in order to prevent the hunk of food from dropping off his fork, he would lean over his plate as though in the middle of a fit of vomiting.

Clea had averted her eyes throughout the meal. Yet he had, she knew very well, a double-bladed knife that he kept for his own special purposes, so far unknown to her, though clearly not for eating. Clea shrugged her shoulders. The immoderate consumption of bread she could just about excuse as a legacy of Konstantin's Russian past, with its centuries of hunger and high mortality from starvation. But he had also refused the main course, a vegetable stew with carrots, blanched cauliflower and cooked tomatoes. He had said: 'I think there is not a cholera epidemic in England at this moment, so why dip the tomatoes in boiling water?' Then why, Clea wondered, had he ignored the side-dish of raw celery, chopped walnuts and sprouting barley? And so on throughout the meal. Yet he knew with what care she had steeped the sprouting barley, being aware of how fastidious Margot and Anthony were about such things.

'There is a little of the horse in all of us,' Margot had joked in Russian, referring to the barley, quoting Mayakovsky to show off her familiarity with Russian poetry. 'Where is that line from?' Clea tried feverishly to place the quotation. 'Is it from Akhmatova – or Pasternak? Perhaps it's from Mandelstam.' Putting on an understanding look, Clea made use of the remark to change the subject, and turned the conversation to people's attitudes to horses, in connection with the bomb that had exploded in Hyde Park and which, in addition to injuring several troopers of the Royal Horse Guards, had struck down several horses.

Clea said that for all her love of animals and her hatred of both the monarchy and the Household Cavalry, she was amazed at the dehumanisation of the British public. The newspapers had reported that voluntary contributions of money towards the treatment of the wounded horses had greatly exceeded the cost of treating the wounded troopers, and that some rich aristocrat had even paid for a hearse and a gravestone for one of the slaughtered geldings. To which

Anthony had replied that for all his contempt for the excessive horse-worship of the aristocracy, he considered that in this particular incident the horses, unlike the men involved, were innocent victims; the Household Cavalry, after all, forced the animals to be used for militaristic and reactionary monarchist purposes, and that whereas the troopers would in any case be cared for by the government, the horses stood in need, as never before, of charitable assistance. But Margot said that Anthony had better keep quiet about his humane attitude to animals – hadn't he driven their cat, Ivan, insane? In the name of kindness to all living creatures he had hung a bell round Ivan's neck so that its tinkling would warn off all the wee birdies and the mice. Yet when those same mice had then started to overrun their kitchen, Anthony, without a moment's hesitation, had bought arsenic at the chemist and massacred all the little mousikins at one fell swoop. And that was called being humane. But the fact that this humane bell perpetually ringing behind his ear had driven Ivan the cat to hysterics and hallucinations, which had led to having him put down – none of this had mattered a jot to Anthony. His only concern was that the cat should never eat a mouse or a bird and thus should not consume the flesh of a fellow creature. In other words, what mattered to him was that the cat, like himself, should be a vegetarian.

Dodging the approaching conjugal row, the sensible Anthony turned to Konstantin and exerted instead his knowledge of Russian: 'Bourgeois democracy eventually made meat easy and cheap to buy for millions of masses. In pre-industrial periods meat was accessive only between aristocrats. In present situation, though, meat, cheap for millions, has made mass aggressiveness from overconsuming meat and leads to wars of popular genocide instead of tourneys between knights of aristocracy.'

Anthony took a deep breath and added fervently:

'But who benefit of this? Industrial aristocracy, how else? Put question, please: is meat accessive for population in Russia?'

And Anthony stared keenly at Konstantin with the fervour

of a committed debater. Konstantin did not even realise that he was being asked a question.

'Anthony is asking you: is meat available to the Russian masses?' Clea could no longer stand Konstantin's idiotic silence.

'Everything is available to the Russian masses,' Kostya at last condescended to reply. And belched again.

'But is that really so?' Anthony replied eagerly, switching to English. 'We know very well that there are meat shortages in Russia. Clea will confirm it. There's simply nothing to eat. Of course I sympathise with the toiling masses, but one must face facts, after all! Either there is unbridled militarism, like here in the West, or there are food shortages, as in Russia. But at least, the result is that the population has not been depraved by eating meat and is consequently not aggressive and the militaristic instincts in their blood haven't been stirred up. I prefer the hollow liberalism of the stomach to the fascist gluttony of the brain. Lack of meat in the shops is a guarantee of the sincere intentions of the Soviet government in its negotiations on nuclear disarmament. That's what Western governments in their blindness can't understand . . .' His train of thought petered out. He could not finish the sentence, because his thoughts were slithering away from him along with the slice of banana which kept inexorably sliding off his spoon back into the viscous syrup of his bowl of fruit salad.

'The other day Margot and I were rereading old Aldous Huxley – his pacificist novel *Eyeless in Gaza* – have you read it? It's not about the Palestinians, although geographically it's the same Gaza, but what I mean is . . .' and he began to explain specially for the benefit of the slow-witted Konstantin. 'The title is taken from Milton's poem about Samson, you know – the biblical hero who was deprived of his hair and consequently of his strength, thanks to his weakness for the fair sex. The Bible is forbidden in Russia, that's why I'm explaining it at such length – it is forbidden, isn't it? And Milton too?'

But Konstantin was looking past him into the distance with a glassy stare, like a blind man poisoned by gas. His hand was mechanically crumbling a piece of bread, and his moving fingers were the only evidence that a man and not a scarecrow was sitting in front of them. The birds, however, took him to be a statue, and ravenous flocks of them were attacking his crumbs of bread, quite undeterred. In this city, by the way, they were all as tame and well-trained as primary schoolchildren. Right under Konstantin's nose was a feathered creature with a red breast and a wagging tail: a wagtail? or a bullfinch? – Kostya wondered idly. Even if it were a wagtail, its Russian name did not correspond to the bird which, had it flown to Russia, would have been called a wagtail, but here it was called. . . . God knows what. Words corresponded to objects only when those objects were carried across a frontier.

'In Russian "*milton*" is a slang word for a militiaman – a policeman,' said Kostya aloud, but the remark was meant for himself, in order to convince himself that he still had not forgotten his mother tongue. He flicked a bread-ball at the wagtail, but missed it, and the missile landed in Anthony's bowl instead.

'Oh, really? . . . Doesn't matter . . .' Anthony mumbled, blushing, as he tried to fish the bread-ball out of his bowl without being noticed. He caught the unwavering stare of Konstantin's impudently blue eyes. This strange Russian – what was he? A barbarian, obtuse but invincible, one of those whose cavalry would trample over his, Anthony's, fragile Western civilisation? Or was he, on the contrary, a cunning and unscrupulous envoy of the new Rome, the Soviet empire, and Anthony an ancient Greek, effete from centuries-old wisdom and the refinements of culture, whose feather-bed was about to be stamped on by this legionary from the land of Scythia? Whichever it was, there was force in this bony Slav, while there was the wisdom of civilisation in Anthony the Englishman, who would have liked to use that wisdom to bridle the latent savagery of this dangerous upstart – or to be seized by that force, impregnated by it, merged with it in a single embrace as had been the wise Greek with the mighty Roman, having first given him nectar to drink and softened him with sweet-smelling unguents in the great baths of the ancient world, with their masseurs, their wines and their fruits.

'Anyway, there is one remarkable saying by Huxley in this book . . .' Anthony addressed himself once more to a stub-end of banana that still insisted on sliding off his spoon. 'An alliance with jingoistic nationalism still seems too vulgar for our liberal intellectuals to stomach . . .' Once again Anthony hesitated. 'Or rather, no, I'm wrong. What was the wording, Margot?' But Margot did not come to his rescue. Finally, losing patience and abandoning good manners, Anthony fished out the piece of banana with two fingers, popped it into his mouth and said, smacking his lips: 'Delicious fruit salad! In other words old man Huxley was right: intellectually our reactionaries are still attached to democracy. Their stomachs, however, their guts – their essential nature, in fact – have long since been ripe for fascism: meat and blood, meat and blood! And no milk please!' He pulled away the cup of tea over which his hostess was obligingly tilting a milk jug. 'The true vegetarian, Clea, doesn't use milk. After all, in what way is milk preferable to eggs, which are simply unhatched chicks?!'

'If I were you I'd stop repeating second-hand ideas from Aldous Huxley. In any case, vegetarianism nowadays is as popular with right-wingers as it is with the left. And when *will* you learn to use a table napkin?' said the sceptical Margot through gritted teeth, who had not failed to notice Anthony trying to wipe his fruit-syrupy fingers on the table-leg.

Aggrieved, Anthony started rattling a teaspoon in his cup of tea, stirring non-existent sugar. It had been on Margot's instructions that he had extracted the aphorism about the liberalism of the intellect contrasted with the latent fascism of the stomach, and he was hoping to insert it into his speech the following day at a protest meeting against the deployment of nuclear missiles on British territory – and thus to make a witty transition to a venomous critique of the generally more aggressive tendencies of the British conservative establishment, with its traditional bloody roast beef on Sundays and its turkey at Christmas. But Margot had upset him with her unkind piece of sarcasm; the fact that there were plenty of right-wing vegetarians somehow didn't fit into the logic of the speech he was planning for tomorrow.

'It's not a matter of left and right or East and West, but the aggressive way that people greet any new idea,' said Anthony in an offended voice, turning to Margot. She had a gift of phrasing everything in a way that made anyone who disagreed with her look mentally deficient. She might well, incidentally, learn some vegetarian recipes from her friend Clea. How deliciously she had prepared that sprouting barley! What's more, she knew the Russian recipe for nettle soup. It was said to be very good for high blood pressure, especially useful in the present international situation. Now that would be a really genuine example of East-West collaboration: Russian nettle soup and American sprouting barley, macerated for twenty-four hours. Fat chance of asking Margot for any such thing, though: she couldn't even boil a potato properly, and they did nothing but eat out in restaurants, so it was impossible to relax properly at home after a hard day selling computers.

Anthony glanced surreptitiously at Clea, with her plucked eyebrows, her ash-blonde fringe and pouting lower lip – until now he had somehow never noticed her slender, schoolgirl figure: at home they were always separated by a crowd of friends or at the office by the hierarchical structure of the firm for which they both worked.

'Anthony is absolutely right,' said Clea, plucking up courage after catching a hint in Anthony's remarks that he was referring to her husband's gastronomic tastes. 'The flesh of animals, slaughtered in true fascist style by a racist of the human species, infiltrates the brain cells with fascist instincts through the gut and provokes the people's brains into committing slaughter among their own kind – which is the vengeance wrought by the wretched victims of the animal world against man, the mass-murderer.'

At this moment Konstantin belched for a third time. Clea again noticed Margot and Anthony exchanging glances.

'Go and drink some bicarbonate!' Barely restraining her hysteria, Clea repeated her injunction in a loud and clear voice, this time in Russian. Just to make sure.

'If you mean soda, say so,' Kostya replied languidly and belched again, this time covering his mouth with his hand. 'Excusato,' he said in apology, using a language known only to himself. He was constantly inventing pseudo-Latin words as one way of camouflaging the inadequacy of his English. Excusato! Clea watched unblinking, as Konstantin heaved himself up from the table and set off – not into the kitchen for bicarbonate, but to the far corner of the garden. She was even irritated by his walk, which had lost the briskness and economy of movement that it had once had in Moscow. Perhaps he had always looked as he did now, but it was only here that he had begun to show such obvious signs of a ponderous stoop, a bull-like slope to the neck and the elephantine gait of a man who has had slightly too much to drink. It looked as if, in passing, he was about to aim a kick, with irritable clumsiness, at the painted earthenware gnome that stood guard, among some decorative cobblestones, over Clea's carefully tended part of the garden.

With a fleeting sense of consolation she swept a proprietorial glance over the silken lawn (her keen eye noticed a certain waviness in the grassy surface: this meant it was time to go over it again with the lawn-mower and fiercely remove the patches of curled chestnut leaves, blown there by the wind from the next-door garden), and she made a careful inventory of the selection of flora around the lawn – from the greying locks of the lavender bush to the funereal majesty of the hawthorn, all laid out according to a colour-scheme, as in a florist's nosegay or a carefully-designed birthday cake. Her gardener's pride was shared by the earthenware gnome, who seemed to wink at her, his Snow White. The detractors of petty-bourgeois kitsch despised her for the gnome: Clea had noticed Margot's ironic smirk when they had been inspecting the house, but she had decided there and then not to yield an inch to the legislators of public taste. The gnome was her shield and defence against the tyranny of her previous enthusiasms – her erstwhile addiction to everything Russian, Maoist and feminist, in other words to everything aggressive in human nature. The gnome was the faithful guardian of the pacifist conservatism of her soul, which had been formed from children's books in the local public library, from the glossy illustrations of domestic bliss in women's magazines glanced at on news-stands, and from the television programmes around Christmas time. A conspiracy between the great powers as they flexed their biceps in the arms race and Margot's snobbery were jointly trying to take that gnome away from her. There had been a time when she had hoped that Konstantin would protect her gnome; the gnome would stand guard over house and garden and Kostya would guard the gnome – he would even, she thought, become a gnome himself, the protector of the little garden of her life. But Konstantin had rudely ignored these horticultural projects, and now the only thing he saw before him was the hefty birch-tree that grew in the far corner of the garden.

Around this 'birch corner' was a patch of long grass and weeds no more than two paces in diameter, but Nuclea felt it was like a gigantic pimple on someone's chin, a leprous blight on a rose-bush – in other words, it was her *bête noire*. Firstly, the birch-tree itself, in her view, should have been chopped down long ago and the stump rooted out. Its big, gnarled, lanky trunk was in any case half-withered; one side of it was paralysed, sprouting a few blackened stubs of dead branches like a tree after a nuclear explosion; on the other side of the tree, half-alive and sagging, a few dry, always half-faded leaves hung like some tinkling oriental ornament. If this ugly monster were uprooted one could plant an elegant cypress or even a palm-tree, just to demonstrate that anything could grow in England's green and pleasant land quite as well as in the former British colonies, which would be one more proof of how the nostalgia for colonial times was waning. But Kostya hung on to that birch like a drowning man clutching at a straw. And it was not because the birch reminded him of his abandoned homeland; it was not nostalgia that made him prefer it to a palm or a cypress. In any case, how could *this* tree arouse his nostalgia for Russian birch-trees, when it was standing here in England and not giving a damn about its graceful Russian sisters – indeed, it had been standing here since before Russia was even literate, and if it was withering that was not because it was pining for its Russian sisters but from sheer old age, since this birch had been there at least since the invasion of the Vikings, who, before setting off from Scandinavia to conquer Russia en route to the Greeks, had first sailed to the isles of Albion. It was obviously they who had planted this soil with birches. Thus argued Konstantin, whenever Clea's slender hands itched to pick up an axe.

Konstantin clung on to this birch-tree for the same reasons that he stoutly defended the long grass and weeds that sprawled at random around this half-dead tree. The 'birch corner' stuck out amid the neatly groomed lawn like an incongruous tuft of hair left in the middle of a fashionable haircut by a careless hairdresser; consequently, in Clea's eyes, it made the lawn look like a punk hair-do (according to Kostya, 'punks' must have been the contemptuous name given by the Polish lords to the shaven-headed Zaporozhian Cossacks who affected a single top-knot growing out of the crown of their otherwise clean-shaven head). But Kostya would not allow this ridiculously ugly top-knot to be shorn – under threat of divorcing Clea and returning to Moscow. Although secretly she would have welcomed either of these outcomes, she could not allow herself such a luxury, just as Great Britain could not, shall we say, concede its South Atlantic islands to the Argentine junta: it was a matter of principle, not of justice. Kostya meanwhile defended his patch in the corner of the garden with excuses about the bees needing the dandelions and burdocks, although Clea was well informed about gardening and knew that these weeds harboured destructive little bugs which together with the caterpillars that throve among the plantations were ready at any moment to devour the flower-clusters of the hydrangeas growing behind the earthenware gnome – and even that guardian of horticultural well-being could not prevent it.

Now, after almost knocking over the gnome on the way, Konstantin was pottering around the birch-tree, bent double as he fossicked among the weeds, sniffing for something like a rag-and-bone man in a rubbish dump. Clea averted her gaze from the distressingly pathetic figure of her husband and caught Margot looking at her with a smile intended to look sympathetic but which in fact signalled contempt. Margot looked away.

'Lovely garden, Klava, lovely!' she said, as though hastening to change the subject of their conversation – or rather, their exchange of looks. She always called Clea by her Moscow nickname of 'Klava' whenever she felt embarrassed for her friend. The reference to Moscow implied the sharing between them of a certain happy past, a certain intimate, secret bond, a foundation of permanent, indissoluble affection and friendship that withstood all the revolutionary changes in their attitudes and in their positions in family life and society. It was as if not Clea but Margot (who had never held a gardening tool in her life, except a watering-can) had done nothing but dig flower-beds, replace turf, transplant seedlings and prune shrubs every minute of her free time after an eight-hour working day in Anthony's office. It was all very well for Margot to be the wife of this pacifist vegetarian, who pulled down twenty thousand a year selling computers. Clea, of course, admired his eloquence; she was ready to listen to Anthony from morning till night, but it was a bit much to have to be his secretary, typist and errand-boy all day long on a salary of three hundred a month, half of which went on the mortgage repayments, on the hire-purchase instalments for the refrigerator, the cooker and the washing-machine (of course they could have managed without the washing-machine – there was a launderette just around the corner – but as a child she had hated the sight of her mother, a laundress, as she staggered along the empty streets carrying bundles of the neighbours' washing). It was all too easy to discuss the demise of capitalism sitting on the balcony of Anthony's smart flat in Kensington, where the lawns and flower-beds were mown and watered by a handyman and there was a porter in a peaked cap at the front door.

'Lovely house, Klava, lovely!' Margot repeated as she inspected the new home, as though it were she and not Clea who had stripped off the old wallpaper, drilled holes in the walls and had fumbled around beneath the ceiling with the curtains gripped in her teeth. For a whole year, penny by penny, scrimping and saving, from armchair to table, from table to couch, Clea had built up her conjugal nest and had finally invited this couple of snobs – for what? For Margot to fawn fastidiously as she fingered the lined chintz curtains? To watch Margot stopping herself from bursting into sarcastic laughter at the fireplace, which was faced with special wallpaper made to look like a brick wall? It was all very well to spit on capitalists from a balcony, but what does one do when both the back door and the front door of the house open straight into the capitalist system and there is no other way out – and no way of getting out from behind a typewriter either, even as a manager's PA, due to lack of the time and energy needed to take a course to improve one's qualifications? No, she was proud that she had risen above trendiness and snobbery and had come to accept certain positive ideals: peace in the world, a husband in the bedroom, toast and boiled egg for breakfast. Admittedly Anthony insisted that a true vegetarian didn't eat eggs, but that, in Clea's opinion, was extremism. It was, of course, sincere extremism, in which there was no hint of a condescending sneer, unlike Margot's hypocritical 'Lovely, Klava, lovely' as Kostya belched away, when Clea was ready to be swallowed up by that English lawn and fall to the other end of the earth, back to Moscow, where at least the belching Konstantin would not be the target of ridicule. How charming and enigmatic he had been in distant Russia and how absurd and unpleasant he was here!

2 A COMINTERN GROUPIE

Of course, if it hadn't been for Margot, she would never have gone to that awful Moscow, whose jackboots had been trampling all over her heart for the past few years. At that first New Year's party she had realised at once that she would never get used to the place, when, almost straight from the airport, having barely had time to register at the hotel, they had entered the flat inhabited by some of Margot's Moscow friends as though being thrust from darkness on to a brilliantly lit stage.

A wave of human warmth hit them as the door was flung open, and in that first moment she felt as if she had gone back to her childhood, when she and her parents used to travel up to Scotland to spend Christmas with relatives. Here in Moscow, too, there was a crowd of people and a Christmas tree – the same sort of tree, with tinsel and paper chains, with coloured glass baubles and tangerines wrapped in silver paper. And the smell of tangerine peel – or was it orange peel? The only difference was that a red five-pointed star was fastened at the top of the Moscow tree. And outside, with their yellow, wolfish eyes, loomed the massive tenements stacked in long streets with long, unpronounceable names, to which they had slogged their way from the hotel for nearly two hours in a journey that had included a change of trams, in tramcars with frost-flowers on the windows, to a district across the Moscow River whose squalor exceeded that of the slums of South London across the Thames; what was more, it was not far away from a prison where, Margot assured her, the heirs of Stalin were wont to knock out the teeth of campaigners for human rights in a manner not unlike that of the hirelings of the Argentine junta – although that was hard to believe. Clea, however, was prepared to believe anything by the time they set out from the tram-stop towards the grim, seven-storey, brick-built block of flats, itself reminiscent of a prison, along a gloomy, deserted street that lacked even a single lamp, where only the moon behind their backs shone like a prison-camp searchlight, while a painfully biting frost flayed their throats like emery paper and the wind whipped their faces like a knotted lash. It was not the famous Russian snow that crunched as they walked but sand, strewn in a crusted layer over the ice-bound asphalt, rustling underfoot as though some prehistoric beast were dragging its tail along the dark, prison-like corridor of the street.

In this brave new world Clea once again felt out of place: this, too, was Margot's doing. In the little room (or was it a kitchen?), with a gas stove in one corner, perching on a couch, on chairs, sitting on the table or on each other's heads, almost swinging from the ceiling, banging their heads against the unshaded light-bulb, were nothing but foreigners (Russians, that is) shouting to be heard over each other and the tape-recording of a French singer, and in this bedlam of sounds and faces Clea immediately felt even more lost than in a near-deserted London pub where, if you wanted to talk to the other person sitting at your little table, you either had to pretend to tread on his toe by mistake or pour beer on his jacket, so that with the excuse of apologising you could start talking – about the weather. Here, it seemed, everyone's soul was wide open for talk, except that there was nothing to say, and therefore they were all doing their best to embrace each other – and Margot above all:

'Margot, hey, Margot – where are you? Come on, old girl, have a drink!' And Margot, the 'old girl', was flying around the room – wherever one looked there was Margot hugging someone and drinking to eternal friendship or simply laughing, roaring her head off, or leaping about like Isadora Duncan after meeting the Russian poet Yesenin.

This, in fact, was the picture of Russia that had been conjured up in Margot's first stories about Moscow – with Yesenin and Red Square in the snow, with the ikons of Rublyov and the underground palaces of the Metro, with vodka, sputniks, samovars and the ideally efficient public transport, with the classless society and the mysterious gatherings of dissidents, who, although they were only confirming the slanderous fabrications of various 'Solzhenyavskys' in their attempts to discredit the picture of a classless paradise on the other side of the Iron Curtain, were also reviving – on *this* side of the Curtain – earlier hopes of a 'permanent revolution', as fondly imagined by the members of British Trotskyite splinter-groups, to whose meetings Margot had once dragged Clea.

Margot had always been the first to do anything new – the first to be on the pill at school, the first, after smoking a joint, to start discoursing about the Van Gogh landscape between her legs. And she had always had the knack of putting things in such a way that anyone who didn't follow her current enthusiasm was made to look like a petty-bourgeois thickhead or an opportunistic, right-wing deviationist. And every time, after having overcome one's initial aversion to Margot's latest craze, one would again join the crowd and latch on to the latest fad and prove to everyone around, and above all to Margot, that one was in step with her in the ranks of the Left. Then it would turn out that Margot had already totally rejected her previous credo and its slogans and was spreading yet another new revolutionary contagion, picked up in some country whose existence everyone else had forgotten.

Russia, for instance, had started to figure in Margot's remarks almost twenty years ago. But then in those days one could hardly hold a conversation without mentioning Marx and Lenin, so it was not surprising that the subject of the Soviet Union should also arise. Marx, after all, had beavered away at *Das Kapital* in the Reading Room of the British Museum, where Lenin, too, had subsequently studied that proletarian bible while he hid in the British Museum from the tsarist secret police; and when Marx's tomb in London was being spat on and desecrated by vulgar graffiti, in Moscow the likeness of that martyr of the doctrine of surplus value had become an ikon for every honest toiler and Party activist. The link between the cradle of Marxism-Leninism in London and its coming-of-age in Moscow was clear. There was no doubt about that. But that link was only recalled as an argument during, say, a row with one's landlady when she raised the rent of one's student digs and it became obvious that these money-grubbing old hags had to be dealt with once and for all by the method used by Dostoyevsky's Raskolnikov – after one had first, of course, studied the works of Marx and Lenin. Everyone knew that in the Soviet Union there was hope for people because in England there was no hope for anyone, thanks to the reactionary system of privileges reserved for the ruling class. On the whole, however, it was the anti-social privileges of British reactionaries that infuriated everyone, and not the hope of fraternity and equality on the model of the distant Soviet never-never land. In other words, the link with Moscow had existed for all those years, but rather as a dream of the insulted and oppressed getting their own back; the link never became a geographical one, in the way that, say, colonial India had been in the days of the British Empire for a London clerk who might otherwise spend his life coughing his lungs out with bronchitis in some office in the City. It was Margot, in fact, who transformed the ideological phantom that Moscow had for so long seemed to be into a geographical reality, into a city that was no further away than a short flight by Aeroflot.

Margot had been the first to go on a package tour to Moscow, after which everyone had listened open-mouthed to her account of it, amazed not so much by the details about life in the other ideological hemisphere of the world as by her decisive reassessment of her previous attitude. Until recently the Soviet Union, in Margot's vocabulary, was labelled an 'imperialist tiger' that should have been long ago branded as such by means of a cultural revolution copied from the Belshazzar's feast of Mao's Red Guards. But a couple of years later, after several trips to Moscow, Margot became disillusioned not only with the Chinese brand of Trotskyism; she also began to point out the failings – not of capitalism, but of Stalinism. A new word began to figure in her vocabulary: *Gulag*, which Clea naturally confused with the Hungarian *goulash*, imagining that Margot was talking about the Hungarian uprising of 1956, which only a few years ago Margot had damned as a typical piece of anti-Soviet sabotage organised by the CIA. Now it suddenly turned out that the fate of the world depended on the KGB's treatment of various Solzhenyavskys and Yevtusenskys, who were languishing in the salt-mines of Siberia. In Margot's descriptions of it, Moscow had come to represent a kind of bottomless barrel, a gaping hole in the fabric of Western civilisation, from which poured a nightmarish horde of Orthodox peasants, emigrating Jews and dissidents, all harnessed to a troika and whipped along by the reins held by Politburo members singing snatches of Karl Marx to the accompaniment of balalaikas.

More and more often Margot had trumpeted away about freedom of religion and the right to emigrate. It was funny to hear her going on in this vein, because it was also being trumpeted with equal vehemence by the most reactionary British newspapers as they drowned out the protests of dissidents in South America and Northern Ireland by exaggerating the hullabaloo about dissident Soviet Jews. Anyhow, what did the reactionary press matter when, only a few years earlier, if someone tried to catch Margot out with a question about the freedom of Soviet citizens to emigrate, she herself used to reply, without batting an eyelid: 'The Soviet Union is not a rest-home for millionaires. Who can afford to travel abroad? I'd like to know how many ordinary English people can afford a holiday in Rome. Capitalism is strangling the Soviet economy and the rank-and-file Soviet citizen simply hasn't the means to pay for such extravagant trips abroad!' And she was right. As for the chosen few who regularly put in appearances in the world's capitals, the Margot of the past had seen nothing unfair in this: 'The state subsidises foreign travel for those of its citizens who labour ceaselessly for the good of socialist society. The people who won't join the Party and the anti-Soviet parasites can stay at home. Would the bourgeois ruling clique in a capitalist country subsidise travel abroad for members of the Communist Party? Or even for ordinary workers?' – And with a triumphant smile Margot would kill any further discussion on that theme. Into what depths of her memory had those shattering rebuffs to ideological opponents now vanished? Clea had long since guessed the meaning of these revisions of one's past views, and now she had even found the strength in herself to resist such mental revolutions and would never give in to Margot's latest 'gulag' caper. But when they had been looking through the photographs that Margot used to bring back from each trip to Moscow, Clea had felt the English soil sliding away under her feet. For it was these very photographs that had fascinated her, bewitched her into accepting Margot's ideas. Those empty streets devoid of shrieking insincere advertisements, the slightly asiatic ornateness of the buildings, alongside which the few passers-by that happened to be caught in the picture were frozen with expressions of frowning concentration – whatever the explanation for those stern looks might be, they were witnesses to the harsh and tragic course of their country's history, and that sternness was a seal that certified what was unique in the fate of the Russian people. Clea was, however, even more fascinated by the photographs of Russians at table: that mixture of despair and laughter in the eyes, those hands clinking glasses in a toast, the shoulders pressed against each other as though just before some irrevocable parting or in presentiment of a fateful meeting – in defiance of everything that was liable to shatter and dethrone all this world's ideals. Moscow began to emerge out of those photographs like the persistent mild delirium that keeps coming back when one has a feverish cold, easily recognisable but insoluble of meaning. And Clea had given way to Margot's persuasion. Instead of the week she had planned to spend in Tunis at reduced rates, she had found herself instead in Moscow for the New Year.

For Clea, the reality behind those photographs of Moscow immediately lost its sentimental aura. The goings-on in that New Year's bedlam reminded her, rather, of a Tunisian bazaar. The people immediately pushed Clea aside, engulfing Margot, snatching from her and passing around various weird volumes and shiny Kafkaesque dust-jackets with screams of hysterical delight. 'Natives' – through Clea's mind there flashed the word from the vocabulary of her missionary great-grandfather, who had spent his life constantly preparing to campaign against heathendom with a suitcase full of trinkets. These heathens, however, were not crawling on their knees for glass beads – standing fully upright they would frenziedly throw themselves at Margot, kiss her on the cheek and then retire into a corner with their booty. Margot had brought with her a whole suitcase-full of remaindered books that she had bought in bulk, by weight, at sales and in the second-hand bookshops of Charing Cross Road.

Two of the natives, who were fighting over a book, erupted into an argument that Clea found incomprehensible: which was better – Faulkner or Hemingway? She vaguely remembered the names of these two pre-war writers, whose books her grandmother had often read. If only Clea had known in advance that these stuck-up twits (who apart from 'goodbye' and 'okay' could not string two English words together) were capable of nearly coming to blows over the printed word, she would have taken care to bring some *real* literature for distribution in Moscow: say, for instance, the feminist novel *The Ruby Fruit Jungle*, which although some of it was mere lesbian *épatage* was nevertheless an uncompromising account of how hard life was for a girl from a working-class family – but not the congealed metaphysical ravings of boring intellectuals or fossilised dinosaurs from the nineteenth century. But of course Margot, the crafty beast, had never told her that in Russia 'a book is a good read', and consequently, when Clea found herself going to some stranger's house with empty hands, Margot had suggested a solution to the problem which had turned out to be a trap – to buy a bottle of gin in the 'Beriozka' foreign-currency shop, where Clea had been well and truly ripped off.

Maybe affluent people like Margot and Anthony could afford to throw these bottles of export liquor right and left around Moscow, but all her London friends knew how much moonlighting and overtime it had cost Clea to earn every tenner saved up for this extravagant trip to Moscow, and that after buying that gin in the 'Beriozka' there was no hope of buying any of that *Gzhel'* pottery or the brightly-lacquered wooden Khokhloma ware, as she had been advised to do by experienced people at her office (computer salesmen who had often been to the Soviet Union and knew the ropes) – not ikons but specifically *Gzhel'* pottery and Khokhloma – which she had carefully noted down before leaving. To say nothing of the fact that not one drop of gin had been left in that bottle for her – and she had probably needed it more than anybody else, since the familiar taste might at least have transported her mentally back to her home ground and given her confidence to cope with this alien world.

The bottle of gin had been snatched from her at the door, with mystifying cries of 'Vermouth! Vermouth!' and her frost-blinded eyes had never seen it again. These barbarians tossed back gin by the glassful – and neat, without tonic. 'They'll all be sick,' Clea muttered to the unheeding Margot, watching with a mixture of repulsion and vindictiveness as these parasites of the world's first socialist state gulped as much spirit in one minute as would have kept one English family in pre-prandial drinks (one finger's-worth at a time) for a whole month.

'Stop gulping all that vodka without any *zakuski*,' shouted the hostess from the other end of the flat. 'Wait for the meat, you fools. Kostya's coming, and he's bringing the meat.' From her corner Clea only caught four words: 'vodka', 'zakuski', 'meat' and the word which she thought meant 'bones' – *kostya* – the bones in the meat, she presumed. Who could have imagined that the woman was in fact talking about her – Clea's – future husband?

She had been learning Russian from the records issued by the BBC. For a whole year she had gone to sleep with her head bulging with new words, but here, apart from 'vodka' and 'meat' she was unable to make out a single word. No one here finished their sentences properly, jumping from one subject to another by a series of half-hints, grins and careless jargon in between explosions of laughter.

Clea was amazed at their extremely bad diction and their inability to express their thoughts in an ordered manner. Margot had not even bothered to introduce her properly, having simply pushed her into the crowd with a casual: 'This is Clea! Welcome!' (whereas according to convention she should have said 'Please welcome her and be nice to her', to which the hosts would have said 'Welcome!') – and had immediately rushed off to embrace someone. Clea had hoped that on coming face to face with real Soviet citizens instead of Intourist guides she would have a chance of exchanging views on the unfortunate instances of repression and persecution that took place on both sides of the Iron Curtain, regardless of the political system or the way of life. She immediately sensed, however, that this mob simply did not want to know, that it ignored the darker sides of life with as much disdain as did fresh-faced Sloane Rangers of Chelsea or the fat-cat bohemians of Hampstead, who discussed revolution with brazen crudity, ignoring the fact that after eight hours behind a clattering typewriter no working girl was capable of absorbing their Maoist gobbledegook.

These Moscow types spoke their own brand of double-dutch with, in effect, the same kind of snobbish carelessness as did the products of English public schools, and when she closed her eyes from a sudden wave of tiredness she could hear the same lah-di-dah intonation, the same plum-in-the-mouth habit of talking through clenched teeth, the same contempt for anybody who wasn't 'one of us' – in fact, the same supercilious, reactionary freemasonry in their local uniform of jeans and sweaters. Had it been worth standing in the freezing cold and humbly returning the steely gaze of Soviet frontier guards, just to land up in the familiar, tedious company of snobs who repeated tirelessly and mechanically: Kafka this and Faulkner that, Proust this and Hemingway that, instead of recalling their own national heritage such as Tolstoyevsky – or even Melnikov-Pechersky, a writer whom a White Russian émigré had so feelingly discussed in a lecture on Russian literature at the Centre for the Protection of Ethnic Minorities, during a festival held as part of a campaign against the extermination of seals?

Squeezed into a corner beside a window-sill, Clea pressed her burning forehead against an ice-encrusted pane that was weeping and dripping, like her own eyes and nose, from an atmosphere made stifling and steamy by the central heating. The radiators were as scorchingly hot as an open-hearth furnace, because, as Margot had explained, heating for the entire population was supplied centrally by the state; consequently everyone squandered the nationalised heat as much as they liked and in the same irresponsible way that the bureaucrats at the top overfulfilled the planned figures for consumption of oil and coal, and just as the guests in this hothouse, ignoring the risk of cancer, puffed away like chimneys at cigarettes that assaulted one's nostrils with a reek like horse-manure mixed with straw, bought cheap by the Soviet government from their Bulgarian comrades.

After the savage, barbaric outdoor cold, the sauna-like atmosphere of the flat, filled not with steam but with clouds of acrid blue smoke, immediately gave Clea watering eyes and a running nose. Within a minute her handkerchief was turned into a wet dishrag, and these admirers of bourgeois freedom had not yet got around to producing paper tissues. As she cooled her blazing forehead against the frostbound window-pane, Clea fondly recalled, perhaps for the first time in her life, her parents' cold house, where the draughts whistled and where, for economy's sake, the gas fire was not lit until her father came home from work; warmth in daytime had to be sought in the public library, which apart from the pub was the only warm place in the whole district – a fact that greatly encouraged a love of reading. Tears flowed down Clea's reddened cheeks, which an onlooker might have thought were tears of envy. She began to edge her way out towards the door on to the landing, from whence a blessed coolness was seeping into the flat.

The landing, where flights of dirty concrete stairs wound their way around the prison-like steel lattice of the lift-shaft, smelled of cats and urine, but at least it was easier to breathe. All the smells in the world came floating up the stair-well, while the magic sounds of new-year celebrations came through the doors, seemingly dulled and muffled by the glimmering of the one feeble bulb that hung from the grime-spattered ceiling. Seeking support, her hand touched the window-sill and instantly recoiled from it: her fingers were smeared with something sticky – 'Blood,' she thought; then her hand hit something round, and with a crash an empty bottle fell off the window-sill and was smashed to fragments. She read the word 'Portwine' in cyrillic letters on the label as she pushed the broken glass into one heap with her foot. The pseudo-English name on the bottle – or rather on the shattered remnants of someone else's party – reminded her of where she had come from and how she had got here. In that filthy, dark womb of a strange house in an alien country there was concentrated such utter misery and loneliness that if she had only made one more mental effort, one more step towards awareness of her ultimate defeat in this alien world, she might perhaps, even then, have freed herself from the importunate assault of other people's dotty ideas and slogans and might have started to live by her own perceptions and without second thoughts. Without Margot. Without Russia.

But at that moment there came from the lower floors down below a clattering and rumbling and humming and the ponderous old lift – obviously a relic of the Stalin period – started to ascend. At first it was a tiny speck of light rising from the bottomless canyon, which grew into a gigantic glow-worm and then finally, casting huge criss-cross shadows from the grille of its wire cage, came to rest at Clea's floor with a clanking of the winch. Swearing as he stepped out face to face with Clea, a creature emerged from the lift-cage wearing a crumpled worsted overcoat and a rabbit-fur hat with ear-flaps. The man was holding a gigantic newspaper-wrapped parcel cradled in his arms like a baby. The home-made wrapping was under obvious strain and in one place had burst, and through the hole protruded an indecently-shaped bone attached to a crimson, frost-coated lump of meat. 'As if he had just hacked someone to death in the street' – the absurd thought made Clea stagger back, at which with nervous politeness she corrected herself in an English fashion, racking her brains to construct something like a Russian sentence, to assume something like the smile that strangers exchange in England when they find themselves together in a lift: a polite smile signalling one's peaceful intentions, or rather one's indifference – no, I'm not planning to put a knife to your throat, you go to your floor and I'll get out at mine, goodbye, all's well, *merci, au revoir* . . .

'I know!' said Clea. 'You must be *kosti*. They told me.'

'Kost*ya*,' Kostya corrected her. 'Not *kosti* – not the bones – but Kostya. Who told you?'

Clea waved her hand vaguely in the direction of the half-open door of the flat. 'Kostia?' she repeated in an effort to correct her pronunciation, though she remained convinced that his nickname really was '*kosti*' – boneman – because he was the purveyor of meat to this party and '*kostia*' was simply a special Moscow way of pronouncing the word *kosti*.

'I'm English,' said Clea.

'I respect England,' said Kostya. 'All the cuts of meat have come to us from England: roastbeef, beefsteaks, rumpsteaks,' and he added, pulling aside some of the paper wrapping: 'And I've brought some beefsteaks – with bones, it's true. We shall eat' – and he clicked his teeth to make his meaning clearer. Every word that he spoke was pronounced crisply and distinctly: 'Kostia' clearly wanted to be understood and to understand, unlike the supercilious snobs in the flat, with their incomprehensible gabble.

But the door was flung open, blowing out the little flicker of mutual comprehension between the two on the landing, and their brief conversation was smothered by cannibalistic cries of 'Meat! Meat!' Kostya's bony figure vanished into a crowd of backs in the corridor, only to reappear, towering like a giant, at the stove. Though crushed back into her corner, Clea managed to disregard the heaving bedlam of grimacing features; she could not take her gaze off Kostya's mighty shoulders, his sinewy elbows armoured in the rolled-up sleeves of his lumberjack shirt, his straining neck bent over the lumps of meat. Every muscle of his broad back was engaged in the mystical procedure of an empty bottle pounding at the pieces of meat, alternating with the strokes of a sharp knife that covered the flattened beef in a network of cuts.

'Rumpsteaks, I suppose. Or are they sirloin steaks?' Clea found herself unexpectedly trying to guess at the purpose of these mysterious passes. She surprised herself, too, with the readiness, even keenness, of her attempts to penetrate the inner world of this gangling prestidigitator – the world of the mysterious Russian soul.

With the assurance of a surgeon, Kostya rapped out: 'Breadcrumbs!' and immediately someone rushed to pound some slices of dried bread into breadcrumbs. 'Onion,' muttered

Kostya, but someone else, as though anticipating the royal will, had already bent double and fished out an onion from a box of vegetables. Godlike in his dexterity, appearing to possess not one pair of hands but ten, Kostya simultaneously manipulated the sizzling frying-pan, the pepper-mill and the butter, dusted the lumps of meat with flour and made a series of magic passes over the hissing onion with a kitchen knife. By his whole appearance – conjuror's swagger combined with imperturbability – Kostya seemed to be demonstrating to Clea, a foreigner, that there was in fact plenty to eat in this country, that there was red meat in Russia despite the assertions of the London sovietologists – the only proviso being that to get it one had to be friends with Kostya, indeed one had to *be* Kostya and not some god-forsaken dissident or highbrow pseud. How gracefully, without false scorn, Kostya ignored the advice offered by these ignoramuses; how benevolently he smiled as he inclined his ginger forelock; how ironically he wrinkled his snub nose, making dimples appear in his prominent cheekbones! Even his check shirt, his protruding shoulder-blades, and the sharp collarbones showing beneath his rumpled collar already seemed dear to her – this Soviet shirt actually gave him the slight look of a Texas cowboy or a Scottish farmhand: in other words he gave off an air of healthy, open-air poverty, something earthy and natural, with none of the grimaces of these intellectuals or the affectations of this crowd of rootless snobs. In a word, there was something *proletarian* about him, and Clea caught herself getting dreadfully angry when the mob of fans of Kostya's culinary art prevented her from seeing his face, half-turned towards her.

The climax came when Kostya unexpectedly picked up the scalding frying-pan with a towel and, without any fuss, without turning round or looking about him, carried it right across the room to the festive table – already loaded with over-salted salads, a dish of marinated herrings garnished with circles of onion like staring eyes, bowls of sharp horse-radish, all mixed together, already half-eaten, prematurely devoured by the impatient guests. All these dishes were swept aside to make way for the gigantic meat-filled frying-pan, in the same way that the mob of guests made way for Kostya's victorious progress, crowding in behind him in their haste to be in a good position to help themselves. Forks were already poised when suddenly from various parts of the company people could be heard arguing, at first quietly, then rising to an impassioned pitch at the tops of their voices as the sound blossomed into a series of furious rows, in the course of which the participants thrust their watches under each other's noses until, finally, someone had the sense to switch on the radio. Along with the rumbling, inarticulate roar from the loudspeaker of 'Happy New Year, com'adz', chaos broke loose in the room – hands reached for bottles, vodka was poured on to the tablecloth, glasses clinked: 'We can see out the old year until the anthem!' There was just time to clink, drink and pour again before the Soviet national anthem thundered out; everyone stood up and once again the glasses met over the hot frying-pan full of Kostya's steaks.

'Now then!' said the hostess, as she pulled away someone's over-impetuous fork, and plates of meat began to circulate along the impatient queue around the table. But the cries of rumbling appreciation amid the crunch of jaws and the tinkle of glasses being filled did not last for long. Quickly sated, people were soon switching on the record-player in a corner of the room and throwing orange-peel at each other, someone was stubbing out their cigarette on a half-eaten piece of meat, while two others, screened by dancing couples, were embracing on the sofa.

Once again Clea found herself squeezed into the corner at one end of the table opposite a plate with the gnawed remains of a bone, which she was spraying with an uncontrollable sneeze from her running nose.

'A girl's crying' – suddenly her neighbour pulled at her elbow and began to prod the revolving spool of the antediluvian tape-recorder, which was emitting a monotonous, guttural baritone singing something oriental on two notes, that sounded like the invocation of a somnolent muezzin. 'Do you understand Russian? They're bards, minstrels – unofficial ones, get it?' The uninvited guide shouted to her over the noise of the room and the tape-recorder. 'I'll explain it to you – listen here. It's about a little girl, see. And she's crying. And the globe is flying through space. The globe means a balloon, like an airship, only small – a child's balloon. But at the same time it's our planet, you see, looking like a balloon. The next verse is about a girl. She's crying like a little girl. But she's also a big, grown-up girl and she's crying too. Because she hasn't got a boyfriend yet. And obviously she never will have, see? They're comforting her.' At this point Clea felt the hand of the tape-recorded muezzin's interpreter sliding up her leg towards her knee. She caught a lecherous glance. Or was it Margot, giving her an impudent wink from a distant corner? 'They're consoling a woman. Her husband has run off with somebody else. And the balloon, or the globe, just keeps on spinning – see? Do you have access to the diplomatic bag?' Clea remained tensely silent, assuming that this wasn't a question but still part of the translation of the song. 'I've brought with me a hand-written volume of poems written by our group of poets, and I want to read them to you,' said the interpreter, fishing out a school exercise book. 'No, no, those aren't the words from the tape-recorder,' noticing that Clea was still staring at the revolving spools. He switched off the machine and thereby switched on the bellowing voices in the room again, but not for long, because as he flicked through the pages of the exercise-book he seemed to have switched on a loudspeaker in his own throat and Clea was literally pressed against the wall by the sound-waves of his howling voice.

Russians generally speak in a sing-song. She had been convinced of this back home in London when Margot had dragged her off to an evening of verse-reading by an émigré poet, who, in a voice reminiscent of the long-drawn-out booming of Big Ben, had declared to the audience that the clocks in London were always going. This was a dubious assertion. Although there were clocks all over the place in London, by no means all of them were always going. Furthermore, the poet had intoned à la Big Ben: 'London town is splendid.' Clea simply could not agree with this. Perhaps the translator had misconstrued it or had been deafened – for this Russian bard was declaiming from the stage at tremendous volume. 'Why does he have to shout so?' Clea had thought miserably to herself, as she waited for the translation. But Margot had said that this style of declaiming poetry was connected with the tradition of liturgical chanting in the Orthodox Church and with the religious role of poetry in Russian history. Perhaps. It was hard to argue with Margot. But as a city London was awful. Moscow, it now turned out, was no better. Clea could not understand a word. 'Do you like it?' – the Muscovite bard would occasionally break off to ask, only to switch on the loudspeaker in his gullet again. 'Can you get it out?' he asked Clea, having bellowed out enough verses and drawn breath. 'Can you get it out? I mean can you send it abroad, export it from East to West – smuggle it out in the diplomatic bag, I mean?'

When Clea finally understood what he was asking her to do, her cheeks began to burn, not from the scruffy, Turkish-bath atmosphere, but with indignation. She was so indignant, in fact, that she could only reply in English. Who did the poet take her for? However sceptical her view of Soviet history may have been (whose victims, by the way, were no less pitiful than the victims of American history, with its genocide of the Red Indians, or of British history, with is mass executions of mutinous sepoys), she would never allow herself to break the laws of the country in which, at the moment, she was only a guest – to say nothing of the fact that she, Clea, wouldn't dream of approaching those arrogant bureaucrats in the British Embassy, those self-important, pompous officials with their pursed, would-be aristocratic lips and impenetrable expressions. Anyhow, they would never give her access to the diplomatic mail. And didn't he realise that Clea would be the first to be searched on the way out? What impudence to try and trap her, a complete innocent in games of political intrigue, into such an irresponsible action whose ultimate aim, after all, was to undermine the achievements of socialism, which though admittedly distorted by Stalin's cult of the personality, were nevertheless the ideal of all the workers of the world at a time when millions of unemployed Britons were queueing up to collect their miserable dole. And was he, a liberal Soviet intellectual ('Kindly take your hand off my knee!') so naive that he didn't realise whose cause he would be helping with his poems? He should fight to have his work published in his own country and not secretly deliver these prophecies about his long-suffering people into such cynical hands as the CIA, who, as everyone knew, financed and distributed Russian-language publications in the West – their trump-card in the dirty game played by the intelligence services in the global conflict of the superpowers – and by no means in order to preserve Russian literature. He should take as his example the fate of such Russian poets as Akhmatova, Pasternak and Mandelstam who suffered heroically in their own country, and not those dissidents grown fat on foreign currency, the tales of whose sufferings were ceaselessly being dinned into us in the West, and who then turned up on our side of the Iron Curtain wearing fur coats and diamonds and immediately started blackening their homeland!

Clea could not bring herself to say all this, but she nevertheless said some of it, furious at herself for parroting Margot's pronouncements of ten years ago. And some of it, though not all, penetrated the poet's consciousness, as his face was increasingly distorted by a grimace of disgusted annoyance, until he finally threw back his head and bellowed to everyone in the room: 'She's a Comintern groupie! Who brought this Comintern groupie here?!'

His scream, in which there was no longer a trace of the Orthodox liturgy, started a whispering across the quietened room, and the instantly sobered eyes of the guests were all fixed on Clea. She was terrified, feeling that someone might hit her at any moment. She realised that what she had said might seriously upset – even offend – the declaimer of those incomprehensible verses. Far from being convinced of the justice of her remarks, she had in fact disliked regurgitating all that demagogic rubbish about the cradle of the revolution and the anti-Soviet conspiracy of foreign intelligence services. She had simply spouted that nonsense because she had been forced to say something in self-defence: to get rid of that insistent poet's stare, the pressure of his voice in her ear and of his hand on her knee. It had nothing to do with her attitude to Russian poetry – she had simply felt that someone was wanting to use her. And so she had tried to defend herself – using the first words that came into her head at that moment. Did they really have to glare at her like that just because of a few words, even if they were hurtful? With such collective hatred in their eyes? At that moment Clea realised that this must be what it was like at Party meetings, those notorious gatherings at which attendance was compulsory. She realised now that she was among *Soviet* people, that this was what it was like to live under Soviet rule. And she felt sick and frightened.

She looked around for Margot. It was time to depart. To leave, while there was still somewhere to go. Margot, however, was obviously circulating somewhere in the corridor. Or she was in the bathroom. Clea had noticed that Margot would now and again lock herself in the bathroom, whence she would emerge looking inexplicably pinker and younger, always to be followed by one of her 'old friends' from previous visits to Moscow. 'Sexual promiscuity is the reverse side of the aggressiveness of capitalist society' – Clea recalled one of Anthony's aphorisms and blew her nose into her handkerchief, avoiding the hostile stares fixed on her. These eyes were from the socialist world, but they too were aggressive. Furthermore, she didn't understand what a 'Comintern groupie' was. Pressing her handkerchief to her nose, as though she had already been hit, she stared at the opposite corner with an unseeing gaze from her tear-reddened eyes – until she finally realised that the corner she was staring at was not empty at all: blinking his ginger eyelashes, Kostya was looking fixedly at her.

For the rest of her life she was to remember how that arbiter of the Russian stomach brushed the crumbs from his knees, slowly stood up and set off across the room towards the spot where Clea was pressing herself against the wall. He moved towards her with exactly the gait that was described by the Russian writer and anti-slavophile, Turgenev, as '. . . the teetering gait of our Alcibiades, Churilo Penkovich, which produced such an astounding, nay almost physiological effect on old women and young girls, and with which, to this day, our loose-jointed waiters mince their inimitable way.' As she watched this proletarian wonder she couldn't decide whether her knees were feeling weak with fright at the approach of her executioner who would turn her, the 'Comintern groupie', into beefsteaks, rumpsteaks or roast beef as the next dish to be served up to this noisy mob, or whether her knees were weakening for quite a different reason – indeed, the feeling was not in her knees at all: a blissful heaviness had begun to creep from her chest to her crotch, and she suddenly decided that, even if he were to punch her in the face (and everyone knew that in Russia, as in Ireland, all husbands beat their wives, or at least they did before the revolution, although she, of course, wasn't his wife and he wasn't a pre-revolutionary husband – oh, how muddled and complicated things were in Russia!), she would forgive Kostya even for this gesture of male chauvinist piggishness towards the weaker sex, precisely because she would never have tolerated any such thing from one of her fellow-countrymen. It was not a matter of the box on the ears and whoever might deliver it; the point was not in the means but in the end – despite the views of bourgeois liberals; and the aim of the impending box on the ears (she felt this in her chest and stomach and knees) was not demagogy or versifying but physical contact between East and West, despite the machinations of reactionary enemies of *détente* on both sides of the Iron Curtain. But the Curtain fell. And no blows followed. Pulling a chair close alongside her and seating himself astride it,

Kostya looked into Clea's face with eyes awash in Russian history. Clea desperately blew her nose again from embarrassment.

'Got a cold?' Kostya enquired sympathetically, and Clea felt his broad hand on her shoulder. Without looking at him, she nodded affirmatively. She lacked the words to go into explanations about her allergy to the reek of tobacco-smoke, further stoked up by the central heating. 'We'll soon fix that' – and Kostya patted her confidently on the shoulder, like a doctor treating a sick child.

Squinting out from behind her handkerchief, Clea watched the business-like way that Kostya reached out for a bottle of vodka standing on the edge of the table, and after delving in his pockets with the same doctorish air he produced a little home-made paper packet; with medical precision he measured out half a glass of vodka, tipped into it some claret-coloured powder from the screw of paper, mixed it all up with a teaspoon taken from someone's plate of cake, moved the glass to the edge of the table and gave the order: 'Right, now drink it down in one!' Entranced by this set of movements, as precisely calculated as the manoeuvres of the superpowers, Clea lifted the glass to her lips without a word. The smell of raw spirit hit her nostrils, her head swam and with a trembling hand she put the glass back on the table.

'The chief thing is not to despair,' said Kostya encouragingly to this foreign woman. 'Do it like this – first breathe right out, then toss it down in one, swallow, don't breathe in once until it has gone down – and immediately eat a gherkin,' Kostya explained to her, holding a swollen pickled gherkin ready in one hand and the glass in the other, graphically demonstrating to Clea the whole procedure for swallowing the vodka. 'Then you can breathe any way you like,' he urged, putting the glass into her hand. Hypnotised by this pantomime, Clea screwed up her eyes and tossed the contents of the glass down her throat, muddling up all the instructions about breathing in and breathing out; the vodka poured over her lips and chin, her eyes turned upwards into her head and, gasping like a stranded fish, she was seized by a spasm of coughing that was only stopped by the iron hand of Kostya thumping her on the back. 'What is it?' she mumbled in English – and in French: 'Qu'est-ce que c'est?' (French was, for her, the language one instinctively used for foreigners).

'It's pepper,' Kostya explained. 'Cayenne pepper with vodka is the surest remedy for the symptoms of a cold. After potato, of course.' Still gasping for breath, like someone who has escaped from a burning house, Clea repeated after Kostya the unfamiliar Russian word for potato – *kartoshka* – with her pepper-smeared lips: 'Artichoke?' But Kostya explained thoughtfully and in detail that he only knew of artichokes from Marcel Proust's novel *Du Côté de Chez Swann*, and that on *this* side of the Iron Curtain you took a potato, peeled it, and having boiled it to a mush in a saucepan, you threw a towel over your head, bent your head over the saucepan like an Arab and having thus separated both your respiratory tract and the saucepan from the outside world, you inhaled nothing but potato vapour until you were completely cured. As he explained all this, Kostya threw a dirty dishrag over his head and used a bowl of half-eaten salad to symbolise the saucepan.

'But in the circumstances, pepper is more efficient,' he said, waving towards the jumble of heads that filled the flat to bursting. Perhaps that dishcloth was a magic one, or the vodka had already started to boom in her ears like a fairground band, but the babble of voices together with the hostile faces of the guests seemed to be receding to a safe distance, while Kostya the magician loomed ever larger in her eyes. 'And you must immediately take a second glass, while the sparks are still in your stomach, as the great Russian writer Chekhov taught us,' said Konstantin, pushing the glass towards her, refilled with its healing alchemy. Clea, her sodden handkerchief already forgotten, and without taking her now undimmed eyes off Kostya, tossed back the liquid, hypnotically obeying his professional instructions: breathe out, throw it down, pause, gherkin, breathe in – this time without even coughing.

'Is this how the Russian people treat a cold?' she enquired in animated tones.

'But of course!' Kostya nodded. 'It's naive, of course, to imagine that these are ancient Russian methods, still less are they true folk-recipes. I am convinced that similar healing mixtures can be found in medieval monastic treatises on alchemy. And pepper came to Russia from Byzantium,' mused Kostya, moving over to sit closer to Clea, 'as did the light of Christianity. Mind you, the theory about pepper has yet to be confirmed, but it clearly wasn't grown in the swamps of Siberia – it is obviously a southern plant. No one can deny, however, that the potato came from America.' Clea agreed and concurred that the potato had also reached Western Europe from America, discovered by Columbus.

'But Columbus was a European,' Kostya pressed home his point, 'and consequently the potato reached Russia thanks to Europe – as did, incidentally, everything decent in the Russian diet.'

'Columbus was not a European,' said Clea, the patriotic sentiments awakening in her slightly tipsy brain. Like all English people, she distinguished the continent of Europe from the British Isles. 'Columbus was a subject of the English crown!'

All this time their conversation had been conducted in a mixture of English and dog-Russian, but even in Russian Kostya had only the weakest grasp of the nuances of geography beyond the Iron Curtain: to him, the West was all one, and in culinary matters he was a firm Westerner.

'Take, for example, the immemorially Russian samovar. It's as immemorially Russian as the Tartar yoke, thanks to which the samovar made its appearance in Russia,' said Kostya, warming to his theme. 'The samovar came from the Tartar khans, and those typically Siberian meat patties – *pelmeny* – were introduced from China – even the word sounds Chinese: pel-men! And the prototype of the famous Russian cabbage soup is to be found, of course, in the German-speaking lands, along with romanticism in Russian poetry.

Russian cooking, if you analyse it, is quite simply nothing but blatant plagiarism!' roared Kostya, while Clea, this time on her own initiative, was partaking of a third dose of the healing potion and was not so much listening to Kostya's words as examining the prominent cheekbones and broad nose of Kostya's physiognomy, which combined in one face all three of those legendary Russian folk-heroes depicted in the Tretyakov Gallery: Alyosha Popovich, Dobrynya Nikitich, and Ilya Muromets, mounted on their three horses, who were either guarding the frontiers of Russia against contraband recipes from abroad or were inspecting those same recipes from under the hands shading their brows, while all around lay the skeletons of their enemies, their armour shattered, their heads bowed in death.

In the dim light, the guests appeared to be leaning towards each other at the most bizarre angles, and through the Joycean double-dutch of Russian speech could be heard the sound of snoring mixed with bursts of laughter and other strange sounds from the depths of the flat; thus it seemed to Clea as if all around there was no one but herself and Konstantin, two plenipotentiary representatives of West and East engaged in a top-level discussion in which the General Secretary of the East was insisting on the primacy of the West, while the lady Premier of the West was obstinately inclined to favour the East. She, in fact, was about to incline herself so far that she would have fallen off her chair, had not Kostya picked her up in time with a strong hand that reminded her of a soup-ladle.

'You need further treatment,' said Kostya firmly, leading her towards the hallway with a less than firm tread. As he thrust his arm into the wrong sleeve and did up buttons in the wrong button-holes, Clea made a last attempt to return intact to her native shores and rushed back into the flat, muttering: 'Margot . . . where's Margot?' and something about their plans to go on a guided tour to Suzdal tomorrow. But to judge by the suspicious squelching sounds and a familiar laugh from behind the bathroom door, it was obvious to Clea that Margot was busy seeing some quite different sights of the capital city. Gripped by a pang of angry jealousy, sharply seasoned with the vodka and pepper that were pounding at her temples, Clea slammed the front door on Western civilisation in the person of Margot and, taking Kostya by the arm, strode out into the Russian frost.

The ground-wind whistling along the street clawed at her face like a cat, and she was again overtaken with depression by the prison-corridor look of the frostbound street and the dim lights of the railway station on the far side of the square – a station from which one could travel neither to London nor to Tunis. But Kostya gave her no time to come to her senses and with a sort of cowboyish whoop, as though spurring on a horse, he pulled Clea towards a van marked with one word – MEAT – in large letters on its side which had pulled up at the street corner. After a brief wrangle with the cap that poked itself out of the cab window, the other door was opened and the biting frost was replaced by the no less biting reek of petrol and overheated metal. Clea, however, was past noticing these changes of climate. A truck and a driver like these might easily have been encountered on a scorching Californian highway on the far side of the Atlantic – which seemed, in fact, to be the reckless driver's destination, and Clea had to press herself against Kostya on the curves, becoming the heroine of a thriller, the captured bride in a Western.

Squinting sideways, the driver muttered: 'Nice jeans the lady's wearing. Foreigner, isn't she? Would she sell them, maybe? My old woman's been nagging me for years now to buy her a pair. I says to her: What d'you want 'em for? How're you going to get those great thighs of yours into those drainpipes? You change your overalls every year for a size bigger. But she keeps going on at me – jeans, jeans, jeans. Would your lady sell them, maybe?'

If Clea had understood this male conversation, she might have decided that Kostya was bargaining with the driver, because his hand, that had been gripping her knee, had crept upwards and was resting on the zip, which must, as we know, be unfastened before one can take off one's jeans. But she was past caring. Her last sober thought was concerned with how she would retell her 'Russian adventures' in London under Margot's envious glare.

The subsequent episodes of her first encounter, however, vanished from her memory, either because of the vodka-induced fog that muffled her perceptions as effectively as the notorious London fog obscures visibility, or because of its excessively intimate nature, which Clea was not brazen enough to have recalled even to herself – not to mention the attacks of fear which sapped her mnemonic powers no less than the Muscovite vodka or the London fogs. She remembered dimly how they had blundered into the lobby of Kostya's shared flat; how Kostya had tried to walk on tiptoe and had, of course, knocked something over with a frightful crash; how she herself had given an unearthly scream when something hairy and bristly had thrust itself into her face (next morning it turned out to have been a broom). Then there was the performance with the folding couch (a relic of grandmother's days, with torn chintz upholstery covered in suspicious stains and worked by a set of evil-minded springs), which refused to unfold and then suddenly sprang apart, hitting Clea behind the knees so that she fell backwards on to the couch, leaving her staring at the ceiling, which reminded her of a yellow sky marked with a spiralling sandstorm that might have been cobwebs or simply soot. Above the couch were shelves full of coiled pipes, test-tubes, flasks and retorts – exactly like the laboratory of a medieval alchemist. Kostya himself, bending over her wearing spectacles (or so she thought in her terror; she never again saw him wearing spectacles), was laying out a set of what looked like empty mayonnaise jars. 'Bare your back,' he said gruffly, in the tones of an inquisitor or an experimental scientist, and began to make magic passes over the jars: holding a jar upside down, he lit a match and started to heat the glass in the flame – and in the flickering light of the match it seemed to Clea that his snub nose was in reality hooked and villainous. 'Well?' he said threateningly, and pulling off her blouse he tried to turn her over on to her front – then came another movement and a jar was being pressed to her skin. Clea felt her skin being sucked into the jar, drawing the soul out of her. All the stories that she had read in the *Sun* and the *Daily Telegraph* about the torture-chambers of the Lubyanka were made incarnate in the figure of Kostya, advancing on her with a lighted match and a jar – yet she felt no pain, although her back started to itch and sting a little, and whether it was from the itching or from the nightmares about the KGB, Clea gave an involuntary twitch that knocked the careful rows of instruments of torture off her back and brought Kostya down on top of her. Then it felt as if a heavy railway train had jerked into movement, because the room started to tremble, rock and slide away to the sound of the creaking of the couch, like the carriage of a long-distance express, while her heart was beating in time with the accelerating click of the wheels on rails – and just as a hot jet of locomotive steam hit her in the crotch, she gave a jerk at the long-drawn-out sound of a train's whistle that seemed to be coming from her own throat.

She fell unconscious, or rather fell asleep thinking how right Freud had been to draw a parallel between sexual intercourse and the movement of an express train, but even so she dreamed of mustard poultices – of which Freud no doubt had never heard – and in her dream she confused these mustard poultices with rooks, exotic Russian birds that were flapping against her breasts with their wings – or perhaps they were simply Kostya's hot, mustardy, rookish hands. The Freudian parallel, however, lost its picturesque metaphorical force when she was woken by the approaching click of real train wheels and started up in panic at the sound of an ear-splitting train-whistle. Through the window at the head of the couch she caught sight of the coaches of an express train, due to the fact that Kostya's house was situated right alongside a railway line. The hands of the alarm pointed to three o'clock – evidently in the afternoon, and the trains had obviously been rolling all night, in both the literal and the Freudian sense. She wanted to rush off to her hotel, but not before she had, at Kostya's insistence, learned the Russian equivalent of 'the hair of the dog', which brought them again to a study of the comparative culinary traditions of different lands and peoples – in other words, Clea found herself naked once more as she listened to a whole list of culinary terms in Russian which Kostya awarded to each part of her body; the fruity simile of 'strawberries and raspberries' did at least arouse certain erotic associations, unlike a kind of humbug called a 'crayfish's neck' which, for reasons unclear to her, he awarded to the primal seat of amorous pleasure. In brief, by the time he had escorted her to the Golden Wheatsheaf Hotel, it was already pitch-dark again. She wanted to take him up to her room so that they wouldn't have to say goodbye out in the cold, and for other purposes, but the doorman barred the way to Kostya and said: 'Not allowed.' Clea tried to explain to the doorman that she had paid for her room and that Kostya was her guest, but the doorman shook his head obstinately: 'The Golden Wheatsheaf is an Intourist hotel for foreigners. Kostya? If he's Kostya then it's not allowed.'

They said goodbye, pressing their lips to opposite sides of the bullet-proof glass screen, and as she watched the stooping figure of Kostya, hunched against the cold, with his shabby rabbit-fur hat with its earflaps dangling over the collar of his thick woollen overcoat (blacks in New York wear the same sort of hat), as she watched her rejected lover trotting away in the gusts of icy wind under the light of the street-lamps that lit the black tunnel of the wintry street, against all logic – both emotional and geographical – she saw in the retreating Kostya a shadow from her past, a London youth running away blindly from the scene of the crime. The youth's name was Colin. She tried to banish that London phantom, but although she had at first recalled that nightmarish episode from her office life with anger and repulsion, now she unexpectedly found herself bursting into tears and, as she leaned against the bullet-proof glass, for a moment she confused Mosow at New Year with London at Christmas. How long ago was it? Who would have thought that she would have to recount even that episode in court?

3 A CHRISTMAS PRESENT

She remembered that winter's day as though it had been yesterday. Something like it was only to be expected in London during the days leading up to Christmas. In the lunch-hour on the day in question all the secretaries, typists and junior clerks had dashed in a bunch to the nearest pub: on such occasions drunkenness, as we all know, practically becomes a religious obligation, and anyone who refuses to join in is threatened with excommunication from the group. Deprived by history of the opportunity to experience fraternity on the revolutionary barricades, people exhibited their unexpended enthusiasm for solidarity in such a way that incurable egotism and an innate standoffishness might look like sincere gestures of each individual's concern for the collective.

Clea pictured to herself the crush at the bar, where everyone, hand in pocket, would be shouting to be heard over the din and, with vigorous use of their elbows, would order a round of drinks when it was their turn. The system seemed to be thoroughly democratic: each for all and all for each. No one had a chance of contributing a greater share to the general happiness than anyone else, just as there was equally no possible way to avoid making one's predetermined contribution; it was a system of overt extortion in the guise of fraternal cordiality and collective generosity.

If, say, ten people took part in this display of collective responsibility, then at the end of it all ten would stagger out of the bar stinking drunk. The girls, of course, would insist on drinking shandy to begin with, but as they warmed up and yielded to the men's insistence they would change to Campari and gin and tonic, while the men, on this festive occasion, after showing off by ordering champagne cocktails, would end up with the usual pints of bitter, as a result of which the second half of the day before the start of the Christmas party would be spent belching and yawning until their cheekbones ached.

This collective moral blackmail in the guise of collective jollity was also in full swing on the street. Through the huge plate-glass window of a snack-bar, with its plastic table-tops in garish pseudo-childish colours, overwhelming in their spurious cheerfulness, Clea, having slipped away from the group, gazed with distaste at the pre-Christmas hurly-burly in the street. Year after year, as in children's Christmas pantomimes, the characters in this crowd scene were always the same, trying with exaggerated guffawing and exaggerated gestures to attract attention to themselves with an excessive cheerfulness that was quite out of keeping with the normal polite glumness of the street crowd.

Clad in a red dressing-gown and a semi-detached cotton-wool beard, Father Christmas from the supermarket across the street was barking into a megaphone to advertise a nickel-plated set of turkey-carvers as a Christmas present. He was clearly being outdone by a Salvation Army choir and band. In their funereal, red-trimmed uniforms, old maids in unison were celebrating the Holy Child on the eve of his birth and encouraging him to suicide through the cruxifixion that awaited him. The band and the commercial huckster were taking it in turns to drown out a gaggle of freezing schoolgirls wearing the badge of their school on the breast-pockets of their wretched little blazers: with mouths wide open as though from sudden pain they were bawling: 'Oh come let us adore him, Oh come let us adore him!'

Collectors of charitable donations were darting back and forth like detectives between the singers and Father Christmas, agents of the once-yearly outburst of goodwill for special causes: for handicapped children and cripples; in support of lesbian pacifists against the rape of whales by American missiles; in protest at racial discrimination against cannibals; in defence of obscure minorities and in the name of humane terrorists. As the whole pack of them jostled through the crowd, clinking their tin collecting boxes, the rattle of coin on tin produced a dull ache in one's temples and set one's teeth on edge like the sound of a fork drawn across a plate. The rattling sound was reminiscent of the shamanistic throbbing of tribal drums, of a witch-hunt that drove one's heart into a corner by moral blackmail so that it might be scooped up, like a half-dead cockroach, by that tin box: the noise in those tins was the rattle of one's harried, petrified conscience changed into coppers. A nation of conscientious extortioners and collectors of moral debts.

Clea opened her purse, counted out the appropriate sum for her hamburger and coffee, wiped her lips on a paper napkin and was preparing to get up when once again her glance met the eyes of a solitary customer sitting beside the door. She had the impression that he had been staring at her for a long time and had taken a seat by the door as though on guard. She did not like the eagerness with which he intercepted her chance look.

She was almost certain that this was the man who, for the last couple of days, had been lurking outside the windows of her nearby office. He might even have been following her all the way here. At the moment, amid the Christmas bustle, he was obviously in no hurry over his lunch, if a cup of murky coffee and an almost uneaten cheese sandwich (the cheapest item on the menu of that establishment) could be called lunch. Even so, he treated both coffee and sandwich with the care of a man who rarely allowed himself to spend money in public places, when the same coffee and cheese at home would have cost him almost three times less. For him to patronise this very ordinary snack-bar was almost an excursion into high society. His pose alone bore witness to this: a carelessly extended hand holding a cigarette; leaning against the back of his chair; his legs crossed – it all lent him, a man well into middle age, a purposely youthful air. This assumed nonchalance only accentuated the pitiful shabbiness of his appearance.

At first sight he looked distinctly like one of London's tramps and vagrants, the inhabitants of doss-houses for the homeless; he might even have come straight from under Charing Cross arches, where there are a lot of ventilation grilles from the Underground which exude heat from the trains and the passengers' accumulated stale breath, and where you can survive the night half-asleep even when the puddles all around are frozen – provided you can also snuggle into some empty cardboard boxes.

His overcoat, shiny from too close contact with street life, his clumsy, weather-worn shoes, and his very features – the alcoholic's wrinkled fold of flesh, eyes pale as though marinated in vinegar – would have announced that this man was a dosser who slept rough, had it not been for the extreme care and attention that had been given to every detail of his appearance: everything about him was scrubbed and clean, from his shoes to his face – carefully shaved, with a few fresh marks where the razor had nicked his skin, the sparse colourless hairs covering his bony skull impeccably parted. In any case, men of his type were to be found in doss-houses too; towards Christmas many of them would camouflage their appearance: from under the mattress they would produce ancient jackets pressed by having been slept on for a year, starched shirtfronts and ties so twisted that they looked like a dessicated stem of ivy; they would shave off their methy's stubble in order to line up, quiet as a funeral congregation, at the Salvation Army's charitable distribution of wafer-thin portions of turkey in gravy; they would smarten themselves in order to queue up as a kind of religious obligation, or rather in silent confirmation of the unspoken non-aggression pact between the charitable givers and receivers of alms, only to vanish again into the ditches, under the bridges, or behind the peeling walls of doss-houses.

Having identified him as yet another sample of the poverty and distress that were on display in England like the wares in a shoe-shop, Clea might even have felt a certain pride, the pride of a connoisseur, if she had not noticed on the table occupied by this gentleman from London's lower depths a paper parcel from W. H. Smith, the book and stationery chain. As though afraid of losing this precious purchase, the man never let the parcel out of his hands. In the couple of minutes in which they exchanged glances, the man opened the wrapping paper a few times, with the obvious aim of making sure that the highly-prized object was still there, to check that it was still undamaged, to admire it once more with the affection of a satisfied purchaser and then to seal up the opening of the package again. His exaggerated care in handling the wrapping-paper indicated that the purchase was intended for someone else. A present. A Christmas present. For a friend? A relative? But vagrants from doss-houses are, by definition, people who no longer have either friends or relatives, who have no one left in their lives to whom to give Christmas presents; the denizens of the lower depths are precisely those who never give presents to others – all gifts, in the form of handouts, are destined to be given *to* them, in order, at least on public holidays and feast-days, to restore a spurious harmony and equality between homeless loners and people with families grown weary of their domestic hearth. The man at the corner table by the door was thus not a vagrant, because he still had something to offer as a gift and consequently something to lose. He was therefore not in need of Clea's sorrowing reflections. For this reason, she would always clearly remember her own astonishment, embarrassment and even fright when, as she passed his table on her way to the cashier's desk, she suddenly heard: 'Excuse me, please.'

She stopped and glanced down at the man, his face turned towards her with an ingratiating look, which she countered by an expression of withering indifference. The lips seemed to be articulating with a very slight time-lag as they carefully uttered, in the respectable accents of the half-educated, the words: 'Excuse me, please,' rather as if he were asking her to excuse him for having failed her examination as a candidate to the ranks of the deprived and the suffering. Still without getting up, not daring to put himself on her level in height and social position, he began to construct, in a muddled way, with frequent apologies, clearings of the throat and pauses, what was really a single sentence. He spoke of how, for the past two days he had not liked to 'take the liberty of asking her a favour', but that her kind face had nevertheless allowed him to hope that she would 'understand his fatherly feelings at Christmas time'. She was already reaching for her purse, having assumed that this was the usual tortuous request for money to buy a drink, when, breaking through his own garbled preamble, the man stood up and introduced himself: 'Colin is my son – I'm his father. You know Colin, don't you?' he announced with a shake of his head that might have been from pride or possibly an apology, either for his paternity or his offspring.

The likeness between father and son was undeniable. Inadequacy was clearly hereditary. One had only to recall Colin's face to be convinced that the similarity between them in poverty of spirit went beyond the bounds of class origin. Colin – a tall, lanky teenager, pale to the point of transparency – had been brought to the office a week ago by the bookkeeper, Mrs Macalasky, a woman of vast lateral proportions and such small stature that when she coughed one felt it was not from smoking very strong unfiltered cigarettes but from asphyxia brought on by having carried in her belly a beanpole of such enormous vertical dimensions as Colin. He was apparently a backward child from birth, with a stunted intellect expressed in a fixed stare that he was to keep all his life, so that even as an old man he would, like his father, still look half a child; in adulthood this vacant fixity of gaze would be perceived as a sign of innocence and ingenuousness, those nostalgically prized attributes of the British face.

'I don't want him mucking about with punks in the park during his school holidays,' the bookkeeper had said, as she introduced her son to her colleagues. 'He can learn a lot here. He's a bright lad, is my Colin. When he grows up he may become a manager – who knows?' – 'Manager!' It was obvious from first glance that Colin would never become anybody, that nothing would ever come of him, just as nothing – less than nothing – had ever come of his father.

The mere sight of both of them was enough to induce the symptoms of a cold – a lump in the throat and a tickle in the bridge of the nose – brought on by the sickening thought that for someone, you, too, looked like Colin and his daddy. For you too had a father – a semi-educated nonentity apt to deliver domestic lectures about what was wrong with the world and the value of education through corporal punishment, strictures that turned into practical lessons as the whisky-bottle grew emptier; you too heard your mother's howls gradually merging with your father's snoring, and next morning there was a cup of tea turning cold because your mother hadn't had time to finish it as she dashed off to work to the sound of slamming doors, while you ate your solitary breakfast before playing truant from school. Never before had sons followed so exactly in their father's footsteps over so many generations as did the Macalaskys. And they were all your ordinary, everyday fellow-countrymen: they were born in the next street, they played truant, they took no 'O' levels or 'A' levels, they never went to a university; and the older they grew, the clearer and more predictable became the pattern of their daily lives – fixed by the route from home to work, from work to the pub, from the pub to home, and back again the next day along the same path trodden by generations of nobodies. 'In place of happiness, 'tis said, Mere habit's sent to us instead,' and it is those for whom habit is a substitute for happiness who are the volunteers in the army of 'ordinary, decent people', that army which is, as politicians tell us, the bedrock of any society – an institution created, like a circus-ring, to display the clownish antics of a small élite. But among those 'ordinary, decent' involuntary volunteers there are occasionally some soldiers endowed with that worst of military defects – a slight surplus, a little extra intellect that is not enough to put one in the officer-class of this world but which exceeds the necessary minimum ration of brain cells that guarantees one a steady place in the iron-fast ranks. That surplus is just enough for a person to be aware that although all the generals of this world call themselves 'soldiers', there are certain private soldiers who will never even make it to sergeant. The small makeweight of brain only serves to drag its possessor down to the very bottom. In any other country this unlucky ranker, cheated by fate, would find his level among his peers, would retire and find a congenial café, pub or club where the half-wits, in spiritual fraternity with the dim-wits, would formulate the basic political creed of these Siamese twins of the intellect as an alternative to the genetic individualism of the elect of this world. But in these islands, where the idea of privacy extends not only to one's dwelling but even to the inside of people's skulls, no one will ever look such an odd man out straight in the eye and he himself will never bring himself to knock on the door of someone else's soul. The only thing left to him is to go out once a year at Christmas, sit in a deserted snack-bar and stare out at the festivities in the street through a plate-glass window.

Clea watched the absurd fandango danced by the adepts of charity rattling their tin money-boxes in the street as though it were a sequence in a silent film: the sound of chinking coins was shut out by the thick glass of the café window – or rather, the Christmas-tide merry-go-round of kerbside altruism went on to the accompaniment of the long-winded yet timid explanations of Colin's father. Finally Clea began to pay attention to his mumblings about the 'dearly loved offspring of a tragically unsuccessful union' with Mrs Macalasky, and it became clear from this plaintive story that Mr Macalasky was terrified of his ex-wife and therefore had been unable to summon up the courage to go into Clea's office, where his son was killing time, and hand the boy his Christmas present. He would have sent it by post, but was afraid that the package would be intercepted by his wife – so would Clea please be kind enough to hand over the present to Colin in person? The wretched man held the cherished object in its wrapping. 'Why don't you give it to him yourself?' said Clea briskly, in an attempt to evade this absurd request. Mrs Macalasky had long since handed out the wages and set off to the shops; she was unlikely to return before the start of the office party. 'You have nothing to fear,' said Clea, and turned towards the cash-desk.

'So do you mean I could . . . come with you?' the delighted Macalasky asked ingratiatingly, and dashed back to his table. Out of the corner of her eye Clea saw him finish his coffee in three gulps, pause for a moment to wrap the remains of his sandwich in a paper napkin with that careful foresight common to tramps and bachelors, and then put it in his pocket. He caught her up in the street and trotted along beside her, now to the left of her, now to the right.

'The younger generation, you know, has quite ceased to believe in a life after death and that's a fact,' he suddenly announced, shouting to be heard over the Salvation Army's choir as they stopped for the traffic-lights at a crossing. 'There's absolutely no respect for old age. I've been reading in the papers how they murder old ladies with razors. Because they don't believe in an after-life, that's a fact. If you believe in life after death, you respect old people because they're on the threshold of that other life – that's a fact, isn't it?' He was again trotting alongside her, apparently not expecting an answer.

'It's possible to believe in an after-life and still hate that life as being something only for the privileged – and therefore to hate those who are about to enter that life,' said Clea, adding, as though to tease him: 'And that's a fact!' Why was it that the victims of injustice – any injustice – were always the last ones to perceive that injustice, just as a wife was always the last person to learn of her husband's infidelity? Clea gave an irritated sideways glance at the classic example of wretchedness trotting beside her. Suddenly Macalasky stopped, as though having sensed the concealed offensiveness in Clea's reply.

'I don't think I'll go any further, if you don't mind,' he said, his gaunt face twisted into an ingratiating smile. 'I'm afraid to, and that's a fact,' he added, apologising for his own weakness, and Clea sighed with the relief of someone whose unkind motives have escaped detection: Macalasky obviously had not guessed what she thought about him. Slackening his pace, he thrust the packet, crumpled and stained by his sweaty palms, into Clea's hands and set off quickly, almost at a run, back to the Underground Station. Dumbstruck, Clea made an indecisive move to stop him, but after a glance at the stooping back hunched into his shabby overcoat, she changed her mind and remained standing on the pavement.

Before diving into the Underground, this absurd creature fumbled in his pockets and dropped a coin into a chinking tin collecting-box deftly held out by a schoolgirl. The girl gave him a little bob of gratitude and Clea twitched, perhaps repeating the girl's gesture, perhaps in a spasm of revulsion or annoyance at the unpredictability of human nature – or was it from envy?

At the office no one was making more than a pretence of doing any work, to judge by the way that the holiday-minded crowd of idling employees had begun to drift and drape themselves around the place like Christmas-tree decorations. Demonstratively placing all ten fingers on the keyboard of her typewriter, Clea glanced at the girls who were hanging Christmas tinsel around the room, which meant standing unsteadily on chairs and squealing coquettishly as the men clasped them, ostensibly to secure their graceful torsos against an imminent fall. Someone was already wandering about in a coloured paper hat, while the general manager was appealing for help to place a white plastic angel on the top of the Christmas tree.

Someone else was already asking for a corkscrew, as the cases of cheap wine were being delivered. The chatter of Clea's typewriter was clearly annoying everybody, or at least she felt it was annoying them. Business papers were swept off desks to make room for batteries of paper cups and paper plates, on which the female staff of the organisation was neatly laying out slightly tired ham and pâté sandwiches, together with dishes of peanuts and potato chips. This was when Colin could have been useful. Clea caught herself not so much watching the festive bustle as looking around for his glum, lanky figure with his father's pale and timorous eyes, and the more she glanced at the passing faces of her colleagues the more she kept noticing the separate features of Colin's face – a protruding chin, arched eyebrows, sunken cheeks, the back of a long neck – as though multiplied in the many faces contorted by the pressures of getting ready for the party. But of Colin himself there was no sign.

All week he had hung around the office, his legs tucked under his chair and clasping his knees, having found himself a place alongside Mrs Macalasky's desk, like an overgrown chick under the wing-feathers of a broody hen. Occasionally she would dig him in the ribs and look in the direction of a secretary who was carrying a gigantic pile of file-covers across the office. Colin would then leap to his feet and rush to help. 'He can learn a lot here,' Mrs Macalasky would repeat to her colleagues in a loud whisper. 'Office jobs are harder to get than ever nowadays.' And she would immediately start to curse computers. After doing his duty as a newly-recruited errand-boy, Colin would go back to his place like an obedient dog bringing his master the newspaper in his teeth, and from his corner would intently watch the secretaries and clerks as they dashed to and fro. The more he felt himself to be superfluous, the harder he tried to be of help. Sometimes Clea would intercept that doglike glance, begging for she knew not what – a glance, it was now clear, inherited from his father, full of a primal urge to be of use mixed with a dull certainty that his services were not wanted.

The beginning of the week had turned out to be a time of disappointed hope for him, a false promise, when some pre-Christmas repairs and redecoration had involved moving desks and steel filing-cabinets; here he had been exceptionally useful, but for no more than an hour. As soon as the workmen had started drilling holes in the wall, he had hung around among the desks for a while and then slunk back, rejected, to his invisible kennel alongside his bookkeeper mother. Whenever a secretary or clerk got up from their desk, Colin would leap to his feet and rush over to offer his services – and the person concerned would shy away in fright, swearing. Colin pretended not to hear.

The disastrous aspect of his desire to be of use was made plain over the business of giving out coffee. An offer to fetch coffee for anyone who wanted it was the last card in his desperate struggle to prove how indispensable he was in the office. Coffee and tea were dispensed in paper cups from an automatic machine on another floor of the building. When you spend eight hours a day bent over a typewriter, to get up and walk to the coffee machine on the next floor is a real pleasure for every typist; in the corridors you can loiter at the notice-board, you can look out of the window at the next-door building, where other clerks exactly like yourself are flitting between the desks of an office exactly like yours; it is some consolation that others are no better off than yourself. Colin, bending over with a well-meaning desire to please, was looked upon with ill-concealed fury. His offer to go for a cup of coffee eliminated people's only chance of getting up, stretching their legs and consoling themselves with the realisation that other office-workers' lives were as bad as their own. But after one look at his spotty face, at the trembling smile on his thin lips and his timid unblinking eyes, one could only give a twisted smile in return and nod with affected gratitude. As soon as Colin's back had bustled out of the door, the look of gratitude gave way to a grimace and a suppressed curse: 'Idiot!' Mrs Macalasky either pretended not to hear, or really didn't hear, as she loudly summed up the character of her filial protégé:

'Helpfulness, I always tell him, is the best way to start a career!'

It was on one such occasion that Colin, reaching the doorway, had unexpectedly turned round, as though looking for confirmation of his mother's aphorism; at that very moment Clea, with a mocking wink behind Mrs Macalasky's back, was tapping her index finger to her forehead in a comment on the mental deficiency of the whole Macalasky family.

Now, as she recalled all these humiliating episodes, Clea was certain that at that moment Colin had been looking straight at her – because it was for her that Colin had set off to fetch a cup of coffee on that occasion. It had been no good for her immediately to pretend that she had lifted her finger to her temple to pat her hair. It infuriated Clea that she of all people, with her exceptional insight and understanding, was the person who should have sympathised with him; but the fact was that she was the one who found Colin most irritating, precisely because he reminded her of herself. Thou shalt love thy neighbour as thyself. But what if you hate yourself? What if you feel revulsion at yourself?

Only when the bosses, shouting above the babble of voices, officially announced the end of the working day, and the thump of disco music began to blare from amplifiers, did Clea get up from her desk, although it had long since been pointless to try and drown the clink of bottles with the tapping of her typewriter keys. Someone handed her a paper cup full of thin wine, and with a face that felt like dry paper she started to push her way to a corner where she might stand for the appropriate length of time required by the conventions of group propriety.

Depression welled up inside her like the heartburn induced by the cheap, sour wine. They would all get blind drunk, simply because the bosses were paying for the wine: the only active form of the class struggle – at the expense of one's stomach; and instead of revolutionary songs there would be an infantile chorus of 'Merry Christmas and Happy New Year' with foot-stamping and clapping – culminating in belching and vomiting. At Christmastime the entire population of these islands was given a warrant to lapse into infantility: everyone regarded it as their duty to act like a naughty child. It was the annual mass reversion to childhood, sanctioned by religion or, alternatively, it was the annual premature display of senile dementia, a licence to drool. All around, the atmosphere gradually became that of a children's playground, in which drunken teachers played with tipsy infants in a cat-and-mouse game of false equality and fraternity. As though it were their duty, everyone became unduly familiar: subordinates clapped their bosses on the shoulder, and with forced guffaws the bosses swallowed their subordinates' once-a-year legalised familiarity along with the cheap wine. In reality, however, every step, every remark was strictly calculated. One only had to overstep the mark by a fraction in one's tone of voice or make the wrong gesture, and one was immediately the target of several beady pairs of eyes.

Clea instinctively edged away when her friend and boss, Anthony, a director of the firm, came over to her and laid a friendly hand on her shoulder. Splashing wine over an impeccably understated jacket that had cost a secretary's monthly salary, in an expansive, egalitarian gesture he described a circle in the air with his paper cup and, shouting over the noise and hubbub, revealed his intimate thoughts to Clea: 'Only four years ago, how many were we? And how many are we now? But the atmosphere in the firm is the same, a family atmosphere – a family collective, a collective family.' Humming the tune that was snarling out of the record-player, he began to push his way through the crowd to Mrs Macalasky the bookkeeper. This lady, crushed between the backs of several of her colleagues, was simultaneously choking and calling out 'Merry Christmas' as she devoured crackers spread with pâté and cheese with the greed of a starving Ethiopian baby. As her boss took her by the arm, Mrs Macalasky, giggling like a schoolgirl, started to gyrate on her thick legs in an old-fashioned twist.

Amid the salvoes of musical gunfire from the disco, Clea caught herself constantly looking for Macalasky Junior among the clouds of tobacco smoke. Colin was one of those creatures of the lower class who appeared in one's life and disappeared again like the blossom of London's trees in the spring. But now it was the middle of winter. And as the bosses droned on about the family atmosphere among the firm's staff, Clea finally realised that Colin had not been allowed, on principle, to attend this party. He might be permitted to turn up during the working day thanks to the management's indulgent attitude to their bookkeeper's family situation, but no one had thought of inviting him to the Christmas party – it was not a party for real families but a party for the staff, which was a pseudo-family. And before long Clea was feeling just like Colin – an uninvited relation at someone else's party.

Outside in the street it was as unnaturally dark as it had been unnaturally bright in the office, as though this frosty street was a purposeful invention, a visual aid for teaching a moral lesson to those who absent themselves from the collective on such an occasion, in weather like this, in an age such as ours. In other countries, where summer is summer and winter is winter, on a dark night at this season snowflakes are falling, inviting one to join in the dance of life, despite the cold – as, no doubt, was happening in Moscow. But here in London, where the seasons simply merge imperceptibly into one another, as do perceptions of the differences between the male and the female sex, and where even the weather has become a transvestite, there was not even any snow to soften the harshness of the frost-bound asphalt gloom, a gloom that did not end with the street: at the end of one's journey there was still a freezing cold room. How was one to reconcile this outburst of goodwill, these fraternal embraces to the clink of glass, audible even through the curtains of lighted windows, with the misery and loneliness that succeeded it here, out of doors, on the frost-bound asphalt? If only these manifestations of love and friendship were not meant for others at all, but were simply a public demonstration of entirely personal spiritual longings, as in an oral examination at school – everyone can hear your voice, but only the examiner is listening to you. Is there not, surely, some other island in the world, some other civilisation, where one is not always threatened by that schoolmaster's ruler called personal responsibility – responsibility for one's own life, for one's own conscience, for one's own death – that ruler which cracks you over the knuckles and the heart whenever you forget yourself and imagine that either everyone is guilty or no one is guilty, and therefore one need not worry about one's own guilt . . . ?

He emerged from behind a mountain of black rubbish sacks piled up at the foot of a flight of steps, as though these dully gleaming polythene bags, stuffed with the detritus of everyday existence, were cocoons for incubating the misbegotten freaks of the human race, creatures that hatched out at night and became garbage again at daybreak: the moths of an underground world.

'Colin!' Clea exclaimed with affected enthusiasm. 'I've got something for you . . .' she went on, intending to tell him about his Christmas present, but her voice dried up. She did not like the look of him. Colin was not looking straight at her, but his gaze was wandering all over her with the eyes of an indecisive murderer. 'Go home, Colin,' she whispered almost to herself.

Clutched in Colin's little fist, a knife flashed in the light of the street-lamp – not a proper knife, but a penknife, a thing one takes to school for sharpening pencils, or whatever people do with penknives (sharpen quills?). 'Go home, Colin!' she repeated as she backed towards the lamp at the foot of the steps, saying it loudly this time in the hope that someone might hear her, at the same time trying to suppress her hysteria lest he think she might give him away by calling for help. With one leap he managed to gag her mouth from behind with his hand, and they both staggered backwards as though retreating from a savage monster in the form of the lamp, its single eye swaying in the darkness. They drew back from the terrible danger, violator and victim pressed together by the hostile emptiness of the deserted alleyway that offered no escape to the bright street. Clea's heel broke, and as she stumbled they both fell on to the sacks of rubbish. She should have shouted, but somehow she could not, and not only because fragments of anecdotal advice were floating through her head: lie back, shut your eyes and think of England; nor from fear of the penknife, especially as that little blade had clattered from his trembling hands as his fingers ran over her body, aimlessly tearing at her silk blouse and clumsily trying to pull up her tight narrow skirt. A little longer and it would come to the tangle with her tights and knickers.

Her fear had quite gone now; instead came the tedium of waiting, as when one has an appointment with the gynaecologist or before an interview for a job. A mysterious object was pressing into her side, having fallen out of her handbag – it was the Christmas present intended for the creature who was now panting, straining and heaving over Clea's unyielding body. She thought anxiously that the gift wrapping, over which Colin's father had taken such care, was probably now completely torn from being dragged over the asphalt, and she started to wonder what was inside that coloured paper – a box of sweets? A set of writing materials? A box of dominoes? Whatever the object was, it was now lying among the sacks of garbage, digging painfully into her side and reminding her that she had failed to hand it over. In all her life, in fact, she had never given anyone a present, just as no one ever gave anything to the down-and-outs who spend the night under bridges, in ditches and on rubbish-tips, huddling into empty cardboard boxes, wrapped in garbage-sacks – in the same way that she was now sprawling, covered as though with a coarse blanket by this youth crazed from awareness of his own wretched inadequacy. Was he one of those who use razors to test for the existence of an after-life on old women pensioners? Was she, in his eyes, one of those old women? No, she was a rejected present on a heap of refuse – an abandoned Christmas present for the human race, meant for someone who never received a present from anyone.

'You bitch, you bitch!' Colin swore, half groaning, half whining, as though in response to her unspoken thoughts.

Quite unable to penetrate her, he could only press himself to her crotch and clumsily rub against her, causing her pain; he was like a famine victim incapable of swallowing even the longed-for crust of bread offered to him by some miracle of charity. The damp, sticky hairs of his fringe gave off a strong smell of cheap eau-de-cologne – the smell of school dances and first meetings with girls, a sickening reminder of one's years of ineptitude, humiliation and hopeless emotions, when one expects everything from the world and one wants it *now*, only to get contemptuous kicks, sneers and jabs in the stomach instead. He twitched and stiffened, breathing in gasps, as Clea's hand groped for and felt the little lump of helpless flesh, wrinkled with shame and fear, that hung between his legs. Like a child having a nightmare he ground his teeth as Clea tried to squeeze from that piece of flesh the force pent up within the recesses of his body – a force which, if he failed to release it, would leave him forever an embittered and ineffectual supplicant for the kindness of others, for Clea's compassion. His face swayed before her eyes like a huge blind moth, a creature that you simultaneously fear, despise and pity, and which you try by every possible means to put out of the open window. As he beat himself against her like a moth against a pane of glass, after a few hopeless jabs a stream of hot, sticky liquid squirted into Clea's hand – a fluid that for one instant felt like blood. Colin squealed as though he had been stung and began to crawl away from her on all fours. His face, half of it in a black shadow caused by the play of lamplight, was twisted into an ugly grimace of bared teeth like the muzzle of a panting dog. But Clea felt that she herself looked still more repellent; even if hers had been an act of compassion, she knew she had not done it out of kindness: her unselfishness sprang from the fact that she felt even greater revulsion for herself than for him.

His mouth still gaping open, Colin picked up the knife from the ground. Clea got up too, and waited, kneeling, for the short jab to her heart that she knew she deserved. Despite the darkness, she could see for the first time that he was looking her straight in the eyes. Finally his throat uttered a sound that was half grunt, half sob; he suddenly turned round and began to move away, at first at an unsteady walk, then at a jog-trot, stumbling, his back bent like a beaten animal.

Clea got up from her knees, slowly and with mechanical carefulness smoothed down her skirt, tried to straighten the seam of her torn blouse and finally began to do up the buttons of her overcoat right up to her throat; the coat was now filthy from being rubbed over the frost-coated asphalt. She was bending down for her handbag when her fingers, fumbling in the dark, came across a torn, crumpled piece of gift-wrapping. 'Jean-Jacques Rousseau – *CONFESSIONS*', she read on the cover by the light of the street lamp, after she had extracted the book from its wrapping. *Egalité, fraternité, liberté* – or was it the other way round? The social system was to blame for everything. Clea recalled that this precursor of the French Revolution had taught that all evil is the fault of society: it is society that makes us what we are and we ourselves are not guilty of anything. Rousseau must have been gratified that he had served tonight as bedding for an act of humiliation that illustrated his precept: he – Colin – was not guilty; we were all guilty. The well-fed features of the French thinker smirked vaguely from the cover of the book, a face totally unlike that of his humble English disciple, who had spent the last of his money on this book in the cause of educating his son and heir in the spirit of humanism.

Clea walked over to one of the huge, man-high steel refuse containers that stood behind the pile of garbage sacks and swung her arm back, intending to throw the absurd, useless Christmas present into it. But her arm stopped in mid-swing and she staggered backwards in horror: out of the square, tomb-like metal box arose two monsters of the subterranean world, two ragged down-and-outs from the lower depths. Unshaven, with sunken cheeks and dishevelled hair, looking like left-overs of half-eaten human flesh, they were scavenging among the rubbish with hands encased in black cotton mittens, so that in the darkness it seemed as if their wrists and palms had been cut off and their protruding fingers were moving of their own accord. The two figures looked to Clea like aged, decades-old ghosts of Colin and his father. One of them was pawing a broken plastic doll that he had just pulled out of a heap of trash at the bottom of the container. The other, teeth bared in a grin, was scratching the doll's stomach with his fingernail and laughing with his toothless mouth, at first quietly and idiotically, then in a bestial neighing that grew louder and louder. Clea giggled hysterically. They both turned towards her and, roaring with laughter, threw the doll high into the air. It fell, the celluloid making a dull thump on the asphalt. One of its arms had been torn off, its stomach was split open and its neck twisted; only its glass eyes stared at Clea with the timeless, divine, commercialised blueness of the Holy Child that had been born that night.

4 ROUSSEAU EXPOSED

'The establishment is putting it about, in the hope that people will believe it, that if it hadn't been for pacifists like Aldous Huxley and Bertrand Russell, Hitler would never have been able to carry out his holocaust. And we, they say, are playing into the enemy's hands in exactly the same way. The implication is that if it weren't for our peace movement, totalitarianism wouldn't be on the rampage, and that we are simply providing grist for their mill . . . I shall leave aside for the moment the question of who is *really* aiding and abetting totalitarianism in our time, and I would point out that at the worst we are only supplying grist, and not pouring oil on to the flames of future wars,' – and Anthony spluttered as he choked on yet another slice of banana. Margot slapped him on the back. As though spurred on by this gesture, Anthony continued with the rehearsal of his speech for tomorrow's anti-nuclear protest meeting. 'And incidentally, if we had all been pacifists like Aldous Huxley, there would never have been a Hitler and his acts of genocide: the king of Denmark, for example, pinned a yellow Star of David to his own coat and the Jews in his kingdom were saved. If everyone was like me – I mean, like us – there would be neither Soviet totalitarianism nor American imperialism in this world. That is, of course, a somewhat metaphysical statement, but the time has come to stop blinkering our minds with notions of national security when there will soon be nothing left of this nation but a heap of radioactive dust – that way, our security *will* be guaranteed! And don't let people tell you that our demonstrations in defence of peace are being exploited by the enemies of freedom behind the walls of the Kremlin. Now is not the time to be thinking of how your words and actions are being utilised by the enemy. It is time to reject the concept of an "enemy" altogether – it is time to vindicate our own categorical imperatives! Let the Soviet people work things out for themselves. I am convinced that there are enough people of goodwill in the Soviet Union who understand us aright; at least if it happens they will know that *we* didn't want war. Meanwhile they should be inspired by our example. Certain irresponsible Russian dissidents hate the achievements of socialism so much that they are prepared to drop an atomic bomb on the heads of their own children, mothers and old people. Let them try and find ways of peaceful co-existence with the Soviet regime and stop accusing us, British intellectuals, of failing to agitate for a suicidal blockade of the Soviet Union. And by the way, a certain movement that shares our ideas is already detectable in Russia: the other day I read in *The Times* that Russian pacifists had unfurled a banner in the street with the slogan "Peace to the World!"'

'That's an official Party slogan,' Margot the know-all interrupted him. 'Slogans like that are draped all over the place, and it wasn't pacifists who displayed that banner but people marching across Red Square in an official First of May demonstration.'

'Like Aldous Huxley, I would rather remain alive under

Soviet tyranny than be a charred corpse under our pseudo-democracy, which is turning itself into fascism as part of the growing incitement to a third world war.'

'You've just misquoted Aldous Huxley, and kindly note that it wasn't Aldous Huxley who said all that. It was a character in his novel – who was, incidentally, an out-and-out scoundrel. In the story he seduced his best friend's fiancée and the friend ended up by committing suicide. Some pacifist!'

'It's too easy, Margot, to discredit ideas by blackening people. It's time you learned to appreciate progressive ideas even if you find the people who utter them repellent. And moreover, you must learn to live in the world not only with people but with ideas that you may find repellent. The people who live on the other side of the Iron Curtain are, like it or not, human beings, and not monsters from another planet, as certain people imagine who hypocritically hold forth on the differences between totalitarianism and bourgeois democracy. None of us are perfect!'

'Of course, we are all capitalist sharks, but even so it's a mistake to confuse a boiling saucepan of fish soup with an aquarium,' said Margot between gritted teeth.

'An aquarium?! And what's so marvellous about our insular little puddle, inhabited by a bunch of middle-class frogs that croak with ecstasy every time they are shown a wax mummy called the British monarchy? Even the hawks in the Kremlin are not fooled by these syphilitic remnants of the British empire as it slowly sinks to the bottom of the sea! Rule Britannia! Britannia rule the waves!'

Anthony pulled a face and puffed out his cheeks as he sang the patriotic words with ironic enthusiasm. Clea noticed that Anthony's squealing tenor made Konstantin, apparently asleep on his feet beside the birch-tree, raise his head and gaze in their direction with a long, absent-minded stare. Clea had the impression that Margot's constant interruptions of Anthony's monologue were not so much intended to refute what struck her as false ideas as to attract Konstantin's attention. Anthony, too, was clearly giving frequent sideways glances at the ambiguous dummy standing in the far corner of the little garden. Either they didn't understand what Konstantin was really like or they may have been nervous about what they were saying in his presence. And were they competing with each other in an attempt to win his approval?

Periodically the clouds would roll across the sun, and together with the puff of wind that accompanied this natural phenomenon the conversation would be interrupted by the twittering of birds, as though to blot out Anthony's sententious maxims and Margot's caustic rebuttals and remove them to a safe distance away from Konstantin. In these moments of twittering birdsong, Konstantin's lowering silence in the background became less unsettling and oppressive. His very presence and the fact of his Soviet provenance were distracting Anthony from making his brilliant deductions and arguments in favour of unilateral disarmament. He reminded them of the existence, in the background, of that country whose government was akin to the frost, the sun, death – akin, in fact, to nature itself, a force whose aims and actions we are notoriously powerless to influence. Every reminder of this hindered Anthony's efforts to induce his fellow-countrymen to see the light.

'Men are bored, they want to go in for a bit of fighting – to crush a few bones. Rule, Britannia! What are we, weaklings? Are we any worse than the Yanks? We're a superpower too, they say – we've got the wherewithal to give the commies a bloody nose! . . . Do you realise what all that propaganda is based on?' said Anthony, turning to Margot and Clea, as though they were a crowd of pacifists, thousands strong. 'As a cover for all this aggressiveness and male chauvinism they are using the idea of the "sinister hand of Moscow".'

'Thank God they've got something to cover. Not like some people.' Clea had no idea whom Margot might be attacking with this cynical remark.

'And what is there to cover?' Anthony said, starting to fidget. 'All that falsehood, hypocrisy, cruelty, greed, intolerance and envy?'

'And lust,' Margot put in.

'Yes, and lust. But the main thing is aggressiveness. Did you hear what our Secretary of Defence said this week? Both sides in the nuclear rivalry must intimidate each other in the hope that their mutual threats will never be put into practice. Therein, according to this monster of human morality, lies the guarantee of peace. And they expect us to live in this state of mental absurdity? Someone has to say, openly and out loud, that the emperor has no clothes!'

'You mean – the queen,' Margot giggled.

'Soviet emperor, British queen,' Anthony brushed her aside. 'What does it matter? We're all naked and defenceless against each other. We're all offspring of the human species, irrespective of race or political systems. If only we could admit our own errors and failings and convince the rest of mankind to do the same, to realise that none of us is any better than his opponent. If only West and East could bare themselves to each other, throw off the spurious garments of their mutually hostile ideologies! And someone has to be the first to start what you might call this self-exposure. By that I mean unilateral disarmament.'

'Rousseau also wanted people to go back to nature and called on them to throw off the hateful vestments of civilisation,' said Margot, as she picked up a paperback edition of the *Confessions*, lying on the grass near the table, and began idly leafing through the pages. 'And how did it all end? With the French Revolution. And yet it started with nothing but a harmless bit of flashing. Did you know, Clea, that Rousseau was rather fond of exposing himself? He would stand round a corner, let down his breeches and flash his prick at passing girls – damn, I can't find the place where he describes it,' she said, as she flicked through the book she was holding.

Anthony, apparently out of humour as a result of Margot's remark, said nothing. Clea bit her lip. She could not forgive herself for having left the book lying alongside the garden table that morning, and now she did not feel able to snatch the *Confessions* from the hands that were mauling the book. She had become very familiar with Jean-Jacques Rousseau. He had been, as it were, the sole witness of that disgustingly humiliating episode with Colin; old Jean-Jacques, crumpled during the attempted rape, smeared with dirt from the asphalt near that rubbish-dump, was someone she could trust. Margot's outrageous treatment of his *Confessions* was, it seemed, the culminating humiliation ordained by fate for this preacher of merciless sincerity about oneself, this bard of individual freedom, this philosopher of personal salvation, this denouncer of clerical and governmental authority – of all those, in fact, who foist upon us a perception of truth as bureaucratic expediency, of which Clea, together with Rousseau, saw herself as a victim. She, however, had not so much studied his philosophy as the human image of this man with his embarrassed smile on the small, slightly effeminate lips of the face that gazed helplessly from the tattered cover of the book.

With him she had shuddered with a spasm of degrading lust when the hand of his governess, having first lowered his breeches, had lashed him with a birch-rod; and when he undid his fly to stand waiting round a corner for passing girls, knowing that the day would come when he would be soundly thrashed for it. With him she was filled with disgust and indignation, but at the same time with curiosity, when a Jesuit had tried to accustom him to sodomy; with him, too, she would masturbate at night in order to keep herself from worse forms of debauch. With him, in spirit, she had run away from the house of soulless relatives to be a servant in another household and to sigh alone at night as he recalled the dazzling social gatherings in the drawing-room of his master and mistress. With him she had indulged in some petty pilfering from his employer's boudoir and, fearing disgrace, had slandered an innocent servant-girl, only to suffer for the rest of his life as he attempted to redeem his guilt. For several years now, as she re-read Rousseau's *Confessions*, in each successive episode of humiliation she had seen herself and the pathetic Colin, and it was hard to say on whose account she had suffered most: Rousseau's, her own or Colin's. In the endless vicissitudes of Rousseau's years of wandering in exile – full of physical sufferings, of real and imaginary fears, full of the genuine humiliations that were the lot of a refugee and of his own self-distrust – Clea had perceived her own years of voluntary exile in Moscow. Even Jean-Jacques' relations with Mme de Warens, which at times touched the extremes of morbid exaltation – the woman whom all his life he had called 'maman' – reminded Clea of her own relationship with Konstantin, especially the episode during a meal when 'maman', who had just put a piece of meat into her mouth, had been frightened by Jean-Jacques' shamming performance of showing the intensity of his love for her. Rousseau had cried out that he had noticed a hair on the meat; 'maman' had spat out the half-chewed piece on to her plate, whereupon Jean-Jacques had greedily seized the rejected morsel and swallowed it with amorous passion. Rousseau had been obliged to place his own children in orphanages; how could he, a persecuted exile, bring up his offspring? And wasn't Colin just such an orphaned child? Clea remembered the mocking, contemptuous glance with which she had looked Colin up and down when he had been hanging around the office and offering everyone – and Clea most of all – his well-meant but unwanted services – and she was seized by the same sense of guilt that had preyed upon Rousseau when he recalled his children, scattered among several orphanages.

As Clea's glance wandered from corner to corner of the garden, encountering the figure of Konstantin lurking by the birch-tree, in her imagination she could see only Colin's orphanage-boy's back, bent in humiliation at his own crime, and she was ready to forgive him everything – the knife in his hand, the pain between her legs and the stab of mortal fear in the pit of her stomach – if only Colin would forget the scornful looks she had once given him. In her own defence she could only say that she had been punished for all that by Konstantin's appearance in her life, he whose shadow seemed even now to be stretching as far as her.

The setting sun was shining through an oncoming cloud

with slanting rays, casting moving shadows over the birch-tree, the fence and the house, and for a moment Clea had the impression that in this play of shadows the figure of Konstantin, bent over the weeds beside the birch-tree, had turned into the stooping Colin, who was hiding behind the trees of the next-door garden – or was there someone really hidden behind the fence, peering through a crack at her present humiliating way of life?

'Where is that page, where he flashes his prick at girls?' said Margot, still hunting through the book with greasy fingers. Clea knew all the pages by heart, including the number of the page that Margot was looking for. But she naturally kept silent. She wanted to wrench her *Confessions* out of Margot's blasphemous hands. 'I wanted to use it to show that a ballistic missile is a phallic symbol. It is, isn't it?' Margot giggled. 'So all your discussions about arms reductions are like little boys showing each other their willies and measuring them. Who's is longer? Who can piss the farthest? So unilateral disarmament, Anthony, is voluntary castration. The desire to become a eunuch, while others are in the grip of an innate fear of castration. And you know what eunuchs are used for, don't you, Anthony? Perhaps you'd like to tell us about it, would you, Anthony?'

'You've changed terribly over these last few years, Margot,' Anthony grunted, adding suddenly, with no change of tone but with unexpected aggressiveness:

'How could you forget my gumboots? It's going to rain tonight, tomorrow I shall have to walk a good four miles over cart-tracks and through woods in order to get to the missile base – so what sort of state shall I be in for the meeting?'

'You can borrow a pair of gumboots from Kostya – as a first step on the road to mutual castration by East and West.' And Margot exchanged conspiratorial glances with her old friend Clea.

'Konstantin will never lend his gumboots to anyone,' Clea reacted in a tone of unexpected grimness. She wanted to complain about Konstantin's sudden nocturnal sorties, from which he would return nearly twenty-four hours later, his boots smeared almost to the knees with mud, to which several huge stains on the carpet invariably bore witness. She had been obliged to put up with these stains and the foul smells that came from the kitchen. No, he most certainly would not lend his boots: he needed them for some secret purpose of his own, as he also needed the huge knife that he always took with him. How could she tell all this to Margot and Anthony? They would think she was insane.

With the same flickering, unseeing gaze – in the way we look at people who are not quite normal – Anthony had listened to Clea's complaints about the Soviet way of life in the days when she was living in Moscow. He had obviously not believed her, and in response could only mumble that of course Soviet socialism had its internal shortcomings. The service in the Hotel Rossiya, for instance, left a lot to be desired, to put it mildly – but one had to remember that these hotels for foreign tourists were being built at a time when the Soviet government's chief priority was a big programme of housing construction for their own working people, and foreigners had to put up with the situation, just as he, Anthony, was putting up with the minor irritations of his trip to Moscow.

They had met on that occasion in Sokolniki Park, where Anthony was representing his firm at an international trade fair – or something of the sort. They had wandered among the black tree trunks flanking the pathways dug through the snowdrifts by park attendants, as though strolling through a stage-set for Glinka's opera *Ivan Susanin*. Anthony, who had been to the Bolshoi Theatre the previous evening, was expressing his views on that Russian classic with mixed feelings: on the one hand Ivan Susanin had dealt with the enemies of his country by demonstrably non-violent means – by leading them into snowdrifts in the depths of a forest from which there was no way out; on the other hand, though, he had been led to perform this patriotic feat by a feeling of blind hatred for the enemy and blatant xenophobia – of which Anthony, of course, could not approve.

'In general, I must say, this patriotic attitude among certain elements of the Soviet intelligentsia worries me. Patriotism is only one step away from idiocy,' said Anthony, stepping cautiously through the snow, 'to say nothing of fascism. In Russia, however, one shouldn't confuse official propaganda with the religious longings of the Russian people. For many Russian intellectuals, a patriotic leaning towards religion, which in the West is undoubtedly a reactionary tendency, is at times the only hope for a non-violent restructuring of society in a spirit of pacifism. The Orthodox Church, with its emphasis on communality, is, I believe, the only alternative to rootless dissidence, which breeds renegades who are so implacably hostile to Soviet society that they place all their hopes on a military *coup d'état* – or on military intervention from outside, as I became convinced during a series of meetings with *émigré* representatives of this movement in England. Believe me, Clea – those people are feeding disinformation to public opinion in the West. And it's not surprising: most of them were failures where they came from, with an unconcealed hatred of the ideals of their people, and once having betrayed their own country they have deprived themselves of the right to judge Soviet history objectively. They purposely blacken their own path in order somehow or other to justify running away from the land of socialism. I don't deny the shortcomings of the Soviet system, but believe me, Clea, they can't be compared with the ills of capitalism, to which Soviet dissidents are completely blind. I hope your Konstantin isn't a dissident, is he? I tell you frankly, Clea – we can't go along with those people,' – argued Anthony, as they made their way towards the edge of the park. Having come to meet Anthony in the hope of discussing with him the chances of getting Kostya's 'culinary treatise' out to the West, Clea said nothing.

It was hard to accuse Anthony of being fickle in his views: he was quite ready to repeat in Moscow what he propounded in

London. And in return Moscow obviously fascinated him by its unchanging character – at least where its cold weather was concerned. The frost and sunshine on that day seemed, like the words in Pushkin's poem, fixed and hardened for ages to come. The landscape around them instilled into Clea a fear that was akin to her fear of the Soviet government, as hardened and unchangeable behind the walls of the Kremlin as the tree-trunks in their frozen shrouds of hoar-frost. Anthony hunched himself into the collar of his City businessman's camelhair overcoat, crowned with a sable fur hat with ear-flaps that he had bought on arrival at a foreign-currency shop. Clea, unprepared for such a long walk in the snow, was shivering in her hooded, Czech-made duffle-coat, aware at every step that her tights-clad knees were freezing to her jeans, already coated with hoar-frost. Feeling as deep-frozen as a cod-fish in a freezer, she listened dully as Anthony, for the umpteenth time, appealed to both East and West to bare themselves and to strip off the fictive garments of their mutually hostile ideologies.

This appeal suddenly appeared to receive a practical response: a whooping sound came from behind their backs and a crowd of men thundered past them, pushing them into the adjacent snowdrifts. The men were naked. That is to say they were wearing swimming trunks and bathing-caps, but otherwise they were naked – huge, fat, hulking creatures with bulging muscles and pot-bellies. They pounded onward into a glade between the trees, trotting through the snow on bare pink heels towards a frozen lake that glinted white between the trees. It was clearly a lake and not a field, because in the centre of this gigantic open space there yawned a hole in the ice, showing black amid the snowy expanse like the ragged-edged pupil of an enormous eye. When with much guffawing and whooping these fleshy hulks began diving into the hole, for a moment Clea thought she was witnessing the inauguration of a new form of political protest, of mass suicide, on the lines of self-immolation by fire though using the very opposite means. But in a moment the men's knobbly heads in their bathing-caps started bobbing up to the surface from the water singing out something optimistic like '. . . the great thing, lads, is to stay young in heart!' Then the men clambered out on to the ice and began to run around the hole, pushing and egging each other on, starting mock quarrels and throwing snowballs at each other until finally, panting and snorting, they began to rub each other's backs with snow. Their bodies suffused from within by a claret-coloured incandescence, like scalded crayfish or a newly-flayed carcase, they were loathsome yet at the same time fascinating in their carnivalesque, naked state of being. A minute later they were on their way back: Clea caught sight of drops of melted hoar-frost on hairy chests and clouds of steam issuing from the mouths of these reanimated monsters from the ice-age. One of them, playfully showing off as he ran, biffed Anthony with his shoulder, making him fall into a snowdrift amid the passing hoots of laughter. Anthony's fur hat fell off. He picked himself up, floundering knee-deep in the drift, and began to brush the snow off himself, a helpless, apologetic smile on his face. For the first time she suddenly felt terribly sorry for him.

On the way back, Anthony complained about Margot: for the umpteenth time she had refused to go with him on a business trip to Moscow. He invited Clea to his hotel 'for a cup of tea', and Clea agreed, but the doorman refused to let her go up to Anthony's room, taking Clea for a Soviet citizen – on that occasion she did not have her British passport with her.

5 *BARTER*

All Clea's emotions were being expended in the long-drawn-out affair with Kostya – and not only her emotions: all her money was going on the constant trips to Moscow. For the first months she consoled herself with the fact that in the eyes of her London friends she had become someone special. Behind the mask of an ordinary secretary was a first-hand witness to the legend of mysterious Russia. In fact more and more of her energy and money were being spent on proving the mysteriousness of that Russia. At one time there was no end to the invitations to dinner and lunch, at which the 'Russian question' would inevitably arise and she would throw off a casual explanation of the recipe for 'prison swill' in the works of Solzhenitsyn or describe the menu enjoyed by the Kremlin leaders, supplied on special order from the Party's restricted-access food shops.

Without noticing it herself, whenever the talk turned to Russia she would constantly revert to one single theme: food –

simply because this was the only thing that interested Kostya. This, in turn, was the only thing that made Kostya interesting to his friends. Ah, those friends! They only showed their friendly feelings when Kostya arranged one of his evenings of culinary extravagance for them. As soon as there was nothing left of the meat but bones, their interest in Kostya evaporated, just as Clea's London friends' interest in her Russian stories declined and vanished, unmoved as they were by the disappearance of sausage or cottage cheese from the counters of Moscow's grocery shops. What worried them was unemployment in Great Britain, but since unemployment was forbidden in the Soviet Union, and a man could be sentenced to prison with forced labour for 'parasitism', interruptions in the supply of food could not dim the light of socialism in their eyes.

It was even harder for Clea to demonstrate coherently and conclusively the permanent shortage of foodstuffs suffered by the working population of the land of socialism. In the opinion of Kostya's friends, meat had vanished from the shop counters simply because all the Russian cows and bulls had been given jobs as Party officials. But this was obviously just a cheap political joke, whereas Clea always found their tables well supplied with ham, or if not ham then best-quality sausage or smoked herrings (known in England as 'kippers'), not to mention tinned cod's liver and 'Rodina' brand aubergine pâté, which Clea never liked, despite Kostya's persuasive lectures on the wealth of calories and vitamins in these tinned foods. His exhortations were sadistically echoed by Kostya's so-called friends, who clearly disliked Clea because in their view she exerted a harmful influence on Kostya, with her ultra-leftist deviations and drove him demented with her stories about the West; in fact they regarded her as virtually an agent of imperialism who was trying to abduct their country's best cook and connoisseur of 'Rodina' brand tinned foods. At such moments they became pure chauvinists. 'Try some smoked herring,' they would say, smiling sweetly as they slipped a reeking fish on to her plate. 'They say you can't get smoked herring for love or money in Europe.'

'Smoked herring is first mentioned in the Scandinavian sagas. Therefore this food was originally European and not Russian at all,' Kostya observed in an authoritative tone, using the herring, in his own peculiar way, to defend Clea's Western European heritage.

'Russian this, European that – but Russia is part of Europe, isn't it?' – the guests insisted. 'And what about black bread? All Russian émigrés complain about the lack of black bread abroad,' they claimed, attempting to discredit the West in Kostya's eyes. And Clea, choking, would eat smoked herring and gulp down 'Rodina' brand aubergine pâté. In fact, towards the end of every stay in Moscow Clea felt so starved that her allergy to 'Rodina' practically disappeared. Exactly how all this exotic produce found its way on to the table in every home, when the only things on sale in the shops were potatoes, soap, galoshes and tins of stewed pork, remained a mystery to Clea, despite the explanations given by loquacious hosts proud of their black-market connections in the food trade. At first she couldn't understand a word of their resourceful and highly practical advice, full of slang expressions like 'orders' desk' or 'under the counter' and mysterious terms like 'a bit of grease' or 'to bag a place in a queue' – everything that in Russian is called *blat*. She discovered that this word had a whole spectrum of meaning from friendly connivance to outright crime, and at first she had confused it with another widely-used slang word – *blyad'*, which, although it means a whore, Russians would even confusingly use to abuse a man.

Given such a well organised system of plundering the socialist economy, it was hard to understand why people spent their whole lives doing nothing but making telephone calls, greasing someone or using *blat* to bag a place in a queue under the counter.

Strangely enough this exhausting activity became, at times, almost a form of national rejoicing. One day, on the advice of his neighbour, Kostya went to queue up for some tinned herrings. After standing in a queue for nearly a whole day, he proudly carried home the hard-won booty, opened the tin of this scarce commodity with trembling hands and almost fainted: beneath the label marked 'Herring' the three-kilogram tin turned out to be full of red caviar. There at once began a flurry of telephone calls to all and sundry, the news was spread to every corner of Moscow, and Kostya, at the head of a party of his loyal subjects, rushed back to queue up again in the fish department. Obviously someone at the factory had by mistake canned a batch of red caviar in herring tins, although more likely it was not a mistake at all but had been done expressly for black market purposes and maybe even for sale abroad.

Everyone was terribly excited and discussed the prospect of a life of pre-revolutionary luxury for a year ahead, with caviar to accompany their vodka, but they were all let down by the stinginess of the poet Mandelstok. Standing in the queue, the miserly Mandelstok announced that he couldn't afford a whole tin and decided to share his prize fifty-fifty with someone else, which he proceeded to do in a corner of the shop for all to see. A bystander immediately spotted that the 'Herring' tin was full of caviar, and this started such a stampede that the salespeople themselves were threatened with being turned into caviar. Immediately realising what had happened, the counter staff closed the department. The cash desk, too, was closed, and the manager, shouting down the mounting uproar among the workers, personally made a speech to the crowd. White in the face, he begged the public to put themselves in his place and to return the tins of herring, or rather the wrongly labelled tins of caviar, and he even offered a small reward – otherwise, he declared, he was likely to be shot for misappropriation of national property.

It is hard to say just how much the contents of the tins were a surprise to the manager; what may have been a surprise was that these special tins had been put on sale to the general public without the manager's knowledge, and that for this error he really would be made to pay by the mafia that ran the black market. One way or another, Kostya's friends managed to lay their hands on enough tins of pseudo-herring to vanish smartly before the manager had time to call the police. Flushed with excitement as though after an act of revolutionary expropriation, they all crowded into Kostya's room, carrying the coveted tins under their coats. But the first tin, opened to help celebrate the coup with vodka and caviar, aroused a suspicion which gradually increased as the other tins were opened and turned into an ominous mood of hostility towards Kostya. Of all the tins, only Mandelstok's contained caviar; the rest corresponded to the label, which showed Atlantic herrings trying to swim to America but getting caught on the way by Soviet fishing-nets. Someone even proposed subjecting Kostya to a show-trial for spreading disinformation, but as usual it all ended in a booze-up, in which they ate all the caviar and later took the remaining herrings home in their shopping bags. There were enough of these, however, to make the washing-up smell disgusting for a month, and the reek of herring seemed to settle in people's lungs for a lifetime.

The tinned foods on which Kostya chiefly subsisted were little help in getting rid of the after-taste of herring. Clea would not have been surprised by the mere fact that Kostya's diet consisted of so much tinned food; the British working class, after all, ate nothing but tinned food because it was cheapest. In Moscow, though, it was in short supply – all those tins of sprats and ladies' fingers were simply not available to ordinary people; but Kostya was in a privileged position, and in his home there was an endless supply of the canned goods that were so damaging to Clea's digestion. And not only to her digestion: they undermined Clea's faith in the legendary Kostya whom she had first seen on that new year's eve – Kostya as the true representative of proletarian Russia. It was not so much that both his parents were gynaecologists; the really damning thing was that in Clea's eyes his job in a factory was nothing but a piece of bluff. Yes, he worked in a factory – but as what? As a guard on the main gate. And in what sort of factory? A cannery. And what for? Not in order to merge with the toiling masses, but so that he could pinch as much tinned food as possible. The point wasn't in the misappropriation of national property – everyone pilfered everywhere; Kostya's motive was that he worshipped the West, and he regarded tinned food as almost a symbol of the industrial progress of Western civilisation compared with the barbaric backwardness of Russia. It was useless to try to convince him that all these partly-cooked tinned products were a symbol of the inhuman automatisation of Western society, in which cheap commodities and cheap ideas, such as tinned soup and the concept of the Iron Curtain, were used to stupefy the stomachs and brains of the necessarily thrifty proletariat, whilst the manufacturers paid millions to a pop artist like Andy Warhol to advertise their tinned soup. To these exposures of capitalist chicanery, couched in Marxist dialectic (in which Clea herself believed less and less), Kostya responded only with a crafty smile, as with maniacal enthusiasm he would examine every tin with a new label that he had sneaked out of the factory under his coat, then would open it and sample the contents.

In the course of his tinned-food banquets Kostya would tell her the latest news that he had heard at work – for example, about the unprecedented zeal shown by the guards at the main gate of a distillery and the tragic incident in which a friend of Kostya's had been involved. In response to a tightening-up of the system of anti-pilferage checks on the employees, Kostya's friend had devised an original means of smuggling out spirituous liquors – with the help of a condom! He would swallow a condom, while gripping one end of it with his teeth; the spirit was then piped into the condom through the open end – and without an X-ray apparatus no security guards could ever spot it. Having poured in three litres of brandy by this method, Kostya's friend had boldly set out for the check-point at the main gate with the much-expanded condom suspended in his stomach. 'You've got yourself one hell of a gut, haven't you? Don't you do your physical jerks to the radio every morning?' – said the guard, roaring with laughter as he hit Kostya's friend in the belly. If Kostya's notoriously foul-mouthed friend had replied to that punch in the gut with an appropriate four-letter word, the story would not have ended as tragically as it did: in opening his mouth, the spurt of brandy would have blasted out of his mouth into the guard's face and Kostya's friend would have been sacked from his job. Well, and maybe he would have been fined, maybe given a suspended sentence with compulsory deductions from his pay. But the friend decided not to give himself away; he restrained himself, kept his mouth shut – and pop! The distended condom in his stomach burst from the punch, the brandy flooded through his alimentary tract and the friend died next morning from alcoholic posioning.

'How unreliable condoms are in the Soviet Union' – Clea thought to herself in perplexity, wondering why Kostya was telling her these grotesque stories. Perhaps this story contained a hidden reference to the fatal lack of freedom of speech in the USSR – because if that friend had dared to open his mouth he would still be alive! But what was the significance of the condom? Was he hinting at something, on the very eve of their wedding at the register office, after which there would be no turning back? 'Belly, condom . . .' Was he perhaps hinting at the undesirability of her getting pregnant? At all events, these stories contained more than a hint of contempt for ordinary people – of that there was no doubt at all. The more her knowledge of Russian improved, the less she understood this culinary pervert. Even the Russian word for tinned food – *konservy* – was becoming associated in her mind with the Conservative Party in England.

It transpired that Kostya's job as a factory gate-keeper was not a change or a promotion from manual work, but merely a consequence of his dismissal from the Academy of Sciences, where he had worked in a highly paid job as an economic statistician. And he had been sacked for disagreeing with his boss over culinary matters. Konstantin might well have remained a Soviet citizen all his life, standing in queues for hours at a time, not wishing to risk years of imprisonment, had he not happened to be present at an official lunch given by his boss at the Academy in honour of a delegation of Arab exchange scholars. The academician, a frequent visitor to the lands of Arabic socialism, while offering hospitality in his office to the Arab comrades in the form of some Georgian *shashlyk*, ordered in from the 'Aragvi' Georgian restaurant, had remarked that a whole range of meat dishes used in Near Eastern cookery formed a link between the Arabs and several of the non-Russian republics of the Soviet Union. *Chekhartma*, for example. 'What is *chekhartma*?' enquired the Arab comrades. '*Chekhartma*,' said the academician, 'is a Caucasian dish, basically a form of roast meat.' – 'Nonsense!' said Kostya, rashly intervening after a closer study of Georgian brandy than of roast meat. '*Cheremsha* isn't meat at all – it's a plant, something like our onion.'

Trying hard to restrain himself in front of foreigners, the academician gently disagreed: 'No, my dear fellow,' he said to Kostya, '*chekhartma* is not an onion, but roast mutton.' Kostya, however, was adamant: '*Cheremsha* is an onion!' – '*Chekhartma* is mutton!' insisted the academician. '*Cheremsha* is an onion!' Kostya maintained, his voice rising. 'Look here, I'm not going to argue with you,' said the academician indignantly. 'You've never been to the Caucasus and you haven't eaten *chekhartma*.' This was the last straw for Konstantin: 'I've never eaten it because I can't stand it. *Cheremsha* reeks like garlic . . .' (although, be it noted, he himself always put garlic into every meat dish that he cooked) – and without further ado he threw a long, pointed *shashlyk*-spit at the academician. Unfortunately he scored a hit – only not on the academician but on the head of the Arab delegation. Luckily the spit was caught up in the Arab's headdress, which saved the man's life, and although Kostya avoided being deprived of his freedom he was deprived of his job with a black mark on his record. Apart from becoming a watchman or a security guard, therefore, he could not get a job anywhere, and even as a gateman the only place that would take him on was the cannery.

At the time, Clea could not of course grasp the essence of the argument about *chekhartma* and *cheremsha*, but she was already beginning to get an inkling of her future husband's true nature. What she had at first taken for an innocent predilection for matters gastronomic (like being keen on gardening or breeding tropical fish) was a real illness, the attacks of which were prone to lead to absurd incidents that caused embarrassment in others and put Clea in an unpleasant position – such as, for instance, the incident at the French embassy during a reception for a certain Vladimir Vysotsky and his wife Marina Vlady.

One can imagine what hypocritical smiles and flirtatious advances she had to make to her toffee-nosed superiors in order to gain an invitation to this super-élite gathering. Clea only submitted to these humiliations because the date of her marriage was approaching and she knew perfectly well that Soviet bureaucrats were capable of pulling any kind of trick. For bureaucratic reasons the marriage ceremony had already been put off several times, on one occasion because the register office was being redecorated but chiefly as a result of the endless queue – as though on hearing of Clea's intention all Soviet maidens had decided to follow her example without delay. By now she had been kept hanging around waiting in Moscow for three months; Anthony, thank God, had fixed her up with a secretarial job in the office of one of the British commercial representatives in Moscow, through whom she had managed to wangle the coveted invitation for an evening with Vladimir Vysotsky and Marina Vlady at the French embassy.

She was not interested in either Marina Vysotsky or Volodya Vlady; she did yearn, of course, for starched table-cloths and waiters but her chief motive in getting the invitation was the hope of making connections in diplomatic circles, just in case any complications should develop over her marriage and subsequent departure for England with her husband. Kostya, it would seem, should have been grateful for Clea's successful efforts, which had cost her so much humiliation, from an insincere flirtation to scrimping and saving every kopeck to buy a party dress. And indeed Kostya had agreed to the idea at once, even with a display of enthusiasm that was somewhat excessive for a function of this kind. As a result, Clea put herself in an ambiguous position with regard to the

KGB by taking Kostya, a Soviet citizen, to a diplomatic reception.

As soon as they entered the embassy, Clea immediately began to suspect that there was something odd in Kostya's behaviour. She led him over to the buffet table in order to make friends with people who might prove useful contacts. And what a table it was, after *bouillon* cubes and tinned fish from the food factory! The spread was positively Gogolian in its abundance and sophistication, Clea was thrilled by the maelstrom of tailcoats and furs, the aroma of mingled scents and the buzz of the French language. It was all so theatrical that even conventional thoughts of the falsity of so much gilt on life's gingerbread immediately vanished from her mind. Kostya, however, did not share her Cinderella-like excitement. Standing in a corner by the door, through which waiters dashed in and out, he was nervously fiddling with his tie, which Clea had had such difficulty in making him wear and had then tied for him. Every time a tray of delicious canapés was brought round, Kostya would turn away in irritation, giving no more than a sidelong glance at the tasteful array of exquisite morsels on bread and butter. She was doing her best to pull him towards a group that was holding a lively *à la fourchette* discussion of *samizdat* – and who better than Kostya to join them and play the part of Solzhenitsyn, but he was simply blind to her secret winks and urgent gestures. Nor did she want to miss the opportunity of contact with the Vysotsky-Vlady constellation, around whom literally the entire party was orbiting. According to rumour this couple had played together on two guitars in the famous Taganka band, which Clea had heard about from Margot in London even before coming to Moscow. But whenever she tried to entice Kostya in the right direction, she was firmly rebuffed.

'I must be nearer to the kitchen,' he whispered conspiratorially into her ear. 'The kitchen's at the other end of the building. They don't go in for glass screens, so you can't watch the cooks at work, like in some of these fast-food joints,' he added, almost to himself. 'If the chefs work in secret, that's because they've got something to be secretive about.' Glancing furtively around, he wagged his forefinger wisely.

Clea did not immediately grasp the full sense of this enigmatic remark. Kostya twitched and his expression changed when the waiters began to hand round the next offering, a dish of salad. If it had not been for Kostya's twitch and the positively erotic sighs of a few gourmets in various parts of the room, Clea, who had already sampled most of the delicacies on offer, would have completely ignored these tiny little plates with their miniature portions of some finely-shredded gastronomic frivolity. Only one plateful was handed out to each guest, with no second helpings, and when Kostya had seized a little plate from the tray he hurried off to a distant corner, thrusting aside tailcoats and the trains of priceless dresses as he went. There, with a face as pale as the hero's in the ball scene of Griboyedov's *Woe from Wit*, with trembling hand he lifted the contents of the plate to his lips in tiny amounts, which he then chewed slowly and carefully. His jaws seemed to be stretched forward like an animal's muzzle, moving not only up and down but from side to side.

The fashionable assembly had long since forgotten the salad; coffee and liqueurs were already being served, cigars were being puffed here and there and people were moving into the adjacent drawing-room to listen to the bard of the Taganka, but Kostya was still in his corner, eating his salad with an air of intense concentration.

Nervously cracking her fingers, Clea walked round and round the almost empty room in circles. Glancing about her, her face twisted into a fixed, social smile, she finally decided to tug at Kostya's sleeve: 'What are you up to?' she whispered into his ear. 'We'll miss Vysotsky!' Kostya did not reply but only stared at her in firm refusal as he continued to extract fragments of salad from his plate and move his jaws in a circular motion. Clea looked into the little salad bowl, which Kostya was holding in front of his nose, in the way that one might hold a spittoon or an alchemist's dish. In it lay the last fragment, with a wisp of some greenstuff sticking to it. With a deep sigh Kostya picked up this magical herb, chewed it, smacked his lips, frowned and finally gave out a victorious 'Aha!' which caused the few remaining tailcoats in the room to cast astonished looks in his direction. Kostya, however, was already dragging Clea towards the front door. Pushing aside doormen and lackeys, he rushed towards a taxi-rank outside the embassy gates. In the taxi Kostya uttered not a word but only smacked his lips.

Bursting into his room, he practically pushed Clea out of the way and began grabbing various little packets out of drawers, rummaging through his shelves and unscrewing the lids of jars and bottles; he then shook out the contents of some boxes, mixed them up, the spoon tinkling on the side of the glass, then ground something in the mincing-machine, stabbed at a mortar with a pestle, stirred, mixed, shook it all up, sprinkled something and poured something else, until Clea had the feeling that at any moment the bowl in which he was mixing all these ingredients would start emitting an evil-smelling vapour. But Kostya was working with ever greater calmness and calculation, and finally, with slightly trembling hands, he placed the bowl in the middle of the table. Removing his frilly woman's apron he gave a nervous sigh and spooned out a tiny portion of his concoction. Smacking his lips again and whistling through his teeth, he looked thoughtful for a moment, wrinkled his forehead and then suddenly jumped up, almost hitting the lampshade that hung from the ceiling. 'But of course!' he kept repeating, at first in a whisper and then more and more loudly, as he dashed back to the shelves full of jars and boxes, where he rummaged once more, sniffed, mixed in a bit of this and a bit of that and tasted it all again until finally a beatific smile lit up his face.

'The answer was quite simple,' he cried, as he pranced around the room, stamping his feet and clapping rhythmically. 'There it is, there it is!' he shouted joyfully, tapping the bowl lying on the table. He thereupon scooped some of the salad out of the bowl and almost forcibly thrust the spoon into Clea's mouth. After chewing it obediently she shrugged her shoulders and said that she had been eating the same salad an hour ago in the French embassy.

'That's the whole point!' Kostya exclaimed excitedly. It emerged from his somewhat incoherent remarks that this salad was something special: for centuries it had been a strict secret of the kitchen of the French embassy in Moscow. Rumours about this salad had been in circulation for hundreds of years and every Russian diplomat had raved about it in their memoirs – from Vyazemsky the poet to Litvinov the People's Commissar of Foreign Affairs – but only he, Konstantin, at this very hour, in this year, in this century had succeeded in correctly guessing the secret recipe and reconstituting the ingredients of that magical dish. Leaving Clea standing in the middle of the room holding a dirty spoon, Kostya grabbed a fountain pen and sat down to enter the recipe into his record-book.

It was probably that evening that Clea began to suspect the maniacal nature of her future husband. For a year before that she had been touched by Kostya's culinary passion, and she still kept a fresh memory of that domestic image of him on New Year's Eve – the sight of Kostya at the gas stove, giving orders to an eagerly helpful mob of pseudo-intellectuals. Only recently Clea had patiently endured a row with the Soviet customs, who took her for a drug-smuggler: the customs officers would unscrew the lids of innumerable little earthenware jars containing rare, expensive spices, open packets and shake out exotic mixtures, so that for months after one of her regular Moscow visits Clea could never escape the smells of cinnamon, tarragon, cardamons and similar rarities. Kostya was crazy about spices, which according to his theory symbolised the imperial culture of Western civilisation, whereas instead of spices Russian cuisine preferred nettles, with which they had flogged the serfs and then stirred the resulting nettle soup with birch rods, while they made tea out of the birch-switches used in steam-baths.

'Is there any flavour in the Russian pancake?' Kostya would enquire angrily. 'What civilised person is going to eat that tasteless concoction of flour and water? Exodus is over and we're not living in the Sinai Desert any longer!' And he would quote well-known passages in the classics of Russian literature, from Chekhov to Leskov, which described in detail how Russians used to reduce Englishmen, Germans and Frenchmen to helplessness by feeding them on these same pancakes, blackmailing these foreigners through the laws of hospitality with the aim of suppressing Western influence.

It gradually became clear that he regarded all literature from an exclusively culinary viewpoint. He only recognised, say, Gogol as a genius because Gogol had described Ukranian dumplings in sour cream – a dish of obviously non-Russian origin, because the Ukraine had long been polonised and Poland herself had been westernised for even longer. He appreciated Marcel Proust purely for his description of *temps perdu* while in search of French asparagus, Brussels sprouts, artichokes and suchlike exotica which existed only *du côté de chez* Swann, whereas on this side of the Iron Curtain there was nothing but abstract proustianism without any of his vegetables. Kostya's attitude to historical figures and to politicians was the same. He was prepared to forgive Stalin for his reign of terror, because he had given national status to Georgian cuisine. Khrushchev, on the other hand, earned Kostya's approval because he had brought back from America the idea of milk in waxed paper cartons and cornflakes. He condemned Peter the Great, however, because he had introduced the Russian people to the habit of smoking tobacco. Here he would produce examples of barbarity in Russia, where everything – from the food to the alphabet – had been introduced by force: as when, for instance, the Empress Catherine decreed that her people should be compelled to eat potatoes in view of the economic advantages of this newly-discovered fruit of the earth. 'And how many of our dimwitted population died as a result of that decree?' Kostya would enquire with malicious glee, before informing Clea, who was being driven mad by these stories, how the stupid Slavs, fearing the imperial displeasure, had rapidly sown all their fields with potatoes and had died in tens of thousands after the first harvest: they had eaten the leaves of the potato plant – it had never occurred to them to dig up the tubers – and potato leaves, as we know, harbour a poison more venomous than arsenic.

As the months of their acquaintance went by, Kostya's stories grew more and more weird. No one knew where he picked them up, and outsiders sometimes felt that they had only the most tenuous connection with food and cookery – for example, the nauseating story that *Pravda* had printed during the 1920s. He had acquired this copy of the newspaper from an old junk-dealer and would read it out on all suitable occasions; eventually he even had it framed and hung it over the couch:

> 7th April 1922.
> The appearance of an old Jew named Gindin on Lubyanka Square and then on Theatre Square carrying the corpses of three children gave rise to a large number of unfounded rumours.
>
> The People's Court decided to put an end to these rumours and ordered the public hearing of the case to begin on the following day, 5th April. Long before 4 p.m. a large crowd had collected outside the Polytechnic Museum, where the trial was to take place. They quickly filled the huge auditorium and galleries, and sat waiting patiently.
>
> In came the first accused, Gindin – a decrepit old man who could hardly drag one foot after the other, a tattered little cap on his tousled grey hair, the charge-sheet held in the bent fingers of his gnarled hands.
>
> The examination of the accused began.
>
> 'Gindin, what is your occupation?'
>
> 'I work for the synagogue,' the old man lisped with an effort. 'When a person dies, I read the psalter and help with the burial . . . I do good works . . .'
>
> 'Who directs you to conduct burials?'
>
> 'Who? Fuchs, God grant him health. I do nothing without Fuchs. He is the boss . . .'

The court questioned Fuchs, who is in charge of the Dorogomilovskoye Jewish cemetery.

'Why did you appoint old Gindin to bury the deceased persons?'

'I was asked to name someone, and I suggested him – I wanted to give him the chance of earning his living.'

It was meanwhile explained that according to Jewish custom no great significance was given to funerals, and bodies might be buried in whatever manner was available.

'The next accused!'

An elderly woman got up from the bench in the dock – Tatyana Romanova, a points-woman on the tramways.

General laughter – 'Some surname! Must be a member of the Tsar's family!'

She knew nothing.

'I just change the points: the trams run so often now. I looked and saw people running, so I ran too. I looked again and saw an old man with a sack at his feet and there was a little corpse . . . And everyone was shouting and shouting . . .'

'And what did you do?'

'I don't remember.'

'She hit me,' Gindin stated to the court. 'She hit me and shouted: "The Yid's murdered a baby".'

Next to be questioned was the youth Serafimov, a ticket-speculator. He was selling tickets under the colonnade of the Bolshoi Theatre; he heard people shouting 'Beat the Yids!' and ran to look.

The accused Yefremenko stated that he had found himself in the crowd by chance.

'I'd just had my lunch and was walking along the street. I heard people shouting: "Beat 'em, bash 'em up!" Well, so I went over and said "What's it all about?" – "The Yids have murdered a baby!"'

'And did you shout?'

'Yes, a bit. That old girl –' he indicated the points-woman – 'she told me, and I blabbed about it to someone else. And so it went on . . .'

The last accused was Lipovetsky, commandant of Check Point No. 195. He had failed to take the necessary measures to provide the mortuary with proper equipment, as a result of which rats had gnawed the corpse of the infant Rabinovich.

Blagoveshchensky, a priest of the church of the Holy Virgin, was questioned as a witness. He stated to the court categorically that the corpse of the infant Kaplun had not had so much as a scratch and was circumcised.

The parents of the infant Kaplun testified that their son had died of pneumonia: he had caught a cold when he and his mother had been travelling from Yelizavetgrad to Moscow to join her husband. The Kapluns were poor refugees and had sought the services of Gindin because they had been unable to bury their son on their own . . .

Late that night, after 4 a.m., the court considered the verdict and pronounced sentence.

Regarding it as proven beyond doubt that the infants Rabinovich and Kaplun had both died a natural death, the court found all the accused guilty and pronounced sentence as follows:

> Romanova, Yefremenko and Serafimov – guilty of anti-semitic agitation, but since they were all unwitting tools of experienced adherents of the 'Black Hundreds' movement and enemies of the Soviet régime, they were sentenced to a severe public reprimand. Gindin – his guilt was proven, but it was impossible to punish a decrepit and hungry old man, engaged in carrying corpses to the cemetery to earn a crust of bread. The court could not punish him, but recommended that the Social Security administration should immediately ensure that he was supplied with the necessary means of subsistence.
>
> The sentences made a tremendous impression on those present, which was increased by the closing words of the president of the court, who appealed for a struggle against medieval prejudices and ignorance.

Clea could not understand the connection between children's corpses and cookery: 'The story is all about anti-semitism, the blood libel,' she said. 'Jewish blood as a sauce for Soviet propaganda was not offered on the counters of Party ideology until much later,' Kostya objected, 'and that is why, in the nineteen-twenties, an old Jew on Lubyanka Square with a sackful of corpses was acquitted. But what had happened to the corpse of the third child in the sack?' And Kostya pointed out with tedious insistence that there had been three children's corpses in the Jew's sack, whereas only two had figured in the trial. 'What happened to the third little corpse? *Pravda* says nothing about that. But I can tell you what became of it: it was eaten!'

With a fanatical gleam in his eyes, Kostya would feed Clea with stories of cannibalism, ranging from bonfires of human bones in the Volga steppelands to the alleyways of Leningrad during the blockade, where in the pitch darkness of the blackout thugs armed with boat-hooks and stevedores' grapplers would lurk in wait for someone weakened by hunger, grab their victim and drag him into a cellar, where they would cut him up into steaks and sell them on the black market. Clea began to be afraid to go out into the street at night, although she didn't really believe these macabre stories of cannibalism, in spite of *Pravda* – which in any case no one in that country believed, except, apparently, Kostya, although Kostya was reading into the story things that *Pravda* had never published.

With all the assiduity of a monkish chronicler Kostya would regularly enter his anti-Soviet fabrications into his record-book, the mere sight of which gave Clea attacks of unaccountable fear and depression. It was a greyish-yellow volume made of cheap, lined paper with margins printed down the sides of the pages. In the 'credit' columns Kostya would enter recipes of foreign cuisine, while on the 'debit' side were juicy versions of slanderous legends about how the Russian diet had mutated from eating normal food into cannibalism. He entitled this culinary treatise: 'Russian Cooking – A Story of Terror and Cannibalism', and he had apparently been engaged on writing it for almost an entire decade. He referred to his treatise with that peculiarly Russian sort of mockery which Clea never did manage to decipher – a mixture of self-deprecation, irony and, at the same time, wounded pride. The contents of the treatise remained a mystery to her, because it consisted of fragmentary, disconnected entries, where recipes were found alongside passages that she would have regarded as sheer pornography had they not alternated with pages of anti-Soviet writing on food and cookery.

In the long evenings, to the sound of a blizzard howling outside, Clea would sit for hours translating these macabre texts. Kostya's aim was to have his treatise published in the West, so that the whole world should be made aware of, as he put it, the crimes of Russian cookery. 'Synyavsky and Daniel – and Solzhenitsyn too, incidentally – have failed to identify the essence of the tragedy of Russia: its *gastric* character, in the literal sense of the word,' Kostya would say, pacing up and down the room as it shook to the rattle of train-wheels outside. The vibration would cause phrases to dance in front of Clea's eyes, phrases untranslatable into the language of Shakespeare, such as: 'The process of dekulakisation of stomachs and cannibalism as a form of collectivisation,' followed by recipes for cooking human flesh, from shredding it on the lines of German sauerkraut to a French-style marinade and aspic made from human bones.

Clea was beginning to guess why Kostya had chosen her as his intimate companion. He was making use of her as an ingredient in his recipe for the salvation of Russia through the westernisation of the Russian stomach. For Kostya, Clea was a guinea-pig from the West – could she or could she not swallow all his libellous ideas about the land of socialism? He himself was obviously incapable of swallowing the Russian people.

She was even prepared to accept this position. The individual was right to combat the servile traditions of his people, the conservatism of that society and the conformism of a Soviet bureaucracy that had corrupted the proletariat in the course of its victorious progress towards communism. And once having taken the path of dissidence, one should step out on to the high road and not settle down, entrenched behind jars and recipes, at a crossroads near the Lefortovo Prison. The life of a dissident was, of course, a form of escape and flight from the everyday tedium of work and discipline into the narcosis of revolutionary activity, into the ceaseless round of meetings with foreign journalists while still at liberty and encounters with the outstanding men of one's time during prison sentences, in conditions that were sufficiently humane to permit metaphysical dialogue, especially since the exposure of Stalin's autocratic crimes. But it was nevertheless possible to avoid this escapism and the infantile disease of communist leftism, and there was a host of examples of this to be found in Moscow. She had heard of such examples when she had been living in London, from connoisseurs of Moscow life, who at that time were breeding in the British capital faster than the increase of the unemployed under the present Conservative government. Many of them knew the poet Yevtusensky, who also regarded himself as a dissident (otherwise how could he have become famous in the West?), although according to rumour he had a magnificent dacha in the south of Russia called 'Babii Yar', and in Moscow he had built himself, at the Tishinsky Market, a hundred-foot-high ivory tower. Officially this tower had been erected as a monument to the friendly peoples of Africa, but in its bas-relief of carved hieroglyphics, supposedly spelling out a revolutionary slogan from the Ivory Coast, an experienced eye could discern the outlines of Hebrew letters; thus the tower became a symbol of the Jewish contribution to Russian culture. Furthermore, it was possible to receive foreign journalists in the tower; there was a public lavatory just around the corner, so that a WC and a water-supply were unnecessary, and the tower was quite habitable.

Another example was the artist Glazoment, who officially painted portraits of members of the Politburo, but if one looked carefully, all the faces on these portraits were a cryptic mosaic of ancient Russian cult-objects, such as carved wooden ducks and distaffs, which in itself was a protest against the Party's propaganda for soulless atheism.

Even the persecuted Solzhenitsyn, so it was said, lived an interesting life at Rastropovich's dacha: Tvardovsky would read him bedtime stories from *Novy Mir* while Rastropovich accompanied him on the cello. In other words, even under a dictatorship certain people were able to combine a form of dissidence with a full and active life. Only Kostya was incapable of it.

There was, of course, a third way – to go to the West. With the greatest ease Konstantin could have been reading his political cookery book into the microphones of all the Russian-language radio stations in the West, thus re-educating the stomachs of Russia by brainwashing via the ether. But Kostya wouldn't hear of an ethereal existence in the West. Clea could not understand how it was that, given his gut hatred and cannibalistic attitude to the Soviet régime, Kostya refused to emigrate and live among the Yorkshire pigs. Obviously that hatred was for him a kind of gastric juice that caused his spiritual metabolism to function. That year, in trying to understand Kostya, she had read a great deal of the Marquis de Sade and Sacher-Masoch. It was obvious that neither de Sade nor Masoch would have spared either themselves or their countries in order to implant their sado-masochistic ideas into the minds of all humanity. Unfortunately the society that they were attacking began to indulge, in petty-bourgeois fashion, in the practices of these two but not their ideas: society reacted to Masoch masochistically (they spurned him but they read him) and to de Sade sadistically, by first shutting him up in the Bastille and then in a lunatic asylum. But at least society did not ignore them. Kostya's sado-masochism was obviously of a masturbatory kind: the object of his attacks – Russia – had no inkling of his existence.

Nor had anyone, except Clea, guessed of the existence of his record-book and its catechism of accusatory recipes – the book was kept hidden from even his closest friends. Even so, Konstantin had got it fixed in his schizophrenic brain that the fate of Russia depended on his gastric constructs and that his stomach was virtually the soul of Russia. '*La Russie – c'est moi,*' was clearly his motto and with an enigmatic look on his face he would observe that Rome had been saved by geese. The fact that no geese would save Moscow had long been obvious to Clea, since they had vanished from the counters of the food shops for all time. With increasing frequency the salty marks made by Clea's tears stained the recipes of the record-book as she sat at home translating them into English. 'Go awaaay, awaaay,' the trains would wail outside the window. But it was too late to retreat. Her russophile English girlfriends, having amused themselves long enough with Kremlin exoticism, had long since run away to get married at home in Sussex or Middlesex or Devon, and feeling a premonition of the anguish and humiliation that their pitying glances would cause her, a grass widow, Clea preferred the anonymity of marriage behind the Iron Curtain. Apart from that, she had also decided that one could not abandon a mentally ill man to the mercy of fate – a man who imagined that Russia was lodged somewhere in his rectal passage. And Clea decided to extend her stay in Moscow for a further year.

That year in Moscow was to remain in her memory as a kind of prolonged nightmare, in the way that some people shudder when they recall a winter's enforced stay on an ice-floe, a spell of sharing a Turkish prison-cell with the rats or a first abortion – times when both pride and shame are destroyed and no degradation can stand in the way of attaining one's sole objective: to survive, to claw one's way out, to clamber to safety.

When her marriage was solemnised in a register office (where a woman looking like a sack of cabbages hung with medals gave a long speech about the role of the family in the struggle against the fascist aggressors), Clea simultaneously lost her secretarial job at the British trade delegation – either on security grounds or due to reduction of staff. There was nothing left for her to do but stay at home for days on end, especially when the really cold weather began and the first blizzards started to howl. As the wall of snow grew outside the window, so those discussions in London about permanent revolution and inflation began to freeze solid in her memory and in her eyes the Iron Curtain rose ever higher in the shape of the fence along the railway tracks, behind which the trains would pound along, shaking Kostya's room, coming she knew not whence, going she knew not whither. Time, too, had shifted, because Kostya's job involved shift-work and he would sometimes return at midnight, sometimes towards morning, marking Clea's time in Moscow by his erratic homecomings – she had no other point of reference.

It was not only her hours of sleep, or rather of her nightmares, that depended on Kostya. Like a prison warder, Kostya naturally dictated her food rations, largely consisting, as was to be expected, of tinned foods stolen from the factory, not counting the insubstantial delicacies that Clea had managed to bring back from London. While Kostya, sipping bouillon made from cubes, mixed with Brussels sprouts from a London tin, would read out the appropriate Brussels-sprouts quotation from Proust, Clea would be trying unsuccessfully to banish the single word that rang ever more loudly in her head and which drowned out both the burbling of Kostya's reading and the rumbling of her own stomach. That word was: meat. At first she had tried to renounce the frivolous, petty-bourgeois thought of scrounging food from under the counter, but when the last mentions of meat vanished from Kostya's culinary experiments, bloodstained visions of Chicago slaughterhouses and Yorkshire mincing-machines began relentlessly to persecute Clea in her nightmares, and by morning the edge of her pillow was liberally moistened with her saliva.

Once she even dreamed of Gindin the Jew and his sack in the middle of Lubyanka Square: he was offering her the corpse of a baby, gnawed by rats, as suitable for roasting, saying that he would let her have it cheap as they were going to arrest him anyway. 'Take it and eat it, may it bring you good health,' the

Jew with the sack was saying. 'You're allowed to be a cannibal: you're a foreigner.' But Clea had shaken her head: 'I'm a Soviet citizen by marriage,' pushing away the little cold baby, yet thinking: 'Perhaps I should take it? Kostya's a cannibal, after all.'

During their meals taken *à la Kostya*, Clea would sit at table as though half asleep, holding an empty spoon poised in the air in one hand and propping up her chin with the other, with a gaze as blurred as a frost-bound window, sniffing the aromas that floated in from the corridor through the keyhole until her head began to spin. Out there, Kostya's neighbour Tonya was cooking up something that clearly differed from Kostya's tinned-food diet. More precisely, Kostya's menu was directly dependent on whether Tonya was feeling favourably disposed towards him.

Tonya worked in the butchery section of a large food store, and Clea gradually began to realise how the myth had arisen of Kostya as the chief national purveyor of meat to his friends' festivities. All those chickens' drumsticks, legs of mutton, lamb chops and fillet steaks had come straight from under Tonya's counter. These supplies, however, depended on the highly complex nuances in the relationship between Kostya and his neighbour, and for a long time these nuances remained a mystery to Clea. At all events, the first few months of Clea's residence in the shared flat as Kostya's wife resulted in Kostya being obliged to limit himself to the tinned goods that he could scrounge from his work-place, and Clea, completely demoralised by her longing for meat, began to think up possible moves towards *détente* – in other words towards Tonya – in the kitchen. And Tonya, despite a show of reserve, clearly welcomed these steps. She had become a figure of temptation to Clea, a temptation that sent her confused mind back to the moral teachings given during religious instruction at her Quaker school. The very smells floating out of the kitchen, unusual for an English sense of smell, she found dizzyingly exotic and therefore seductive; she was drawn to them as to the treasure island in a children's story-book. As she listened to the rhythmic tapping of a native's knife shredding cabbage, or to the burble of a heated frying-pan full of hissing oil, she would wonder – could one really cook fillet steak in such a gigantic lake of oil? Or perhaps it wasn't fillet steak at all, but a pork chop sizzling in its own fat? Or was it liver? Perhaps she was cooking a meat pie? This though immediately brought her up short: how could it be a pie when this was a communal flat in Moscow and not a Yorkshire country pub?! The spoon fell from Clea's weakened fingers; justifying the shameful calls of her deprived stomach by a missionary idea (she should teach Tonya, that culinary barbarian, how to cook a delicate English pudding), Clea made an excuse aloud to Kostya: 'I'm going to rinse my spoon.' Picking up her spoon from the floor, she went out to the kitchen, her knees weak and trembling.

Tonya, a sturdily-built girl in curlers, wearing a navy blue dressing gown patterned with peacocks, was busy performing at the stove. 'You can't trust rump steaks,' she gurgled in a throaty voice that still had half a country accent. 'I swore I'd stop pinching rump steaks, but the devil tempted me again.' Clattering the saucepan, she nonchalantly threw into it several slices of meat thickly coated with breadcrumbs. The breadcrumbs floated in a cloud above the stove. 'They say they're prepared for frying in breadcrumbs, but underneath what is there? I prodded the breadcrumbs with a fork, it felt all right, then I started to fry it – and so much melted fat came out I had to throw it into the rubbish bin. And apart from the fat there was nothing but bones!'

Clea gave her a sidelong glance as she pretended to rinse her spoon at the sink. 'Shall I pour out some of this fat for you to fry your potatoes in, Clea love?' As though hypnotised, Clea nodded agreement, staring at Tonya's plump, dimpled elbows as she conjured with the frying-pan. Every time she caught that misty gaze on her, Tonya would screw up her eyes a little and say with a smile of compassion on her big lips: 'Why are you looking so pale today, Clea?' Returning to the kitchen after slamming the door of the refrigerator in her room, she loomed up again beside Clea like a temptress-genie out of a bottle: 'Would you like to try a little pork brisket? Nice and lean?' – and she almost forced into Clea's mouth a piece of crackling that gleamed like patent leather, fringed with layers of smoked pork. Catching a smell like that of English bacon, Clea bit hungrily into the hard, unchewable morsel and devoured it, almost choking, tears starting out of her eyes from the determined working of her jaws. 'And are all you English women so frenchified? Do you all diet?' – said Tonya, giving the choking Clea an affectionate pat on the back, as though tipping a weighing-scale that was measuring a quantity of meat and bones. 'Back home in the country, miniature women like that would stay virgins all their lives. But Konstantin is a townee, he likes miniature women, that's why he's keeping you on tinned food and clear soup. When your tummy starts to rumble, Clea my love, don't you bother looking to that husband of yours – knock on my door any time of the day or night, I'll find you a bit of something. No point in turning yourself into a bag of bones just to satisfy your husband's foreign tastes for English jellies. I've known Konstantin for quite a while now: a man likes a woman to have something on her he can get hold of!' – and with modest pride she wrapped her blue synthetic-fibre dressing-gown over her pneumatic, heaven-bound airships of flesh.

Wearing the same foreign-made dressing-gown (acquired under the counter from her friend Zina, who worked in a haberdashery shop), she soon started to appear, without knocking, in Kostya's room, bearing a parcel of food that was bursting out at the sides quite as much as her well-fed body. When she unpacked the parcel on the table, there was revealed a sight incredible to the eyes of the starved inhabitants of a Moscow communal flat: a whole leg of lamb, say, or a pristine log of smoked sausage. Kostya would start to bring out his usual disparaging remarks about Soviet meat-processing factories, where, apparently, rats spent the night in the mincing-machines, but Tonya seemed not to be listening; sitting down on a wobbling stool and letting Kostya have his say, she would cut him off. 'Eat, you aristocrat! Eat and shut up!' she would exhort Kostya, straddling the stool as though she was offering him not the leg of mutton on the table but her own ample thigh, gleaming from under her dressing-gown. 'You can't feed a wife on nothing but your mucky foreign recipes – look, you can almost see through her!' – and with a maternal gesture, although she was about ten years younger than Clea, she gave her a hug. 'And don't try and pay me,' she added. 'We're all friends here. You scratch my back, I'll scratch yours,' and giving Clea a smacking kiss on the cheek she set off down the corridor to her own room.

'How generous and unselfish Russians are!' – the thought went round and round in Clea's sleepy brain, while her stomach digested Tonya's latest offering. 'Would Margot be capable of such generosity?' Even during one's student years of 'struggle against bourgeois prejudices' one only had to bring a friend a cup of coffee at lunchtime for them to put ten pence into one's hand and one did the same in return: the rule was tit for tat. Tonya always categorically refused money, although it was not a matter of a beggarly cup of coffee but a whole leg of pork. She did not, however, refuse a packet of soap that Clea had brought from London. 'The manager of the consumer goods department just loves foreign soap in its wrapping,' Tonya would say, in one of her enigmatic remarks concerning the complex Soviet procedures for the distribution of goods. 'How about a bottle of that whisky from the foreign-currency "Beriozka" shop, eh? It's my hairdresser's birthday tomorrow, I'm taking her some Hungarian salami and a bottle of scent as well, but I really should take her something really nice from abroad, shouldn't I?'

After the hairdresser there was the manager of the shoe-shop, not to mention a visit to the Writers' Union bookshop to get a copy of Alexandre Dumas' *Twenty Years After* for the entertainment of the manager of a dress-material shop on Gorky Street; it was as though the entire socialist economy depended on the wines and spirits department of the 'Beriozka' shop, and that without that form of 'grease' the country would have long ago reverted to the primitive barbarism of a cave-dwelling existence, with its mammoth-hunting and the communal cooking-pot on the campfire.

Whenever she accepted an offering of food from Tonya's fleshy hands in exchange for some foreign 'souvenir', Clea soothed her conscience with the thought that perhaps this was what communism was, namely a return to barter on a basis of mutual assistance. Tonya in her turn always repeated her 'Oh no, I couldn't! No, you mustn't! You scratch my back and I'll scratch yours!' But after stammering her thanks she would reward Clea with a juicy kiss and immediately start to describe how she would 'grease' the manager of the travel department for a booking at a boarding-house in Truskeniki, where all the managers of the Moscow food stores would foregather at the New Year and divide up the perks amid clouds of steam in the local sauna baths.

On every occasion (and these occasions happened again and again, since hunger is not a maiden aunt who visits us but once a year) Tonya refused less and less to take a gift in return and demanded with growing insistence that Clea should concern herself with the state of Tonya's soul. She was anxious to have answers to many varied and urgent questions: 'They say there are crowds and crowds of blacks in your streets. Is that really true?' she enquired, looking thoughtfully at Clea. In some perplexity, Clea tried to explain that in London people didn't walk around the streets in crowds but as individuals or in twos and threes, irrespective of race. Tonya nodded eagerly. 'I only asked,' she said, getting to the point, 'because I wanted to know if they have black pricks, those negroes.' Clea blushed. 'Don't blush,' Tonya patted her on the knee – 'I was just interested out of international solidarity. But it would be interesting to try it and see. Just for international solidarity. I suppose black skin is rougher, isn't it?'

Conversations on such international topics grew more and more frequent. 'They say you can even buy artificial pricks in the West. Synthetic ones. With an electric thing at one end. Is that true?' With eyes downcast in embarrassment Clea explained that the electric ones were not called pricks but vibrators. 'And they buzz?' Tonya giggled. 'I wouldn't mind them buzzing. When a man's on top of you grunting and groaning as if he was being strangled, is that any better? And then it's bang! – and he's snoring, and you're tossing and turning all night, unsatisfied.' She sighed. 'But your Kostya's not like that. Kostya's so tender and thoughtful.'

Tonya's mysterious sighs were finally explained when one day she came into the room with a black eye: 'My old man's back from being away. I made him some bortsch,' Tonya reported, wrinkling her nose. 'Well, he tasted two spoonfuls and says: "What's this," he says, "pea soup?" – "Yes," says I, "it's pea soup!" He ate another two spoonfuls. "What d'you mean – pea soup?" he says, "when it's bortsch!" – "Well," say I, "what do you think it is if it isn't bortsch – pea soup?" – "So why'd you say it was pea soup, then?!" And he fetched me one, the old cripple, from here to here.' She sighed, feeling the black eye with her finger. Clea could not fully understand the reason for this family conflict, but the black eye was there for all to see and not for the first time.

Tonya's husband had been crippled either in the War or by his own fault – which was also the reason why he had spent half his life in corrective-labour camps for having embezzled national property from a fur-trapping collective. To get Tonya a Moscow residence-permit he had obtained permission for her to join him as a domestic servant, but he had refused to carry out the marital obligations that were assumed to be part of that unwritten agreement. 'Anyway, he can never get it up,' Tonya explained, 'and the terrible cold in those camps froze all his sperm for good. So without one of those vibrators from abroad I'll never be really satisfied. Now and again our loader at the shop has it off with me, but only when he's not stinking drunk, and he's stinking drunk seven days a week. And sometimes you can get poked by the auditor – but that's part of the job, there's no avoiding it, and you can't call that love, can you? He's terribly proper, a family man, just buttons himself up and goes away again, so where's the loving and cuddling?'

Since she saw no chance of getting hold of a vibrator, Clea pretended not to understand Tonya's hints and requests. She had used up all her foreign currency and had long since changed to barter: first her sweaters went, then her jeans, after which she was reduced to trading her bras and knickers. Gradually everything she wore was Soviet-made, as though she had acquired a new skin, and Clea tried feverishly to think what other foreign article she had in reserve except her own body. She had even begun to doubt the foreign origin of her soul, especially since one could hardly exchange one's soul for foreign currency in the land of Soviet atheism. Clea, however, had underestimated the great, patient, persistence of a woman of the Russian peasantry when she knows what she wants.

The next time that she gave Clea a present of fillet of beef, in reply to Clea's expressions of gratitude Tonya mumbled her usual: 'Oh, come on, we're all friends – you're one of us!' She did not go back to her room, however, but remained seated as though expecting something and fiddled with a corner of the tablecloth. Then, taking a deep breath, she sat down on the couch beside Clea, whose hands she clasped in her own fat palms, and started talking about the joys of family life, about how happy Clea and Kostya were without a vibrator – because despite his weird ideas about recipes for saving Russia, Konstantin's male potency was in no way affected by them; she knew that well enough, having lived in this flat for quite a while. Then, after a silence, she turned to practical matters. Since Clea and Kostya could look forward to a conjugal life together until the hairs around their working parts turned grey, while she, Tonya, faced a prospect of widowhood, would Clea not lend her Kostya to Tonya for a few hours – for bodily amalgamation? 'Don't get the wrong idea!' Tonya hastened to explain as Clea started to choke on a piece of fillet steak, with tears in her eyes caused either by choking or by outrage. 'Don't think I'm planning to start an affair with him. It'll simply be to take away the hot feeling I get – I haven't slept for nights. If I had a vibrator, Clea, would I have asked you for such a favour? But just think: Vasya the loader is on the bottle again, there's no audit in sight and my old cripple, is a dead loss as you know. And of course I don't go with just anybody. It's got so as I can't control myself when I'm behind the counter using the weighing-machine. Instead of cheating the customer, I find myself adding a bit *extra*. And when there's a man at the counter, I feel as if I've got red-hot dumb-bells on my chest – yesterday I felt so dizzy I almost fell into a barrel of sour cream. So I'm asking you this, you might say, like you ask for medicine at the chemist: as sort of a treatment. Especially as I know Kostya has his day off tomorrow and I'm on second shift. It won't take up much time, and while he and I are at it you can spend the morning looking at our Lenin in his tomb. You ought to go, you know.' Dumbstruck by what she was hearing, from the very tone of the request, half plaintive, half briskly businesslike for all its improbability, Clea found herself nodding her head to confirm that indeed she never had visited Lenin's tomb . . . and, well, in general, yes – 'You scratch my back, I'll scratch yours.'

On the morning of Tonya's first 'session' with Kostya, Clea tramped around the frostbound Moscow streets, her eyelashes stuck together with frozen tears, and pretended that she wasn't crying with jealousy and humiliation but was suffering in sympathy with the unsatisfied women of Russia, victims of male chauvinism Soviet-style.

From her student days Clea had trained herself not to give way to the petty-bourgeois emotion of jealousy, to a false sense of possessiveness. Perhaps Tonya's request had been sent from above as a sort of spiritual testing, of trial by shock, to see if she was ready to renounce the principle of individualism, inseparable from Western civilisation, and to acquire the difficult art of communal living, where one had to share not only one's thoughts but one's bread and salt with others. As she set off that morning for Lenin's tomb, she strove with all her heart to identify herself body and soul with Tonya, with the hunger and cannibalism of her rural childhood, with the internal passport system and the need of a residence-permit to live in Moscow, with her crippled husband who had turned into a human wreck through no fault of his own but as a result of the curse of his people – prison – the eternal fate of that nation of slaves, God's convicts.

The greater the warmth of her noble feelings, however, the lower grew the temperature of the air in Red Square, and the nearer she drew to the mummy of the leader of the revolution, moving forward a step at a time in a gigantic queue across the frosty cobblestones, the more keenly she felt an emptiness in her stomach, since the hour of the English lunch was approaching and all around her was nothing but the grim, frost-flecked walls of the Kremlin, whose ruddy colouring reminded her of meat – stale, weatherworn, deep-frozen meat.

Holding her breath, she passed the sentry with his fixed bayonet, afraid that he might rip open her stomach with that bayonet in order to put a final stop to the indecent rumblings that were so shocking in someone going to meet the leader of the revolution. But the young sentry's chilly red cheeks beneath their youthful down reminded her of the fluffy, golden hair on Tonya's neck as she bent over the stove stirring a potful of aromatic broth. And she began to have a persistent vision of Tonya's meaty hips, and with a little imagination – the August cherries of her nipples, unobtainable in winter (except at the Central Market), the peaches of her cheeks, the pineapples of her buttocks, and, most vividly of all: the strawberries and cream that Kostya was busily whipping into a froth with his mighty tool, and which, as he completed his work on this luxurious dish, he was smothering in his own sauce. And Clea wanted to devour Tonya's ample frame whole, guts and all, in a kind of surge of hunger for human warmth and flesh in this freezing climate that turned sex into cannibalism.

As though catching her out in these cannibalistic thoughts, someone roughly nudged her forward, breathing heavily down her neck: she realised she was holding up the procession filing past the tomb of the leader. Her glance flickered over the mummy's small wax-like face, with its little beard that seemed to be stuck on. The queue bore her onwards and out again on to the cobbled square. The nagging emptiness in her stomach gave way to a dull, rising nausea, as though that mummy were in her stomach. She went into a public lavatory, where she vomited long and painfully.

What was it that had made her agree to Tonya's insistent persuasion – was she giving in to the calls of her stomach, or was it sympathy with the unhappy lot of a lonely woman? She felt as if she were the incarnation of all Russia: unable to feed herself, but giving love in exchange for food, and when Tonya's requests began to be repeated with the regularity of monthly periods, Clea even started making enquiries as to the possibility of taking out Soviet citizenship, in order, as it were, to register officially her own sacrificial status. Obviously, however, not all the insulted and oppressed of the communal flat shared such a sense of pathos at her self-sacrifice. The next time that the familiar languorous restlessness showed in Tonya's eyes – because Vasya was blind drunk, no audit was in the offing and her crippled husband was absent for the second week running – Clea decided not to go out for a walk but to stay in the kitchen, the more so as it was so cold outside that even the schoolchildren were being kept at home. There was also another excuse: a mountain of dirty dishes had piled up in the kitchen, which would occupy the half-hour of her 'appointment', as Tonya called her visits to Kostya's room.

As Clea stood at the kitchen sink, with its black wounds where the enamel was chipped, casting sidelong glances at the accumulated dirt and kitchen grease on the window, she rattled the crockery in an attempt to drown either the clicking of train-wheels outside or the loud creaking of bed-springs next door accompanied *crescendo* by the puffing of steam locomotives. In order not to hear those groans, sobs and creaks she actually wound a towel round her head, but nothing would muffle the sounds of action on the bed, and these invocations, sham or real, began to make Clea go weak at the knees, and the cake of soap (detergents being unknown in that civilisation) flew out of her coarsened, reddened, hang-nail-adorned fingers and fell on to the creaking, splintered floorboards.

The humiliation of it was not that Kostya was now engaged next door in culinary rituals with Tonya's hot body but that Clea wasn't there, that they would not let her join in this feast of Russian warmth amid the Soviet cold; she wanted to be Tonya entwined with Kostya, or Kostya entwined with Tonya. Every time she hoped they would call out, invite her in and initiate her into the mysterious ritual of physical sharing instead of making her always stand guard outside.

The sourish, musty smell of the kitchen, unventilated for years, reminded her of a pigsty, and the wail of a locomotive whistle merged with the sounds of Tonya squealing like a stuck pig. What *were* they doing in there? Why was she standing guard? Was she a guard at all? What if all the ideas, hopes and ambitions that had brought her to this mystic land of Soviet Russia were nothing but bluff? And had her aunt been right in declaring, to Clea's uncle the missionary, that savages had to be treated savagely otherwise they would eat you?

Once again the scrap of soap slithered out of her fingers and as she was picking it up from the sticky, blackened floor Clea caught sight of her blurred reflection in the steamed-up mirror above the sink. And she did not recognise herself. With a towel wrapped round her head, with her face weatherbeaten by the Russian winter, with broken nails and dressed in something like dungarees since her jeans and polo-neck sweater had migrated to Tonya, nothing was left of the London Clea. What remained was a woman dressed and prepared as a human sacrifice – in fact, a familiar case of Russian cannibalism. At that moment she sensed something rustling behind her, which then prodded her shoe and started crawling up her leg, something firm yet springy, like a rat. And why shouldn't there be rats, since the flat was already swarming with bed-bugs and cockroaches, however much one put down disinfectant and pesticides; whenever you went to the lavatory at night and switched on the light you were almost set upon by an army of busy centipedes, crowded in every corner into their own queues at their own variant of the food distribution system – so how could there not be rats too? She twitched, as though someone had dropped a wet piece of soap down her collar and it was slithering down her back in a sticky, slippery lump. Grasping an unwashed plate as the only available weapon, Clea turned slowly round in order to attack the parasite that was creeping over her shoe.

'Don't be frightened, English girl.' A creature, his teeth bared in a grin, was standing in the middle of the kitchen swaying back and forth on crutches. With the rubber ferrule on the end of his crutch he was rubbing Clea's shoe, but at the sight of the plate clutched in her hand, he took the crutch away. In his appearance Tonya's crippled husband looked liked a cartoon of one of London's unemployed in the Soviet satirical magazine *Crocodile*: a fringe of damp, matted hair protruding from under a cap with ear-flaps, an alcoholic's haggard face spotted with eczema, a nose like a rotten potato, and a chapped harelip that permanently revealed his crumbling, nicotine-stained teeth. It wasn't clear where the filthy body ended and the hideous rags began, where the coloured material of his shirt merged with the unwashed neck and the unshaven stubble.

To Clea this monster was like the ghost of one of these London down-and-outs, the outcast mongrels of British society who dossed for the night under railway bridges. Once again she remembered Colin and his Christmas present. The cripple was swaying in front of her like the spectre of English injustice, the personification of her social conscience; but because he also looked so exotic, to Clea's eyes he was unexpectedly transformed into a parody of an English lord, a Victorian judge in a wig who was shaming her for forgetting all the insulted and oppressed in her own country and letting herself be enticed into the foul and debauched customs of another people. Only a moment ago, her hands filthy from washing up crockery covered with other people's food scraps, she had been indulging mentally in lust and fornication, into which she had been drawn by her perverted devotion to her native husband. It was as if she, a neat and disciplined schoolgirl, had been caught in her Girl Guides uniform smoking in the lavatory, or found in the dormitory under the bedclothes with another girl, and now the headmistress (or the bewigged judge or the Lord Chancellor) was swaying back and forth in front of her, threatening her with the crutches of history.

Clea stared at the moving lips while they cursed her with incomprehensible oaths, until she finally realised that Tonya's crippled husband was asking her a question: 'I've been wanting to ask you for a long time, English girl, what the working class in England use to get stinking?' – 'The working class does *what*?' Clea was so frightened that she couldn't grasp what he meant. 'What do they mostly like to *drink*?' explained the swaying victim of social injustice. 'Everything,' Clea replied after a moment's thought, and added: 'Everything – and cider as well.' – 'Cider? What's that – cider?'

Straining her knowledge of Russian to the utmost, Clea tried to explain that cider was a kind of weak wine made from apples. 'So there's not much alcohol in cider – is that it? Why drink it, then?' said Tonya's husband in perplexity. Clea explained that the alcoholic effect was obtained by the quantity you drank. 'I suppose it's a wholesome drink, is it?' the cripple enquired thoughtfully. 'Well, what sort of snack do they eat when they're drinking it? What does the English working class eat when they're drinking?' he asked, advancing a little towards Clea. 'Nothing,' replied Clea, taking a step backwards. 'Ah, now that's a real man's way of drinking!' – the cripple banged his crutch on the floor. 'There's something we, the proletariat of the first socialist country, should learn from the English proletariat. Not to eat when we're drinking!' He was silent for a moment. 'But then it's easier for the English proletariat. If there's not much alcohol in the cider stuff, what's the point of a snack when you're drinking? No need. But if you take vodka, now' – he stabbed the air with his finger – 'or if you take pure spirit, we're well ahead there. We don't eat, either, when we drink vodka. 'Cos there's nothing to eat anyway. If it weren't for Tonya!' – and he hiccupped.

During this puzzling dialogue Clea, as any foreigner would, suspected that there was another, hidden meaning concealed behind these absurd remarks. Tonya's husband was purposely hinting that Clea was an alien in this society, a stranger to his Russia. And for the first time in all these months she suddenly found herself giving full rein to her accumulated resentment and jealousy, and she wanted by any means to have her revenge on the plump-bottomed Tonya for her gift-offerings of meat – for the fact that because of her sufferings in Russia she, a proud daughter of Britannia, was having to stand over a pile of dirty crockery in front of this wooden-legged denizen of the swamp and answer his crafty questions.

'Have you seen my Tonya? I feel like a bite to eat,' grunted the cripple and turned towards the kitchen table. 'It would be a good idea to set this brute on that couple next door,' Clea thought, but she immediately came out with an answer that belied her malicious intention. 'She is not yet coming back from shop,' she muttered, murdering the Russian language as though in contrition for her vengeful thoughts.

'What d'you mean she's not back yet, when there's two pounds of beef rotting on the table?' – and Tonya's husband pointed inquisitorially at a piece of fillet steak that was oozing blood on to a plate. At that moment a duet composed of Tonya's cries and the creaking of bed-springs came from the door of Kostya's room with redoubled volume.

'That's Tonya's voice,' said the crippled husband, frowning and cocking his ear towards the door. 'Only my Tonya squeals like that when I set her peasant brain to rights with my crutch.' Growing more and more certain of what he was guessing, he now started swaying and limping towards Kostya's room. Clea, too, began to edge out of her corner, trying to use her body to conceal the existence of the door leading into the inferno of carnal sin that lay behind it. 'Out of the way, English woman,' the cripple threatened her. 'I don't cause you any trouble, so I don't let anyone else knock my Tonya about. I'm her lawful husband.' Thrusting Clea aside with his bony shoulder, he knocked open the door with one blow of his wooden leg.

Clea thought (if she was thinking at all at that moment) that she would see some sinful orgy out of Anthony and Cleopatra's Egyptian nights, but as she peered round from behind Tonya's husband what she saw was something more like a scene of industrial production. Facing the door, Tonya was on all fours, the sweat-soaked curls of her permanent wave sticking to her forehead, her eyes rolling and her tongue sticking out. As though pounding laundry on the bank of an invisible river, the powerful shuttling movements of her buttocks were inducing a violent swaying motion in both the bed and Kostya, who was grasping her backside with every available member in obvious fear of falling on to the floor. 'I'm just coming, I'm just c-o-o-o-ming!' screamed Tonya, as though explaining to her husband that she was about to finish her working shift and would then be at his disposal. Passion is blind. It was only when her crippled husband laid a heavy hand on her permanent wave and pulled at her hair that Tonya, her eyes rolling upward in amazement, came to her senses and let out a groan or a wail, either from fear or in fulfilment of her promise to come. The wail turned into an animal squeal of pain as the cripple gave a wrench, threw her on to the floor and dragged her by the hair, naked and wriggling, all the way down the corridor, like Bluebeard taking his latest victim into the cellar. He did not even bother to shut the door of their room, from whence came the sound of a series of steady, dull blows.

Clea rushed to the door. Heavy grunts were coming from Tonya's husband; he had taken off his wooden leg and was steadily thrashing Tonya all over her white body, not excluding her face. Glancing round when Clea appeared in the doorway, he tore himself away from his exhausting occupation for a moment and said threateningly, shaking his crutch at Clea: 'You keep out of our internal affairs, you lump of foreign shit. Start up capitalist competition here, would you, shameless English bitch! I will not allow my family to be broken up!' – and he resumed work with his wooden leg on Tonya's ample form. Kostya, after watching this scene with the indifference of an experienced zoologist, had to call the police.

Later came the visit to Tonya in hospital. There were endless checks on the patient's identity and a mix-up about the number of the ward; cracked oil-paint and threadbare linoleum; a smell of floor-mops, unwashed saucepans and dirty bandages, the smell of death. Clea made her way along corridors lined with patients' beds due to lack of space in the wards, as though during a war or a revolution. A nurse with a moustache like a brothel-keeper pointed out Tonya's bed to Clea in the overcrowded ward – otherwise Clea would never have recognised her neighbour. Tonya was lying on the bed swathed like a mummy, encased from head to foot in plaster and bandages.

The mummy sighed between lips discoloured and swollen with bruises and looked at Clea with the eyes of a dog that had been scalded with boiling water. Clea was about to pick up the carafe of water and the paper bag of apples that were on the bedside table, but the eyelids, swollen from their battering, closed again. Clea sat down on the little chair alongside the bed and for a while listened to the groans coming from the neighbouring beds.

Just when she was getting up to go, Tonya suddenly moved and her eyelids fluttered beseechingly. Like a sister of mercy, Clea bent her ear close to those wounded lips as though she were the executrix of the last will of a dying person, and heard a voice that was half whisper, half groan: 'To the country . . .' and then again, after a gulp of air: 'Want to go back to the country . . . home, to my village . . .' Tears welled up under her swollen eyelids and spread in yellowish blobs on the bandages . . . 'To England! Back to England!' Clea urged herself, her heels clicking along the hospital corridor towards the exit.

Returning home from the hospital, however, and seeing Kostya's back hunched over the table, she decided to say nothing about her intention to leave Russia. In the middle of the table, as though it were a valuable antique, lay a green cucumber, at which Kostya was staring unblinkingly. The cucumber was of an incredible hothouse length, but thick and marked with the pimples of an outdoor-grown ridge cucumber. Against the background of light reflected from snowdrifts outside the window it seemed an exotic fruit brought from lands overseas – and it gave off a powerful head-spinning aroma of spring and England.

Clea watched fascinated as Kostya stretched out his hand to the cucumber and began to stroke its pimples with his index finger. With an aggressiveness that she had never suspected in herself Clea grabbed the cucumber, bit off an enormous chunk and began, with a loud crunching nose, to chew this live piece of nostalgia for the English spring. 'That cucumber hasn't been washed,' said Kostya between gritted teeth, looking up at her from under his eyebrows. And from the tone of his voice and the look in his eyes Clea finally guessed where the cucumber had come from: it was Tonya's last offering, a souvenir of the era of barter, payment for her last 'appointment' with Konstantin.

The whole scene of love-making, with its gynaecological details, with the creaking of the bed and Tonya's squeals, arose again before Clea's eyes, and her mouth went dry as though instead of a cucumber she had been chewing hospital bandages. The cucumber, with a large bite taken out of it, dropped from her hand and rolled across the floor. 'From now on I'm a vegetarian!' said Clea, as though taking a solemn oath never again in her life to behave badly, and she turned away towards the window. Konstantin picked up the cucumber from the floor, and turning it over and over in his hands, he said, as though nothing had happened, as though encouraging her in her resolution to turn vegetarian:

'Why don't we make some Greek *tsatsiki* tomorrow?' For *tsatsiki*, he explained, all one needed was a fresh cucumber and some dill, of which there was still some left, in dried form, from the days of Clea's visits to London, and there was also some of last year's garlic hanging on the wall. The only thing lacking was yoghurt, but that was no problem either: one only had to plunge a spoonful of sour cream into some milk and next morning there was your ready-made yoghurt. 'Let's hold a wake for Tonya with some Greek *tsatsiki*,' said Konstantin in conclusion, and as he set off for the night-shift at his cannery entrance-gate he gave Clea his instructions: 'Buy some sour cream!' – 'Where?' Clea blinked uneasily. 'Oh, in the food shop near the depot,' Kostya shouted back to her as he went out, slamming the door behind him.

After wandering around the empty flat for a while and shedding a few tears outside the door of Tonya's room, which had been sealed by the police, Clea put on her duffle coat, wrapped a scarf round her neck and set off into the freezing cold to buy some sour cream.

She took a route that led down side streets and through courtyards, like a legitimate inhabitant of her district accustomed to cutting illegal corners. She couldn't understand why she was trudging off to get this sour cream, why she was obediently following Konstantin's instructions, nor why she didn't just pack her bags and leave this human sewer for ever. In general she found it had become hard to answer her own questions and to make logical deductions. She had somehow grown more accustomed, along with millions of Soviet toilers, simply to drag her body from one day to another, like papers being carried from office to office along the corridors of some vast organisation. She no longer had any thoughts about merging herself into some communist commune of the insulted and oppressed, but she simply waited passively for some change in the circumstances, having taught herself never to take the first move, to suspect that in any such initiative lay the threat of future trouble lurking around every corner – waiting only to jump out and whirl one off into a St Vitus' dance of exhausting explanations, show-downs, rows, traumas, hospitals and funerals. It was easier, as though screwing up one's eyes against the cold and holding one's breath, to plod with one's string-bag to the food shop, which in this case was called – there being no private ownership – by its geographical location: the tram depot, say, or the District Office of the Party.

Back home, in the life she had left behind, every house and shop or the most insignificant product shrieked the name of its owner, founder or manufacturer: along with all objects of consumption, she loved or hated hundreds of human names. In this land of nameless shops, however, she was beginning to hate all objects as a whole, unattached as they were to proper names, except perhaps for abbreviations such as CC for Central Committee; life in this country forced one either to thrash oneself into convulsions of loathing or to bow down in worship before huge, global abstractions: people, Party, idea. And with every step that she took Clea felt she was gradually forgetting the name of the exit from this vast namelessness.

All around loomed multi-storey brick buildings, their grim facades leprous with hoar-frost; the frost-bound street reminded one of newsreel shots of wartime London before a bombing raid. People were running here and there as though in response to an air-raid warning, bunching into groups and dispersing again – with grim, grey faces, wrapped to the nose in scarves, ear-flapped hats pushed down on their foreheads, and wearing bulky winter overcoats. Spun around by the ground-wind, they would collide, talk, gesticulating and bending close to each other's ear, and hurry on, past old women, with scarves tied around their waists, stamping their feet in felt boots to keep warm at the front of queues.

Clea passed a line of freezing citizens moving forward at a funereal pace with their clinking shopping-bags to the little booth where empty bottles were handed back. A janitor set her teeth on edge with the scraper that he was using to remove the ice from the pavement, divided from the roadway by a gigantic fortification and anti-tank barrier made of piled-up snow. The other side of the street had already been strewn with salt and grit, and this mixture, combined with slush, stuck to one's shoes in white patches like leprosy. But the real scum, as bad as a crowd fighting to get into an air-raid shelter, was awaiting her in the food store. The slush from the street, trampled by hundreds of feet, was spread over the tiled floor in huge puddles. Oblivious to the swearing and pushing, a charwoman in a blue overall, armed with bucket and mop, was pushing her way through the crowd and throwing handfuls of sawdust over the floor, mostly aiming it straight at the customers. Although they swore at her, all their attention was concentrated on the spiral, invisible amongst all the pushing and shoving, that formed the queue in the dairy and meat department. Another invisible spiral led to the cash-desk, and where these two circuits ended and where they began and where they were entangled was impossible to determine; even so, with steely intuition people followed each other in the invisible hierarchy of queues, and were quick to tick off anyone who dared to call that sequential order into question. It very soon emerged that sour cream was available, but it was being given out to the joint queue that was also striving for some 'doctor's' sausage – food stores in the Soviet Union were obviously combined with chemists, and there were a lot of patients.

'No more than half a kilo to one customer!' – now and again the cry would ring out at the place that was to all appearances, the front of the queue. Try as she might to convince this queue that she, Clea, was a vegetarian and didn't want any sausage, still less 'doctor's' sausage, but only sour cream, no one would believe her. The sausage queue involved a three-hour wait. There was one other possibility: to try one's luck at the delicatessen near the Communist Party District Office. But there it turned out they were only selling cottage cheese with raisins, and there was no sour cream to be had – it hadn't been delivered; by now starting to panic, slipping and sliding on the icy pavement, Clea dashed back to the 'tram-depot' foodstore and, with vigorous use of her elbows, took her place in the queue for the cash-desk. Half an hour later, when there were only about ten people between her and the cashier's window, the piercing voice of the saleswoman in the dairy and butchery department came ringing over the heaving ant-heap of heads: 'Sour cream is sold out!' Since Clea had never learned to apprehend shouts in a foreign language unless they were directly addressed to her, this warning passed her by until it was repeated to her personally, this time by the cashier: 'Sour cream's sold out! Are you deaf, or something?' – 'But I've been queuing,' said Clea. Indeed she had been queuing, fatalistically allowing the surrounding crowd to prod her in the back, push her in the chest and shoulder her aside, until this maelstrom pressed her up against an old woman with a kind little face who was standing in another queue. 'Run over to the "Energy", my dear – they always have sour cream. And my neighbour told me they're selling pork sausages there, too, today. You can keep a place for me in the sausage queue there. I'm getting some "doctor's" sausage here, then I'll pop over to the "Energy" for the pork sausages,' the kindly old woman whispered to her secretively. Clea started to push her way to the exit.

A certain desperation and a purely English persistence, nay obstinacy, induced her not to turn for home but to head for the Institute of Energy Supply, where the 'Energy' delicatessen was presumably to be found. It was not hard to find it among the other gloomy doorways: a queue was bursting out of it like the intestines of a corpse, blistered with shopping bags. After standing in it for the customary hour and a half, Clea finally emerged in front of the saleswoman, the coveted cashier's receipt for half a kilo of sour cream clutched in her hand. Without looking at her, the saleswoman began to pull out a string of pork sausages, like a conjuror producing something out of his sleeve.

'Next!' she barked, impaling Clea's receipt on a sharp spike, a weapon evidently intended to repulse Clea. Garbling the words, Clea mentioned that she wanted sour cream. '*Banka!*' yelled the saleswoman, throwing away the string of sausages and seizing a gigantic ladle. 'Banka? What Bank?' Clea enquired in perplexity, having long since grown unaccustomed to both banks and cheque books. 'I've already given you my receipt from the cash-desk,' she reminded the saleswoman. 'Am I supposed to twist the receipt into a paper cone for your sour cream, or what?' roared the woman in fury, waving her ladle. 'Where am I to pour your sour cream?

Where's your *banka* – your jar? Or are you going to take it away in your hands?!' Clea became aware of the ominous fact that in this country sour cream was only sold loose. She needed a pot for it. Or a jar – *banka*. There were, of course, no jars to be had. 'Shall I pour the sour cream into your mouth?' the saleswoman went on relentlessly. 'What's the matter with you, don't you understand Russian?' Clea did understand a certain amount of Russian: she understood the loud swearing that was coming from the queue pressing against her from behind, the yells of 'You're wasting our time!' and she tried to explain to the people her problem with the jar and the sour cream. 'Run home for a jar and I'll keep your place in the queue,' – the kind old lady from the 'District Office' delicatessen had materialised beside her. With her 'doctor's' sausage in her string bag, she explained to the raging queue that Clea was her daughter and that they were shopping together: her daughter had come for sour cream and she, the mother, wanted a string of pork sausages.

'Remember me,' Clea begged the saleswoman and the people in the queue, 'so that I don't have to queue all over again.' The old woman gave her a friendly shove on her way, and the queue growled: 'All right, all right, off you go!' The saleswoman was already screaming: 'Next!'

Once more Clea ran along the icy, salt-strewn pavements and then back to the grocery clutching a large jar in her outstretched hands, like the cup-winner after the final lap of a relay-race. But when she reached the 'Energy' grocery it was shut for the lunch-hour. She decided to stay put, and stood outside the door for an hour, clutching the jar in her frozen fingers. In anticipation of the shop's reopening, she was already being pressed on all sides by a newly-formed queue for sausages, but she defended herself with her elbows and refused to allow anyone to push in front of her, pressing her forehead against the glass door with its prison-like protective grating. When the door was opened, the crowd, pressing hard from behind her and streaming towards the counter and the cash-desk, carried her forward over the tiled floor covered with a soup of slush and sawdust, and Clea, as though being thrust into a circus arena by a push in the back waved her arms to keep her balance and slid forward on one heel; the jar, slipppery from the cold, flew out of her hands, curved through the air in front of a mob of gaping mouths and hit the bare tiles: there was a crash, immediately followed by a burst of foul language from the crowd as their boots crunched over the fragments of glass.

That tinkle of breaking glass, the sound of her dashed hopes, together with the ear-splitting squeak of a janitor's scraper, accompanied her all the way home. Entering their room, with one movement she swept all Kostya's jars and tins of spices from the shelves; the smell, sharp and intoxicating, began to bore into her temples and tickle her nostrils, making her eyes water and masking her own tears. It was the stench of the Russian stomach, the essence of Kostya. The crunch of broken glass seemed like the crunching of bones as Clea walked up and down amid the destruction and, page by page, ripped Kostya's record-book into tiny fragments, scattering the torn pieces around the room with the same systematic persistence with which the snowflakes outside attempted daily to camouflage the ugliness of the surrounding townscape. 'I'm leaving!' she moaned, weeping. 'I'm going home – alo-o-one!' – and a passing locomotive echoed her with a hoot.

But when Kostya appeared in the doorway she got a terrible fright: his face was as much a picture of ghastly destruction as was the mess that she had made in the room; it was as though her hatred of all Kostya's paraphernalia had been transferred to his face, which was swollen, covered in scratches and bruises, and with a broken lower lip – much as Tonya's face must have looked, in fact, if her bandages had been taken off. Without saying a word, Kostya flung himself down on the couch and lay looking up at the ceiling. Blood was trickling from his nose, which he was wiping with a dirty handkerchief. Clea ran around the room, organising lotion, iodine and wadding. Finally, plastered and bandaged, as though made up to look like Tonya, Konstantin spoke, hardly moving his shattered lips. He described how it had all happened because of a meeting held at the factory to protest against Israeli aggression, at which attendance was compulsory. Kostya, as usual, was sitting it out in a corner in the back row and dozing in between reflections on his latest exotic recipe. Just as chess geniuses can play blindfolded, so Kostya was capable of experiencing the taste of culinary combinations in his mind.

The speakers on the rostrum were meanwhile painting in lurid colours the atrocities of Zionist genocide against Palestinian babies, and Kostya, following the orators, switched his thoughts to the cuisine of the Near East – from *houmous* to *shakshuki*. All would have passed off as normal – with the audience half asleep and yawning – had it not been for a propagandist from the Regional Committee of the Party, who did not limit himself to listing the sinister facts but plunged into a historial excursus on Zionism.

This propagandist pointed out that the poisonous brew of rampant Zionist militarism had been fermented by the yeast of the vicious doctrines of Judaism from the Nile to the Euphrates, with its eye for an eye and King Herod's order to knock out the teeth of innocent babies, supported by the reactionary Pharisees and Sadducees, and the use of babies' blood for making the Passover matzos, not to mention the trumped-up affair of the doctors in the era of Stalin's cult of the personality, whose condemnation by the Party's general line had been so timely. Kostya cared not a fig for the doctors or for the blood of Palestinian babies as such; but the speaker had rashly included blood in the recipe for matzo. And it was there, with respect, that Zionism stopped and quite a different cuisine began, if you'll excuse me. Kostya jerked into life and asked permission to speak. This was granted to him – out of sheer surprise. It was the first occasion in the history of such compulsory meetings that the spontaneous expression of the will of the working class had extended beyond snoring in the back rows. Having mounted the rostrum, Konstantin announced that he was not going to talk about genocide, in which he had never taken part, but on the subject of cookery in Judaism, and in that connection he wished to correct the speaker from the Regional Committee on the matter of the use of blood. The main principle of kosher cookery was precisely that there should not be a trace of bloodiness in either meat or poultry. Therefore when he has, for instance, slaughtered a chicken, the kosher butcher keeps the bird upside down for several hours so that the blood drains out to the last drop. At first sight it might seem that an Orthodox Jew could eat a Palestinian baby, having first cut off its head to allow the blood to flow out, but human flesh is also non-kosher, because Palestinian babies lack the hooves required to make them kosher; either that, or – though he could not personally vouch for this – they had cloven hooves, which would also put them in the non-kosher category. Either way, whether they had cloven hooves or not, the blood of babies and of all other *artiodactyla* was excluded from Jewish cuisine, and the rumours about Passover matzos were based on absurd prejudice, known historically as the 'blood slander'.

Konstantin was not allowed to finish: the chairman interrupted his speech, declaring that today's agenda did not include a discussion of the myths of Ancient Greece. Kostya did not argue, reckoning that he had said his piece; he obediently stepped down from the rostrum, and made for the door. As he was going out, someone tugged at his elbow:

'We wanna word with you,' grunted a stoud lad from the dried-fruit department, without looking him in the eye. From behind his broad back appeared two comrades of athletic build, and, urging Kostya forward with a box on the ears, this trinity led him off, at the brisk pace of a military escort, towards the packing warehouse. There, amid the deserted rows of tins of pineapples destined for the Kremlin's special restricted-access grocery, a lanky redhead picked up Kostya by the collar of his jacket and, holding his fist to his victim's nose, hissed: 'So you're in favour of the Yids and their aggression, are you, you lump of dog-shit? Show solidarity with the crimes of the Zionist fascists would you, Yid-face? We're going to make you into a piece of bloody beefsteak, you lousy little nit. Don't worry, we'll let the blood drain out of you before we hand you over to be put in tins,' – and with each ideological affirmation he rammed his fist into Kostya's nose, which from looking like a new potato was transformed into one of the stuffed marrows produced by the 'Rodina' canning factory. But it was stewed pork that came to Kostya's rescue. Home-produced. Non-kosher. As he sprawled on the floor, doubled up with pain under the boots of the patriotic trio, he noticed it standing right under his nose. His hand groped blindly for the large tin, and equally blindly he swung it at the three faces bent over him in sacred and bloody trinity. The faces howled and fell back, just as a burst of applause from the nearby hall announced the end of the meeting. Kostya reached the main gate still holding the heavy tin – which was the cause of a report being drawn up, accusing him of attempting to remove finished produce from the grounds of the factory. This resulted in his dismissal with an adverse note in his work-record. For some reason, no one paid any attention whatsoever to his battered, bloodstained features.

Several hours later, when after the repeated application of damp compresses Kostya's eyes began to open a little, he gazed round the room with a dumbfounded look and mumbled: 'What happened? I thought I was having hallucinations – what's being going on here?' Clea ran up and down, whimpering, and began to shout in English that she was leaving, then in broken Russian she started hysterically describing the misfortunes she had suffered in her attempts to buy sour cream, trying to justify her outburst of despair and to show the connection between the jar that had been smashed in the shop and the mess in the room. Kostya, however, either didn't understand her or simply wasn't listening. He limped around the room, bent down and turned over the broken fragments, sniffed the scattered powders and herbs, sighed, muttered and swore. After trying unsuccessfully to put several scraps of the torn pages together again, he groaned: 'And they destroyed my book, the bastards!' He was convinced that the room had been searched and ransacked by the KGB. He could not forgive the destruction of his record-book. When Clea finally realised that the target of Kostya's flow of obscenity was the KGB, she decided not to disillusion him. After all, the Russians themselves blamed their misfortunes on the KGB, so why shouldn't she exploit this Soviet devil's brood as a convenient scapegoat to solve her own spiritual conflicts? A month later they had gathered together the necessary papers and Konstantin submitted a request to be united with his British spouse in her place of residence – London.

6 THE WHITE SPRING

'Aha! Oho! Haha!' – the piercing cries of triumph came from the far corner of the garden. Breaking off his brilliant exposition of the sinister absurdity of the arms race, Anthony looked around in perplexity. Kostya was leaping about in childish excitement beside the birch-tree; he then squatted down on his haunches, dug around in the grass, and rushed at full speed back to the tea-table. The run made him pant jerkily and almost asthmatically, and his eyes were starting out of their sockets, as though what he had found in the grass was nothing less than a human corpse.

'Found it!' he kept saying maniacally as with trembling hands he thrust what looked like a gigantic snail under each person's nose. In his other hand a knife glittered in the sunlight. 'Why does he always have that knife with him?' flashed through Clea's mind.

'Put the knife back where it belongs,' she said to Kostya like a schoolmarm admonishing a naughty pupil, and sternly pressed her lips together. Without arguing, Kostya threw the knife down on to the table and with both hands held his precious find up to the sun, admiring it in the afternoon light. 'A birch boletus – see?' he whispered blissfully, glancing round at everyone with a triumphant look. Without waiting for the fanfare, he turned to Clea and started lecturing her in a reproachful recitative: how right he was to have insisted on careful treatment of that patch around the birch-tree on the principles of environmental conservation! He would like to know what would have happened to that boletus if he had allowed Clea to mow everything flat with that buzzing machine that had levelled the flora with such crass egalitarianism, regardless of whether the rest of it was burdock, buttercups or bluebells. She had even been prepared to reduce the birch-tree itself to a stump – only fortunately, thank God, she lacked the necessary tools. As for the boletus, what chances of survival would there have been for that delicate mushroom, one of the most remarkable pickling mushrooms in the world? For pickling, probably the only thing superior to the cap of the boletus was the white mushroom, but in mushroom soup the boletus produced a strong broth unlike anything else, while if you fried it, especially with some onion and potato – and vodka to wash it down . . . ! Kostya sighed sweetly, his eyes closed in ecstasy.

'If a birch boletus has managed to grow there, soon there'll be some orange-cap and then before you know it the white mushroom will get established in this little plot too,' he summed up, hopefully casting a sweeping glance all the way from the table to the neighbour's fence, – 'provided, of course, that you allow all the weeds to run wild and you root out all those damned hortensias and lupins that are depriving the mushrooms of their place in the sun!'

'Kostya is our fungophile,' Clea explained in embarrassment, noticing that Anthony was fidgeting in his chair, fearing the onset of a family row.

'Fungophile?' Anthony enquired, blushing for no apparent

reason. Then he added: 'Oh!' and smiled sympathetically at Kostya.

'What did you say to him?' said Kostya, reacting suspiciously to Anthony's smile and turning to Clea. Margot hastily intervened in the role of intermediary.

'She didn't say anything. She merely said you were fond of mushrooms.'

'Then why does she say it in such a stupid way? Really – what a word to dream up: fungophile! What on earth is a fungophile?'

'Kostya loves discussing mushrooms,' Clea explained in English to Anthony, who had been reduced to baffled silence.

'Ah, yes – the atomic mushroom-cloud!' Delighted, Anthony returned to his favourite theme.

'Careful!' Kostya barked at him, as Anthony, with the abstracted curiosity of someone preoccupied with his own thoughts, pulled the boletus towards him by its stalk.

'It's a poisonous mushroom, I suppose,' Anthony remarked innocently, having completely missed all Kostya's preceding remarks about the boletus. Putting on his fashionable John-Lennon-style, steel-rimmed spectacles, he sniffed at the mushroom from a distance and then fastidiously pushed it away with his little finger. 'I prefer our traditional British mushrooms.'

'What's he muttering about?' Kostya turned to Margot for a translation, who interpreted for him the remarks about poisonous fungi and British mushrooms.

'Poisonous?! A boletus – poisonous?' Kostya retorted indignantly. 'British mushrooms! They're not British at all, by the way, but French: *champignon*. Napoleon brought them to Russia with the mud on his soldier's boots. Nobody in Moscow even bothers to eat them; they grow in Gorky Street between the cracks in the pavement and the people tread them underfoot. Because they don't taste like mushrooms – they taste like rubber galoshes! But the boletus now, especially pickled, is as tender as a suckling baby.'

'You mean a suckling pig,' Clea put in, determined to show off her knowledge of Russian.

'I know better which is the more tender. Which of us, I'd like to know, has eaten a dog in cookery – you or me?'

'What *are* you talking about?' said Clea indignantly, catching his words about 'eating a dog'.

'I thought they only ate dogs in China – surely they don't eat them in Russia too?' asked Margot, with the interest of a specialist on Russia and a former enthusiast for the Chinese communes.

'Who said they eat dogs in Russia? Have you gone mad here in England, with your fantasies about Russian bears and sinister KGB men?' Kostya flared up.

'What has the KGB got to do with it? You said the words yourself!' said Clea.

'What did I say?'

'That you'd eaten a dog!'

'Oh God, it's just a saying, a metaphor: if I say I've eaten a dog, it means I know what's what, I know what I'm talking about. Really – and you're supposed to have studied Russian! If Russians ever go in for that sort of thing, they prefer straight cannibalism.' And Kostya lapsed into thought, while Clea remained on her guard.

'At least they're not worm-eaten,' Anthony remarked in English.

'What aren't – babies?' said Margot in a blasé voice, yawning.

'My God, can't you change the subject?' groaned Clea, almost in tears.

'To what? Your beloved vegetables? Call yourself vegetarians? You don't know anything about mushrooms!' said Kostya, frowning.

'I was talking about English mushrooms,' Anthony explained gently in English. 'At least there are no worms in them, as there are in this – what d'you call it?' – And with obvious disgust Anthony prodded the fringe of the boletus, which was peppered with little holes.

'Hey, hey – steady on!' Kostya leaped to the defence of his mushroom. 'What if there are worms in it? Worms are meat too. And if you're such strict vegetarians, put the mushroom in salty water and all the worms will crawl out. Then you can fry the mushroom vegetarian-style. Oh, why do I bother to talk to you?' he sighed, and turned to stare at the birch-tree.

In the awkward pause that followed, everyone listened to the singing of the birds and looked at the sun, sinking into a fluffy duvet of clouds, taking with it the slightest hope of reviving the conversation. Putting a cheerful face on it, Clea started rattling the teacups as she poured out the remains of the tea. 'Don't you dig tea, feller?' Margot asked Kostya, jabbing him playfully in the ribs. Kostya moved a little away. As a result of her contacts with Leningrad black-marketeers and unofficial artists in Moscow, Margot liked to show off by talking in something resembling Russian semi-underworld slang, which she took to be the language of the Soviet intellectual élite. Kostya, however, was irritated by something quite different.

'Who made this tea?' he enquired sternly, sipping from his cup with a grimace of disgust. Clea, of course, had made the tea. 'As usual, I suppose, you poured fiercely boiling water on to it?' said Kostya contemptuously, knowing the answer in advance. 'No, people in England don't know how to make tea,' he sighed bitterly. Margot winked at Clea and burst out laughing. Clea said nothing, but blushed the colour of what Kostya called 'Krasnodar brick tea'.

'Tea?' Anthony repeated like a polite parrot, trying to follow this Russian dialogue. 'How else should one make tea? With boiling water, if I'm not mistaken.'

'Kostya was saying that the English don't know how to make tea,' Margot explained to him in English.

'Oh!' said Anthony in astonishment, and started twitching in his seat again.

'You may well say "Oh!"' Kostya frowned. 'Only in Russia do they know how to make tea,' he said, 'because tea came to Russia much earlier than to Western Europe.' And he proceeded to deliver a whole lecture about the Cossack chieftains Petrov and Yalyshev, who had described the strange Chinese beverage as early as the fifteenth century. He then droned on about Vassily Starkov, the traveller and envoy of the tsar's court, who in exchange for sables was given half a hundredweight of tea by the Mongol khan, a substance then unknown in England, as a result of which the tsar and the boyars were already drinking quantities of tea in the sixteenth century – and not only the boyars, but even ordinary Muscovite townspeople were able to buy 'the khan's potion', along with soap and hemp, on Red Square. Thus tea as a drink was first democratised and reached the lowest levels of society in despotic Russia and not in England . . . 'with its vaunted parliamentary democracy,' said Kostya.

'Interesting thought,' said Anthony, who had picked up the one word that he understood – 'democracy' – in the whole of Kostya's monologue.

'It's time to abandon the crude division of the world into totalitarianism and democracy. To divide the globe into zones of tea and coffee reflects the course of history far more profoundly,' Kostya interrupted him. 'Europe, by the way, under the Bourbons and Habsburgs, who from the very beginning made coffee a state monopoly, turned its bourgeoisie into keen admirers of the coffee bean, and thereby shut off all routes whereby tea might have been distributed eastwards to the Slav lands. If it hadn't been for that envoy, Vassily Starkov, and his supply of tea from the Mongol khan, Russia, too, would have become slavishly addicted to coffee. Thus Europe pushed Russia into the oppressive embrace of the Tartars – the "Tartar yoke". That's pure legend – about Russia acting as a shield protecting Europe from the Tartar hordes! It was all invented by Pushkin and Chaadayev, and the West took it up simply to console itself for an unforgivable omission that lasted for centuries; whichever way you look at it, Europe ended up in the coffee zone, whilst Russia, thanks to the Tartar khanate, strode in seven-league-boots into the tea zone.'

'And what about America? What about the other nuclear superpower?' said Anthony eagerly.

'Oh, you and your nuclear this and nuclear that! There never will be a nuclear conflict between America and Russia, because they both belong to the tea zone. Tea came to America from Russia: via the Chukchis and the Eskimos – through Alaska, on dog-sleds.'

'In other words, ultimately from the Tartar khanate?' Anthony exchanged nervous glances with Margot; Kostya was obviously off his head.

'Everything came from the rule of the Tartar khans. For some reason people refer to it as the "Tartar yoke". Impudence! Did you know, you Westerners, that during that period of the so-called Tartar yoke there were already bath-houses in Russia, in which the steam was fed in through pipes? At a time when enlightened Europe was washing itself once a year in a tar-barrel, the wild Slavs – thanks to the Tartar yoke – were steaming themselves in a tiled bath-room, or, as you would call it, a sauna.'

'So that's where "birch tea" comes from!' said Clea, delighted at her own flash of insight.

'What do you mean – "birch tea?"' Kostya queried.

'Made from a birch-switch,' Clea explained.

'What have birch-switches got to do with it?!'

'Well, in a Russian steam bath they use birch-switches, don't they?'

'They climb up on to the upper shelves and beat each other with birch-switches in the steam,' Margot explained to the baffled Anthony, who had by now completely lost the thread of the conversation.

'What for?' Anthony enquired, reasonably enough.

'It was Dostoyevsky who described a Siberian steam-bath in which he was doing penal servitude,' Margot continued, showing off her knowledge. 'The Russian people like to achieve spiritual purity through physical suffering.'

'In my view, that's simply masochism – as a sign of protest against the sadism of the authorities,' said Clea, unwilling to let Margot get away with her apparent omniscience. 'And then, after a bath, they drink tea – isn't that so, Kostya?'

'Yes, they do,' Kostya confirmed gloomily.

'They steep a birch-switch in the tub of water that supplies the steam for the bath, and then they drink that infusion. It's called birch tea.'

'Lime tea, you fool!' Kostya cut her off. 'You're mixing it up with lime-flower tea. Apart from that, there's the expression: to fleece someone like stripping off lime-bark. And there's lime tea, but there's no such thing as birch tea!'

'No doubt she's confusing it with "birch porridge", which is what Russians call flogging people with birch rods,' said the all-knowing Margot, hypocritically coming to Clea's rescue.

'In Russia they flogged people with birch rods in the last century,' Clea persisted. 'Now they beat children with a bunch of nettles. And then they make nettle soup. They say it's good for high blood pressure.'

'And they don't drink birch tea, but birch sap,' said Margot, not to be outdone. 'There's even a Soviet song that goes: "I was drinking birch sap in a pine forest," – isn't that right, Kostya?'

But Kostya was staring hard at the birch-tree and did not answer. His eyes went glassy and he belched loudly.

'When did you manage to get drunk again?' Clea could not resist asking him.

'Right here and now,' Kostya barked. 'From drinking your ghastly tea. This "birch tea" of yours is guaranteed to give you heartburn . . . Europe will be destroyed by radioactive poisoning,' he concluded unexpectedly.

'We were just talking about that,' Anthony agreed with him enthusiastically.

'Europe will perish because she will insist on making tea with fiercely boiling water from a kettle, having rejected the tradition of the Russian samovar – which was also, by the way, a legacy of Tartar rule, along with steam-baths,' Kostya added as though in revenge at Clea as the personification of Europe, and went on to a panegyric on the samovar, the 'Russian tea-machine', as the samovar is rightly called in the West. The samovar, Kostya explained, thanks to its unique shape, which increases its resonating properties, has a remarkable characteristic: when the water is just coming to the boil, the samovar gives off a barely discernable sound on the note of 'G' – it sings; but then gradually the quantity of bubbles, which start out at the bottom and rise up to the top, increases more and more until finally the second stage of boiling occurs: it is marked by a massive upward surge of bubbles, which at first make the water slightly cloudy and then actually produce the effect of turning the water white, in a way reminiscent of the rapidly flowing water of a spring. For this reason this stage is called 'the white spring'; and at that point the samovar, thanks to its resonating properties, starts to give out a special sound. And Kostya made a noise somewhere between a buzz and a hiss.

'It is very easy to miss that barely detectable moment. But thanks to the samovar . . . The samovar makes this noise to tell us: "Now's the time to make the tea, or you'll be in trouble!"' And Kostya looked round triumphantly at the others, who had fallen silent from the effect of his graphic description of boiling water in a samovar.

'You said: "You'll be in trouble." Why will you be in trouble?' Anthony enquired nervously.

'You don't understand, do you?' Kostya gave him an ominous stare. Could civilised English people really not understand that if you let the 'white spring' stage pass, the molecules of water start to break down from over-boiling? Gigantic quantities of hydrogen start to evaporate from the water, and the longer you boil it – as English housewives, such as Clea, are apt to do – the resulting tea will contain corresepondingly more deuterium – heavy water – which is an isotope of ordinary water.

'What?' Anthony asked in alarm.

'Heavy water – that's what! If you boil water too long you get heavy water, and what you drink is not tea but coloured heavy water. And you know what heavy water is used for, don't you?'

'For a hydrogen bomb!' said Anthony, his mouth gaping.

'Exactly,' Kostya confirmed grimly. 'You're filling yourself up with heavy water, not tea. Your stomach is gradually being transformed into a walking hydrogen bomb! Aaarrrgh!' – he suddenly uttered a dreadful roar, a sort of atomic howl, and flung his whole body forward across the table, sending cups, saucers, sugar-bowl and milk-jug flying. The fact was that Anthony, as he was listening to Kostya's dissertation on the samovar, had been nervously picking at the boletus with his fingernail, and, on hearing that drinking tea was turning his stomach into a hydrogen bomb, had convulsively clenched his fingers and – the gorgeous mushroom in his hand was reduced to nothing but a damp mess of skin and fibres.

'I warned you! I told you to be more careful!' Kostya almost whimpered as he bent over the squashed mushroom, like King Lear over the dead body of Cordelia, in an unsuccessful attempt to reconstitute fragments of mushroom in the hope of resurrecting the shattered masterpiece. With pale, frightened faces Clea and Margot bustled to and fro, picking up, in their turn, fragments of the broken tea-set and wiping off tea-leaves spattered over clothes and chairs, as though the teapot had indeed exploded like a hydrogen bomb. Kostya paid no attention to them at all. With a glazed look he surveyed the scene of the disaster, groaning: 'Oh, you . . .!' With back bowed in grief he strode away from the table, stopped halfway and returned to grab his knife before going into the house. He slammed the door. Clea straightened up and hissed after him: 'He's gone into the kitchen. He'll get drunk again, like a bloody Scottish miner. Or an Irish barber.' She couldn't bring herself to use the appropriate Russian expression – 'like a Russian cobbler' – because she regarded herself as an internationalist and not a xenophobe.

It was no coincidence that Kostya had begun to hold forth about the Tartar khans and samovars, for he had started to behave like a Tartar himself. At her first appearance with Kostya in public, Clea realised that the creature she had brought to London was an Asiatic with a greedy, slit-eyed look. The reception, or, as the English call it, 'the party' in honour of their arrival on the shores of Albion, had been arranged on Margot's initiative and held in Anthony's elegant flat in Kensington. Clea had hated the whole idea from the start; she hated Anthony's new flat for its trendy bareness, its glossy and expensive fittings, its open fireplaces and its bar. She had guessed in advance, when Anthony was showing them round the flat, that he would casually draw their attention to a brass candlestick, bought for a fortune in the Portobello Road, stressing that he had bought it in a flea market, as if no one knew that it had long since ceased to be a 'flea market' and was now a collection of smart antique shops for rich eccentrics and tourists; that he would complain about his neighbour, an 'oil magnate from the sands of Arabia', one of those *nouveau riche* Arabs who were buying up the best houses in London with the result (hypocritical sigh) that ordinary citizens were unable to find a decent, modest place to live because the price of property had been so inflated; that he would say: 'Margot and I decided not to carpet the floors but just to leave them as they are – it's so much nicer and simpler without carpets,' although any fool knew what a fortune it cost to sand and polish these oaken woodblock floors – his guests could see themselves reflected from head to foot, simply in order to be reminded of their own insignificance; that he would casually straighten in passing a nineteenth-century engraving that depicted a coal mine complete with Victorian winding-gear, saying as he did so: 'Look – the coalminer's lot hasn't changed since Dickens' time, has it? Ah, the horror of it! With ice or without?'

She had also detested the prospect of a crowd of her girlfriends from university days, whom she had not seen for years; they would all, she knew, come running for the opportunity to peck her on the cheek and then to go into idiotic raptures about this happy solution to her peculiar and difficult ordeal in Russia, whereupon they would whisper to each other in a corner about this absurd foreigner, this Asiatic Tartar whom she had dug out of some Russian garbage-tip for lack of other matrimonial alternatives.

All this, of course, was beyond the reach of Kostya's understanding. Like any newcomer, it was doubtful whether he understood the difference between fashionable Kensington and humble Kennington, just as he was unable to appreciate the difference between cheap carpets and varnished parquet – indeed he perceived it in exactly reverse terms, regarding carpets as smarter because in Moscow one had to queue for them whole days and nights, whereas everyone there had parquet floors even if they were not quite of the same quality.

He was, however, amazed at the variety of drinks and, above all, by the way they were served: from a bar-counter, where there was even draught beer in a barrel that was delivered to one's home. This touched him. For the rest, he understood little – who these people were, why they had come and what they were talking about. When questioned, he would mumble a vague reply, grinning politely, nodding in answer to a nod, smiling in response to a smile – in the way that every foreigner, to be on the safe side, apes the grimaces of his interlocutor when he understands neither the language nor the customs of the natives.

Defeated in their attempts to extract from Kostya an analysis of the difference between totalitarianism and democracy, the guests finally left him alone. Clutching a large mug of beer, he settled himself comfortably in a corner on some large cushions against the wall, which were even more pleasant than an armchair, and where he was finally able truly to relax after all the problems and rows induced by leaving Moscow and travelling to England, accompanied as it had been by a permanent chorus of advisers and inquisitive onlookers. A forest of English legs flickered in front of him as the guests danced away their 'party'. These 'party members', as he mentally dubbed them, were also drinking beer, but in a strange way - without eating anything, as Russians do, and if they did eat as they drank then only roast peanuts; in other words, they were eating something sweetish, whereas it was obvious to anyone that beer needed something salty to stimulate one's thirst, so that one could then satisfactorily quench that thirst by pouring a deep draught of beer down one's throat. But Kostya was in luck: alongside the cushions he found an elegant little stool made of some obviously precious kind of wood, and on that graceful piece of furniture was an equally graceful china saucer, upon which, in pleasant if disorderly profusion, someone had poured a heap of small black rusks. The rusk-bearing stool was thoughtfully placed at such a height that anyone reclining on the cushions had only to stretch out a hand to pick up a supply of rusks without even looking. And the rusks turned out to be exactly what was wanted: salty, but not too much so, just right for this light beer that the guests for some reason called by the Russian word for 'prison camp' – *lager* – apparently in Kostya's honour.

Kostya luxuriated in his corner on the cushions, sipping his beer and nibbling rusks. It was a good thing that Margot and Anthony had been to Moscow – they obviously knew the proper way to drink beer. Anthony, however, in passing by, stopped and raised his eyebrows in astonishment. Pointing to the rusks he enquired hesitantly: 'Er . . . do you like them?' To which Kostya hastened to explain how one's gullet was stimulated by provoking thirst with something slightly salty when one was drinking beer. Anthony obviously had trouble in understanding Kostya's little discourse and moved away with an odd sort of smile, shrugging his shoulders. And he was not the only one. Kostya noticed that many of the guests were glancing round and giving him amazed looks; some were obviously trying to push their way over to his cushion-filled corner, and having seen for themselves that Kostya really was eating these rusks as he drank his beer, would go away again, hiding embarrassed smiles behind their hands. Clearly the Russian way of drinking beer struck these islanders as comical and absurd – although it was of course possible that these curious onlookers had simply walked over to stare at Kostya himself, a specimen of *homo sovieticus* in an English zoo. Finally it dawned on him that maybe he was not alone in liking these delicious little rusks, but that everyone was too shy to say so and they were all amazed at the obtuseness of this Russian who was monopolising the whole bowlful of this rare delicacy.

Such was indeed the case, to judge by the look of dismay on Clea's face, who was pushing her way through the crowd of guests, making enigmatic warning signs to Kostya from the other end of the room. Before this she had been circulating animatedly from one little group to another, and by the selection of words reaching Kostya's ears, such as 'politburo', '*Pravda*' and '*apparatchik*', she had been kindly describing to the guests the horrors of totalitarianism and the Soviet censorship. Now, though, her face was distorted in a spasm of disgust. Reaching Kostya's corner, she pointed at the china bowl and hissed in his ear: 'Do you think those were put there for you? Why are you eating them?' Since Clea could not be suspected of ignorance of Russian beer-drinking rituals, she was obviously accusing Kostya of having cornered these rusks for himself and refusing to share them with others. 'Why are you behaving like such a clown?' she went on, shaking with fury. The matter was obviously more serious than Kostya had supposed. 'Are you trying to make me into a laughing-stock? Don't you realise who those rusks are meant for?' Kostya did not realise; but at that moment the answer provided itself: with a tinkle of the little bell fastened to its collar, a huge ginger tom-cat jumped up on to Kostya's knees, bent its well-fed face towards the little stool and began systematically to devour the rusks in the china bowl, glancing around hungrily and licking its chops.

'Why didn't anybody tell me it was the cat's bowl?' Kostya muttered in a hurt voice as Clea was taking him to the bus-stop.

'Why? Because this is not the Soviet Union!' snapped Clea. 'This is a free country. You can eat dog-shit if you like and no one will say a word to you – especially since, as far as the English know, that's what the Russian population eats anyway.'

It was, perhaps, from that evening onwards that Konstantin's inclinations and preferences, both culinary and ideological, began to change. Suddenly he firmly rejected first English cooking and then Western cuisine in general. He began to describe English dishes as nothing but left-over cat-food. Even the variety and abundance of foodstuffs soon palled on him. His initial enthusiasm only lasted a few weeks, when he had run, goggle-eyed, from shop window to shop window – from the trendy delicatessens of Covent Garden to unremarkable suburban supermarkets – and had come home worn out. At night he would babble aloud as he mentally lined up the thousands of labels on all the tinned goods he had seen. He devoured with his eyes the dozens of varieties of apples and pears, which shamelessly flaunted their pink flanks from inside their pleated, skirt-like paper wrappings. Prawns, with whiskers like guardsmen's moustaches, tempted his gaze on fishmongers' slabs, which replaced the lack of rainbows in London's skies with their palette of colours that recalled distant islands: from amber-coloured haddock to the bronze tints of kippers. He would voyage through the exotic herbaria of greengrocers' displays as though in a museum, where salads like palm leaves enveloped mounds of brussels sprouts with their haloes and fortress-like ramparts of avocadoes were shaded by little woven Red-Riding-Hood baskets full of strawberries. He would circle around them, sniffing the aromas and whispering to himself the names of these gifts of nature like an incantation, and when he went to bed he would toss and turn for a long time, thinking up dishes for almost a year ahead. But the more he talked of them, the less he did.

Quantity was converted into quality, in the sense that the sheer variety of these rarities lost its mystery and they no longer held the attraction of the whiffs from some distant, foreign kitchen-stove. There were too many enigmatic labels to be able to perceive each one of them as something. What then was unique about his laborious journey towards culinary truth, which had once peeped tantalisingly through cracks in the Iron Curtain? Konstantin began to look for flaws and defects. And finally he found one: dill.

'Did you know that they don't sell dill in this country?' he announced to Clea one day over dinner, as though this were some joyful piece of news. Clea said that you could buy dill anywhere in dried form in jars, just as you could buy cardamoms, tarragon and any other herb or spice you wanted. But Kostya said that the stuff in those jars didn't even smell of dill; it was nothing but dust, and you might as well rub oak-leaves into your soup. 'In Moscow that dill in jars from England suited you perfectly well when you wanted to make *tsatsiki*. You didn't send me out for dill – you sent me to get sour cream!' Clea recalled with pain. To combat her husband's pessimism, Clea nevertheless found some fresh dill – in a Greek greengrocery, whose customers needed it for *tsatsiki*. 'All right,' said Kostya. 'You can get dill from the Greeks. But there's no sturgeon here, is there?' It was true; sturgeon was nowhere to be found. 'But was there any sturgeon in Moscow?' said Clea, making excuses for London. 'Did you ever eat sturgeon in Moscow?' – To which Kostya replied that you couldn't get anything at all in Moscow, and perhaps the reason for him leaving the place was that there was no sturgeon there; but he had *not* come so far just to arrive here and find there was no sturgeon! In fact, they did find sturgeon – in Harrods, whose food department catered for millionaires, where everything cost a month's pay and sturgeon was ten times dearer than anything else.

'I could get anything in Russia if I tried hard enough,' Kostya sighed plaintively. 'But here I don't feel like trying. And even in that store "Horrors" you won't find a plain, ordinary herring.' – 'The store is called Harrods, not "Horrors",' Clea naively corrected him, but Kostya obstinately persisted in garbling English names. His favourite reading was now Leskov's *The Left-Hander*, from which he extracted a mass of insulting expressions about England, such as 'wadding' instead of 'pudding', and he would say that those English jellies served with cream made his guts stick together. He got into the habit of going to restaurants where there was foreign cooking, such as French or Italian restaurants, until Clea announced that if he wanted to continue going to restaurants, he should get himself a job as a dishwasher, because they would soon be evicted for non-payment of rent. As a protest, Kostya practically stopped going out of the house.

He also started making strange experiments – so strange that Clea wondered whether he was planning to poison her. Coming home from the office one day, she smelt a strange smell when she was still only at the corner of their street. It was a weird smell, as though tear-gas were seeping out of every crack in their house. She found Kostya in the kitchen, standing over a saucepan the size of a bathtub and throwing shredded onion into it. A gigantic mountain of onion was piled up on the kitchen table, no less than about ten kilograms of it. Using the bony fingers of his huge hands like a rake, Konstantin was transferring this mountain into the bubbling, boiling water, and with each batch a cloud of evil-smelling steam billowed up from the saucepan, floated up to the ceiling like the mushroom-cloud of a nuclear explosion and then spread all through the house. When he had finished loading a year's onion-harvest into the saucepan, Kostya sat down beside the stove with the scraps of paper on which he had been writing his recipes in a spidery Old Slavonic script. 'Shoulder of beef, Samoyed-style!' he proudly informed Clea. Laying aside his recipes, he pleasurably inhaled the steam from the saucepan with both nostrils. He then settled himself more comfortably, as though preparing to go to sleep.

'How long is all this supposed to cook for?' Clea asked, trying to breathe through her nose. 'About three hours,' replied Kostya, 'so as to produce a thick infusion of onion. And then the shoulder goes into it.' – And he pointed towards a stringy, almost Russian-looking piece of beef that was marinading in the sink.

Clea barricaded herself into the bedroom and sprinkled herself with eau-de-Cologne, but the scent did no good, and either from humiliation or from the caustic, acrid smell tears welled up in her eyes. Around eleven o'clock at night, when she had almost attained a state of oblivion by putting the pillow and a blanket over her head, Kostya burst into the bedroom. He dragged her downstairs, half-dressed, and sat her down opposite him at the table. To her horror a vast bowl appeared between them, in which a shoulder of beef was protruding from a yellowish swamp of fatty stock. 'Take it and eat,' Konstantin urged her, his features distorted by the nauseous fog. With his bare hands he tore lengths of gristle from the boiled meat and crammed them into his mouth, wiping his face with the back of his hand. 'This is how the Samoyed people eat. And while you're chewing, you simultaneously wash it all down with vodka,' and smacking his lips he drank vodka, not tossing it down in one in the usual way but sipping it, like water, from a cut-glass tumbler.

'No, no, not like that! Tear it with your hands!' he shouted angrily at Clea when she reached for a knife. The knife clattered to the floor, having cut Clea's finger as it did so. Ignoring Clea's frightened cry, Kostya tore off a lump of gristly meat from the bone and began stuffing it into Clea's mouth: 'Suck it in, suck it in and sip the vodka through your teeth,' he muttered with irritation. Clea choked and jumped up from the table. She vomited for a long time.

From that night on, everything in the house reeked of onion: the stench of onion pursued her everywhere and at work she even stopped going to the canteen. The onion smell had soaked into the walls, the furniture and their clothes. She was perpetually opening windows and creating draughts, despite Kostya's protests that he was suffering from a cold. She even repapered the walls – to no avail. Finally they had to move out of the flat. This cost money, putting off once again the day when they could buy their own house.

Their move caused Kostya to develop an interest in the achievements of Western technology in everything to do with kitchen equipment. He made Clea buy him a humidifier. Indeed, the heat that summer was such that all the grass had withered. Kostya made a long study of the instruction-booklet; it described how distilled water, when poured into the humidifier, was converted by electricity into an invisible vapour, which humidified the atmosphere that had been dried out by excessive heat. On the first night he installed this unusual apparatus in the bedroom. Next morning Clea could not lift her head from the pillow. Molten lead was swilling about inside her head and rats had spent the night in her stomach.

Konstantin was staring at her with the broad, blissful smile of a half-wit, and holding a glass of beer in his hand. 'Would you like to chase away your hangover with some beer?' he asked, winking. 'How did you manage to get drunk?' Clea asked, overcoming the pain of her aching head. 'The same way as you,' said Kostya, 'in the conjugal couch.' He proudly explained that he had poured a bottle of whisky into the humidifier the previous evening, and all night long the mixture of whisky and distilled water had been dispersed into the air, intoxicating and refreshing simultaneously.

It was hard to say which element was uppermost in this and other shenanigans perpetrated by Kostya: daftness or buffoonery, gut nostalgia or carefully calculated sadism. He clearly could not forget his first appearance before the London public when he had accompanied his beer with a snack of cat-food, because during that first summer he took advantage of the unheard-of heat to prepare a food that Russians traditonally eat with their beer: he set about curing roach. 'So you *can* get sturgeon and fresh dill. But have you ever seen roach in London?' he said to Clea when she found him hanging out some disgusting-looking little fish by their tails on the washing-line. Every morning he would go out and admire them, prodding and sniffing them. The fish started to give off the most appalling stench, and Clea had dreams about morgues full of decomposing corpses. Once, waking up in the middle of the night, she could resist the temptation no longer; she went downstairs to the back yard and, suppressing her revulsion and childish fear, she went up to the little fish gleaming in the moonlight as they dangled from the washing-line. At that moment she staggered back with a wild, hysterical shriek: the bony ribs of the gutted, flattened fish were alive with little white worms. She paced up and down the room for half the night, shaking and feeling sick. At dawn she plucked up courage, unpinned the fish from the line with the fire-tongs, trying not to look, and incinerated them all in the back yard. She had decided on this step because that night Kostya was not at home: autumn was approaching and he had started to disappear regularly, every time taking with him the double-bladed kitchen knife that was used for cutting up meat.

7 *HOMESICKNESS*

Only when he had fastened the kitchen door behind him with its little hook could Kostya breathe freely after a long day full of irritating English sounds. The kitchen was not only his fiefdom, to which entry was forbidden to strangers; the kitchen was like going home. Opening the door of the refrigerator he cast a proprietorial glance over the stoppers and corks of various kinds of vodkas and liqueurs, and selected a bottle of home-made pepper vodka – to revive himself through his stomach. He poured himself a cut-glass tumblerful (it was like a glass from a pre-revolutionary Russian tavern, a chance find that he had bought from a London junk-dealer), tenderly fished out a fragment of cayenne pepper from the glass and set off to the back door leading to the cellar. There in the cool, mysterious twilight stood his tubs and jars, containing salted cucumbers; salted green tomatoes and pickled red ones; sauerkraut, coarsely sliced and mixed with carrots; and macerated apples, of a large, sharp-tasting green variety almost like a Russian *antonovka*. He tipped some pepper vodka into his mouth without swallowing it, thought for a while, scooped out a salted tomato, swallowed the pepper vodka that stimulated his palate as he savoured it nostalgically, and crunched the aromatic, nose-tickling tomato.

'Not enough garlic,' he muttered, clicking his tongue in disapproval, and selected a healthy grey head of garlic from a large string among the bunches of herbs hanging from the walls. The garlic turned his thoughts to other delights in his collection of home preserves. He opened the refrigerator again and took out a jar with a screw-top. Raising the jar to the light he gazed lovingly at the choice caps of marinated white mushrooms as together with a bay-leaf they lay maturing towards the perfect condition. An image of the boletus, crushed in an Englishman's fingers, rose again before his inner eye. 'No matter, no matter,' Kostya muttered to himself. 'We'll get our own back.'

Outside the window there appeared a man in a familiar peaked cap of Eastern European cut; striding past with purposeful gait, he waved a greeting to Kostya.

'Pan Tadeusz, Pan Tadeusz!' Kostya flung open the window and waved back to his neighbour with a welcoming gesture. 'Why don't you drop in?' And he flicked his forefinger under his cheekbone in an alcoholic gesture. Pan Tadeusz, Kostya's and Clea's neighbour, was the owner of a Polish delicatessen (round the corner in the High Street) and Kostya's sole drinking-companion in his hours of glum, nostalgic reflection. They had first made each other's acquaintance as buyer and seller; it had started with a discussion of 'Polish' garlic sausage, of the kind that was on sale in Pan Tadeusz's little shop, and had culminated over a bottle of Tadeusz's 'Wyborowa' on the territory of Kostya's empire – the kitchen of Clea's house. On the next occasion Kostya had given Pan Tadeusz a practical demonstration of the superiority of 'Stolichnaya' vodka over 'Wyborowa', which Pan Tadeusz had countered with some Polish 'Zubrowka'. In short, they had drawn closer to each other on a basis of alcoholic tête-à-tête meetings in which they swore mildly at their pet hates, as is proper in the great family of brother-Slavs.

'Where's Clea?' Pan Tadeusz enquired cautiously, as he shifted indecisively from foot to foot outside the window. He knew as well as Kostya did how Clea reacted to these fraternal drinking-sessions.

Kostya jerked his thumb contemptuously backwards, meaning 'It's OK – come on in!' and ran to open the front door for Tadeusz. Having tiptoed through the house into the kitchen, once inside Kostya's domain they immediately settled themselves down in noisy, festive mood at the table with all the business-like enthusiasm of a couple of Gogol's landowners. 'Well now, let's see!' said Pan Tadeusz as he unbuckled the straps of his large briefcase and proudly banged down a preserving-jar on the table.

'Ha, ladies' fingers! Fancy that!' Konstantin wheezed sceptically, scarcely glancing at the jar of pickled okra. 'No,' he sighed, laying out plates, forks and two small cut-glass tumblers. 'You may indulge yourself in your Turco-Bulgarian ladies' fingers, but I recommend our pickled *antonovka* or a Russian pickled cucumber to have with the first glassful – by the way, shall we start with vodka? Lemon vodka? Or coriander and cinnamon? Or some of this pepper vodka that I've just been sampling? It has turned out really well. Or . . . I know what!' With a mysterious look Kostya turned towards a dark bottle in a corner, the cork of which had been rammed in with a piece of rag around it to ensure that it was hermetically sealed. 'A drop of home-distilled vodka, perhaps? You know, Tadeusz, I have rejected all these Western high-tech novelties with coiled pipes and activated charcoal for filtration, and I do it the simple Muscovite way: two saucepans, one inside the other; it evaporates out of one and drips off the lid into the other, and it makes the most splendid moonshine, I can tell you – it may tickle your nose, but it's as pure as the tears of a repentant enemy of the people.'

'There's an American drink in the West called "Pepsi-Cola",' mused Pan Tadeusz in reply.

'And not only in the West. Pepsi-Cola was brought into the Soviet Union long ago – in exchange for emigrating Jews,' Kostya interrupted him. 'It's nice and sweet – good for washing down Cuban rum! But with vodka the best stuff is pickling-brine.'

'Yes, Pepsi-Cola is sweetened with sugar, that's my point,' Pan Tadeusz continued his train of thought. 'So I was thinking: since there's *so* much sugar and even some drug in Pepsi-Cola – don't you think you could make a very special sort of moonshine from it, Kostya, if you distilled it by your two-saucepan method?'

'Interesting thought,' said Kostya pensively.

As usual, the first four glasses passed in talk of new recipes for distilling moonshine and continued in concerted moaning about their mutual *bête noire* – English cooking.

'They boil the taste out of everything, the swine,' said Kostya as he washed down some of his home-cured smoked salmon with a glass of pure spirit.

'Where did you get this salmon?' Tadeusz enquired with studied casualness as he modestly picked up a slice of it by the edge. Kostya, however, did not reveal his culinary discoveries to everyone, especially as he was wary of Tadeusz: he was not just a neighbour but the owner of a delicatessen. Kostya therefore ignored the enquiry.

'They even overboil tomatoes, the monsters!' he went on, as though he had not heard the question. 'I can't complain about potatoes – every nation boils potatoes. But will someone kindly tell me why they steam leeks? And as for scalding tomatoes in boiling water – I'm sorry, but that's sheer barbarism! And no amount of parliamentary government can justify such barbarism! Another drink?'

Both now went on to curse British soups, consisting of boiled carrots floating in a disgusting kind of gravy; they swore at British sliced bread, which reminded them of a soggy rag used for wiping down dirty tables. Nor did they forget the notorious English fish-fingers. 'In our wretched country, deprived as we are of every sort of food, one eats anything that is tasty and nourishing – one might even eat those fish-fingers,' Kostya sighed gloomily. 'But how British fishermen, who catch megatons of lobsters, crabs, tender little squid and other delicious gifts of the sea, can bear to eat nothing but fish and chips, passes my comprehension. And it's not *gefilte* fish, mind you, but frozen cod, and the chips are not crisp *pommes frites* but God-knows-what fried for too long in fish-oil mixed with petrol, and then on top of that – they soak it in reeking vinegar and eat it straight out of cone of rolled-up newspaper! They export containers-full of delicious seafood abroad, while they themselves chew away at frozen cod covered with grated beetroot. So who buys all those colonial delicacies piled up on the counters of their grocery shops? Foreigners – that's who! Typical British hypocrisy: it's done so that foreigners can stare at it all and exclaim that, ah, the British are quite as civilised as the Parisians. The British can't get over their imperial past. They want to pretend that because of all that imported tea, cayenne pepper, avocadoes, artichokes and what have you, Britannia still rules the waves. But far from enjoying all these fruits of empire, such as artichokes, their stomachs are in a state of artistic shock: they stuff their refrigerators with all this exotica, and then they systematically ruin it, destroy it completely by boiling it in order to remove any flavour and make everything else taste like baked potato. And along with this total contempt for foreign refinements, in this frenzy, one may call it, of culinary chauvinism, they don't realise what precious delicacies they're throwing into the cat's bowl . . .

'Literally into the cat's bowl,' Konstantin went on. 'Not long ago, I was walking past a fishmonger's shop and saw the assistant gutting a fresh salmon for his customer, an old lady (they are the ones, by the way, who are the inquisitors of sterility; they want fish to be like the kind that comes in a plastic bag from a supermarket). So there was the fishmonger gutting it. And I saw him, along with the guts – snick-snack! – cut out the roe and throw it into the waste-bag. I was literally stupefied: the waste-bag was transparent and in it were the innards, guts and swim-bladders – and all sewn together, as it were, by a ruby-red thread of globules of fresh roe. That lovely red roe was glinting in the light like pearls cast before swine. I don't need to tell you, Tadeusz, that you only have to sprinkle that roe with a little salt and in twenty-four hours you have the most delicious fresh roe that's fit to be washed down with champagne: the very same red caviar, in fact, that you find in a few special shops and where a jar the size of your little finger costs a month's pay. When I came to my senses, I said to the salesman: why are you throwing away the roe along with the guts? He didn't hear what I said about roe, and he said: "Who needs these innards?" I said: "My dog likes eating all that muck." I explained this in English: "You know . . . dog . . . woof-woof, bow-bow!" He immediately understood about the dog – they like animals better than people here – and the fool put aside those fish-entrails for me, that's to say all that caviar in its pure form,' – and with a little self-satisfied guffaw Kostya put a litre jar of red caviar on the table. 'Go on – have some; I don't want any. I feel like a relative of mine who lived in the Soviet Far East before the war: first bread was rationed, then it disappeared altogether but they could get caviar by the barrelful, and soon they couldn't bear to eat caviar. Ah, you can't get real black bread here, Borodino bread for instance, so we'll have to spread it on white bread. Go on, eat, Tadeusz, don't stint yourself.' Unmoved by Kostya's nostalgia for black bread, Tadeusz put a tablespoonful of caviar into his mouth and clicked his tongue in appreciation.

'Does this fishmonger of yours often gut fresh salmon?' he enquired with ill-concealed envy.

'Now, Tadeusz, don't you try getting round me with your hints. I won't tell you the address anyway, but I can console you slightly. He has stopped putting aside those fish-guts for me. I went to see him the other day and he said: "I'm sorry, but I threw all the offal away." He couldn't be bothered to sort out salmon-guts from cod-guts. He couldn't be bothered, do you realise?! So it all went to waste. Stupid people!' They poured out more drinks and took another snack, but this time it was dill pickles with black bread. 'You have to buy black bread from the Germans. The Danes have it too: the Danes stole the recipe from the Slav boyars when the Varangians used to voyage southwards through Russia to Greece. And the Greeks, on the way back, stole dill from us, and now in London they sell it in Greek shops,' he observed glumly. 'It's sad, by the way, that you Poles, our brothers, spurn the use of dill when you pickle cucumbers. Now you, Tadeusz, just spear yourself a pickled cucumber from that jar' – and watching the expression on his companion's face as he munched a cucumber, he enquired impatiently: 'Well?'

'Not bad,' said Pan Tadeusz, chewing thoughtfully. 'Not a bad cucumber. We, by the way, also put dill into our pickles.'

'I can't taste it!' Kostya objected sharply. 'I, for instance, bought some pickled cucumbers in your shop. On the label it said: with dill. I opened it and there was no taste of dill at all. No garlic, either. And as for a bay-leaf, you had forgotten about that altogether. Nothing but vinegar, so strong that it tickled your nose – what sort of pickle is that?'

'I don't think Polish pickling-liquid is very different from Russian,' frowned Pan Tadeusz.

'As different as heaven from earth, as your head from your stomach!' shouted Kostya, pouring out some more moonshine vodka. 'Of course it's not a Western marinade, which is nothing but vinegar and sugar – enough to distil vodka from it. You Poles have at least taken some account of the historic brotherhood of the Slav peoples, and a real cookery expert or gourmet like myself can detect a little bit of dill in your pickled cucumbers. But what will an ordinary, simple Russian say when he bites into one of your Polish cucumbers? Vinegar – that's what he'll say! That pickle expresses a typically Polish approach to the confrontation between East and West: on the one hand the recipe is Russian, with dill, but it's also full of vinegar to give it a thoroughly Western taste. Now that's not nice! It's precisely the vinegar and not the hypocritical pseudo-presence of Russian dill that the ordinary man tastes in your pickled cucumber!' After the fourth glass Kostya was inclined to transform things culinary into the metaphysics of national character.

'I don't understand,' said Tadeusz, offended, 'how such an original and sensitive gourmet as yourself can rely on the opinion of the plain man in the street. People like that can't tell the difference between a Slovak *spikačka* and a frankfurter.'

'And what, pray, is the difference between your famous Slovak *spikačka* and a frankfurter? Really – just because they cut it criss-cross from both ends and fry it instead of boiling it as a normal human being would, they make out it's a unique national dish! Well, perhaps they do add bacon and garlic to it, but the idea is not very original, I must say.' Konstantin shrugged his shoulders. 'And why do you Poles have such aristocratic contempt for the man in the street? Ordinary people are the safeguard of a healthy stomach. For example, Tadeusz, take the simple Russian – let's say a merchant from the Zamoskvorechye district of Moscow.'

'A merchant from *where*?' asked Tadeusz baffled.

'Zamoskvorechye,' Kostya repeated.

'Are there any merchants in the Soviet Union?'

'There is everything in Russia,' replied Kostya, without blinking. 'But there's no Yorkshire pudding. Because if you served this simple Russian merchant with a French artichoke and Yorkshire pudding, he wouldn't touch it. He might be dying of hunger, but he wouldn't touch it. Sprinkle as much sugar as you like on that sort of muck, his stomach would still rebel. He would spit out all these foreign fancies, go into his kitchen-garden, dig up a potato, pickle a cucumber and happily do without all that muck from abroad as long as he could have his familiar, home-made plain local food with his own butter and salt. When I was in Moscow I was keen on foreign foods too and I used to argue about the divide between East and West, but only here, in voluntary exile, have I come to realise that the secret of great cookery lies in familiarity, habit – in what you're *used to*. Habit is a gift from above. Do you know, Tadeusz, what dish I miss most here? *Pelmeny*. Plain old Soviet *pelmeny*, with their slimy dough, each one with its heart stuffed with meat, onion and any old muck.' Kostya licked his lips. 'Those *pelmeny* will lie in some battered, cast-iron Soviet stomach like bullets in the barrel of a gun, but what those bullets are stuffed with – now there's a mystery for your student of cookery! Do you think I haven't tried to unravel that mystery, Tadeusz? I've tried every sort of meat, I've added fish-bladder, changed to a different mincing-machine. None of it was any good. The essential element of muck was missing – that familiar staleness, decay, stagnation. Whether that's good or bad, I don't know – I'm not a moralist. But one thing I do know: the whole Russian cookery rests on that element of muck – therein lies its mystery, impenetrable to rationalistic foreigners. No, the mind alone can never understand Russian cookery. All we Slav peoples are bound by that secret, from the Russians to our brother nations – the peoples of the Baltic principalities, even including the Varangians, who are today's Scandinavians. And the proof of it is – our age-old Russian salted herring is common to them all. All the Slav peoples feed on it – from the Volga barge-haulers to the Varangians of Scandinavia. Where in England, Tadeusz, will you find herring with *that* smell, that unique admixture of filth with its inimitable stench? Search as you will, go to Lapland and bang your head against the Iron Curtain – but you won't find salted herring in the British Isles.'

'Why not?' Tadeusz objected, ever the optimist. 'They do have something like our salted herring here: they're called rollmops.'

'Exactly: something like! Rollmops – dog-shit, ha!' said Konstantin with bitter irony. 'Tell me, Tadeusz, why do they soak herring in vinegar? Now try some of my home-made salted herring, take a nice fat piece,' Kostya pushed the plate of herring towards him. 'It's as simple as can be: I just rubbed sea-salt into the fish, put it in the fridge in a plastic bag – and a day later . . . what a fragrance! But they put God knows what into their rollmops, and then vinegar, vinegar and more vinegar to stop it from going bad – but the whole secret is in the decay! I've noticed for a long time that you Poles have taken a fancy to rollmops. You're breaking away from the Slavo-Varangian tradition. And that's a pity, because there aren't many of us left who understand the point of it.' Kostya's gaze clouded over with nostalgic gloom. 'Sometimes I'm overcome with such loneliness, Tadeusz, that I can't describe it. I've only ever found anything similar in the letters of Leo Tolstoy. When these moods come over me, I get behind the steering-wheel and drive off to the woods.'

'To the birch-woods?' Tadeusz put in sympathetically.

'Why to birch-woods in particular? Trees as such don't affect me. I'm interested in what's to be found under the trees.'

'What – berries?'

'Stop playing the idiot, Tadeusz! As if you hadn't guessed. I'm not talking about berries. I'm talking about mushrooms. Take a look at this . . .' Kostya turned around, took something out of the refrigerator and slammed the door shut again. 'Have you seen anything like that?' And he put the jar of pickled mushrooms on the table, banging it down with a solemn, carefully calculated thud. 'Boletus – see? Cap to cap, stalk to stalk – like a ballet at the Bolshoi Theatre!' And he turned the jar around in a ray of sunlight shining through the kitchen window.

The keen eyes of Pan Tadeusz glittered and narrowed – and not only from the sunlight reflected off the jar. With the gaze of a fanatic the Pole admired this well-ordered mushroom ballet inside the glass jar, among which a clove of garlic could be seen giving off the dull gleam of pearls in a dress-circle box or a bay-leaf floating theatrically like a black swan.

'Well,' said Kostya, holding his breath, 'what do you think? Shall we open it?'

'Right now?' Pan Tadeusz muttered with fearful joy. 'Perhaps it's a bit soon?' He licked his dry lips.

'If one were orthodox in these matters, I would say it was a bit soon. But I am an irrationalist, Tadeusz, and my intuition prompts me that now is the very moment. These are boletus of unusual perfection. Not a single little worm, not a single snail – pure as newborn babes: you could eat them raw,' Konstantin muttered excitedly, opening the jar neatly and firmly. 'And you, Tadeusz, pour us out a little more. There now!' After a theatrical pause, he removed the lid from the jar like a conjuror. 'What an aroma, eh?' he said, taking a long sniff.

Both were silent, nostrils wriggling in ecstasy. Then like two religious sectarians performing some heretical ritual, they armed themselves with forks, uttering not a sound.

'Right, Tadeusz, you can have first go,' Kostya pronounced at last, pushing the jar, with typical Russian generosity, towards his younger brother in the family of Slav peoples.

'Why should I be the first?' Tadeusz lowered his eyes. 'No man should plunge into the thick of the fight before his father, as your Gogol's hero, Taras Bulba, used to say.'

'Taras Bulba wasn't interested in mushrooms. He chopped the Polish knights into shreds, like sauerkraut. To feed the worms, if you'll pardon the expression. So go on, Maria Walewska – spear yourself a mushroom,' said Kostya, egging his neighbour on while impatiently holding his fork at the ready.

Obviously offended by the remarks about Polish knights and Maria Walewska, Pan Tadeusz was about to put down his fork but in the end, after a short altercation and mutual offers to go first, they both stuck their forks into the jar simultaneously. Exchanging looks, they each speared a mushroom, fished it out into the light of day with solemn simultaneity, held it up in the sunlight to admire it and, having downed a glassful with equal synchronicity, dispatched the mushrooms into their mouths – Tadeusz politely devouring a stalk while Konstantin, as master of the house, ate a cap. Holding their prey in their mouths, both chewed it gently, swallowed it and exclaimed together:

'Aaah – mmm?!' whereupon they sighed in chorus 'Yeee-sss!'

After some head-nodding and smacking of the lips, each stuck out his lower lip in the approving grimace of the connoisseur. There was a long, blissful pause. Tadeusz then enquired casually:

'I suppose you picked them early in the morning, did you?'

'Yes,' Kostya nodded. 'On April the First.'

'At the edge of the wood?'

'Yes. And in a clearing. And in clumps of hazel-trees.'

'A lot of hazels grow in the woods around Oxford,' Tadeusz remarked in a throwaway, man-of-the-world tone.

'There are hazel-groves in the woods near Cambridge, too. Not to mention Sussex, Middlesex and Essex – there are lots of hazels in any "sex".'

'Ha, ha – that's a good one about sex!' Tadeusz laughed ingratiatingly. 'Not sex in a hazel-wood but a hazel-wood in a "sex" – very funny.'

'Flattery will get you nowhere. I'm not going to tell you where I pick my white boletus, Tadeusz, so don't build any hopes. And don't try to catch me out with your crafty little questions,' Kostya warned him.

'Me? Try to catch you out?' Tadeusz gave a forced laugh. 'I have enough mushroom-places of my own, thank you!'

'One wouldn't think so, to judge by your delicatessen. I went there yesterday – nothing but those tasteless English mushrooms. I even prefer the Chinese black mushroom. At least the Chinese mushroom has a flavour and makes a good, thick soup. No wonder they sing: Russians and Chinese are brothers forever!'

'Well, of course, you only need us Poles as one argument in the dispute about the spiritual pre-eminence of Orthodoxy. You're always trying to convert us: we annoy you with our Catholic obstinacy. You're even prepared to kiss and cuddle with the Chinese so that you can put us out of your mind,' Tadeusz sighed gloomily.

'All right, that's enough of playing at being the poet Mickiewicz! I'm not talking about religion,' said Kostya indignantly. 'I'm talking about mushrooms! You can eat as many English mushrooms as you like. But you try to be on both sides at once: you run with the hare and hunt with the hounds. What would happen if one allowed a brotherly Pole into one's mushroom-places? Why – the very next day there wouldn't be a single mushroom left in the British Isles! And it's not as if you cut them neatly with a knife and leave the mushroom spawn in the soil, so that with the first shower of rain a new mushroom will raise its head in the same place – no: you tear them up by the roots, you slaughter them like clumsy ruffians so that other people shan't have any more. But worst of all, having savagely wrenched the mushrooms out of the ground, what do you do to them? You souse them in your Polish vinegar until they lose all their taste. And it's not just mushrooms, either – you can't even pickle ordinary cabbage properly, but you insist on imitating the West with your sweet-sour marinades. Sauerkraut should have a healthy smell, the reek should hit you half a mile from the open tub – but you turn your noses up at our Slav flavouring; the vinegary West makes you feel ashamed of the family of Slav peoples. Your stomach may not be able to take the stinking roach the way the Finns cure it – all right, that's excusable, it's an acquired taste. But why have you rejected Russian sour-cabbage soup? Incidentally, that soup made from sauerkraut is the greatest Russian invention. As a cure for a hangover.'

'Cabbage soup?' Pan Tadeusz cut off Kostya's chauvinistic tirade. 'But cabbage soup is a Polish dish. We've been eating cabbage soup in Poland for ages.'

'Ages – shmages – who's counting? But only the Russians know how to cure a hangover with sour cabbage soup.'

'What nonsense you do talk, Konstantin! Cabbage-soup?! Why, you only have to go to the Polish club – you'll find two hundred different sorts of it on the menu!'

'Two hundred? So what? And how many sorts of *rasstegai* pasties alone were there in pre-revolutionary Russia? Made with sturgeon-gristle, for instance, or with anything else you like to name. I've been to your Polish club, though, and to be frank you've lost touch with the cuisine of your Slav cousins since you've been in emigration. And what is there that's original on the menu? Except, perhaps, for the fish, which is good – but even that's Yiddish-style.'

'What do you mean by that?'

'I don't mean anything. I mean that the club is Polish and the fish is Yiddish!'

'Well, so what? Where's the contradiction?'

'Nowhere. Yiddish-style. One couldn't think of a better name for it!'

'As it happens, I am a Jew myself,' Pan Tadeusz announced, with unexpected sternness, after the pause that followed.

'And I, you imply, am an anti-semite? Is that it? No, Tadeusz, you won't wriggle out of an argument between Slavs quite so easily. It's you Poles, by the way, who have called that sort of fish "Yiddish". Not "Jewish", but specifically "Yiddish".'

'I don't see anything wrong in that. A Jew in Polish is called a Yid. There's no other word for Jew in the Polish language.'

'Really! You can use linguistics to prove anything!' Kostya drummed his fingers on the table. 'Do you know, Tadeusz, what these infidel foreigners called me today?' he said in an unexpectedly hurt voice, nodding towards the garden.

'What did they call you?'

'A fungophile! Have you ever heard such a thing? A fungophile!'

At that moment there came a cautious knock on the kitchen door, indeed not so much a knock as a tap, a scratch even, as though the twig of a bush, blown by the wind, was scrabbling at the door. In the doorway stood Anthony.

'I decided to come and apologise for upsetting your feelings as a fungophile,' he stuttered, with an embarrassed smile on his bearded, eternal-student face.

At the word 'fungophile', Kostya swore incomprehensibly, exchanged glances with Tadeusz and spread his hands, half helplessly, half invitingly. Sitting down on the very edge of a chair and glancing fearfully at the spread on the table in front of him, Anthony began a muddled apology for 'disturbing a private party'; it emerged from his russified anglicisms that he had come to express his 'embarrassment' at the episode with the squashed boletus. He assured Kostya that he shared his devotion to any form of vegetarianism; even if mushroom-eating did threaten one with gastric poisoning, this Buddhistic way of suicide by devouring poisonous toadstools was, in his personal opinion, more honourable than destroying the white cells in other people's blood by dropping an atomic bomb. He had already got up to leave, when Kostya tugged him by the elbow.

'It's easy enough to encourage others to commit a pacifist form of suicide, but are you ready to try it yourself?' said Kostya, nudging him towards the table.

'Try what?' Anthony murmured in polite unease. 'What must I try . . . ?'

'A mushroom. A poisonous mushroom. And would you risk sampling a boletus yourself?' Kostya cut him off, a gleam of *Schadenfreude* in his eyes. Realising what this kitchen-table interrogation was leading up to, the Englishman paled. He dithered, tried to pretend that he didn't understand a word of Russian and generally behaved like a false prophet or an *agent provocateur* who has been shown up.

But Kostya had already pushed a chair under him and opened and shut the refrigerator door; in a moment Anthony found himself holding a fork on which was impaled, like a black eyeball gouged out of its socket, a slimy cap of a small boletus. Into his other hand Kostya thrust a glass measure of vodka.

'Well, is it so terrible? Is it terrible to take on personal responsibility for saving the world by putting this into your mouth – at the risk, so to speak, of your own pacifist life?' said Kostya, winking at Tadeusz. 'Or are you in favour of producing the hydrogen bomb through a concentration of heavy water from overboiling the kettle?'

'I'm against it,' gulped Anthony.

'Against what?'

'Against the bomb.'

'Then eat the mushroom at once!'

'I can't!' Anthony's Adam's apple quivered in a spasm of nausea.

'Does that mean you prefer an atomic mushroom to a pickled mushroom? And heavy water to Stolichnaya vodka?' Kostya pressed him.

'No,' Anthony declared firmly, moving the glass aside with a shaking hand and placing fork and mushroom neatly on a plate beside it.

'No! No! Why do you refuse everything I offer you?' said Kostya angrily, pacing around the kitchen in circles.

'In a choice between a mushroom and a bomb, if I don't prefer one it doesn't follow that I prefer the other,' said Anthony carefully in his own defence.

'None of your medieval syllogisms! You said yourself it was better to eat a poisonous mushroom than to exterminate babies at Hiroshima with radiation, didn't you? So drink up and eat your boletus at once!' Kostya insisted relentlessly.

'I can't,' groaned Anthony, as he raised the fork to his mouth and let it fall on to the plate again with an ominous clatter.

'I can't!' Kostya imitated him maliciously. 'But *I* can? *I* can? If I can, then why can't you? That's not pacifism – that's double standards!'

'Everyone fights the fight of peace by his own form of pacifism,' said Anthony, in an attempt at reaching a compromise. 'Let the Russian people protest to militarism with vodka and mushrooms. We prefer unilateral disarmament.'

'So *we*, in other words, can drink ourselves to perdition with vodka, weakening our military potential and our male potency, while you over here can bloat your bellies with heavy water, turning yourselves into the most powerful hydrogen bomb in the world? What sort of *détente* will *that* be, for heaven's sake?' asked Kostya indignantly.

'I won't do it any more.' Anthony groaned.

'What won't you do?'

'I won't drink overboiled water,' said Anthony like a guilty schoolboy. 'But then you must abolish the samovar.'

'Why on earth should I abolish the samovar?'

'Because the samovar boils water!' declared Anthony sententiously.

'Of course it does. And the main thing is that it bubbles. First it sings, then it bubbles. When the samovar bubbles it means the boiling water is at the "white spring" stage,' said Kostya, starting to mount his favourite hobby-horse.

'And then you must drink the tea,' Anthony prompted him, as though repeating a well-learned lesson.

'And then you must *make* the tea,' corrected Kostya.

'So the samovar bubbles. They drink tea and the samovar bubbles on,' Anthony prompted him again with a sly look.

'What are you getting at?' said Kostya, on his guard.

'I once saw a Chekov film. *Three Sisters*. They drank tea. And the samovar bubbled. They made tea. Then they topped up their glasses with hot water. It bubbled again. They topped up their glasses again. They made a fresh pot. And the samovar boiled. Glowing red charcoal. Smoke came out of the top of the samovar. Or steam. It was boiling for six hours, maybe even for days on end – with overboiled water. How long have there been samovars in Russia?' he suddenly asked Kostya directly.

'It must be about a thousand years. Since the days of the Tartar yoke,' said Kostya thoughtfully.

'Aha?' Pan Tadeusz suddenly roused himself. 'I see now! I see what Pan Anthony is getting at. Over those thousand years of drinking tea from a samovar the entire Russian people, according to your theory, Kostya, has been turning itself into a hydrogen bomb!' His forehead broke out in sweat at the appalling thought.

'All you Poles can ever do is blame the Russians,' growled Kostya. 'As though you didn't drink tea yourselves.'

'The Poles drink coffee. Like the French. Now I see clearly what this has led to.' Nervously he poured himself a glass and drank it down.

'You all make yourselves out to be sophisticated Europeans, of course! In Russia, by the way, they have long since ceased to drink tea made from a samovar. The foreigners have bought up all the samovars to take home as souvenirs. Even Anthony has a samovar at home – haven't you, Anthony?' Anthony nodded shamefacedly. 'So now they're filling themselves with heavy water quite as much as the Russians.'

'And coffee-drinking Poland finds herself squeezed between the tea-drinking superpowers!' declared Pan Tadeusz, banging his fist on the table.

'You Poles do have a weakness for the French, don't you! What was there left for the Russian people to do?' cried Kostya. 'The Chinese invented gunpowder, Leonardo da Vinci invented the cannon, so how were we to defend ourselves? Willy-nilly we had to adopt the Tartar samovar! But at least we didn't drop that samovar on the heads of babies in Hiroshima. And we weren't the only ones, by the way, who made tea by overboiling water. America is a tea-drinking power too.'

'So what will happen now?' Anthony asked in alarm.

'What will happen is that the whole world will be turned into one big samovar, where people are teapots, all covered by one big lid, so there won't be any need for nuclear umbrellas!' giggled Kostya, pouring more vodka into all the glasses. 'We shall simply have to dilute the heavy water with vodka. We'll soak up the vodka, and you'll have to get pissed on it too. If it's a question of getting sozzled in self-defence, then let it be bilateral. So drink up, Anthony – drink to mushrooms in the stomach instead of a nuclear mushroom in the sky. Come on, now – ' he urged Anthony, who was sitting dumbfounded by this flow of barely comprehensible gibberish, ' – one, two, three and – !'

'I can't drink vodka,' said Anthony obstinately. 'I drink wine.'

'The English obviously haven't yet discovered that simple piece of folk-wisdom: "When wine on vodka does sit – a man isn't worth shit,"' Kostya sighed.

'But I haven't drunk any vodka yet,' Anthony objected.

'You haven't – but we have! And if I gave you some wine now, what would we do? Sit and watch you? No, we'd knock back some wine too, and what then? When wine on vodka does sit, a man isn't worth shit – is that what you're trying to do to us?'

'Beer, perhaps,' Anthony suggested as an alternative.

' "Vodka and beer – jolly good cheer" – I quite agree. But I'm sorry – I haven't laid in any beer. Anyway, one good thing about the Soviet regime compared with pre-revolutionary Russia with all its variety of fancy foods and drinks is that it has at least taught the Russian people to stick faithfully to vodka without exception.'

'I could pop out for some beer,' suggested Pan Tadeusz politely.

'Sit down, Tadeusz, and don't twitter, or my Nuclea will explode like a warhead. I order you to stay where you are. Dictatorship is healthy for the stomach in general. Look – all the liberals of East and West decided to expose Comrade Stalin's "cult of the personality"; but I say to them: after that "cult" had been abolished, what became of the brandenburg sausage?' And he swept his companions with an inquisitorial glare.

'It emigrated to Brandenburg,' said Pan Tadeusz, attempting to joke.

'Not funny, Tadeusz, not funny! That masterpiece of a smoked sausage from the Stalin era was ground up into mincemeat in the process of democratisation. Khrushchev himself turned the handle of the mincing-machine at the notorious Twentieth Congress. The common people wanted their democratic bite to eat, so there had to be cheap and nasty food for the rank and file, and not Brandenburg concertos from the Johann Sebastian Bach of the food industry. Out of one kilo of that brandenburg sausage you could throw together a ton of rissoles made of minced pork, bread and pig-fat. But I tell you: even then you'll never satisfy the mob! And the brandenburg sausage disappeared from the people's memory: they have forgotten the recipe and they'll eat any muck instead – the Russian people are reverting to savagery, savagery . . .' And Kostya sighed.

'On the other hand, Leninist norms of Party life were restored,' said Anthony in an attempt to console him.

'Huh – under those "norms", if you said the sort of things that you say about your government here, you'd have been liquidated long ago, just like the poet Mandelstam, only without any preliminary discussions about it on the telephone between Stalin and Pasternak,' barked Konstantin.

'We have killed our poets, too, by the way. We had our own Gulag in Victorian times.' Insulted, Anthony had finally switched to English. 'Oscar Wilde, for instance, was thrown into prison. Do you know that on his way to jail he was purposely kept standing in chains on a railway platform – and all the passers-by spat in his face?'

'Which Oscar Wilde was that? The one who had fun with little boys? The pederast?'

'Well, yes . . .' Anthony stammered, blushing. 'Yes, he preferred single-sex love. That was entirely his personal affair. I'm talking about English poetry, which in his person was spat on and clapped behind bars.'

'But why do you have to bugger poor Russia in order to defend your Oscar Wilde's poetical arsehole?'

'Do you want me to encourage crass slander of the Soviet government in the cause of reactionary self-congratulation? That's an example of the morality of complacent affluence that I detest,' said Anthony, frowning in outrage.

'And so you felt drawn from that affluence to hungry Russia, did you? To look up her arsehole, as if you were looking at the mirror-image of the revolution you want in the West, is that it?' Kostya pressed him relentlessly.

'I should only like to observe,' said Anthony, beginning to lose control, 'that the arsehole of this Russia of yours is by no means the dirtiest. You don't know what it's like to be a person with a black skin in this country. Or in the United States. In your blind hatred of communism you're prepared to defend the hangmen of El Salvador and the Chilean junta.'

'Well, you can stuff that chilli pepper up your junta! Why do you always throw Russia into any discussion of justice? Russia is not for your stomachs. You couldn't swallow her, still less digest her. Look – you can't even take that morsel of boletus!' – and Konstantin provocatively waved the fork, the boletus speared on its prongs, in front of Anthony's nose.

The Englishman jumped up from his chair. Furious, teeth chattering, he wrenched the fork out of Kostya's hand, bit the wrinkled mushroom off the end of the fork and with a fixed stare began to chew it, his jaws working slowly and intently. Then his Adam's apple quivered, then again, and again, until finally, his eyes popping, Anthony swallowed the mushroom. Uttering what could have been a grunt of victory or a death-rattle, he plumped down on to his chair, crossed his legs with demonstrative nonchalance and stretched out a shaking hand towards a cut-glass measure of vodka. With a weak but triumphant smile – the smile of a wounded hero going to his death – he sipped the vodka in the English fashion, as though sampling a goblet of hemlock. He immediately choked, jumped up and began circling the kitchen, doubled up as though in the grip of a deadly poison. He coughed and his face broke out in to red blotches. Pan Tadeusz supported him under his arms, while Konstantin began thumping him on the back, pretending that he was helping Anthony to stop choking.

'Who drinks vodka like that?' Kostya shouted at him. 'The English! You have to knock back vodka in one, not in sips – down in one and *then* eat your mushroom – but you do everything the wrong way round, that's the trouble with you foreigners!'

Having finally stopped coughing, Anthony muttered that he wasn't dying from the vodka, which had gone down the wrong way, but from the poisonous mushroom, because he, unlike the Russians, had not yet acquired an immunity against it. Kostya, however, assured him that the trouble wasn't in the mushroom or the vodka but in the way they were swallowed and in what sequence, and even if the mushroom were poisonous, the best antidote and disinfectant against such an eventuality was – vodka.

'First breathe in deeply,' Kostya lectured the Englishman as though giving a class in physiotherapy, accompanying it with a routine practical demonstration of how to swallow vodka. 'There are three stages, do you see? Breathe in, swallow, breathe out – got it?'

A minute later, Anthony, like a professional acrobat, was juggling in turns with a glass, a fork, a cucumber and a bottle; it was hard to say what predominated in this feverish series of gestures – the enthusiasm of the convert or the frenzy of a man condemned to death.

'Wait, don't be in a hurry, don't try too hard,' Kostya said, checking him. 'The stomach needs greasing, so you have to line it with a bite of food: drink – eat; layer of grease – glass of vodka; vodka – grease; grease – vodka – but you keep muddling it up . . . you're a muddler, my Tony, my dear Tonya . . .' Kostya mumbled, thick-tongued, momentarily forgetting where he was as he caressed Anthony's neck affectionately. Then a thought suddenly appeared to strike him: 'Let's drink to Tonya!' barked Kostya and pushed back his chair noisily, a glass in his hand. Anthony blushed, smiled and stood up too, clinking glasses with Pan Tadeusz. 'No, I'm not raising my glass to you, Anthony, but to my neighbour Tonya. Let's drink to the memory of Tonya! To Tonya, with her charms and her magic power!'

'To Soviet power?' Anthony eagerly raised his glass.

'Tonya was,' said Kostya, swaying, 'every kind of power: Soviet power and atomic power, she was the finger on the button, she was mutton, she was fillet steak, she was the guts of the people, she was spring amid the winter frost in the shape of a fresh green cucumber, she was my grocery and my house committee, church and state, unity of body and soul – and how she gave herself: now that really was a samovar! She hummed, she roared, she bubbled! In other words, for me Tonya was – Russia!' Kostya tossed down a glass, banged it on the table and sat down heavily. 'And she would have stayed my Russia, had the West not intervened in my internal affairs,' Kostya announced, as he concluded his panegyric to Tonya with a twisted grimace.

'I must tell you frankly' – Anthony summoned up what was left of his sobriety and courage – 'I am against the Soviet invasion of Afghanistan.'

'And what about Clea's invasion of our communal flat?'

Konstantin fixed him with a stern, glassy look. 'She seduced me with fraternal aid in the form of frogs' legs, she entwined me from head to foot with dried octopussies, she powdered my brains with infidel foreign spices and all kinds of culinary evil spirits – and then when I was bound hand and foot she presented me with the bill. That's her Western way – everything's calculated: money, return visits, emotions. And chiefly emotions: how many times I copulated with Tonya, and how many times with her. No spiritual generosity, you see! Why did she want to worm herself into my confidence, if she couldn't accept our Russian breadth of spirit? She tried to entice Tonya away from me with her jeans. She didn't realise that you can't seduce Russia with frippery and trinkets!'

'So the three of you . . . lived together?' murmured Pan Tadeusz in amazement.

'What does it matter? Two together, three together! Who's counting? I tried to get it into Clea's head: human warmth cannot be divided up into allocations and coupons, it is not given out on ration-cards. But she needed an insurance policy on her sex life, so that no one should encroach on it. The trouble with the West is that girls here don't have any friends of their own sex!' Konstantin announced, sweeping his drinking-companions with a bleary stare. Anthony and Tadeusz kept a respectful silence, amazed by this enigmatic proposition. 'You don't understand, do you? I'll explain. In Russia, now, you make friends with a girl – and before you know where you are, her girlfriend starts to make up to you, then that girlfriend's girlfriend and so on, and little by little a sort of clan is formed, one big united family, living a communal life. But what happens here? A girl is nothing but a cul-de-sac, as they call it here, or in Russian – a blind alley. Even if she does have a girlfriend, it's – hands off! And what's the result? Apartheid! The separate couples sit tight in their little houses, eyeing each other suspiciously, and if they ever look out of the window at the neighbour, they hang themselves out of envy.' Konstantin poured himself a vodka and, without clinking glasses, drank it down.

'I agree,' Anthony concurred enthusiastically. 'Western individualism is a breeding-ground of suicide!'

'But is it only suicide?' Kostya hiccupped. 'What about murdering one's neighbour? And doing it stealthily, by degrees, having first gained their confidence, as Clea did. First she drove away all my friends, broke up the collective, as it were, and then she set about Tonya, my neighbour, and brought this poor, simple creature down to the grave – first it was bribery, then she did for poor little Tonya by straight blackmail!'

'What *are* you saying, Konstantin?' Pan Tadeusz shook himself, suddenly sobered. 'Are you accusing Clea of murder?!'

'I'm not accusing anyone of anything,' Konstantin cut him off. 'Everyone will be judged by the court of their own conscience. I am merely stating the facts. An Englishwoman did for our Tonya. Denouncing her wasn't enough, the bitch! She shopped her to a miserable old sod. Who would have thought that a Westerner could stoop so low?' Konstantin's eyes were filled with tears.

'She reported her to the KGB?' Anthony enquired sympathetically.

'What has the KGB got to do with it? Why are you all so fixated on the KGB, as though it wasn't KGB but DDT and we were nothing but a swarm of stinking bedbugs? No, Clea found an even more terrible accomplice – Tonya's husband. That's the old sod that she shopped her to, the one who had got Tonya a Moscow residence permit when she was under age to come there as his maid, and then, for her so-called unfaithfulness to him, he beat her to death with his crutch when Clea had shopped her to him. So the poor ruined girl had to go back to her village.'

'But you said that she had *died*,' said Tadeusz in astonishment.

'Well, so I did. Back to her village, figuratively speaking; that means – to the other world. Otherwise why would I have pushed off to the West? The usual trouble started: police, investigation, trial and so on. I must say I was thinking of myself least of all. I felt sorry for Nuclea – she couldn't help it, she was a victim of this society: innate Western egotism, spiritual under-nourishment, call it what you like. She couldn't have survived Siberia. So we had to leave the country together.'

'So if it hadn't been for Clea, you wouldn't have emigrated?' Anthony asked.

'Who leaves paradise of their own volition?' Kostya shrugged his shoulders. 'Dostoyevsky's character Svidrigailov said about paradise (or eternity, or something) that we imagine it as something vast and bright, but what if in actual fact it's nothing but a fusty, cobwebby cupboard full of spiders? Svidrigailov put that forward by way of a hypothesis. But I actually lived in exactly that sort of paradise – reeking with the stale smell of fried onions, with rot in the woodwork, the wall-paper discoloured and soot-stained from cooking, with cockroaches rustling, the floorboards creaking in the corridor and the water in the pipes rumbling all night. That was my paradise!'

There was a rumbling in one of their three stomachs, but Kostya did not move: staring straight ahead, he seemed to be talking to himself. Nor did he notice that with every word that he spoke the smell of alcohol, onion-laden belches and the stale vinegar from pickled herrings grew thicker and more nauseous. Anthony was clearly looking unwell, but he was afraid to move lest he encounter Konstantin's dangerous glare.

'I lived in that eternity – or paradise – that the Soviet people built with its own hands,' Konstantin went on, 'in the name of universal social justice. And I accept that justice. I was comfortable in it. I have felt at home in it since childhood. In my parents' communal flat there was a sort of box-room, where they kept all kinds of junk; when you opened the door, out came a smell of mothballs, old leather, suitcases, fur coats, old rags that had soaked up years of cooking-smells – the smell of human existence, but belonging to another world, unearthly. We children would always shut ourselves in there when we played hide-and-seek. You shut the door and you didn't exist in the normal world any longer, you were in a different universe, in paradise. And that box-room comes to my mind more and more often, whenever I think of Tonya's paradise. What a cretin I was! I shouldn't have wasted my time getting tied up with foreign women and writing treatises on cookery, when all I needed was simply to get a kick out of sensing the unseen presence in that box-room, where there was neither God nor tsar. To hell with reality: what did it matter whether there was democracy or dictatorship out there? And one didn't have to think about national frontiers either, because there weren't any, because there was nothing beyond them: there was no "abroad" – and there were no frontiers.'

'I like you, Konstantin,' said Anthony with drunken but heartfelt feeling. 'I like you! To hell with the difference between dictatorship and democracy. Let's all unite in a single brotherhood, a single family, a commune – do you see?'

'Where?' Kostya barked back with unexpected harshness, and hiccupped.

'Everywhere!' Anthony swung his arms wide, almost falling off his chair. 'In a commune that's not geographical but mental, spiritual, outside national frontiers, in some extra-historical time, in a paradise that's been rejected, as you said, by rationalistic *homo sapiens*!'

'And where is that paradise? In Jean-Jacques Rousseau's balls, perhaps? In a female womb as big as the whole world? No, Anton, don't try and make a cosmopolitan out of me: mine is a Soviet paradise, behind the Iron Curtain – to preserve my virginity. I'm not planning to exchange it for any other womb.'

'Do you feel the urge to go back?' Anthony pressed him.

'Where?'

'To your homeland.'

'Back to the womb, you mean? Too late. We used to do that when we were children. And do you know how?' Konstantin moved his chair close to Anthony. 'When we were teenagers, my pals and I used to shut ourselves in the attic, take off our trousers and show each other how we could give ourselves a hard-on. But what we were supposed to do with our stiff pricks, we had no idea. We thought that a hard-on by itself was a sign of manliness. If you touched it, it tickled, but it also made a strange feeling of pride start to rise up somewhere in your belly. At first it frightened us: we thought it was some incomprehensible illness. But a second-year kid from the next block told us that this was as it should be: if your cock got stiff and hard, that meant you were a man. But he never told us what to do with it. He only told us that his was longer than ours. So we continued to live in total ignorance, until all the kids in the block learned that babies were born out of a woman's belly by means of your prick getting a hard-on. But how – we still didn't know. I remember how my friends and I used to spend whole days sitting on the bench outside the entrance to our courtyard, watching women pass by and wondering: in which of their bellies would it be nicer to be? And that was the sum total of our sexual excitement: to wank each other while we imagined ourselves inside a woman's belly, where it would be so cosy – you would curl yourself up and look out at the world through her navel. And then a friend suggested I should take it in my mouth, so that he could really feel that he was inside. Taking it in one's mouth was still no problem then: although it was as hard as a bayonet, it was no bigger than one's little finger. We hadn't even thought of sucking each other off at that stage. You just took it in your mouth and sucked it, and you felt you were in the womb. The whole of it went into your mouth. So tell me, Anthony, why did one have to take it in one's mouth in order to imagine oneself inside a womb?' Konstantin enquired with false naïveté.

'The explanation is simple.' Embarrassed by Kostya's piercing stare, Anthony spoke with professional nonchalance. 'According to Freud, the sucking impulse is a manifestation of subconscious sexuality. You know, like the attraction to the female breast – to the nipple. There was no female breast to hand, and the sucking impulse was replaced by an attraction to the penis. Apart from that, you were guided by subconscious jealousy of your father's penis, which penetrates your mother's vagina in the act of insemination. By sucking someone else's penis, you were putting yourself in the position of your mother's vagina, i.e. identifying yourself with the womb. Not to mention the subconscious transference on to your friend of the castration complex and a suppressed urge towards sexlessness by means of "eating" his penis . . .' Anthony found himself getting into deep water, and blushed.

'But *I* thought we sucked each other off because we lived in starving Russia,' Konstantin interrupted him, giving a nasty little laugh. 'After all, teenage sperm tastes something like mother's milk, sort of sweetish, doesn't it? And then it gets thicker and tastes more like your yoghurt or our buttermilk, isn't that right? I suppose you know what sperm tastes like, Anton?' There was a pause.

'I won't deny that we did the same, too, when we were teenagers,' Anthony finally conceded. 'It was common in the dormitories of private boarding-schools. Which is just one more proof, Konstantin, that human nature is the same everywhere. Ultimately, we are all striving towards a single womb – a single paradise. To go back to the womb is a drive that's shared by mankind in general, regardless of race or political systems. You're not going to claim, are you, that a Marxist society has some different, Marxist womb as its ultimate ideal?'

'Stalinist. Not a Marxist but a Stalinist womb,' Kostya corrected him drily.

'I must say quite frankly,' said Anthony, in an attempt at bold directness, 'that I have a strongly negative attitude to Stalinism. I am delighted by the cheapness of Soviet public transport. I admire your free medical treatment. And above all I admire the generosity, warmth and expansiveness of the Russian character, devoid of self-importance, pomposity and snobbery. But I am bound to say that my feelings about Stalinism are negative in the extreme.'

'So you don't respect Stalinism?' Kostya echoed him grimly. 'Therefore you don't respect me, is that it?'

'What have you got to do with it? Personally I find you rather likeable,' Anthony mumbled.

'What have I got to do with it?! But I *am* Stalinism. At least, I am its legitimate offspring. The experts say that if a dog, as a puppy, is brought up away from human beings it grows up into a wolf and will never be domesticated. But the opposite is also true: if a dog grows up among people, then however much you may beat it, that dog will never show any desire to go off into the forest and live in freedom like a wolf. You were talking about totalitarianism and democracy a moment ago; but this is not a matter of ideology – my *biology* is Soviet, do you see? It has been imprinted in my brain-cells – since I was first taken on a May Day demonstration in Red Square. I can remember it as if it was yesterday: everything around me was red calico – banners and slogans, the crowd surging forward ever more tightly packed, pressing all around you, shoulder to shoulder, all in step, all together in step, horse-shit mixed with confetti. I felt I would burst at any moment like a red balloon, I'd burst like a blown-up condom – then all at once a roar went through the crowd, a roar of victory, and I joined in, shouting my head off, and suddenly I was lifted up by somebody above the shimmering, calico-red haze of the demonstration – as though I had jumped out of the womb. And I realised: this was how my mother must have shouted when she was giving birth to me, and I shouted too. And through the fog of the birth-waters, whom did I see in the pink distance? Stalin! He was standing on top of Lenin's tomb with a pale, stern face, like a gynaecologist, and he was watching me being born in the agonies of a socialist festival. And that's why the womb, for me, is a Stalinist womb, do you see? And your attitude to it, Anthony, is strongly negative. Would you be more comfortable in a Marxist womb? Well, sit in it and good luck to you, but don't poke your nose into my womb!'

'Me? Poke my nose in? Never!' Anthony hastened to offer him his drunken assurances. 'It would be interesting, though, in connection with your idea of your country as a womb, to carry out a psycho-analysis of Marxist Russia as a woman.

Since the proletariat, as I understand it, is the moving force of progress in a Marxist society, it must be regarded as the libido. Whereas in a capitalist society it is presumably the equivalent of excrement, the faeces, isn't that so? Therefore emigration from Marxist Russia is the process that corresponds to the excretion of faeces, I would say. Or should emigration be regarded as menstruation? In that case, the ending of emigration is equivalent to the menopause. Or is it constipation?' Anthony giggled, but stopped as he caught Konstantin's disagreeable stare.

'Suck me off,' said the Russian quietly, with a menacing hoarseness in his voice.

'What does that mean?' Squirming in his chair, Anthony turned to Tadeusz for a translation. Pan Tadeusz stammered and muttered something vague about untranslatable vulgarity.

'I'm terribly sorry,' said Anthony squirming again. 'I didn't mean to compare you, the *émigrés*, with shit. It just came out like that in the terminology of Marxist-Freudian analysis, which I personally don't believe in. It was a joke. A metaphysical joke. I'm not at all xenophobic. If anything I'm a slavophile. You know – Ivan Susanin, and so on? As I was saying, we have all come out of a single womb – blacks, Pakistanis, Jews, Russians . . . Well, I'm not too sure about the Jews, but even they, in my view, coming as they do from a separate womb, just like you, Konstantin, have no objection to being reunited in a single womb after the second coming. Or am I mistaken? Oh my God, what an absurd, insane conversation this is!' he groaned helplessly, and tried to get up from his chair. But Kostya's heavy hand was pressing down on his shoulder.

'Suck me off!' Kostya gritted through his teeth, towering over Anthony at his full height. Pan Tadeusz could only see Konstantin's broad back, but he then saw how the latter grabbed Anthony by the hair at the back of his head with one hand, while with the other he did something mysterious. Sensing that something nasty was going on, the Pole ran round the table and there saw a monstrous pantomime in progress. According to his evidence in court (although I don't have complete faith in what Pan Tadeusz said, he being an interested party in the affair), the first thing he noticed was Anthony's face, distorted with terror, his chin forced upwards. Konstantin's hand was pulling back Anthony's head by the hair. Konstantin himself, legs a-straddle, was holding Anthony's knees in a pincers-grip so hard that Anthony could not move. With his free hand Konstantin began to undo his fly. Robbed of speech and able only to groan miserably, Pan Tadeusz dashed around this sculptural group in panic. Paying no attention whatsoever to the Pole, Konstantin reached into his trousers and pulled out his wrinkled penis. Stroked by his hand, however, the penis soon straightened up, stretched itself, stiffened and began to sway triumphantly over Anthony's pallid, upturned face. 'Like it, eh?' Kostya said as the process took place. 'Like a Soviet sausage, is it? Like one of Stalin's brandenburg sausages? Or maybe it's like a Slovak *spikačka*, eh, Tadeusz? Especially if you consider the neat little slit in the end?!'

'Stop this disgusting behaviour at once!' screamed Tadeusz in a voice that he didn't recognise, and hurled himself at Konstantin. With an easy movement, like a horse pestered by a fly, Konstantin twitched his shoulder and Tadeusz, upsetting a stool with a crash on the way, staggered and fell down in a corner on all fours.

'Well, Tonya, are you going to suck me off?' Konstantin patted Anthony on the cheek. 'And what about subconscious jealousy of your father's penis? Or your big brother's? Do you feel it? Are you putting yourself in the place of your mother's vagina, eh? Do you feel yourself turning into a womb? Where's your sucking impulse?' Konstantin loomed over Anthony's upturned face, whose mouth was wide open in a grimace of pain, fear and revulsion, and when he licked his dry lips the top of his tongue involuntarily touched the penis. 'Aha!' Konstantin exclaimed in triumph, noticing how his penis gave a jerk at this contact. 'Aha! Do you feel you're inside our Russian womb now? Do you feel the folds of the red banners fluttering like cunt-lips, do you sense my balls tightening like balloons, can you see the members of the Politburo thrusting their arms upward in greeting? Can you feel my Stalinist will penetrating the womb of Mother Russia?'

As he masturbated with one hand, Konstantin's other hand began fumbling between Anthony's thighs, seeking for his crotch. 'Why aren't you getting hard down there, eh? I somehow don't detect any enthusiasm for merging in a single womb. When you talk, you're at one with the blacks, the Pakistanis and all the Slav peoples, but when it comes to a practical demonstration – suddenly you're all choosy and sensitive. Everyone does their own thing, imagines their own private womb – no admittance to strangers, is that it? Perhaps you agree with Tadeusz? Well, then, you Westerners can suck each other off!'

'*Psia krew*!' roared Pan Tadeusz and flung himself out of his corner at Konstantin, who merely rocked slightly from the impact and sat down on his chair with his penis still pointing upwards. Pan Tadeusz was ready to swear that at that moment a thin stream of sperm glittered in the air and landed on Anthony's lips: his Adam's apple jerked in a swallowing motion. Then Anthony slowly slid off his chair on to the floor, drooping and crumpling just as Konstantin's penis was doing in his trousers.

The door was flung open, its retaining hook torn off: her face pale and contorted, Clea stood on the threshold. For nearly an hour, in the rays of sunset in her tiny back garden, sitting on her chocolate-box pathetic little lawn, Clea had been trying to drown out the noise and laughter that had been issuing, in increasing volume, from the kitchen windows, her voice growing louder and louder as she had discussed every imaginable and unimaginable topic with Margot – from the problems of the Vietnamese refugees to a new form of contraception using a sponge-treated with a recipe dating from the pharaohs of Egypt. Margot, however, had only been listening with half an ear while glancing sideways towards the kitchen, where Kostya was presiding; and the lower the sun sank in the sky as it set into a huge cloud that was slowly moving in their direction, the stupider it became for them to be talking like this, sitting as they were in a rising breeze, on the darkening lawn, with a damp mist creeping towards them like the vapour-swirls of a German gas attack from the trenches along the neighbour's fence.

The remains of a cake, a puddle of milk spilt on the plastic table-top in the middle of which was the slimy blob of the squashed mushroom looking like a crushed snail, even the very tea-things themselves, which the pre-sunset shadows made to look as if they were broken – all this, by its very existence, was tangible proof of the hopelessness of her effort to lend a semblance of normality to her conjugal life with Kostya, of her hope that everything might be ordinary: Sunday lunch on the lawn with close friends; the wife neatly bringing out the tea-tray complete with sugar-bowl and milk-jug; a sly look catching the affectionate gaze of the old friend of the family; the husband, as he cut the cake, kissing her on the cheek; the mock-jealousy of her girlfriend as she took the teapot from her; in short, the naive attempt to live a normal, 'human' existence, as they would have said in Moscow, with a cannibal. Recalling the cannibalistic overtones to the Russian word 'human', Clea shuddered.

'I think they'll be at each others' throats at any moment,' said Margot, glancing towards the kitchen, from whence was coming a renewed outburst of shouting and breaking crockery. 'Oh, nonsense!' Clea replied lazily, pretending to yawn. Remarking casually that it was time to go into the sitting-room, Clea nevertheless set off for the kitchen.

Hiding her curiosity behind a mask of the concerned friend, Margot hurried after her. Despite the brisk determination of her initial gesture, Clea stopped at the kitchen door and, putting her ear to the keyhole, listened to what was going on inside – like a schoolgirl, late for a lesson, standing at the classroom door.

Clea's face flushed red whenever Kostya now and again repeated his mocking distortion of her name: 'Nuclea'. Less for Margot's benefit than for her own, she pretended that the talk was not about her. Even so, to have to listen to all this in front of witnesses was intolerable, and when she heard the dull, heavy thud of a body falling to the ground, Clea wrenched open the door.

The scene that met her eyes was the quintessence of everything that Clea had been trying to conceal even from herself: there, exhausted by drink and raucous argument, was Kostya, looking like some mad potentate presiding over a meal at which every dish was poisonous – bits of half-eaten pickled mushrooms, their stalks clinging to filthy plates like leeches: uncorked bottles, apparently giving off some foul-smelling vapour that had soaked into the fish-bones and lumps of bloody, half-chewed meat that littered the table . . . It was a black mass, a vampire's orgy. Nor was it by chance that the word 'orgy' sprang to Clea's mind: Kostya sat sprawled in his chair while Anthony was kneeling in front of him, his face buried in Kostya's crotch, the crown of his balding head leaning against the Russian's thigh in a pose that was enough to make anyone instinctively turn about and slam the door behind them.

At the moment that Clea appeared in the doorway, Anthony, as though blown by a draught, fell away from Kostya's lap, sat down on the floor and then collapsed sideways under the table. In a moment a loud, whistling snore was coming from his open mouth. Clea had a momentary impression that the Moscow nightmare was repeating itself, that now, as in the fracas with Tonya, she would see Kostya's wet, gleaming, muscular penis jutting impudently out of his trousers. But Kostya's fly was firmly buttoned up.

'Why's she pulling such a hideous face?' Kostya enquired, shaking his head as he stood up and straightened his trousers; he was addressing Margot, as though Clea were a complete stranger. Standing before her, he struck Clea as the personification of some sickening episode from Russian literature – this Gogolesque character out of Tolstoyevsky, with his puffy, greyish face, his leaden and unseeing stare, as ugly and useless as his crooked birch-tree and its carpet of weeds, as repellent as his squashed mushroom.

Clea turned round, pushed Margot aside and ran out. Margot shrugged her shoulders. 'Why? No doubt because she was born with it,' she said in answer to Kostya's question.

Suddenly – 'What's that noise?' asked Kostya, instantly sober as he pricked up his ears.

In the solemn silence that ensued, the buzzing clatter that came from out of doors sounded like the noise of a descending helicopter – as in spy films, when it comes from nowhere at the critical moment to snatch up our secret agent after he has accomplished some risky mission. The rising noise was soon accompanied by repeated dull booms, like salvoes of artillery amid bursts of machine-gun fire, as though someone were carrying out a single-handed attack against the enemy, advancing all along the front, all of it punctuated by the snores of Anthony as he lay sprawled under the table like an expiring corpse.

In this atmosphere of international tension, Kostya acted like the experienced strategist that he was. Moving over to the window, he pulled aside the blind. Unfortunately he could not discern anything outside: the deepening twilight was further darkened by the approach of a thundercloud – or perhaps it was not a cloud but the lilac-bush that overhung the kitchen window; this nostalgic lilac had been the only compromise acceptable to Kostya in matters of English horticulture. It was behind this very lilac-bush that there grew the notorious crooked birch-tree, surrounded by its patch of thistles, and it was in *that* direction, to judge from the noise, that the enemy's – or was it an ally's? – machine-gun was firing. Suspecting the worst, Kostya abandoned all caution and strode out of doors towards the battlefield, towards the territory of the accursed enemy that, in his drunken brain, Clea had now become.

The cloud was indeed creeping up over the neighbours' roofs like a gas attack, and only a single ray of sunlight, quivering with uncertainty, was still piercing that smoke-screen of noxious vapour. This lone anti-aircraft searchlight had picked out the small figure of Clea at the far end of the garden, alongside the little lean-to shed in which she kept her gardening tools. Like a solitary terrorist, Clea was slowly moving forward, pushing in front of her the most terrible weapon of English civilisation: a lawnmower. It was this old mower, with its spluttering petrol-engine, that was giving out the machine-gun-like rattle mingled with artillery-salvoes of reeking smoke – the reek of everything inhuman and metallic, the clank of rusty cog-wheels. Clea's face, lit by the thin shaft of light, was fixed in a mask of doomed heroism – indeed, there was heroism in the mere fact that she had managed to start the lawnmower at all. Now she was advancing step by step, as Kostya the vigilante had instantly guessed, towards his cherished plot, where, in his fevered imagination, along with the blissful if inaudible rustling that accompanied the invisible growth of a crop of burdocks, plantains and dandelions, the curious little buttons of as yet undiscovered mushrooms were peeping out of the soil, pushing their velvety caps through the grassroots like new-born babes emerging from the verdant fringe of Mother Earth's vagina: damp and gleaming, entangled with grassy fragments of the placenta, they were pushing their way upwards into the bright Stalinist future. His lips trembling, Konstantin took a determined step forward and positioned himself in their defence – in defence of everything that was opposed to the philistine smoothness and rationalism of the English lawn, while the birch-tree covered his rear.

'Hands off, you little fool!' in a spasm of anger he barked in his hoarse, drink-sodden voice, shouting above the ominous rattling and banging from the other end of the garden. In reply, with a sharp push from Clea, the lawnmower gave an aggressive roar and, jerking in its mistress's shaking grip, bouncing over the tiny hummocks and bumps, it pressed forward, leaving behind it a sinister trail – a ribbon of freshly-cut grass. Along with the first drops of rain the sharp smell of mown grass reminded Konstantin of the sense, forgotten since he had been in London, of the difference between town and country, between the ordinary people and the intelligentsia, between Westernisers and slavophiles. Straightening up and bracing his shoulders, for a moment he looked to Clea like the forgotten Russian Konstantin that she had first caught sight of; once more her knees began to grow weak and once more a Moscow queue began to wind itself around her like a hangman's knot – but in a second she was pulled free of this Russian noose by her native English lawnmower which, as it tried to wrench itself out of Clea's hands by its own iron will, summoned Clea to stifle the rising delirium of her memories. All she could do was to give a push in the right direction to the blades that were slicing through the net of madness, and with a renewed faith in her own rightness Clea swung the mower head-on towards the evil spectre of her Russian past – the crooked birch-tree with its ugly retinue of weeds. Between Clea and Kostya the gap was now the traditional duelling distance – while the horror-stricken Margot was standing, frozen, a little way off in the role of a second, and Pan Tadeusz, dashing up and down beside the fence, resembled an observer from a UN peace-keeping mission caught unawares by a local conflict that before his eyes had escalated into a confrontation between two great powers. Someone had to be the first to make a preventive strike, and Konstantin, pushing himself off from the birch-tree behind him, lunged forward at the lawnmower like a Russian war-hero tackling a machine-gun-nest head-on.

As in some cheap melodrama, a flash of lightning burst from the off-stage skies and lit up the two angry, hate-contorted faces of Clea and Konstantin, gripping the handles of the lawnmower from opposite sides. The ensuing clap of thunder could not deaden the sound of Clea's scream and Kostya's snarl while they both, as though in a clumsy country dance or some witchcraft ritual, started a tug-of-war with the petrol-spitting mower. Finally, Russian fighting skill overcame Western sang-froid; having acquired the terrible weapon, with a titanic wrench Konstantin raised the lawnmower over his head, swinging it around with the movement of a discus-thrower.

Screaming, Clea fell down and waved her legs in the air as

though fending off the clattering blades swinging above her; but as they twirled on the spot, Kostya's legs also gave way under him and he collapsed alongside her, letting go of the mower, which flew off by the force of inertia and, after jerking convulsively in mid-air like a shot crow, described an arc before crashing to the ground near the fence, barely missing Pan Tadeusz. Covering his head with his hands, the Pole retreated towards the gate, heading for home. Margot, transfixed by this circus act, finally came to her senses and rushed to separate Kostya and Clea, who were punching and scratching each other on the trampled grass, which the pelting rainstorm had transformed into a bare patch of mud. At that moment the lawnmower, up-ended beside the fence, snorted, coughed and – echoing the roll of thunder that came from the sky – blew up with an ear-shattering explosion. The warring parties froze for a moment and turned their heads towards the miniature atomic mushroom-cloud arising in a column of evil-smelling smoke from the eviscerated bowels of the lawnmower. The funereal drumming of the rain in the ensuing lull supplied an appropriate epilogue to this war of the worlds, and instead of the wails of bereaved mothers there came Clea's hysterical sobbing as she rubbed her eyes with her filthy hands. Konstantin got up, spat out the lumps of grass and soil lodged in his mouth and limped off towards the kitchen. Margot lifted up Clea from her knees and, like an army nurse clasping a wounded soldier around the waist, led her indoors beneath the lashing rain. Turning round for a last look at the battlefield, Clea again saw a familiar mirage through her tears – the shadow of a man was flitting among the bushes along the fence. It might, though, have been her Polish neighbour or simply the dense wall of rain that had been whipped into the likeness of a shadow in a gust of wind.

8 *BEAUTY AND THE BEAST*

She lay on the bed, without even a sheet over her: a woman stripped bare, feeling herself to be a woman perhaps for the first time, naked in every respect. All her clothes and underwear were strewn in a dirty heap on the bathroom floor, where Margot had washed her all over like an invalid and had bathed her scratches and bruises with swabs of cotton-wool soaked in eau-de-Cologne. Clea had even thrown aside the dressing-gown that Margot had offered her: after that filthy, nightmarish struggle on the lawn any clothing, she felt, would have taken her back to her previous life, which had now come to such a messy end, culminating in a pile of grubby underclothes and a mass of scratches in the most unsuitable places. The smell of eau-de-Cologne was mixed with the reek of singed dust on the red-hot element of the electric fire, and this, together with a damp, chill breeze from the open window – a permanent feature of English bedrooms – increased her sense of dislocation, recalling the smells of railway sleeping-cars, public lavatories and school changing-rooms – all the places that spoke of contrived discomfort and rootlessness.

'OK? Everything all right now?' said Margot, like a nurse who has done her duty, and got up from the bed. In silent fury Clea turned away from the wall and, clasping her hands behind her head, she looked at her friend with that limpid, glassy stare in which hatred is mistakenly perceived as distress. Margot responded by twisting her lips into a sympathetic smile, sympathising not so much with the injuries suffered by the body spread out before her as with its defenceless nakedness, emphasised by the expression in Clea's eyes. It was Margot's sympathy that was so humiliating. Clea shamelessly examined Margot's face, a face with the features of a well-groomed thoroughbred horse: big cheekbones and lips, a matt, almost suede-like sunburnt skin, breasts pushing abruptly at the wrap-over front of a towelling dressing-gown – her whole body was taut and obedient, like that of a horse in perfect condition. This impeccable harmony was visible proof of the psycho-physical inequality to be found between different creatures of the same human race.

The sheet slid to the floor and Clea pulled up her knees and brazenly opened her legs wide – challengingly, as though demonstrating to her sleek friend standing by the door the extent of her own female inadequacy – from her breasts, looking like two saucersful of melting ice-cream with a couple of nibbled glacé cherries floating in the middle of them, to her pale pubic mound, so pale and hairless that as a girl she had long been terrified because in her, as distinct from other fully-formed creatures of both sexes, that place was bare and defenceless, like an eye lacking an eyelid. Not to mention her pure horror at the word 'hermaphrodite', which she had surreptitiously found in the *Encyclopaedia Britannica*, reinforced by a similar anatomical description (with a picture of that pallid sexless creature) in a book by Krafft-Ebing that Margot had borrowed from her parents' library. Together they had studied the incomprehensible words and the illustrations of sexual freaks. Margot had giggled, and Clea too –

trying to imitate her friend's squeals, but in fact struggling to suppress an upsurge of hysterical terror: supposing she, too, was a congenital hermaphrodite? Later next summer, in Dorset, where Margot's parents had kindly invited her to join them for the holidays, she and Margot had hidden themselves among the clumps of heather in the big, steep-sided dunes and had studied, on each other, the anatomical information they had acquired from reading books. How strange it had been to discover that flat pebbles from the shingle on the beach would fit neatly into the damp little hollow between your legs, and that if you pressed your knees together the heat from the sun-warmed pebble seemed to travel right up to the crown of your head.

They would lie for hours side by side in the dunes, staring up at the blue sky, a senseless smile on their lips, squeezing a flat pebble with their hips in the warm place between their legs, afraid to open their knees and let go the source of this mysterious feeling of bliss. One day, Margot the know-all, to refute Clea's fears about the dreaded hermaphrodite, had parted her friend's knees, thrown away the pebble and in its place had begun slowly to insert her finger. At first Clea had almost screamed with fright, but then bit her lip, because even though it hurt a little it was also nice and it tickled – in fact it tickled so much and in such a funny way that she almost bit Margot, who was pressing herself against Clea's shoulder. Margot's shoulder was as sharp and bony as her own; in those days they had seemed to each other equally absurd in their immaturity – equals in ugliness, they had perceived this as friendship. The sense of their own ugliness was shared and therefore not a source of envious discord.

Margot, her glance following the sheet as it slid to the ground, stepped away from the door and gave Clea a quizzical look, her head cocked to one side like a listening dog, as though trying to discern what her 'best friend' wanted from her. Her friend wanted nothing. Clea didn't want her friend, who had reneged on their common fate of inborn ugliness, who had decided to grow up into something different, something unattainable by Clea's ungainly body. The world of which Margot had become a part did not want to be a part of her, Clea's, undistinguished body. Clea turned towards the wall. Staring at it with a fixed, unblinking gaze, as when she had been put to bed with a fever as a child, she began to trace the pattern on the wallpaper with her finger; in those days, in childhood, the wallpaper had been printed with little girls in sun-bonnets carrying baskets of flowers, while now her finger was wandering over circles and triangles because little girls in bonnets with flower baskets were out of fashion, and in her memory they had faded and merged into abstract circles and triangles. Those colds, fevers, inflammations and rashes in childhood had been, perhaps, the only truly happy moments of her life, when there had been no need to look at others as though into a mirror, there to find nothing but the reflection of one's own inadequacy and shortcomings. Illness meant freedom: just as leprosy had once wholly absolved one from social obligations, so when she was ill as a child she could finally stop feeling shy and ashamed of her own body – her physiology, the natural functions of the flesh, with its repulsive protuberances, hairs and absurd orifices, with menstruation and sweatiness, with everything that one's mind, drilled into certain attitudes by others, condemned as unspeakable, indecent.

Now, pushed beyond the permitted limit by having been savagely humiliated, as though stricken by some childish illness, she had finally stopped feeling ashamed, she no longer feared being left alone in a wretched little child's bedroom, excluded from the grown-ups' talk in the next room. A certain sense of ultimate doom, which had bruised her heart as an eye turns black when it is punched, together with a smarting cut on her stomach (what had it been? A root of that damned birch-tree or Kostya's boot?) had finally liberated her from that female sense of duty that had been foisted on her by God knows who and had persecuted her all her life: the habit, drilled into her since childhood, of caring about her outward appearance, of keeping up the proper image in the eyes of other people –

which was to be charming and say what one was supposed to say.

Words – it was all the fault of words. All her life she had had to say words that were forced on her by someone else. And afterwards to recall with disgust her face, contorted in the obliging grimace of the listener, the eyes narrowed understandingly, the lips assenting obediently and irrelevantly. The terror of finding herself alone – and to combat that, one had to learn and repeat, and even to re-invent what was said by other people: people who didn't want to hear about those days when you were half-starved as you raced, like a squirrel in a wheel, between your part-time job and your studies, nor about your unheated room and your damp, cold sheets, nor about the depression that came with your monthly periods, nor about the migraine that laid you low in between them. Or rather . . . that wasn't the real truth, either: everyone, from parents to colleagues, would have been only too glad to hear all these details, all this stale news of the Victorian era in modern, miniature form that gathers dust in the archives of every English person's soul, lodged in the crevices of their brain – their own little, personal Victorian horrors, that exist parallel to the Viking invasions, the swinging sixties and the world-wide arms race. But she had not wanted to add her mite of unhappiness, one more little item, to the archive of the collective island soul. Words had separated her from herself, from that wordless anguish and morbid langour that for her were also the only truth; everything else was just made-up phrase-mongering about the disorders that plagued the world. But without those invented, borrowed words it was impossible so much as to hint at what it was that tormented her and no one else. So she had to agree, to assent, to argue about feminism, Marxism, pacifism – in the hope that she would also say something about herself. But instead – every word somehow turned inside out whatever it was that really worried her in her moments of introspection.

Words took their revenge. Words made a shameful secret of those episodes in the past which her unconscious mind had learned to accept without particular pleasure but also without revulsion. Even now Clea was trying to pretend that Konstantin's tirades, overheard through the kitchen door, had not been about her, had had nothing to do with her. She had learned to recall the nightmarish affair with Tonya as an exotic instance of the uncouth manner and morals of that barbaric country, Russia. She had schooled herself to remember that episode as though someone else were describing it to her, as if it had been something she happened to have read in an ethnographic study on the behaviour of savage tribes: she had never been in that Moscow kitchen. It was not she who had dashed between that terrifying cripple with his wooden leg and the screaming Tonya, not she who had heard the thwack of those dull, lethal blows in the next room – it had not been Clea but someone else who had been involved in all that physical and metaphysical mayhem. She was prepared to acknowledge only her feelings of pity for Tonya, which had remained intact after that nightmare; for the absurd way Tonya had dressed and talked, and for her absurd death in hospital, her dreaming of going back home to the country. In that pity there was also pity for herself: she had put herself in Tonya's place, she had allowed herself to condescend to her and to imagine what would have happened to herself if she had been born Tonya. It had been, in fact, extremely difficult to imagine this; it had required an enormous effort of the imagination and of the emotions, and she had been aware of her own spiritual generosity in the attempt. At such moments she felt sorry for herself.

During these upsurges of compassion she had even been prepared to admit that she had played the role not only of witness but of participant in that nightmare. She and Tonya had been in the same boat, afloat on that murky Russian lake – or rather, swamp. That was no doubt how Hemingway had felt towards Spanish communists or bullfighters: he had shared bread, salt and blood with them . . . But to blame her for the whole affair?!

Kostya's kitchen tirade, though, had assumed that Clea's role in Moscow had been that of yet another home-grown

Soviet freak, on an equal footing with the others – or rather, equally devoid of all rights – as a participant in the unending, grotesque squabbles in that communal flat, which was how she now saw the whole of life in Russia. Konstantin had deprived her of her position as a foreigner, the role of uninvolved observer, sympathetic to both sides in the conflict. Thus it now turned out that Clea had deliberately set the crippled husband on Tonya. A thought of this kind, brought on by jealousy and by the loneliness of someone banished to the kitchen sink had indeed flashed through Clea's offended soul. But it had only been the thought not the crime itself; if thoughts alone were criminal, you could punish every schoolchild because everyone, in a burst of teenage hatred, has thought to themselves: 'I wish my parents were *dead*!' And in that appalling situation in the Moscow flat she had not even imagined how she might put her jealous, vengeful thought into effect. Nevertheless, the idea had passed through her mind. And now Kostya's words had given it concrete form. They had put the seal on it. Now it would be remembered for ever as the cause of that pathetic, well-meaning Tonya's death. It was all the fault of words.

It was all the fault of those forms of words, those set phrases that prevent one's impetuous mind from retreating a single step, those formulations that turn a vague thought into high principle and turn oneself into a traitor to one's own principles – into an apostate. It was all the fault of those accursed things – convictions. It was all the fault of the philosophers, the religious thinkers, of all those self-appointed prophets. Had it not been for all those words that pronounce ultimate judgment on our acts, she could have somehow continued to survive by living her own humble life, feeling neither unfounded guilt nor false shame: unaware and untroubled, like the grass on the lawn which, when the due time comes, is simply cut down by the lawn-mower.

By being uttered, the words spoken by Konstantin had hardened and made the verdict on her final: now, at least as far as she herself was concerned, she would bear that brand, almost the mark of Cain, for the rest of her life. Branded as a murderess. Even if no one believed it, that accusation had been scorched into *her* memory in red-hot letters. She felt certain that Tonya would have forgiven her if she had known what Clea had had to go through in those years since Tonya had whispered to her from that hospital bed: '. . . I want to go home, back to my village.' Life with Konstantin had been full and final punishment, with no remission, for the cruel thought about Tonya that she had once so carelessly allowed herself to think. Konstantin was the punishment for all her grovelling to other people's ideas and phrases, the scourge of God for her apostasy, for her lack of belief in herself – she who in truth was untouched, pure, innocent, blameless, who had known nothing but the green hills, the gardens and the sweet-smelling turf of England, that would cover her over when the time came. And it seemed to her that the time *had* come – the time of release, since she had served out her sentence in full. For the first time, the thought of divorce came to her mind.

'Does he sleep with you or doesn't he?' The mattress gave a creak as it sagged under Margot's considerable weight, and in order not to roll towards her, Clea moved over until she was right up against the wall. She should have bought a more expensive mattress, of the pneumatic-orthopaedic type; it didn't cost a fortune, but as always when she bought something on hire purchase she had been unwilling to spend the extra twenty pounds, and in less than six months the mattress was already giving way, even before the last instalment had been paid, and it was collapsing into a pit in the middle, just as her hopes of modest family comfort and conjugal happiness were collapsing. Margot had put her question in a 'common' voice that Clea detested, imitating her friend's pronunciation as she had done at school, where rudeness and a working-class accent were regarded as the ultimate in chic; the difference was that Clea had had that accent all her life.

Margot was now trying out a ploy of imitating the long-forgotten tone of the older and more experienced schoolfriend, the tone of whispering on the school bench, of giggling in the street, of walking arm-in-arm down Oxford Street, where both had once had Saturday jobs as shop-assistants and had strolled along drinking fizzy lemonade from cans and eating fish and chips out of newspaper. 'Does he sleep with you or doesn't he?' The tone of this question was no longer one of schoolgirl prurience or of a serious need for intimacy and confidentiality. Behind Margot's question there was only insincere sympathy masking a curiosity to hear a new story of someone else's misfortune, just as in her kiss behind the ear, under a little curl on the edge of Clea's short haircut, there was only a contrived imitation of their previous friendship, a fictitious sisterly solidarity. Equally false was the jolliness with which Margot tousled the hair on the back of Clea's neck and the phoney solicitude with which she rearranged the sheet that had fallen on to the floor. It was as though it was all just a continuation of that madcap night in the Oxford Street store, when, at the end of one working day, when everyone else had gone home, they had both hidden behind the racks of dresses that cost ten times the wages of both of them put together, and they had romped among the fox-fur and mink coats and the silk underwear – all at their disposal for one night as they played at being millionairesses for a lark to celebrate Clea's birthday. They had fooled about in front of a mirror, gulping champagne out of a bottle, trying on the most fabulous dresses one after another. As she was helping to button up a dress, Margot's fingers had slithered down her friend's back and Clea, finding it ticklish, had shuddered, staggered, stepped on the train of a dress, teetering on one foot (she could remember every movement, like a well-learned arabesque in a ballet), had collapsed on to the thick carpet of the fitting-room, pulling Margot down with her. It had not been Margot's features, however, that she had then seen swaying above her but the insolent face of a security guard, bending over and lighting them up with his torch as they floundered, half-dressed, on the carpet; and the sound that Clea had heard was not the echo of her own heart coming from within Margot's ribs but the footsteps of the night-watchman – the guardian angel of a hostile world, the world outside her skin, her thoughts and her entrails.

Now, as though an echo of the past, Kostya's boots were heard clumping, with uncertain tread, up the staircase and stopping outside the bedroom door. Clea squeezed Margot's hand, which was delving in the silky wetness of the place where at that moment her soul began and ended. That hand had seemed to promise to lift Clea out of herself, but now she was being pushed down again to the very pit by the relentless tread of the night-watchman, summoned up by the sound of Konstantin's boots as he blundered noisily and unsteadily about the house. At that moment a burst of hatred for Kostya blinded her as much as fear had paralysed her on that idiotic night when the watchman had appeared from nowhere, dazzling her with his torch as if she had been some noxious insect that one examines with cold revulsion before crushing it with one's foot.

Once again that heavy male footfall signalled a return to the miseries of isolation – only on that earlier occasion it had been a return to the dreariness of the parental suburb and drunkenness at Christmas and desperate loneliness at weekends. Now, the sound of Kostya's tread carried her back to the communal flat in Moscow, forcing her into complicity in the horrifying maelstrom of crime and punishment, vileness and repentance that ended with the bandaged Tonya whispering of her village paradise with lips that had been beaten to pulp. 'I won't, I won't!' Clea muttered feverishly, burying her head in the pillow. She had heard Kostya approaching the door, heard his heavy, hoarse breathing with its alcoholic wheeze, just as Tonya's husband, when he had crept up on Clea invisibly from behind, had breathed down her neck and tapped the heel of her shoe with his crutch. She heard the handle of the locked door rattling as Kostya tried it.

'Why don't you get divorced?' Margot asked languidly, paying no attention to the fumbling at the door, raising herself on one elbow and examining Clea's sharp, bare shoulder-blades. Under the sheets, Margot's hand was still trying to bring Clea back to a blissful state of mindless surrender, but suddenly the bodily silk under her fingers seemed to coarsen, twitch and shrivel into dry, lifeless folds. Clea sat up with a jerk, pushed her friend's hand away and pulled the sheet around herself: she was trembling. She listened intently to the noise outside the door. After stamping up and down for a while and rattling the door-handle, Konstantin grunted something, swore and started to go downstairs, stumbling and cursing as he went. Then from down below, as though from the infernal regions, came his malicious braying laugh. The same insolent laugh had been lurking in the eyes of the store manager on the morning after their escapade – eyes in which there was also something else: either the fury of an angry administrator or cold curiosity, when with a polite smile his lips had pronounced the ready-made formula of dismissal while also presenting her with the bill for the champagne-soaked carpet of the fitting-room and for the torn dress.

It had taken her nearly two years to pay off this debt by working in the even more humiliating job of a waitress. It had never even occurred to Margot to ask Clea how she had managed to settle the bill for that ridiculous night. Margot, it seemed, had completely forgotten about it. To her it had not been a disgraceful scandal but just another amusing episode, a zany incident for which Anthony, her fiancé, had paid the bill; an extravagance of this kind was just one more piquant detail of her life-story, a detail that people of her circle could not resist, valuing eccentricity as they did, no matter what the cost might be. Her attitude to her job in the store had been the same. For Clea it had been a necessity, for Margot a modish pastime, a gesture of fraternisation with the working class, an entertaining interlude before going up, perhaps, to Oxford, or perhaps – why not? – to Cambridge. No doubt she had described the whole episode to her sleek university friends as a huge joke, a delicious piece of kitsch. With equal success Margot might have pulled faces at a schoolmaster behind his back or impudently smoked a joint in front of Buckingham Palace or poured champagne down the back of someone's neck and then burst out laughing, collapsing on to the carpet and waving her legs in the air, as though everything around her had been created purely as a pretext for some hilarious, rather risky, outrage, and that only she, Margot, was allowed to play the fool in front of a shocked public. As likely as not, Margot had known about the night-watchman in advance and that he would be liable to catch them at any moment; but she couldn't have cared less, she was having fun, she was getting a kick from the absurdity, the riskiness, and the fact that this adventure would provide such a marvellous story to be recounted afterwards.

Clea's lips and chin began to quiver on the verge of tears, and she could not stop this quivering. All her complaints, which a moment ago she had been ready to pour out into Margot's busy fingers, had turned into a stupid joke. They were nothing but a joke – all those idiotic scenes in the kitchen with Kostya, his culinary escapades, those long nights when she had been unable to sleep for the crash and clatter of saucepans and frying-pans that came from the kitchen along with the sounds of Kostya's drunken altercations with Pan Tadeusz. He cared not a jot that she had to get up every morning at six in order to get to work on time. He snoozed on till noon. And then there was his snoring at night and her humiliating attempts to squeeze some human warmth out of that lump of snoring, gristly beef lying beside her on the pillow, when she, almost without admitting it to herself, had caressed the limp, wrinkled appendages of his flesh.

The thoughts that came to her, hungry for human warmth during those sleepless nights! Clea shuddered. Hadn't it been a particularly hideous joke, when on one of those nights she had shaken the snoring Kostya, had knelt beside him in her white nightdress and implored him: 'Hit me! Hit me, the way Yesenin used to hit Isadora Duncan!' And Kostya, blinking at her half-awake, had flopped back on to the pillow and mumbled before starting to snore again: 'We're not in Russia. And you're not Isadora Duncan.' It could all be retold and made to sound a joke; other people's lives, seen from outside, are always a joke. And Margot was outside. For Clea, Margot had long since become a foreigner, speaking another language, living with other people in another world, where they even ate and dressed differently. In fact, it was with clothes in particular that Clea had never managed to be on an equal footing with Margot: from the jeans of a dozen or so years ago to leather trousers now, Clea had always tried to dress in the way 'one does', and the results were as they should have been – yet at the same time they weren't. From Margot's barely noticeable, fleeting looks askance at her, she had always felt that she was dressed wrongly, that for all her painstaking efforts she looked like a dowdy freak – in the way that any foreigner, trying desperately to look like the local natives, always manages to get one or two inconspicuous details wrong, which turn all his earnest, well-intentioned attempts to 'be like everyone else' into humiliating absurdity. How absurd Clea had looked in Moscow. How ridiculous Konstantin looked here.

'Why do you hang on to that monster? Why do you make yourself into a victim?' – Margot's voice came from behind her back, like a ready-made echo to her thoughts. 'All right, if you don't want to get divorced – go and live on your own, as though he didn't exist. Take a lesson from me – do you think it's easier to live with a homosexual than with an uncouth Russian?' Clea jerked her face up from the pillow and stared at Margot in silence: what rubbish was she talking now, this past-mistress of the art of false consolation? 'What – didn't you know?' – Margot stared back at her in genuine amazement. 'You don't imagine that Anthony went into the kitchen to apologise to Kostya out of the goodness of his heart, do you? He's fancied Kostya for a long time. What maddens me most of all is that he equates all this with political ideology. Anyhow, why do I need to tell you all this, when the whole affair with a certain youth was going on under your very eyes, in your office? What was the name of that half-wit? Keith? Kevin?'

'Colin,' Clea whispered, almost soundlessly.

'What? Can't hear. Anyway, it doesn't matter. Where on

earth did Anthony dig him up? He used to drag him around everywhere with him, he foisted him on everybody, used to read Aldous Huxley and Oscar Wilde aloud to him, stuffed his pathetic little head with the principles of utopian socialism and pacifism – he even started to teach him Russian. In any case, the boy was obviously not all there, and what became of him after all those mental and sexual gymnastics under Anthony's tuition, God alone knows. And how did it all end? We all know how it ended. Anthony got bored with him. He was exhausted by all his fruitless efforts with the boy. His pupil, you see, failed to live up to expectations. And he also got too big for his boots, apparently – by which I mean he started to demand to be treated humanly, to have a genuine relationship. So Anthony very quickly showed him the door. Now he bombards Anthony with heart-rending letters and lies in wait for him around every corner, still trying to find out where he stands with him. I'm certain he'll try and come to the CND demonstration tomorrow. I only hope he's not seriously intending to commit suicide. It often happens with them, you know – either they commit suicide or they kill their lover. Have you seen him lately, by the way?'

Instead of replying, Clea turned away towards the wall. So that was the meaning behind Colin's hungry, longing looks in the office. He had not been seeking any crumbs of human comfort from her, Clea. For all the feeble clumsiness of his attempts at flirtation, he had obviously been trying to annoy that stupid fool Anthony and make him jealous. And on that night before Christmas he had not been lying in wait for her by the rubbish container in order to force her to respond with some sexual frisson in the cold and dark of his loneliness; he had simply been having his revenge on Anthony because he had rejected him. It was obvious, now, why Colin had not shown up at the office party – he had planned to take his vengeance in the most repellent, humiliating way possible: through a woman. And he had had no need of Clea's self-sacrificing compliance, as she had lain there spreadeagled on the filthy asphalt beside the garbage-bins; he had run away from her, rejecting her 'Christmas present'. The sensation produced by Clea's caress had only been a sickening reminder of Anthony. Clea, as a person, had been completely irrelevant to him. She had been used. Yet again. That time, however, had been out of turn. For all these years, she had seen Colin as the only creature on earth whom she had no reason to envy, who was lower than herself on every scale, towards whom, strange as it might seem, she had felt a sense of guilt, even though it was he, Colin, who was the offender, he who had degraded her in the most terrible way possible for a woman. She had kept alive that feeling of guilt in herself, balanced out as it was by the painful humiliation to which Colin had submitted her. She finally admitted to herself that for years she had been cherishing the memory of that one night when a bond had been formed between the oppressed female and the insulted male, the insulted offender and the oppressed oppressor. It was her very own, inviolable secret, her shame, her guilt, her hope – or rather her failed hope, her paradise unattained, to which one returns in one's thoughts when it seems that all is lost and the only consolation is the knowledge that there had been something to lose. She might have been wife and mother and sister to Colin, his teacher and fellow-pupil – because even though life had made them equal by humiliating them both, Clea was nevertheless evidently the stronger and better able to withstand any future humiliations. And Colin, who in Clea's imagination over the years had become the incarnation of universal misery and helplessness, would have accepted Clea's gift of matrimony with touching, devoted willingness – a gift almost that of a goddess who has perceived and forgiven him for his earthly insignificance.

Lunacy! It had been lunacy to imagine that she might allow herself any such spiritual privileges: even that 'Christmas present' in the person of Colin, unwanted by anyone in its insignificance and degradation, was somebody else's spiritual property, lent to her on hire and then snatched rudely out of her hands as soon as she had dared to imagine herself to be on an equal footing with the lender. People like her could only seek consolation beyond the bounds of what was conventionally acceptable. With Konstantin, at least, she had nothing to be shy of. The combination of her fatal inner flaw and his insane whims made up an amazingly harmonious picture, an idyllic symbiosis of two deformed embryos spawned by East and West. They were both freaks! For the first time she now thought of herself and of him as related – two lonely monstrosities, eternal pariahs of this world, doomed to the end of time to roam hand in hand from one unwelcoming place of refuge to another, to be greeted everywhere by contemptuous mockery.

'I'm going downstairs, he's obviously fretting,' said Clea with the apologetic grimace of a nun who has newly found her vocation. She got up and began to pull on her jeans. Margot went and stood in front of the door, as though barring her way. She was clearly annoyed.

'Do you know who you remind me of?' It was obvious from Margot's tone of voice that Clea was at last going to hear what her 'best friend' really thought of her. Clea would have preferred not to hear it, but Margot had her own ideas about that. 'Of course you know the fairy tale about Beauty and the Beast, don't you? Beauty found herself by force of circumst-ances behind the huge walls of the Beast's castle, and so on. When Beauty was touched with sympathy for the Beast's sufferings, the Beast revealed his secret to her: in a past life the Beast had been a handsome prince, but an anti-monarchist sorceress had made a monstrous revolution in him and the Beast would remain a monster until a Beauty fell in love with him and freed the prince from this evil spell by kissing him. Beauty, moved to tears, opened her arms, shut her eyes and kissed the Beast.'

'And what happened then?' asked Clea, like a child who cannot wait to hear the end of a long-familiar fairy tale.

'Didn't your experience in Russia suggest a new ending to this old parable? When Beauty opened her eyes, what she saw was not a prince but the very same Beast as before. The Beast held up a mirror to Beauty's eyes and instead of herself Beauty saw a toad! Soon the toad-maiden learned to croak, and the Beast became covered in lice. They lived happily together and died on the same day. You may go and join your Konstantin.'

Clea swung her arm and gave Margot a powerful slap on the face.

She slammed the bedroom door behind her and leaned her back against it, as though to protect herself from Margot. Then on tiptoe, trying not to make the floor creak, she went several steps down the stairs and leaned over the banister-rail. Framed in the open doorway below, Kostya was bending over the kitchen table – or perhaps not over the table, but over Anthony's snoring body. No, he was leaning over the table: a map was spread out on the table alongside a large wicker basket. His clenched jaws covered with a day's growth of ginger stubble, Konstantin's face was frozen in that mask of mindless concentration with which people take their last look at the old homestead before setting out on a long journey, trying to remember what they have forgotten to take with them: was it the love and hatred of their family, or a reel of thread and a safety-pin? The electric light cast its glare on a battered felt hat on his head and a waterproof, fastened around the waist with an old army leather belt – the same old clothes in which he had first landed in the British Isles from Moscow.

There was something uniquely Soviet in his whole appearance, but his huge shadow on the wall took no account of Soviet clothes-labels, and consequently his shadow looked like a pre-revolutionary peasant pilgrim. He was preparing to leave this world, carrying his plaited basket. 'Like Leo Tolstoy,' thought Clea. 'Like Leo Tolstoy in his bast shoes.' Kostya, it is true, was not wearing bast shoes but rubber boots. Leo Tolstoy had been a pacifist, and Kostya was no more a Tolstoyan that he was a vegetarian. Even so, it was pitiful to see this creature as he prepared to depart from this world – despite the fact that this creature was a monster. She wanted to call out to him when Kostya, as though awakening from a stupor, shook himself, folded up the map and began to search briskly through his pockets. A moment later Clea noticed that he was holding a knife. With a familiar sharp movement he uncovered the blade, weighed the knife in his hand and then tested it for sharpness on his thumb. Peering at Kostya's profile from the semi-darkness of the staircase, Clea saw in him the fateful resignation of a suicide staring into the muzzle of a pistol. At that moment, his huge ungainly figure in his ridiculous old raincoat became a symbol of a farewell to this world – the world that had dealt him so many painful blows; this creature was going away in order to put an end to himself in secret, like a dying cat looking for a secluded spot in order to die unseen by human eyes. Like an outcast, despised and rejected of men. At that moment Clea was ready to throw herself headlong downstairs and deflect that fateful knife-blow on to herself: it was not Kostya but she, with her perverse, inhuman heartlessness who deserved to be dispatched in this fashion. Just then Kostya shook his head sceptically; without looking round he reached out towards a shelf and picked up a stick of carborundum – a whetstone.

Settling himself comfortably on a stool, Kostya placed the whetstone on his knee, muttered something in a pensive tone, flourished the knife in the air and began – whiizzz – whiizzz – to sharpen the blade with a broad, rhythmic, back-and-forth movement. His lips pressed together, a vein began to swell on his forehead, and his expression of tragic farewell gave way to one of vengeful determination. Now, with all these sinister movements, in his moth-eaten felt hat and his grubby raincoat, he no longer reminded her of Tolstoy but of the repulsive old Jew, Gindin, with his sackful of dead babies in the frostbound streets of Moscow. How many babies had there been, according to *Pravda*? Three. And only two had figured in the trial. So what became of the third one? It had been eaten. No doubt old Gindin himself had eaten it. A starving old Jew in a yarmulka. A poor man, whom one could only pity – like the Beast. Like Shylock. Poor Shylock, another old Jew in a yarmulka. Another monster. Everyone had mocked him, humiliated him, taken away his daughter, the daughter of his people. He had won the right to plead in the high court. By the law of 'an eye for an eye, a tooth for a tooth' he had won the right to cut a pound of living flesh from the body of his adversary. They had taken away his daughter – his own flesh and blood. Having broken his heart and stolen away his dearest, they had granted him the right to a pound of flesh. To roast and eat. Fleshly cannibalism for spiritual cannibalism: the cannibal Jews have been sent into the Christian world to show up how we behave to each other: we devour each other by making one another's lives intolerable; we roast people alive with napalm, we skewer them with radioactivity after serving an atomic mushroom as hors d'oeuvres. Perhaps Kostya was a Jew too? In the Soviet Union you never knew who was what: in the West, we lumped them all together as Russians, but in fact he might come from, say, Uzbekistan. Comrade Shylock Gindin. Like Shylock, he was too calm, pretending to have come to terms with his situation, whetting his teeth the while on all sorts of meat, just as he was now whetting his knife on the carborundum: whiizzz – whiizzz . . . Perhaps he was avenging not only the Jews, but all the national republics of the USSR. The whole Soviet Union, the land of the Soviets, the first workers' state in the world, which all Europe had mocked, had tried to smother at birth, to starve to death, to stuff its mouth with gold, to thrust it alive, bound hand and foot by the thongs of finanacial liabilities, into the debtors' prison. And now the Soviet Shylock was sharpening his knife in order to claim his due, a pound of the live flesh of Europe. Her Europe. She, Clea, was Europe in his eyes. In the eyes of the Soviet Union. And he wanted his due. How many pounds of living flesh were there in her body? But Shylock had forgotten about blood. He had had the right to a pound of flesh – but without a drop of blood. He had forgotten about the blood. Meat with blood is not kosher: that was what had stopped Shylock, the merchant of Venice. But blood was nothing to this Soviet avenger: after Stalin's purges, after the cannibalism in the Volga provinces, what was blood to him, and what did he care about the laws prescribing what is kosher? He would simply slit her throat and leave the house wearing his waterproof and hat and cross the frontier, back to his Soviet *lares et penates*, back to his lair.

Clea clutched the banister-rail, swaying from the fear that was hammering in her temples. A stair creaked; Kostya the monster stopped sharpening his knife and listened. He stood up, put away the knife, having first tested it with his finger for sharpness, and slapped his pockets. After pensively scratching his stubble for a moment, he turned round and began to climb the staircase. Clea, in a panic, was about to dash back into the bedroom, but then remembered about Margot and dithered: she imagined her contemptuous face, her mocking smile, the smile of someone who is always right. That smile was sharper than Kostya's knife. Risking a clash with her bloodthirsty husband, she ran down the stairs and darted into the sitting-room right in front of his nose. Locking the door with the bolt, she began noisily to push the divan bed towards the door. Then, clambering on to the divan, she put her eye to the keyhole and immediately fell back: a blue eye was staring back at her through the keyhole, a cold monster's eye – Kostya's. As she listened to his heavy breathing on the other side of the door, his muffled, slightly hoarse voice growled: 'You've gone completely barmy, you little idiot!' She was not such an idiot as to open the door, though. The monster behind the door rattled the handle and swore foully. She then heard the clump of footsteps on the staircase and some inaudible whispering, followed by an impudent giggle. That was Margot and her shameless laugh. She was laughing at Clea – who else? As usual, she was delighted at having been proved right. After a little while she could be heard swearing from the kitchen, followed by the sound of a slap in the face and Anthony's hysterical, unintelligible, high tenor voice. Then came the crash of a falling body: obviously he had not fully come to his senses – or was Margot the prima donna, who was on backslapping terms with everyone – from trotskyites to cannibals – now engaged with Kostya in eliminating a superfluous witness so that the two of them could then dispose of Clea? But the slamming of the front door a minute later and the roar of a car engine showed that the English couple had washed their hands of the whole business and driven off. Clea recognised the steady snarl of their Jaguar (a bargain of course, bought second-hand, naturally, but however much Margot and Anthony might disparage the smartness of their car, Clea's dilapidated, spluttering Ford, put next to the Jaguar, looked like a mangy old mongrel alongside a pedigree greyhound – and cars, after all, live no longer than dogs). This silly, envious thought about the Jaguar only made Margot's treachery worse in Clea's eyes: her 'best friends' had driven off for a joy-ride leaving her expiring on the verge like a dog that has been run over. Later there would be newspaper reports about a marital fracas that had ended with the wife having her throat cut, and Margot would retail the intimate details of what had happened with her usual Marquis-de-Sade-like relish.

While the window-panes were still rattling from the car's roaring departure, Konstantin's footsteps came back into the house. A surge of intensified fear made Clea get up from the divan and renew her efforts to barricade the door. She dashed to the other end of the room and, exerting all her strength, began to move a heavy, polished sideboard towards the door. In her hurry she forgot to remove from the sideboard a decanter of port – one of the trappings of cosy domestic bliss – and at the next push the decanter slid off the top of the sideboard and poured a puddle of the thick, sweetish liquid all over the new carpet. Housewifely instinct proving stronger than fear, Clea forgot about the ominous rustle of footsteps beyond the door and reached into the sideboard, whence she took out the best Sunday-lunchtime salt-cellar and strewed the puddle of port thickly with salt. The ruby liquid was soon soaking up through the salt like a bloodstain on dirty snow, coagulating at the edges into a crisp, dry crust. Clea was overtaken by a wave of nausea at the sickening sight of this stain on the carpet; her knees gave way, she fell to the floor and burst into tears. In fact, she did not so much weep as whimper – from awareness of the utter uselessness of all her attempts to defend her wretched life against this monster who was tramping around her house in his dirty boots with a knife in his fist. She should have given it all much more thought long ago. Had she really not perceived earlier exactly what she was taking under her roof? Soon there would be nothing left of her except a ghastly stain on the carpet, which, as everyone knows, can *not* be removed with salt. It was absolutely clear that resistance was useless.

She had barricaded herself in these four English walls, waiting for this monstrous Russian to come and cut her throat. It was pointless to try and cajole him. Unlike the brutal account of their relationship provided by Margot, there was not even a chance of Clea being turned into a toad – would Konstantin ever allow himself to be kissed? He would simply murder her and boil her down for soup, as one means of building up his strength before leaving for Russia, the homeland of cannibals like himself. To Kostya, Clea had long since turned into a frog: she croaked, according to him, because none of the English can talk properly but only croak. He, incidentally, with his cast-iron stomach, would not mind eating a frog. Then she could croak inside his belly. No one would ever know that there had once been an English girl who had lived a life in which, for all her faults, she had been independent, had thought as she wanted – and had suddenly found herself inside a Russian belly, in the rumbling, ever-hungry, ill-tempered belly of Russia.

Her thoughts were growing confused. Even if she did succeed in getting out of this prison in which she had immured herself – through the window perhaps (there were, after all, no bars on the windows) – from whom could she beg refuge? And how? What would she tell the police? That she had been turned into a toad and somebody wanted to make soup out of her? That her husband was a cannibal and was planning to escape to the USSR? 'Why to the USSR?' – the British bobby would undoubtedly ask her – 'there are cannibals in Africa, too, so why are you so certain he's running away to the USSR – with his anti-Soviet views?' And she would stand on tiptoe in front of the policeman on her webbed frog's feet and say: 'Croak, croak!'

It was then that she remembered Pan Tadeusz, maybe because the face of that Polish *pan* – not unlike a punk with his long, reddish nose and his upturned moustache – reminded her of a cockroach or perhaps a starving water-rat, in other words a reasonably close relative of the frogs. At first she had mentally dismissed him as a candidate, since he was obviously a crony of Kostya's. With a shiver of revulsion and fear she recalled how the nimble Pole used to sneak into the kitchen, Kostya's fiefdom, trying to avoid meeting her, the mistress of the house. And whenever they did happen to meet, there was his ingratiating '*Excusez-moi*', always in French for some reason, followed by the inevitable: '*Najdroża pani Kleopatra*' in Polish – he always called her by her full name, which she hated. And then, long after midnight, she would hear whispering coming from the kitchen, the murmur of peevish argument that grew into obscene swearing, whooping and hoots of laughter, then whispering again. And once more an obsequious: 'Goodbye, *pani Kleopatra*,' if, unable to bear it any longer, she had gone downstairs in her night-dress to put a stop to these disgraceful midnight goings-on.

Now she realised that it had not been just a drunken get-together but a plot. Or rather, a summit conference. Between representatives of independent Poland and the communist great power, Russia. Between people's democracy and Soviet socialism. In any case, the difference was only superficial, because all of them in Eastern Europe were in league with the Soviet Union in increasing the number of nuclear warheads, all aimed at the countries of Western Europe. Aimed at her, Clea's, green lawn. Naive lefties like Anthony might insist until they were blue in the face that there was dissidence and schism among the countries of the Eastern bloc, might rabbit on about the 'Yugoslav experiment' and about Romania's flirtation with Western capital, but at this moment Clea was in full agreement with the right-wing British parliamentarians, the Reaganites among the Thatcherites:

regardless of ideological nuances and national interests, the mad dog of communism was only dreaming of one thing – to sink its teeth into the jugular vein of Western democracy and the only way to restrain it was by the threat of a nuclear laser-hypodermic loaded with the vaccine of anti-bolshevik propaganda.

But the mad dog was already on the threshold, here and now, on the other side of the door; instead of a nuclear hypodermic the only thing to hand was an empty English port decanter, and ranting away with impotent anti-Soviet rhetoric was not going to do her any good. Whether or not she agreed with the Reaganite wing of Thatcherism, she had to find an ally in the enemy's camp in order to survive. He might be unreliable and obnoxious, morally suspect and of dubious reputation, like Pan Tadeusz, but an ally had to be found and suborned with no matter what promises and bribes. After all, there was such a thing as the underground 'Solidarity' movement! Of course, those Polish trade unionists, underground or official, were all by nature bolsheviks themselves, and their quarrel was only about who should be the boss in what was nothing but a big conspiracy against freedom. Admittedly those underground 'Solidarity' members were all Catholics to a man: could anyone ever imagine Soviet trade unionists kneeling down to say Catholic prayers – in a mass gesture in the middle of the square – before going on strike? And then there was Jaruzelski: a general – in sunglasses! Could one imagine, say, Brezhnev, wearing those film-star glasses? Or even Andropov – although according to rumour he actually spoke English! No, one had to agree that Poland was a special case. Anti-Russian feelings were very strong in Poland and always had been since the days of tsarist rule; not for nothing had Dostoyevsky so disliked the Poles. And she had to exploit that. Perhaps Pan Tadeusz was not really a lackey of Konstantin's communist state at all; perhaps he was a secret ally of the West and was only waiting for a sign from Clea to join a united front against Soviet 'hegemony', as the Chinese put it. Whichever way you looked at it, Clea had no choice.

Either she must find an ally in the lackey or die in isolation from a blow delivered by that monstrous bear who was stamping and shuffling on the other side of the door. Without reflecting for long, Clea opened the window and, moving in short rushes – across the lawn, over to the hedge, then over the hedge and the wooden fence – she made her way next door to Pan Tadeusz's house.

'*Mon dieu, pani Kleopatra*! What a surprise!' mumbled Pan Tadeusz, half asleep, as he stood before Clea in his pyjamas and hairnet (to keep the few hairs on his balding head in good order overnight). He had been dreaming about the Polish uprising against the Russians in 1863: Polish noblemen firing at the Russian troops with duelling pistols; the grating twang of piano-wires slashed by a cossack sabre; and, to the music of a tortured Chopin waltz, the hangman of the Polish people, General Suvorov, with the face of Konstantin, on his white horse that pawed the ground as he reined it in, raised his long whip and shouted: 'Trample on the mushrooms, my brave charger! Send back the message: I have left not a single mushroom for the Poles and I died bravely for the workers' cause!' All this nostalgic delirium had been evoked by the noise made by Clea as she had dashed from the window to the door of Pan Tadeusz's house, banging on the door-knocker and making the window-panes rattle, while looking around every minute in case Konstantin might be creeping up behind the bushes in order to slit her throat. Then, breathing heavily, he would drag her to his kitchen and throw her into a saucepanful of boiling water. She tried to explain it all to Pan Tadeusz: about Gindin the Jewish cannibal, about the Catholicism of the Polish working class, about the sound of Kostya's knife on the whetstone and General Jaruzelski's sunglasses.

'My dear *pani Kleopatra*!' Pan Tadeusz spread his hands helplessly. 'Put yourself in my position' – and he invited her to come indoors and calm down. Clea, however, did not want to be calmed down: dragging Pan Tadeusz by the sleeve of his pyjamas, she urged him to join her in the last, decisive battle against the mad Russian werewolf. 'He is driven by a merciless thirst for vengeance,' said Clea, trying to sound as logical as possible. 'Today it's us, and tomorrow the whole of Western civilisation will be his victim.' And as though in proof of what she was saying, Konstantin at that moment appeared on the opposite side of the street, in boots and waterproof and carrying his basket. He opened the door of their car and put the enormous basket on the back seat. 'You see? You see?' Clea babbled, clutching at Tadeusz's dressing-gown.

'H'mm . . . a big basket,' Pan Tadeusz muttered as though to himself: neither Kostya's gumboots nor his raincoat had escaped his glance. Pan Tadeusz had his own unambiguous and totally apolitical ideas about Kostya's destination. 'I think you are right, *pani*,' he nodded to Clea. 'Is good idea to follow where goes this Russian.'

Taking only a moment to pull on his own gumboots over his pyjama trousers and to grab his plastic waterproof jacket, Pan Tadeusz sat Clea in his antiquated station-wagon. Clea noticed a large wicker basket on the back seat, similar to Kostya's basket. Anyway, there were a lot of empty cardboard boxes lying around – the usual rubbish to be found in a car belonging to the owner of a grocery-shop.

Konstantin did not turn down their side-street towards the High Street, as Clea had expected. He did not turn in that direction where, soaked after a nocturnal August rainstorm, there stretched the vast and unpeopled sewer of the city, smoking with mists and vapours like a heap of wet grey rags – the dirty and crumpled working overalls of God, who had got fed up with the clumsy and laborious job of improving the lot of mankind, had thrown off this stinking garment of civilisation and gone back to heaven, having first washed himself in a shower of rain and finally slammed the door behind him in the form of a distant roll of thunder. Like drainpipes, the monotonous streets ran down from this high hill in the north of London, squashed low by the lid of heaven, whose yellowish, sewage-like glow lit up the rows of two-storey houses glued together, in which every door, with its letter-box and door-knocker, was traced in endless, unimaginative repetition – like the obscene graffiti on the dreary walls of the Underground. As though abandoned and left permanently at the disposal of the rats, these huge, deserted drainpipes, ditches, tunnels ran ever downwards, heading, along with the urine-like babbling of streams of rainwater, towards the parts where, beneath an insanely convoluted, ugly labyrinth of walls, bridges and pedestrian subways there stirred the night-watchmen and wardens of this city: down-and-outs, sleeping in cardboard boxes under bridges and on the Underground's ventilation-grilles; conductors of all-night buses and prostitutes, united in one sleepless trade union by their hateful shift-work, united, too, in shunning the noisy gangs of punks: those self-elected ruffians with the shaven heads of convicts and the clanking chains, lost by the proletariat in the scrimmage of progress, and now draped and dangling from all the most obscene places – from the flies of their leather trousers to their pierced ears; the punks' clinking chains and foul language occasionally alternating with the purr of Rolls-Royces and the high, black coachwork of taxis picking up smart couples in expensive suits and evening dress, in clouds of scent and cigar smoke, wearing their unseasonable but fashionable sable wraps, from nightclubs and exclusive restaurants with shaded front windows – in short, that whole world of ghosts and spectres, freakish exceptions to the rule who defy the prescribed order of things, according to which the rank-and-file citizen of London is supposed, at that late hour, to pretend that he is dead or should at least be sleeping the sleep of the dead. London's plebeian democracy dies when the pubs shut, and the pubs shut, by a suicidal decree of the democratic parliament, on the stroke of eleven o'clock. Those who dare to venture on to the streets and show that they are still alive after eleven o'clock at night must be prepared to meet Jack the Ripper or Kostya the cannibal.

Such was Clea's attitude to her native city. Kostya, however, did not turn downhill towards the blood-red glow that like a broken traffic-light shines up from the sewer of the city centre, but turned the wheel uphill, towards where the high ground merged at its edges with shreds of rain-clouds hanging above the roofs like laundry put out to dry after a giant's wash-day. Kostya, indeed, had his own, not too rational reasons for hating this city: those corridor-like streets, tightly lined with houses like wardrobes; that string of villages, blacked out as though expecting an air-raid, joined up into one city by nothing but a common name, with their invariable 'High Street', as in a village, with their illuminated shop-signs blazing in pointless all-night wakefulness, always announcing the same things: the launderette; the bank; the fish-and-chip shop; the Mecca betting shop. For all the brilliance of their neon signs, these emporia were all shut. But it was not the deadness of the night-time city as such that depressed Kostya.

'This city should have been ploughed up and turned into a potato-field long ago!' thought Kostya angrily, pressing on the accelerator and hurrying onward, faster and farther, northwards through the deserted streets away from those wretched little houses and their patches of wilting garden, the little squares and suburban 'village greens' which in daylight tried so hard to imitate a rural idyll.

Now, though, in the flickering darkness, they had become what they really were: not a grassy quilt but cheap rags painted green by an undiscriminating nature, bare and mangy in the places where bricks, asphalt, plaster, lamp-standards, plaster and asphalt had broken through them. It was pathetic mimicry, a cheap imitation, an artificial stage-setting but not the countryside. The ludicrous way in which the English imagined themselves to be in the country amid the gigantic, smoky, soot-covered ruins of the London slums – that was what infuriated Konstantin. Having spent his entire life in communal flats, nagged and badgered by Soviet bureaucracies and bored to extinction by stuffy trade-union meetings, like many of his generation of Soviet dreamers and macabre fantasists he cherished the idea of the sacramental quality of nature: all those birches, that deadly nightshade, those bogs, those troubled waters where one could fish with one's bare hands, that soil to go back to – all of this could never be completely eradicated either by the axe of a five-year plan or by the hobnailed boots of corrective-labour camps. The countryside was proof that even the most invincible idea in the world – the doctrine of communism – was capable of sinking into a swamp, of losing its way in broad daylight or vanishing without trace into a deep pool. In fact, Kostya did not so much love the country as hate the tidy civilisation organised by those imbeciles, the religious fanatics of progress who have never understood that the chief element in man is the stomach, skin and bones, which are so near to nature by their very composition, their closeness to dust and soil: the source and the ultimate resting-place of all lunatic, utopian ideas – utopian in the sense of '*après moi le déluge*'. The propagandists of 'progressive' ideas always imagine themselves to be the centre of the universe, that the universe itself is the work of their hands, and they stand guard over their little kingdom like a scarecrow in a kitchen-garden who imagines that apart from crows there are no other enemies in the world. What annoyed Konstantin was the conceit of these islanders, who believed that they could subsist entirely on the work of their own hands. He was annoyed by the civilisation of London, because here even the grass and the trees were the work of a man's hands. For Konstantin did not like people, still less their ideas. So away from civilisation drove Konstantin, mounted on civilisation's most perfect invention – the wheels of a car.

For him, though, the car was merely a transitional phase from civilisation to nature, from city to forest. This was how Konstantin excused the greed and tenacity of his own hands as with faultless, mettlesome skill they turned the wheel, the sureness of his feet on the pedals as they pressed on the accelerator – away from those clustered hamlets of progress and enlightened humanism and onward to the barbarism of the forest. Secretly he had a heartfelt adoration for his masterly control of a car's steering-wheel, for that ravishing power with which the obedient, mighty wheels bit into the asphalt soil and crushed the roots of nature with the same controlled passion with which, say, revolutionaries were prepared to shoot and hang a good half of the human race in the name of love of one's fellow-men. In short, he had a great liking for this transitional phase on the way from civilisation to nature, to the same extent that he was obsessed by the very idea of merging oneself with nature, and it was not clear what it was that fascinated him more – nature itself or the race towards it at the expense of civilisation. So he pressed on the accelerator, his outward as well as his inward gaze straining forward and only forward – along the dark nocturnal road towards the woodland thickets on the horizon.

It never even occurred to him to look back, where, a hundred foggy metres behind him, Clea's hands were gripping a steering-wheel no less fanatically. Beside her, nervously twisting his moustache, glancing now at the road, now at Clea's sharply tense features, sat Pan Tadeusz: the road was wet after the rain and Clea was sparing neither the gearbox nor the brake-shoes; at each jolt of his aged station-wagon, with each howl of the tortured engine Tadeusz would twitch painfully, fearing not only for his life but for the fate of his four-wheeled friend, without which his delicatessen would have long since been bankrupt. Clea had firmly refused to take the passenger seat and would not let the station-wagon's owner take the wheel: she had decided to take complete charge of the pursuit of Kostya the cannibal and potential murderer. Pan Tadeusz, as it happened, was quite content with the role of observer: for months he had been trying unsuccessfully to trace the routes taken on his secret sorties by this culinary mystic, this Russian, this ruthless chauvinist of mushroom-picking. Who would have thought that these secret routes would be revealed under such scandalous circumstances? As a Pole, he knew in any case that the Polish people could only ever wrest concessions from Big Brother by taking advantage of whatever political commotion was currently taking place. And just such a commotion was in full swing right now. His eyelids puffy from interrupted sleep, Tadeusz carefully made a mental note of all the turnings on the way to the secret woodlands.

All three of them – Konstantin in front, Clea behind and Tadeusz beside her – were so absorbed in their own thoughts, their ultimate objectives and the means of obtaining them, that none of the members of this obsessive cavalcade noticed another traveller behind them, who was following and trying to anticipate all the turns of the steering-wheel and the mental moves being made by the trio in front of him. None of the three noticed that at the very first turning leading into the High Street, the nocturnal cavalcade was joined in its northbound progress by a clattering, coughing, dilapidated motor-cycle: too many young people, outwardly indistinguishable from Colin, go roaring around at night-time on these rattling, roaring, infernal machines, preventing people from sleeping who sleep without dreams, without suspecting the existence of others who dream their dreams awake. One behind the other, knowing not what was happening behind their backs, each of the participants in the cavalcade turned off the main highway on to a winding, narrow country road. All around them loomed the dark nocturnal spectres of the woodlands.

9 THE KNIFE IN THE BOOT-TOP

Letting the car roll slowly across a shallow roadside ditch (knocking over, as he did so, a plywood warning sign written in the local double-dutch), his wheels crunching over the sparse, coarse undergrowth, Konstantin then switched off the engine and got out of the car. Having collected his basket from the boot, he slung its leather strap over his shoulder and pulled up his boots. Lighting the way with a pocket torch, he swung his legs over some rusty barbed wire that had obviously been there since World War II. He swore as he caught his trousers on it, but without spite, as this barbed wire represented in his mind the border at which Western – and all other – civilisations ended. He strode off, almost at random and without a compass, sensing the right direction by flair, through a thicket towards the clearing marked on his map. He immediately forgot about the barbed wire or any other obstructions: the forest to him was a no man's land. Each step took him further away from the family quarrels and the posturings in the name of social justice that lay behind him; it was for this reason that he took Pan Tadeusz's torch shining behind him to be the flickering of glow-worms, and the chance crackle of twigs under Clea's heel as being caused by the leap of a frightened squirrel or the movement of an ever-wakeful owl. The forest was a territory in which all claims to ideological fidelity ceased to be valid: here there were neither left nor right, and – in the absence of a compass – neither East nor West. He was running away from cause and effect, from the changes of place and language; he was running away in equal degree from both Russia and Europe, because in its universality – roots, tree-trunks and foliage – the forest could be both Russia and Europe at the same time; as he entered the thicket Konstantin was outside all geography and was returning to himself as he retreated from himself – he was becoming no one in order to become Everyman. We have all come from the forest and to the forest we shall return, back to that second stage – the sperm of the world-wide ocean being the first stage – of the evolution of the human race. If the universal ocean is the sperm, then the forest is the maternal womb of mankind.

Tired and relaxed, Konstantin sat down on a tree-stump amid a small clearing, surrounded on all sides by the hairy flesh of the forest. With his innate owl-like ability to see at night Konstantin admired the silvery foliage of oaks, the dense clumps of hazel-bushes, seemingly swollen from the damp, and the lush fronds of birches in the hazy half-light of a sky that was just preparing for the break of day. Having rained itself dry, and with the curved orifice of the moon looking like a half-hidden way out of this cosmic belly, the sky enfolded the earthly womb in warm, damp swaddling-clothes. After staring awhile at the lunar aperture, Kostya finally lost all desire ever to leave this well-protected no man's land, the irresponsible intimacy of the clearing where all his burdens and cares had been lifted from him. Like every Soviet person, who always has something to hide, he preferred to be amid nature and close to the earth – not for love of the plants and the soil as such, but for the comforting absence of any kind of questions:

where there are questions one must provide answers, and when giving answers on anything to do with Russia one must always lie, evade and dodge. Kostya's stomach began to rumble.

Quickly and skilfully he laid a small fire, less for warmth than to appease a longing to smell the acrid, sweetish smoke from rotten leaves and damp branches. He then produced a couple of cans of beer and a sandwich from his basket: smoothly-laid strips of salted herring mixed with pickled onion. Kostya took out his knife, sliced the sandwich into equal halves, wiped the double-edged blade on a tuft of grass and put the knife away in his boot-top. Slowly and with pleasure he fortified himself with a snack designed to banish his hangover. There were still a good three hours before dawn, plenty of time for a nap in the fresh air: it was, in any case, still too dark to see anything underfoot. He stood up, stretched himself with a cracking of joints, shivered deliciously and yawned, listening to his stomach rumbling in unison with the hooting of an owl. To achieve the ultimate in harmony he still had to relieve himself internally. He walked over to the bushes at the edge of the clearing, unbuckled the belt of his trousers, lowered them, stood for a moment with his trousers round his ankles and scratched his stomach, exposing it to the cool breath of the gentle night wind, as only a man can scratch himself who is convinced that beside himself no one else exists on this earth, in this clearing, among these bushes and trees. Unhurriedly, he squatted down on his haunches.

The enormous bottom that revealed itself to the flabbergasted Clea and the terrified Pan Tadeusz, who were hidden in the same bushes, with its dull gleam and its unearthly whiteness in a dark framework of nocturnal foliage, was like a full moon that had fallen out of its bedding of clouds. The moonlight played on the white buttocks in such a way that one could not tell whether it was a Russian behind or an English moon that was illuminating the clearing in a glimmering light. This cosmological aberration caused Pan Tadeusz, entangled in the branches of a hazel-bush, to have an attack of nervous hiccups, and Clea had to stop his mouth with her hand. The panicky rustling and shushing in the bushes was, however, completely muffled by Konstantin: he was relieving himself noisily and enjoyably, grunting, straining and groaning blissfully, materialising through his anal orifice the bond between his soul – his stomach, of course – and the soil. As he sat there holding a plaintain-leaf at the ready, with each grunt he felt ever more strongly how the blessed emptiness within him was achieving equilibrium with the primeval emptiness of the night-time clearing; how that emptiness was gradually being filled by the consoling thought that Clea, East and West, nuclear disarmament and human rights – all this was insignificant, transient, worthy of only regret, compassion and forgiveness, against the background of the metabolic cycle of the fruits of the earth, basis and superstructure, the ends and means of earthly existence.

If only we, the children of this planet, could throughout our lives keep to that spiritual plane that rules us when we are answering the call of nature squatting on our haunches in a clearing or in a lavatory – that mood of conciliation combined with the intense, heightened awareness of laborious achievement and of the visible fruits of our selfless efforts! How peaceably and amiably the days of mankind would pass – without ambitions and pretensions, tyranny or hierarchy! For when a generalissimo is performing his natural functions his thoughts and actions are no different from those of a private soldier when doing the same thing. It would perhaps be hardest of all to imagine, shall we say, Stalin engaged in such a democratic occupation, but Konstantin, exerting his imagination together with his rectum, was easily able to conjure up a mental image of Stalin walking through the pinewoods around his dacha after a lavish Georgian lunch and – lo and behold! – there was a latrine for the use of his guards! As he settled himself in a crouching position over the latrine, whose 'hole' was in the shape of a heart, Stalin recalled a lunchtime conversation about, say, the link between the religious idea of spiritual community and the Soviet concept of collectivism.

Suddenly Stalin had a flash of inspiration: beneath his haunches, he saw through the heart-shaped hole the prototype of that great Russian idea – there, there, where there were not only white worms like vermicelli, not only fauna and rotting flora but also his own, along with the guards', soldiers' and officers', and 'all the serving personnel's' – nay, the whole country's – crap, turds and shit, like the triple unity of the Hegelian dialectic and its clash of opposites, such as between randomness and order, form and content, particular and general, why, even the shit of yesterday's fraternal delegation from Mongolia: and they were all together, all conjoined in unity, and therefore indestructible.

While Konstantin's inward gaze was fixed on the dialectic of the cycle of earthly existence, Clea's stare was riveted to Kostya's huge white behind, which had lost its moonlight gleam and now reminded her of a gigantic poisonous toadstool, ready to smother her life – *their* life – by dropping its evil-smelling fringe of spores. Unlike Konstantin, who was experiencing the process of unification with the soil purely spiritually, since his back was turned to the products of his rectum, Clea was placed in direct contemplation of this physiological performance: Konstantin, to put it plainly, was excreting before her very eyes, defecating, in fact, on Clea's soul, on the soil of England, on her country, the object of her affection and her civil identity, on English literature and religion – displaying his posterior to the entire national heritage. The physical source of Kostya's metaphysics was now clearly visible from the bushes – further proof that metaphysical speculation inside one person's head can turn into shit on someone else's head. All unawares, Kostya straightened up and, in a summing-up of his cosmological reflections as he contemplated the little heap he had created, he thought: 'And it's good for mushrooms, too!' Then he carefully wiped his bottom with the plantain-leaf as Clea watched. She could restrain herself no longer: seizing the hand of her ally, Pan Tadeusz, by now utterly crushed, Clea strode through the bushes towards her ideological opponent, having forgotten all about the knife in his boot-top and the pain in her heart. Kostya was about to look round at the crack of a twig, but at that instant the silence was broken by a noise of such intensity that it would have drowned out any mere verbal exchange between the two sides.

A heart-stopping crash, a howling, roaring and creaking shattered the pre-dawn hush with such surrealistic unexpectedness that an insane thought flashed through Clea's head: was this Konstantin finally breaking wind as an ultimate gesture of humiliation? This mental absurdity, however, was instantly cauterised by the dazzling beams of several searchlights that suddenly shone out on all sides, swallowing the darkness of the forest and turning the clearing into a circus arena, in which Konstantin was seen stumbling around in panic. These salvoes of noise and light also brought Clea and Pan Tadeusz out of the bushes: the undergrowth all around was crackling and tree trunks were creaking, as a number of tracked, armoured monsters moved in from all directions, each with one cyclopean searchlight-eye. Suddenly these juggernauts began to snarl out a volley of amplified military commands: put your hands up and surrender, don't move, resistance is useless. 'It's war – World War III has broken out,' Clea muttered, panic-stricken, on all fours, shaking with fear as she bumped into roots and tussocks; clutching Tadeusz's trousers, she crawled backwards into the middle of the clearing until – bottom to bottom – she bumped into Konstantin, who had been backing in the opposite direction. She screamed. Both leaped to their feet. A blood-red Very light lit up the clearing, and in that ominous glare Konstantin's face became a rigid mask of revulsion, fear and hatred; seizing Clea by the chin, as though about to strangle her, he hissed: 'You! So you were following me, were you?' Strong, experienced hands pulled them apart as the figures of soldiers, in spotted clothes like green leopards, came bounding across the clearing.

'What were your intentions in penetrating into a prohibited military zone?' A junior officer of the Royal Artillery attempted to extract an answer from his prisoners and failed. When he had started his turn as night duty officer he had received the strictest instructions to keep a special look-out for an expected mass protest demonstration by anti-nuclear activists.

The arrested trio, however, were much cannier than any CND stalwarts. The ginger-haired lieutenant's head began to spin. He could not obtain from them any logical explanation of why and how they had ignored all the warning signs and the barbed wire around the approaches to the missile base. Instead, the prisoners would only bicker among themselves in a strange mixture of Russian and English. They obviously took him for a mere boy, as they tried to pull the wool over his eyes with a succession of cheap tricks, pretending to be naive idiots. They were behaving like clowns. Take their leader, called Konstantin, for instance: he was obviously the key figure in this as yet unexplained act of trespass, which might well be an organised conspiracy. The mere fact that the prisoner was Russian put the officer on his guard. He was apparently the boss of the party. As his accomplice, a person of Polish origin, was brought into the guardroom, Konstantin flew at him with fists raised: he obviously had a bone to pick with the Pole over the failure of their operation. When two soldiers forced Konstantin to sit down, the latter growled incomprehensibly: '*Nu pan Tadeusz, nu khitryuga*!' followed by the Russian word for 'reptile' – '*gad*', which the lieutenant, who had taken an army course in Russian, took to be the American pronunciation of the word 'God'. Perhaps Konstantin was hinting at divine retribution for the collapse of their enterprise. Indeed, the pair were highly suspicious: one of them a Pole, the other a Soviet citizen. In the final analysis, Poland was a Soviet-bloc country; despite such things as these underground 'Solidarities' and the Soviet Jews' struggle to emigrate (which the lieutenant had read about in the *Daily Telegraph*), he fully realised that anti-Soviet campaigns of this kind actually provided Soviet intelligence agencies with perfect cover for sending spies to the West. This 'Konstantin', of course, was making himself out to be ignorant, uncomprehending and slightly drunk; on top of all that, his trousers were undone. He was pretending to have practically no knowledge of English, even though, according to his Soviet passport with a British stamp granting him right of residence, he had been in the country for at least a year. He had established himself in the United Kingdom under cover of being married to this irresponsible Englishwoman, whom he insisted on calling by a nickname taken from atomic physics – 'Nuclear'; she was obviously one of these half-wits who had swallowed the latest fashionable ideology hook, line and sinker – the kind who started with this pacifist nonsense, hating their own, allegedly aggressive, government, demonstrating their love for the enemy by marrying a foreigner and who ended, willy-nilly, by working for Soviet intelligence. In the end this sort of double life inevitably led, slowly but surely, to insanity: no wonder this 'Nuclear' woman was accusing her husband of cannibalism, babbling about some knife and demanding that he be put in isolation. A typically leftist form of madness: disillusion with unattainable ideals, multiplied by the number of joints she had smoked. No knife had been found in the superficial search made on the prisoners. They had, however, found a much more interesting item, hidden in Konstantin's inside pocket.

'What was your mission?' the lieutenant asked in Russian, in order to forestall any further misunderstanding on the prisoner's part, and he waved under Konstantin's nose the map that had been found during the search. Pan Tadeusz made a move to grab the fateful map, but before the lieutenant could speak Konstantin barked: 'Sit!' and Tadeusz retired to his corner in terror. There was clearly a distinct hierarchy as between the Russian and the Pole in the mattter of access to secret information: Pan Tadeusz was obviously not supposed to know the contents of the map. 'What was your mission?' repeated the British lieutenant. The map was marked with a rash of espionage symbols: circles, crosses, stars and triangles. Actually these cabalistic signs were not particularly mysterious: their positions on the map corresponded to the locations of emplacements that housed missiles of varying range and with different types of nuclear warheads. 'And what's the basket for?' asked the lieutenant even more sternly.

'*Dlya gribov*,' Konstantin replied reluctantly, after a pause.

'*Grib*?' smiling ironically, the lieutenant repeated the Russian word for mushroom, which he happened to know.

'Mushroom,' the Polish accomplice hastened to explain in an East-European accent, looking ingratiatingly back and forth between the lieutenant and the Soviet master spy. The mushroom cloud over Hiroshima – well, of course, the usual unilateralist rubbish.

'You have an interesting way of classifying these, er . . . mushrooms.' The lieutenant tapped his pencil on the spy's map with its nuclear warheads. 'Are you going to continue to keep your mouth shut till we get to London, or shall we decode these symbols here and now?'

'They're not atomic mushrooms,' said Kostya, having finally guessed what the lieutenant was driving at as he followed the movement of his pencil. After casting a glance at Tadeusz, he reluctantly revealed the secret that is dear to every dedicated mushroom-picker: 'The stars show where there are aspen boletus – you know, the kind with deep orange-red caps.'

'Aspen boletus.' The lieutenant wrote this rare expression in his notebook. This presumably was what the Russians called cruise missiles.

'That's right – aspen boletus. The kind that grows under aspens,' Konstantin explained eagerly. 'But it also grows under birches too. Just as the birch boletus will grow under aspens.'

'Birch boletus,' the lieutenant repeated diligently, following Konstantin's finger as it pointed to the triangles disposed, as the officer knew, in precisely the locations of camouflaged emplacements of ground-to-ground missiles.

'The only difference is that the aspen boletus has a red head while the birch boletus has a black one,' Konstantin explained to the ignorant Englishman, who knew of nothing more than the common-or-garden mushroom.

'A red head? A black head? A nuclear warhead?' the lieutenant asked, trying to fill in the gaps in the code.

'Every mushroom has a head. It's called the "cap",' said Konstantin, waxing enthusiastic. 'One of the good things about the cap of the aspen boletus is that it never harbours any worms.'

'Worms!' exclaimed the lieutenant in horror. A nuclear missile with a warhead stuffed with worms was a horrible, apocalyptic nightmare.

'In that respect, the only thing to rival the aspen boletus is the chanterelle: never a single worm or maggot!' Konstantin continued.

'*Cantharellus cibarius*,' Pan Tadeusz announced solemnly.

'What's that?' asked the lieutenant in perplexity.

'It's the Latin name of the chanterelle,' Tadeusz hastened to explain.

'*Cantharellus cibarius*,' the officer mused thoughtfully. Did everyone in Soviet Intelligence know Latin? One should never underestimate one's enemy.

'Why do you keep harping on chanterelles and birch boletus!' Konstantin jealously interrupted this duet between the two latinists. 'The white boletus – now *that's* the king of mushrooms!' He sighed as it occurred to him that he would now never be able to pick either chanterelles or white boletus in this place.

'White?' the lieutenant enquired, looking for the corresponding symbol on Kostya's map. As far as he knew, the 'Whites' had fought the 'Reds' after the Russian revolution.

'*Boletus edulis*.' Pan Tadeusz eagerly supplied the Latin equivalent of the white boletus.

'What symbol do you use on this map for white warheads?' The lieutenant bent over the chart of missile geography.

'"White head" is what they call vodka in the Soviet Union,' Konstantin remarked sourly.

'Even so – what is its symbol on the map?' the lieutenant insisted.

'I won't tell you!' Kostya suddenly announced firmly,

sitting up proudly in his chair. He had already given away the locations of the birch boletus, aspen boletus and chanterelles to these fools. That was two winters-worth of good pickling gone. 'I won't tell you,' he repeated.

'In that case we shall have to postpone the rest of our talk till we get to headquarters in London,' said the lieutenant threateningly.

'What for?' Konstantin began to raise his voice. 'You've put your missiles in the best wild mushroom grounds in England – and now you're making me out to be a spy. I don't ask you to give away any secrets about your missiles – so don't you poke your noses into my mushroom-picking strategy!' said Konstantin indignantly. No, he would not give away the white boletus. He pictured that fungoid miracle to himself: there it stood, somewhere under a hazel-bush, its arms akimbo, its reddish-brown cap at a slightly rakish angle, wild strawberries dangling from it like the trimming on a fashionable hat. No, he would *not* give away the white boletus. He said so to the lieutenant, who frowned but decided not to insist on the point. This Russian spy might well be trying to raise his price as a future double agent. Let the people in Whitehall sort out this business of the white boletus. He was already quite baffled by all these mushroom code-names.

'What do you do with them?' the lieutenant asked searchingly.

'With what?' Kostya did not understand.

'With the mushrooms that you've named. Birch boletus. Aspen boletus. Chanterelles. What do you do with them when you've found them?'

'What on earth do you mean?' Kostya was amazed at the Englishman's feeble-mindedness. 'What do I *do* with them? I pick them and put them in my basket' – he pointed to the basket. The lieutenant imagined the basket full of nuclear warheads and wiped the sweat from his forehead.

'Don't try and fool me,' he said. 'To whom do you pass on the information you've collected?'

'I don't pass it on to anyone!' Kostya replied with irritation.

'Pan Tadeusz here has been trying for the past year to ferret out where I pick my mushrooms, so that he can pass the news on the grapevine to his fellow-Poles. But he hasn't found out a damn thing. He can collect fir-cones and boil them in vinegar, that's what he can do. As for my mushrooms, I boil them, salt them and marinade them.'

'You marinade them, do you?' the lieutenant pricked up his ears. In other words, he preserved them. *Marinade* . . . ? In the sea? His suspicions began to take a somewhat unexpected direction.

'Yes,' Kostya confirmed. 'I marinade them. And I make soup out of them. So what?'

'He's a fungophile,' said Pan Tadeusz, throwing in yet another latinism.

'Will you kindly shut up, Tadeusz!' Kostya cut him off.

'So you make soup, do you?' The lieutenant was becoming more and more interested. 'And then what do you do? Chew them?' – and he gave a knowing laugh.

'Well, if the mushroom has been, say, pickled or boiled, I chew it. And if it's soup I drink it with a spoon. In other words, I *eat* the mushrooms. What else would I do?' This time Konstantin was utterly perplexed.

'Yes, yes, I see.' The lieutenant, for no apparent reason, hastened to agree. 'I was simply asking out of interest. Because some people don't chew them – they sniff them.'

'*Sniff* them?'

'Well, yes. They sniff an infusion of mushrooms. Young people nowadays sniff anything – even glue!' And the lieutenant shook his head sadly.

'I suppose the glue make their guts stick together, does it?' Konstantin suggested glumly. The lieutenant nodded:

'They die like flies. Personally I prefer a well-rolled joint of pot – you know, marijuana. What about you?' The lieutenant asked in a confidential tone.

'Tobacco?' Kostya enquired in response. 'I don't smoke at all. It destroys the taste-buds.'

'It's nothing to do with taste. It's for one's soul,' the

lieutenant began to explain, recalling his girlfriend, a flat in Chelsea and various discothèques.

'For one's soul? Then why smoke? The soul is in the stomach.' Konstantin was implacable.

'But these toadstools are deadly poisonous,' the lieutenant began; then remembering that the mescalin mushroom was used as a drug by the American soldiers in Vietnam, he stopped and thought: what if this Russian agent is working on a chemical weapon based on mushrooms?

Meanwhile Konstantin, for the umpteenth time that day, was trying once more to make the lieutenant understand that the poisonous toadstool was a relative concept, with the possible exception of the fly agaric or, shall we say, the white spirochetes from quite a different area of mycology, so that even the black-face or the sow's ear, if you boil them well for several hours, can be excellent for salting down.

'*Caramophillus marcuolus*,' Pan Tadeusz put in obligingly.

'Which one is that?' asked the lieutenant.

'The black-face,' Tadeusz explained authoritatively. 'I should mention, though, that black-faces are not found in Great Britain.'

'They aren't?' Konstantin smiled maliciously.

'No, they are not,' Pan Tadeusz insisted.

'Literally not a single black-face in the whole British Isles?' Kostya clicked his tongue ironically and spluttered with suppressed laughter. On this matter he was obviously of the opposite opinion.

'You can't mean it!' exclaimed the lieutenant, getting agitated, as any professional would, as though the discussion was not about mushrooms as code-names for nuclear missiles but about the black population of Albion. Tadeusz, however, stuck obstinately to his point: black-faces were not to be found in Britain. In France, yes, under almost any bush, but in these islands there was not a single black-face, and Konstantin, greatly though Pan Tadeusz respected him and of whose many-sided mycological knowledge he had no doubt whatsoever, was most probably confusing the black-face with the

British variety, *lepiosta nuda*, or perhaps *russula nigricans*, in other words, to put it plainly, the Eastern European blackening *russula*. The lieutenant did not like either the comparison of the British variety of 'black-face' with the Eastern European *russula* nor the superiority of the French in this kind of toadstool. This Pole had wounded his patriotic feelings.

'And you – what exactly were *you* doing on the territory of a military base?' he asked, addressing Pan Tadeusz in the tone of an interrogator. 'This prisoner' – the lieutenant pointed to Konstantin – 'can at least support his claim that his hobby is collecting dubious mushrooms by the presence of this basket' – and he pointed to the basket. 'But what were you doing here? And you?' he enquired, turning to Clea.

'My husband is mentally ill,' Clea intoned in a dispirited voice, having wearily repeated the same thing ever since their arrest but without the slightest result. She had caught sight of Kostya's gesture when he had tapped his forehead and winked at the lieutenant and the latter had twisted his features into an understanding grimace: even if Konstantin were not a lunatic but a Soviet spy, it was obvious that this male collusion – a collusion directed against her – was stronger than all their disagreements and points of conflict over national politics and national frontiers, military secrets and intelligence organisations. The only sober voice in this mad competition between different varieties of male arrogance – her voice – had been declared irresponsible, had been labelled as the voice of a mentally disturbed, hysterical woman, of a lesbian obsessed with the phallic symbolism of nuclear missiles. Even her sole ally, Pan Tadeusz, had ratted on her and was doing his best to gain the approval of the powers that be.

'I wanted to find out the best mushroom-grounds by following Kostya,' confessed Tadeusz, hanging his head.

'In other words you were spying,' said the lieutenant. Konstantin found himself liking this Englishman more and more.

'Can you ever trust the Poles?' Turning to the lieutenant

Konstantin banged his fist on the table. 'Just now he was holding forth about black-faces. Which of us do you believe: this spy or me – I who have been picking black-faces here by the basketful for the past year?'

The lieutenant was inclined to believe Konstantin rather than these Eastern European theories about the superiority of French over English fungi. Admittedly the lieutenant did find this prisoner's statement that he had been regularly trespassing on Ministry of Defence property for the past year alarming though not improbable. If it had not been for the little fire spotted that night from a helicopter, this Russian would have continued his sorties to plunder the missile-base flora with absolute impunity. Anyhow, when the troops guarding the base consisted of one lieutenant and a handful of men, how could security be maintained in matters of birch boletus and aspen boletus? – assuming, of course, that these mushrooms really existed in the nearby bushes and were not simply a metaphor for the nuclear umbrella or an atomic explosion. Before going any further with his interrogation, he first had to convince himself whether or not these chanterelles and so on actually were to be found on the territory for which he was responsible and whether their locations corresponded to the placing of the symbols on the map. And whether indeed there were any 'black-faces' in Great Britain – apart, of course, from Pakistanis. Perhaps if he were lucky he would find out what this *boletus edulis* looked like, whose whereabouts the mystic Russian categorically refused to reveal. Instead of hanging around in this stuffy office, he would arrange an extremely entertaining excursion that would be good for both national security and his own health. Aroused by the prospect of a search for these mysterious 'black-faces', the British sporting instinct made the lieutenant spring to his feet like a ground-to-air missile, and in a few seconds the whole cavalcade, with the lieutenant heading an escort of soldiers, emerged from the guardhouse and headed towards the edge of the wood on a steep hillside.

By night the clearing had seemed like a mysterious black

hole, the dark, damp womb of earthly life; now, in the intensifying azure of the August morning, it was more like a kaleidoscopic mosaic of sunlight and foliage, which the gusts of a breeze made to swirl into clusters that were like gigantic bunches of grapes from some celestial garden, whose earthly counterpart had arisen in this purely English light – a light that rearranges all planes and changes the rules of perspective so as to present every detail with photographic objectivity regardless of distance or length of exposure. The contours of these serene hills, now touched with flecks of autumnal yellow, were crowned with winged angels draped in sunlight-dappled leopard-skin camouflage – the pale bodies of intercontinental missiles. To Konstantin they seemed like gigantic toadstools from some primeval forest; in this paradise, he was no longer a god. Sitting on a tree-stump and screwing up his eyes from the sunlight in an ill-natured scowl, he watched the lieutenant organise a mushroom-hunt, despatching his soldiers in various directions around the wood, some to the hazel-bushes and some to a dense clump of birches, while he himself searched among the rhizomes of a solitary oak, checking everything against Konstantin's map. From the opposite side of the clearing Kostya could hear these newly-converted barbarians getting excited, these neophytes of fungophilia uttering oohs and ahs as they found another toadstool among the distant bushes. The holy of holies, this temple, this Konstantinople had been seized by the heathen Turk, incapable of distinguishing Christian Lenten fare from Jewish kosher, a toadstool from a *russula*.

'Bullytoes, bullytoes!' cried the lieutenant, garbling the newly-learned word as he came bounding across the clearing. Stopping in front of Kostya, he showed him the fungus he had found with the pride of a keen schoolboy: 'Look – a red cap. A bullytoes, isn't it?'

Konstantin looked at the dazzlingly blood-red, sharp-pointed cap of the mushroom, spattered with dry white blobs that resembled nothing so much as sperm. Looking up at the equally mushroom-red cheeks of the lieutenant, he felt an urge to plant a goodly gobbet of spit on them, to match the pattern of the cap of this mushroom.

'It's a fly agaric,' said Kostya, and spat. He turned the mushroom over in his hands: 'You can kill flies with it if you want to.'

The lieutenant looked hopefully at Pan Tadeusz, who was perched alongside Kostya, but the Pole put on an apologetic smile and spread his hands, as if to say he would be glad to contradict if he could, but an agaric is an agaric. The lieutenant's crestfallen expression was, however, at once replaced by a flush of cheerful curiosity and enthusiasm: he was obviously not planning to give up at the sight of the first nasty toadstool and relinquish this happy opportunity to deviate from the tedium of everyday military routine.

'Why don't they all stuff themselves with fly agaric so that they croak?' Konstantin thought to himself as he fingered the toadstool. His glance was caught by the root-end of the stalk, where the white filaments merged into lumpy knobs edged with crumbs of black soil, torn-up grass-roots and weeds. The fly agaric had been pulled up with its root. If these clodhoppers found a boletus, they would do the same. No new mushroom would now grow on that accursed spot – the spot where, instead of mushrooms toadstool-like missiles, weapons of mass destruction, were now growing. Did that mean there was, after all, some common ground between Russian mushroom-hunters and British pacifists? 'What the hell are they doing to the mushrooms?' Konstantin muttered, and in that question it did not matter who 'they' were and whether mushrooms were meant at all; with the same intonation he might have been asking: 'What are they doing to people?' He nudged Pan Tadeusz in the ribs.

'Ruining all the mushrooms . . . not leaving the spawn in the ground, they're pulling them up by the roots' – and he pointed out the foot of the fly agaric to Tadeusz. 'Stand up, Tadeusz, in defence of the mushrooms. Have you got your knife with you? Hid mine in my boot-top.'

Tadeusz confirmed that he had his knife with him, but he

didn't like to stand up because this would be taken as an attempt to escape, which would lead to further questioning – and then who would serve the customers in his grocery today? But Konstantin was filled with sacrificial resolve: surely Tadeusz didn't regard a few miserable pennies as more important than the future of this mushroom-ground? Why, those pacifists were ready to give their very lives in the cause of world peace, yet when threatened with nothing but the loss of a few pence Tadeusz was making himself out to be a martyr. 'What mushroom-ground?' Pan Tadeusz enquired cautiously, ignoring the political slur about his miserliness and conformism. Konstantin then had to come clean: yes, he was referring to a particular mushroom-ground – yes, and the white boletus grew there. And what 'whites' they were!

'There's hardly a trace of fringe under their caps, I tell you! The caps are as meaty as a veal escalope! Exquisite mushrooms!' Konstantin was arousing Pan Tadeusz's interest. If he and Tadeusz didn't get to those masterpieces first and cut off their stalks neatly with knives, leaving the spawn in the ground – so that in a month or two, even before the winter frosts, the fungi would have germinated again and produced choice new mushrooms for the rejoicing of mankind – then the greedy hands of the infidel would have wrenched them up, roots and all, and that would be the end of the mushroom paradise in this quarter of the globe. Would Konstantin have revealed the secret geography of this mushroom conservation area if it hadn't been threatened with genocide by well-armed barbarians? He, Konstantin, on his own could not save this clearing and its boletus – there were too many mushrooms to be picked, one person alone couldn't manage it. Faced by the possibility of total destruction, he was prepared to share the crop with his Polish brother. Perhaps this was a test visited upon Konstantin and Tadeusz from above, specifically to bring to fruition the centuries-old longing of the Slavs for true brotherhood between each other? It would be in the name of joint resistance to the demoralising rationalism of those who could only appreciate the dull, tasteless, common British mushroom. 'And when we return home victorious, that is to say with baskets full of mushrooms, we will exchange recipes for pickling them' – Konstantin concluded his urgent plea with this idyllic picture of Slav brotherhood.

Pan Tadeusz needed no further exhortation. He was already standing up at his full height and about to make a dash for the longed-for mushroom-ground, and Konstantin, experienced conspirator that he was, had to restrain him, to take him by the elbow and instruct him in the tactics for executing their joint strategic manoeuvre. Practically without changing their languid pose, both men began to move slowly away, with pauses and gestures designed to allay suspicion, towards the bushes at the edge of the clearing, moving backwards, making short spurts and then sitting down again in the attitude of idlers taking a sun-bath. In any case, the military seemed to have forgotten about them; the lieutenant and his myrmidons had plunged wholeheartedly into this new, supposedly strategic exercise of searching for strange items of flora with different-coloured caps under the foliage at the other end of the clearing. Even the soldier who had been detailed to keep an eye on the prisoners was poking in the grass with the muzzle of his automatic rifle, carelessly moving further and further away from his charges. Konstantin only had to pass behind one more bush in order to conceal himself in the safe density of a woodland thicket. Pan Tadeusz, with the impatience of an inexperienced pupil, was tugging at his sleeve, egging him on to make the final dash – only another ten paces – and in a moment they were on the edge of the fateful patch of land, the mushroom paradise. In the twinkling of an eye Tadeusz's back was seen flickering between the trunks of a clump of American oak. He was still hoping to be the first to reach the boletus. But the ideal of Slav brotherhood was unlikely to be attained in the lifetime of Kostya's generation of Soviet Russians: how could they ever trust the Poles? In mushroom matters the Pole was the scourge of God! Let him prance around in the thicket – without a guide, without an Ivan Susanin in the person of Konstantin he would only lose his way and there would be nothing left for him to do but eat toadstools and ferns. Konstantin grinned as he watched Pan Tadeusz leaping around ineffectively on the edge of the wood, pulling questioning faces, waving invitingly to Konstantin and begging for further instructions with every possible mimicry and grimace. Konstantin hid himself out of Tadeusz's field of vision, moving towards a hazel-bush with the stealth of a Cossack scout. He got up from his knees, preparing to make the last dash. He no longer had any doubt about the success of his well-calculated little operation and his muscles, taut as violin strings, were playing a victory march. With a crisp, familiar gesture he pulled his knife out of his boot-top, straightened up to his full height – and in one bound he was past the bush, in the heart of the mushroom kingdom.

There, however, he found a pair of hostile eyes staring straight at him.

'Murderer,' said Clea in an ominous voice. She was standing a few paces in front of him, a damp, sweaty lock of her short haircut falling over her forehead, her lips compressed into a twisted hyphen, her fists clenched so tightly that the knuckles showed white. She seemed to be personally defending not only Pan Tadeusz and any other future victims of Kostya the cannibal but the entire woodlands of England. Either that, or the forest was drawn up in ranks behind her, its commander, in the batttle against Kostya the mushroom-hunter. Noticing the sickly white of her face, puffy from lack of sleep, her eye-sockets hollow as though eaten out by snails, her sparse, ash-blond fringe, he muttered with revulsion:

'Toadstool! You pale yellow toadstool!' and gripped his knife tighter. For in the distance, behind him and to the left, an incomprehensible noise was heard and it was growing louder. Konstantin looked round nervously: from the steep hillside that ran down from the edge of the wood where he was standing he had a clear view of the barbed-wire perimeter and the guardhouse of the missile base. Something incredible was happening down there. Crowds of people carrying placards had filled the training area and, making energetic use of the poles on which their placards were mounted, were boldly smashing a breach in the wire fence. A man had climbed up on to the roof of the guardhouse and had begun, gesticulating ferociously, to address the crowd with an inflammatory speech, now and again pointing to the missile-emplacements behind him. Soldiers of the guard detachment were dashing ineffectively around the base: left without a commander, they had no idea what action to take and were putting up only passive resistance to the rampaging horde of unilateralists. Kostya recognised the orator on the guardhouse roof as Anthony, and he almost waved to him in greeting, being reminded of Stalin on top of Lenin's tomb. He suddenly felt a sense of solidarity with this demagogue, or rather not so much solidarity as a feeling of shared hatred for the lieutenant, who was scouring the bushes in search of mushrooms: his, Konstantin's mushrooms and in his own stretch of forest, now given over to the destructive pounding of soldiers' boots, the boots of militarism. Even though he could not sympathise with pacifism, at least he was glad of the harm that this anti-nuclear demonstration would do to the lieutenant's career personally and to the Ministry of Defence in general.

The panic in the enemy's camp was evident: having torn himself free from the clutches of the demonstrators, a sentry was running up the hillside towards the edge of the wood, waving his arms and yelling his head off as he ran. From behind the bushes to Kostya's right came the alarmed voices of the guard troops, followed by the first brisk, shouted orders; the lieutenant had clearly snapped out of his fascination with mushrooms. 'The charge of espionage will be dropped because it's so obviously absurd,' Kostya thought feverishly, but the infuriated lieutenant would undoubtedly implicate Konstantin in a diversionary conspiracy with the demonstrators to deceive the military with this phoney mushroom-hunt, carefully planned to distract the attention of the guard. Now he would be arrested; he would never see that clearing again and no doubt Tadeusz the Pole meanwhile, under cover of all this fuss, had harvested every last boletus to sell in his stinking little shop.

'Out of my way, Nuclea, I'm serious. Go off and join your pacifist friends, you little fool,' Kostya said hoarsely, glowering at Clea. She did not move. 'Go away, toadstool!' he hissed at her. The blade of his knife gleamed dully in the sunlight as Konstantin strode forward. Without taking her wide-eyed, terrified gaze from the blade pointing at her, Clea screamed. Racked as she was with thoughts of Konstantin's vengeful nature, of the confrontation between two worlds and of the world-wide conspiracy of male chauvinism, how could it ever have occurred to her that the knife had not been sharpened to pierce her ribs but to save the mushroom-spawn in the nearby clearing? In any case, she forgot all about ideological clashes at that moment: she could see nothing but the infuriated face of a foreign barbarian, clutching a razor-sharp knife, and fearing that in a second she would no longer be alive, that she, who had longed all her life for affection and consolation, would soon be a bleeding chunk of dead, flayed flesh; that fear filled her lungs and exploded through her wide-open mouth in a wild, piercing, animal scream. Konstantin lunged forward to silence that scream, hastened on by twigs crackling under army boots behind him. Clea fell to her knees, covering her face with her hands. She saw nothing of what happened next.

She did not see that in full view of the dumbfounded Konstantin and of the lieutenant and his men, who were approaching Konstantin from behind, there jumped out of the bushes behind Clea's back a creature whose boniness and pallid, contorted features gave him the look of a ghost. This long-legged apparition flew out of the undergrowth in one leap without seeming to touch the ground and fell upon Konstantin, seizing hold of him like a gigantic bat and trying to beat him to the ground. Konstantin swayed, staggered backwards in the attempt to throw off this evil wood-demon, tripped, lost his footing and collapsed backwards into a hazel-bush, pulling his live, clawing burden down with him. As he fell he hit his side against a projecting branch, but it felt to him that he had impaled himself on his own knife, which was still gripped in his hand, and that he was now somehow suspended from the blade as though on a coat-hanger. Something like a huge brown lump of nausea swam before his eyes – perhaps because he had seen, a centimetre away from his face, the heap of his own dung that he had deposited there the previous night. 'Good thing I didn't fall slap into it. That was lucky,' he thought mechanically. He half rose and there before his eyes – evidently an effect of hitting the ground with the back of his head – the brown lump was transformed into a gigantic, blood-red fly agaric mushroom, only instead of white blobs it was spotted with black ones. Finally the agaric began to shrivel, its outlines shrank and became distinct: Konstantin discovered that beside him there lay the body of a man, from whose stomach that blood-red toadstool was growing; a moment later he realised it was not a fly agaric at all but a huge bloodstain that was slowly oozing through the torn shirt of the body sprawled beside him. The body was crushing his right arm, and when he succeeded with difficulty in freeing his hand, something fell from it to the ground – a knife, stained with blood up to the handle. His knife. A mushroom-picker's knife. As though he had been using it to try to cull a gigantic, blood-red fly agaric, preserving the spores in the soil – in the stomach – so that more fly agarics would grow there again and again each mushroom season. But this was utterly absurd: how could an experienced mushroom-picker flatter himself at encouraging the spread of fly agaric? There were some mushrooms that one might confuse with toadstools and vice-versa – but a fly agaric?!

It finally sank into his consciousness that the lunatic who had jumped on him out of the bushes had impaled himself on his, Kostya's, knife as he fell. It was at least a blessing that the gnarled branch had not punctured Kostya's side. Otherwise there would have been two corpses, and Clea would not have had enough vocal chords to bemoan two corpses in the way that she was now wailing over one – as though the body belonged to her closest relative instead of some unknown maniac given to attacking Russian mushroom-pickers. Konstantin found even the corpse's outward appearance repellent: a face that seemed to have been daubed with whitewash, the face of an immature but ageing youth with a crest of punk-style hair dyed in rainbow colours like a peacock's tail that stuck out in all directions; with the crimson stain on his stomach he looked like a wild, exotic bird that had escaped from a zoo and fallen into a trap. Clea was kneeling beside this stiffening freak and swaying back and forth as she wailed, without tears, wailed, repeating like an incantation:

'Colin! Colin! Colin!' She was repeating the mysterious word 'Colin', which nevertheless sounded as if it might be Russian. Perhaps she was intending to say: 'Kosyta', meaning 'Kostya did it', but was confusing the names Colin and Kostya? 'Why did he have to fall on my knife?' – Konstantin looked around at the narrowing circle of soldiers and demonstrators closing in on him. From far away came the howl of a police siren. 'Why did he have to fall on my knife? I was collecting mushrooms – why should he want to fall on my knife?' said Konstantin, excusing himself to goodness knows who in Russian, but his words were drowned by Clea's wailing as she repeated Colin's name like a cuckoo, moaning hysterically that Colin had wanted to save her, he had wanted to save her and no one else, no one else – except, perhaps, himself. And Jean-Jacques Rousseau.

Colin's funeral took place near where he lived, in one of those interminable London suburbs that are still called London but in reality are an untidy jumble of rows of houses, rejected by the city's centre and piled up into hamlets, between which stretch waste lands and parks, muddy hollows and abandoned factories. Clea had to make three changes on the journey, travelling first by Underground, then by the ordinary train, and finally by bus. This was the journey that Colin's mother and Colin himself made every day on her way to the office, like pilgrims of some mysterious sect who set off to bow down to an idol at the other end of the earth, only to journey back again to their wild cave-dwellings. As she rattled along in train and bus, Clea could think only of how she would go up to the grave into which they would lower Colin's body and place the copy of Rousseau's *Confessions* on the lid of his coffin, as though that book, which had been gathering dust on her bookshelf for years, was the only debt that she had not repaid to Colin in his lifetime. She had, after all, promised Colin's father to give his Christmas present to his son and she had not kept her promise. She had deceived father, son and Holy Ghost. Colin had followed her every footstep, evidently, because he wanted to get his Christmas present back from her. Everything had started with that undelivered book; she would not have stayed in the office for the Christmas party had it not been for her promise to hand the book over to Colin, and Colin would not have attacked her that night near the back entrance and the refuse-containers. It was because of that, too, that Colin had been thrown off course, the course followed by his parents and forebears, the Pilgrims' Way of the working class – from a cold house by public transport to a stuffy workplace and back – and had fallen into a whirlpool of events that it was not given to him to understand, into a conflict between East and West played out in a forest clearing. She would lay this book in his grave, as reading-matter to take on the journey from the stuffy office of this world to the cold house of eternity.

There was, however, no grave. It had never occurred to her, of course, that Colin's mother could not afford a gravestone and that the funeral would take place in a crematorium. She followed the coffin, among an unprepossessing bunch of relatives, from the gates of the cemetery to the 'chapel' where the officiating clergyman pronounced the prayer about 'ashes to ashes', so suitable for a crematorium, pressed the appropriate button and made the coffin disappear behind a little curtain of mourning material. During the few moments of standing in farewell around the bier she could not bring herself to unwrap the paper around the book; it was out of place – the paper would have rustled and people would have glared at her. Besides, one can hardly throw a book into a crematorium oven. On the other side of the chapel, she noticed Colin's father, huddled in a corner, obviously afraid of coming any nearer to the coffin for fear of his wife having hysterics. Clea caught his eye; his expression seemed to flash her a hullo, and he even twitched his hand in an absurd half-greeting, pretending to smooth his hair, but when the ceremony was over and Clea decided to return the book to him – it was his, after all – Colin's father had vanished. She turned to Colin's mother and began to explain something to her as she proffered the book, but Mrs Macalasky, with her fish-like, tear-reddened eyes and her breath that smelled of gin, suddenly began to shout at Clea, right there in the crematorium, and her voice reverberated in a booming echo from the tiled, vaulted, church-like roof: 'Communist!' shouted Colin's mother. 'Married a communist you did, so as to murder our English boys!' Frightened by these hysterical cries, by the incomprehensible change in her colleague's behaviour and her own total inability to say so much as a word in her own defence, Clea was propelled outside by a salvo of disgusted and hostile looks.

To reach the bus-stop she had to cross a piece of deserted parkland, thinly grown with bushes, stunted birch-trees and uncut grass. She was about to lean against the trunk of a birch in order to stop for a moment and compose herself, but she immediately stepped back, having noticed several huge clots of blood in the grass at her feet. She knelt down and parted the strands of withered grass: there shone a clump of unbearably red mushrooms on snow-white stalks, their crimson caps spattered with blobs of what looked like white, coagulated spit. She had a mental vision of Colin in the grass with his stomach ripped open. Under each mushroom's cap there hung down a white fringe – like the hem of a lace petticoat under a crimson-red skirt. Gripping the fragile stem with two fingers, Clea carefully pulled these mushrooms, nature's bloodstains, out of the ground, made a large cone out of the paper in which Rousseau had been wrapped and, all the way home from the funeral, with three changes, she carried this venomous harvest like a new-born baby.

A letter was lying on the doormat, and as she went through to the kitchen Clea opened the envelope and glanced at the final paragraph of the letter: '. . . when you feel you have fully recovered. May the death of this working-class boy, who, though he was not very bright, was a seeker after the truth, serve as a warning to those who turn our woods and vales into bases for nuclear missiles. Next week, by the way, at my suggestion, we are starting a seminar on mushroom-picking. As our last protest demonstration showed, the idea of gathering mushrooms on Ministry of Defence land is an excellent manoeuvre which we unilateralists could well adopt as a weapon with the aim of causing confusion to the militarists in this country. Why shouldn't we call ourselves "mushroomers"? I know it's a rather crude pun on the expression "mushroom-cloud", but even so – just let the police try and charge us with unlawful assembly when hundreds of partisans of peace turn up in front of the barbed wire of missile bases armed with – mushroom baskets! We're not against missiles – we stand for the freedom to pick mushrooms! That should be our slogan. In this connection, would it not be possible somehow to recruit Konstantin? He could give a short lecture on the various sorts of mushrooms – so that we could know what we were looking for on the ground and be fully briefed if we are arrested and questioned. I think he might be interested in this kind of educational work. I realise that at the moment your personal relations with him are somewhat strained, but I hope you will be able to put the interests of society above your family disagreements. With kindest regards, see you soon – Yours, Anthony.'

Clea folded the letter into four and tore it into small pieces.

Since Konstantin's arrest the house had felt as empty as a woman's womb after an abortion. She went into the kitchen and began to collect into a pile all the preserves, all the smoked foods and pickles in their bundles, pots and jars, the fruits of Konstantin's culinary genius. She carried it all out into the garden, where she heaped it up on the lawn. Straining with the effort, she also rolled out all the tubs of macerated apples, the salted cucumbers and marinaded tomatoes. Then she cut down the branches from the hated, half-dead birch-tree in the corner of the garden, laid them under and around the heap of mixed pickles, poured paraffin over the pile and lit it. Stinking black smoke arose from the garlic sausages and smoked fish; then the pickle-jars began to burst with resounding bangs and spurts of yellow flame when the vinegar poured out of them; the tubs, too, cracked in the fire like ribs crushed in a bear-hug. She had the impression that a human figure was moving and crouching in the pillar of black smoke, a figure in which puffs of malodorous smoke were protruding like human organs, turned inside out by convulsions that separated them from each other – skin from bone, bone from body, body from soul – and that a black soul was belching tongues of flame as it gasped, squealed and howled; it was the fire of her personal inquisition, and in the dense, writhing puffs of smoke Clea recognised Konstantin, venting his fury in streams of pickling-liquid as though it were jets of diabolical sulphur. She was subjecting this accursed stranger to the cleansing fire and now, howling and spitting out his acetic venom, he was disappearing in clouds of smoke to the sound of a vicious hiss.

With a sense of duty done, she returned to the kitchen. There she selected the largest salad bowl and began to slice into it the fly agaric that she had picked, cleaning off only the lumps of earth and the root-strands. Then she poured vinegar and sunflower oil over the shredded toadstools, not forgetting to put salt and pepper on these gory slices and then, having seated herself comfortably, she began with intense concentration to eat this lethal mixture, thoroughly chewing each piece as she had been taught in childhood, her lips, tongue and palate cherishing the intolerably bitter, alkaline taste of the fly agaric. A feeling like heartburn gradually spread from her throat to her chest, oozing thence over her whole body, which was starting to go numb yet tender like a swelling abscess. Or that was her impression when, having emptied the bowl, she neatly wiped her lips with a table-napkin and began to wait impatiently, as she had during chemistry experiments at school, to feel the effects of the mushroom poison. Through the kitchen window, as through the glass of a retort, puffs of black smoke were still floating from the smouldering remnants of the Great Russian Experiment. To kill time (the word 'kill' sounded in her brain like a ridiculous pun), she began mechanically to leaf through the ill-omened volume of Rousseau, or more precisely the scholarly preface to the book, which until then she had never bothered to read; her glance slid over the lines of print as if they were something seen through the window of a train, or perhaps everything was simply floating before her eyes as the agaric poison seeped into her bloodstream:

'In summarising Rousseau's ideology, one might say that, having rejected the doctrines of the Catholic church, Jean-Jacques Rousseau had torn himself away from the body of Christ, union with which is conferred through the ritual of communion, thus also depriving himself of the right to ritual confession, which grants remission of sins through participation in the mystery of the Passion of the Saviour. Religious confession, which centres on God, became a literary "Confession" of which Rousseau himself was the centre. The poison of guilt, no longer expiated through the church's ritual of communion and confession, began to accumulate in his mind as in a sealed vessel full of sin. Hence his self-hatred and fear of exposure, from which it is but a step to persecution mania. His was persecution mania of a particular kind: others, he would say to himself, may guess how sinful I am and exploit my sins for their own selfish ends. Forestalling his enemies, real or imagined, Rousseau proceeded to expose himself, to make his confession to the whole of mankind. This self-exposure took the form either of literal exhibitionism, as in the sexual deviations of his youthful years, or in the allegedly uncompromising admission of his own base acts in his years of maturity. Having, however, placed himself at the centre of the universe, when making these admissions Rousseau was in no way concerned with the fate of the victims of his own baseness: for him it was primarily important to prove to the world at large that he had expiated his unseemly behaviour by his suffering – as, for instance, in the story of the servant-girl who was dismissed from her place thanks to a slanderous accusation made by Rousseau, who had himself committed the theft in question. "I may not be any better than others, but at least I am different from others" – he writes in the opening lines of his *Confessions*. Admission of his own sins thereby becomes an end in itself and is stimulated by a belief in his own uniqueness.'

She tried to penetrate the meaning of what was written, but could not concentrate: not because the words were becoming muddled as they floated before her eyes, but because somehow she seemed to have long ago come to these same conclusions through her own experience – yet she was simply unable correctly to equate her own inner knowledge with other people's words affirming the same things. Rousseau's name when written in Russian somehow sounded russified: *Russo*. Was she a russophobe? She shut the book, then opened it again at random:

'One day we were taking a walk in a part of the countryside that was densely grown with thickets of buckthorn. I observed that the berries on these bushes were ripe; out of curiosity, I sampled one or two of them and, finding the berries tolerably pleasant, slightly sharp to the taste, I began to pick and eat them in order to quench my thirst. The worthy M. Bovier was standing nearby, without touching the berries and without uttering a word. One of our companions approached us and, seeing that I was feasting on these berries, exclaimed: "What are you doing, monsieur?! Do you not know that those berries are poisonous?" – "Poisonous?" I cried, in utter astonishment. "But of course they are poisonous!" heard I in reply. "Everyone knows that. It would never enter my head to touch them!" – I turned to M. Bovier and asked him: "Why did you not warn me of this?" – "Oh, monsieur," replied the latter, bowing respectfully, "I considered it impolite to interfere!"'

Clea tried to remember what buckthorn berries looked like, but all she could remember was Kostya's dictum that buckthorn was a good laxative. The real or imagined cramps in her stomach reminded her of the fly agaric, which seemed to be growing upwards from somewhere under her heart, creeping up her throat and out. She felt a wave of nausea. Doubled up with pain, she dashed to the bathroom, fell on her knees in front of the lavatory-pan and began to vomit. She spewed up everything that had accumulated inside her over all these years: Kostya's sperm and slavophilism, vegetarianism and the radioactive exhalations of tea, pacifism and Margot's condescension, fly agaric and the Soviet regime, East and West, the Third World and the drabness of English life. She got up from her knees, groped blindly for the handle of the cistern and flushed the lavatory. Swaying, she went to the telephone and dialled the number for the emergency ambulance service.

10 THE TRIAL

The trial dragged on for weeks; Konstantin was clearly threatened by a stiff prison sentence, despite all the efforts of his counsel to present the affair as an accident, an absurd but tragic mistake in which no one was to blame. Of course it never occurred to anyone to see Konstantin as a cold-blooded murderer, but from the viewpoint of the judge and jury his degree of responsibility for manslaughter could well mean several years behind bars.

I remember that when I happened to come across the first newspaper reports of the trial, I simply grinned maliciously: another stupid English girl entangled with a Russian con-artist who has been getting up to his tricks abroad. Gradually, however, this criminal trial at the Old Bailey, spiced with an over-familiar 'Russian' flavour, began to expand from a joke into a London scandal. For in the course of the trial, during his cross-examination of witnesses, conducted with typically English doggedness, and in his remarks to the bench and to the jury, Konstantin's counsel built up an image of his client as someone whose life-history and circumstances would, in the eyes of the jury, absolve him of practically all responsibility for the crime that he had committed. All was grist to this lawyer's mill – above all the Soviet origins of the accused. In this he had a completely free hand, since both judge and jury – and, indeed, counsel himself – had only the haziest conception of Soviet life, which in their minds was limited, I should think, to an opera scenario in which the Soviet Army marches across Red Square to bar the way to foreign journalists trying to interview Sakharov, who sits reading Solzhenitsyn in *samizdat*, while the KGB, from a space satellite, watches Baryshnikov dancing a ballet in New York. Brought up in an orphanage where he was fed on putrefying human flesh, the accused, according to the legend spun by his counsel, had lived in permanent fear of labour-camp and prison, of being beaten up or shot by the brutal executioners of Soviet power – hence his constant mistrust and suspicion of everyone around him, hence his readiness to defend himself against the enemy within and without. This victim of the regime had been brave enough to defy the threats of the authorities and the bureaucratic obstacles, and to break through the Iron Curtain. But what had awaited him on the other side of that Iron Curtain? Here counsel began to touch on what was a sore point for the British, which they felt as a national disgrace – their traditional xenophobia. Unable to speak the language, lacking suitable professional qualifications – and which of us has not known the horrors of unemployment? – this freedom-loving foreigner, a political refugee, dreaming of liberty and democracy, had come face to face with a cold and hostile world unwilling to extend a helping hand, a world that regarded him as some kind of foreign freak, thereby exacerbating his already over-developed instinct of self-preservation and making him react to an imaginary threat with redoubled aggressiveness. Whither might such a man turn for support? Here the barrister cast a grim and reproachful glance at Clea, Margot and Anthony, who were sitting in the courtroom. Is it not his wife, counsel enquired rhetorically, who should play that vital role in the life of an immigrant cast up on a cold and unwelcoming shore? What did this victim of the Soviet regime and of the hard-hearted British find in his domestic hearth? At this point the lawyer seized the opportunity to underline what Clea and her friends were: a gaggle of lesbians, homosexuals, irresponsible pacifists and Trotskyites! As he skilfully questioned the witnesses, the first of whom were Clea, Margot and Anthony, he insistently pursued the idea that the political views of the participants in this sorry episode were the immediate result of their moral disintegration and their sexual inclinations, which he invariably described as perverted; in turn, he linked these inclinations with their political views, which he invariably called 'Trotskyite', 'extremist' and generally ultra-leftist, allowing it to be understood that people who held these views were, even if not directly working for Soviet intelligence, clearly serving it unawares.

All this produced an uproar in the press. Protests were flung around from all directions. Photographs of Margot bending over the weeping Clea (two lesbians!), or of Anthony with his hand on Colin's shoulder in the office (homosexual trying to recruit his lover to work for Soviet intelligence!) were splashed all over the tabloids; the newspapers drew everyone willy-nilly into the story of the 'trial of the century', and the daily reports from the courtroom were discussed everywhere – in factory canteens, in offices, on the street and at home around the television set.

Nor did I escape this media hullabaloo: in a series of interviews in the national press I explained to the naive British the subtleties of the Soviet passport system – how difficult it was for ordinary citizens to leave the USSR; how, once having left the country by marrying a foreigner, it was often very difficult to get permission for a visit to the Soviet Union, to say nothing of the fact that even those who had emigrated officially were still classified as enemies of the people. In other words, I concluded, with my characteristic gift for aphorism – the Iron Curtain is far from rusty.

The Soviet embassy, put on the spot by the rumours that began to grow up around this trial, decided to show its hand: the embassy issued an official protest note, in which it was stated that the proceedings against Konstantin were a show-trial – an act of political revenge on a Soviet citizen, an attempt to blacken the Soviet system by crude juggling with the facts so as to prove the allegedly criminal character of the accused; the embassy insisted that his guilt or innocence should be decided by a Soviet court, and that if he were found guilty, Soviet law would punish the accused according to his deserts. In conclusion the note demanded the immediate repatriation of this Soviet citizen to his own country. This immediately produced a statement in parliament by a Labour MP: while it was true that he did not wholly share the Soviet embassy's viewpoint on the matter, this member nonetheless took the opportunity to accuse the corrupt system of British jurisprudence of having become a pliant tool in the hands of the Conservative government, which was creating an anti-Soviet furore about human rights around the extremely dubious figure of the accused, at a moment when the striking workers of Great Britian were being battered insensible by police truncheons. This parliamentarian was in turn supported in the press by a spokesman for the Campaign for Nuclear Disarmament, who announced that this trial of a Soviet citizen was one more example of the fostering of aggressive attitudes towards the Soviet Union; Great Britain, he declared, was blindly copying the United States in its propaganda campaign for a liberalisation of the East European regimes, without possessing either the moral basis or the strategic superiority to do so; the current trial of a Soviet citizen, therefore, served no purpose except further to increase international tension and the risk of a third world war. This was countered by a Conservative member of the European Parliament in an interview with *The Times*, in which he called upon the British public not to be taken in by biassed interpretations of the Soviet legal system and not to repeat the tragic mistakes of the past, when after the Second World War thousands of Soviet prisoners of war had been handed over to the Soviet authorities and had been immediately shipped off to the labour camps or simply shot in the cellars of the Lubyanka.

In short, the political point-scoring and the misinterpretations of the case in the press reached such dimensions that counsel for both prosecution and defence vied with one another in requesting the court that this prejudicial press treatment of the trial be stopped until the end of the proceedings. Several newspapers were fined for contempt of court, but it did no good; Konstantin's counsel then made use of this to demand a retrial with a new jury and the calling of more witnesses for the defence. His tactic was to postpone the hearing for as long as possible, at the same time gaining the bench's leave to release the accused on bail pending the opening of a new trial. No less than counsel, the judge had been infuriated by political interference in the judicial process and without much hesitation he granted permission for a retrial.

Imagine my astonishment when one fine day I received a letter from the solicitors representing Konstantin; on a sheet of heavy, expensive, watermarked paper embossed with the firm's name and a two-column list of its partners, in a flowery style full of elegant syntactical *longueurs*, the letter informed me that I was invited to be a witness for the defence in the capacity of a literary expert. Would I therefore agree to a preliminary meeting with the accused and his counsel, in order that an explanation might be given to me of the extremely important role that my appearance in court might play in the course of the trial? Intrigued, I gave my consent. It was in any case pointless to refuse, since the solicitors had already taken out a subpoena in the name of Elizabeth II, By the Grace of God etc., etc., etc., according to which I was summoned to appear as a witness before Her Majesty's Justices of the Central Criminal Court – a summons that in England, as we know, may only be declined in case of death.

During my visit to the remand cell in which Konstantin was being held, I was surprised not only by his manner of speech and his ideas – of that more later; having read the daily newspaper reports of this scandalous case, which had been hogging the front pages of the yellow press, I was expecting to see a semi-literate halfwit, a classic Russian peasant lout. But instead of a potato-like nose rendered spongy by alcohol, flabby cheeks and patches of baldness, I saw a thin-lipped monster holding every wrinkle and crisp fold of his face under tight control; he was a direct descendant of Rakhmetov and Bazarov, those grim, humourless, puritanical radicals of nineteenth-century Russian literature, who in the Soviet epoch had requalified from home-grown zoologists dissecting frogs to being engineers of human souls. What surprised me most of all were his tortoiseshell-rimmed spectacles: they somehow did not tally with the Konstantin of whom I had been hearing from newspaper reports. His spectacle-frames emphasised even more strongly the circlets of his greyish eyes, the irises of which were flecked with a fierce, cat-like yellow. Unlike most Russians, he did not shift his gaze, but on the contrary would fix his stare on you and wait until you, no longer able to stand the ensuing pause, would begin to mumble something compromising or apologetic. He felt himself under no obligation to act out a charade of mutual comprehension. 'Take me as I am – like it or lump it,' his whole attitude proclaimed.

This impression was perhaps intensified by the fact that at the moment of our encounter he was in solitary confinement, a prisoner in a one-man, white-tiled cell. Had it not been for the bed and the minimal bedside locker, the place could have been an isolation cell for violent patients in a mental hospital, or even an aquarium from which the water had been drained. A hypocritical list of the prisoner's rights was fastened to the door, including the right to receive visits, correspondence and food parcels; its only effect was to register officially the fact that Konstantin was cut off from the outside world and could, in consequence, allow himself to disregard that world. In particular, he could disregard me – although it might seem that it was he and not I who was interested in our meeting.

People like him frightened me: over the years that I had lived in England I had grown used to a certain ritual of responsiveness from one's collocutor, as when, on hearing something that you find unacceptable, you nevertheless try to understand the other's point of view by a nod of the head in token of temporary agreement, by a well-meaning 'Well, yes, I suppose so,' allowing the other person to formulate his thought in an atmosphere that is not one of attack with its subsequent blockade, but in freedom, without embarrassment; and only gradually do you bring into the conversation those inevitable 'buts' or 'excuse me's' with which you attempt by degrees to make your opponent change his mind. In Konstantin's eyes, however, intransigence had frozen into a kind of permafrost, a conviction rooted once and for all, that it was impossible to make anyone change their mind and that each person should stick to his own opinion. He possessed the smug, cast-iron pessimism of a man convinced that he is surrounded by knaves and fools. I had a choice: to number myself among the knaves or to enrol as a fool. Naturally I was not attracted to either alternative, and from the very first minutes I found this meeting extremely painful.

'Why did that dimwit have to skewer himself on the knife? Who could possibly have imagined that I was going to murder Clea? Except Clea herself, of course,' he argued irritably, as he carefully spooned Greek yoghurt out of a small plastic tub. 'It restores the white cells in the blood, or maybe the red cells, I'm not sure. Anyway, it fortifies the body's defensive system. Would you like a spoonful?'

I can't stand yoghurt. I was regretting that I had given way – for the last time, I hope – to a false sense of Russian solidarity in agreeing to our meeting. The lawyer's initiative and my role in this trial struck me as more and more ambiguous. In the hearing so far, Konstantin's barrister had, as I have said, tried to cobble together for the jury's benefit a kind of surrogate for Konstantin in the shape of something like a Karamazov brother who had lived through Tolstoy's war and peace and had dreamed of marrying one of Chekhov's three sisters. I had now been summoned by counsel to attest to the complexity of Konstantin's Russian soul and, in particular, to the fact that he belonged to that peculiarly Russian clan, the creative intelligentsia, obsessed as it is by the ideals of freedom and justice. To that end I had been given a thick manuscript – half novel, half philosophical treatise: this work, when interpreted by my skill as a reviewer, was supposed to serve in court as proof that its author, Konstantin, was no ordinary accused but a Russian dissident writer, indeed almost a friend and companion-in-arms of Solzhenitsyn.

With the *naïveté* of a foreigner who perceives foreign countries rather as does, shall we say, a spectator at an opera, the lawyer had actually been prepared to make a similar request to Solzhenitsyn himself: it had never occurred to him that this opponent of any kind of contraceptive measures, whether in bed or in public controversy, would refuse. Solzhenitsyn's candidature for the task, however, had not suited him because of the Soviet fundamentalist's well-known political views – views which would have only poured oil on the flames that were already raging around this trial. Having made the appropriate enquiries, the barrister had therefore chosen me. I was suitable in every respect: on the one hand I was regarded as a Russian writer of fiction and therefore able to judge both the philosophical and literary virtues of Konstantin's treatise; on the other hand, I was known to the Western public through my novels that had been translated into French and English (though without, I must admit, any great success). Apart from that I had a modest name from having published short essays in English in a certain prestigious London literary weekly. My chief value, however, was that I was politically neutral: I had never openly expressed my political views in a single interview – indeed, I apparently had no such views; in short – Russian; a very high reputation among the élite; no extreme political views (i.e. a moderate conservative) – an ideal candidate from the standpoint of Konstantin's defence counsel. His only miscalculation was in the matter of my literary tastes and preferences, since he had not taken the trouble to read a single line of any of my works.

Written in a ledger and entitled with brazen simplicity *Homesickness*, the bulky manuscript that I was given to read put me off from the start by its obtrusively simplistic, I would even say 'village-idiot' tone, a certain consciously vulgar language that was meant to sound as if written by a plain-speaking simpleton from the lower depths of the working class – a tone very widespread among writers of the generation of the 1940s, to which Konstantin belonged. They had been born in the era when the colloquial speech of the intelligentsia – the speech of friends at a civilised dinner-party – had finally disappeared from general use, replaced by the barbaric jargon of compulsory political meetings. The users and propagators of this mode of speech had been arrested, and the erstwhile *habitués* of metropolitan 'salons' had vanished into a literary underground. Those who survived and continued to speak in public now held forth in Party gobbledegook, the new Soviet duck-speak, and were regarded as traitors to Russian literature. Thus the proponents of delightful chatter, of that wonderful inconsequence in conversation, of the 'sparkle lurking in the depths of the eyes' had discredited themselves – both from the official standpoint as enemies of the people and from the standpoint of the literary underground as the venal class in Russian society that had been the initiator and activist of bloody revolution. Thus in semi-official literary circles there arose the need for a new hero, a new Soviet conversational model: a kind of Soviet hick, who had to have served in the army (which from the authorities' angle made him a loyal citizen) but simultaneously having a streak of the populist peasant victim who had endured much at the hands of Soviet bureaucracy, imbued with a primeval hatred of revolutionary 'infidels', and who slipped in pearls of anti-Soviet wisdom between the lines. But most important of all – this personage always talked through dummy figures, in order always to leave open a line of retreat and to be able to deny his own words. A character who hid, as I have said, behind consciously vulgar speech that was always reported, never direct; who did not converse but told stories – as if they were documentary evidence – that were supposedly not his own but on the instructions of and in the name of someone else, like some literary simpleton who could only repeat what he had been told.

Such heroes are inclined to ignore their own times as something temporary, transient, and if they refer to them at all then only ever via historical analogies with other epochs, thereby driving any clear thoughts about their own country into that dark forest of parallels and meridians that is the general historical geography of our planet. It was therefore not surprising that Konstantin made his hero to be a historian – of indeterminate philosophical persuasion but possessing on the other hand an inexhaustible capacity for peering through the prism of other epochs – a prism unclouded by the political prejudice characteristic of those whose civil education was obtained by time spent behind prison bars or in long talks with officers of the security forces. Konstanin's hero was above all that. While remaining a Soviet citizen, he was both married to an Englishwoman and living with a mistress. Neither the Iron Curtain nor the Soviet Visa Office existed as far as this professor was concerned; nor did the Soviet regime as Solzhenitsyn understands it – namely one huge prison-camp – exist for him either. A Russia of course, did exist; a Russia with its special peculiarities: its traditions and its religion, its history and its political upheavals; but it was only one of the many countries in the world. Not until he came to England did he rediscover that same Russia as something unique, tragic, messianic and chosen. Through 'homesickness', through the experience of parting and the agony of separation, he had, in the wake of the hero of his historical research, discovered that Russia.

Once in England, this professor of history studied the biography of an eighteenth-century Russian serf, a certain Appeles Zyablov. This Appeles, a bonded peasant belonging to the Boyar Struisky (a petty tyrant notorious for having a torture-chamber in the cellars of his country mansion, equipped with the last word in the Marquis-de-Sade technology of the time), amazed his master with his unique culinary skills, his congenital talents as a chef, which had been revealed quite by chance when the Boyar Struisky had entered Appeles Zyablov's cottage to give him a whipping (without the slightest cause; merely for the sake of good order and to relieve the stiffness in his arm), and had found the serf engaged in frying the tubers of an exotic American fruit known as the 'potato'. It was with potatoes that the Boyar's late wife, Boyarina Struiskaya, an erstwhile concubine of Peter the Great, had poisoned herself by making soup out of the leaves and stalks of this exotic fruit from the West Indies. The serf Zyablov, however, had been frying these same tubers, cut into slices of equal size, in butter, and had pressingly invited his master to sample this infidel recipe with him. The Boyar Struisky, for all his severity, was a lover of the arts and appreciated experiments of various kinds, and although he gave Appeles a flogging for potentially ruining the Russian serfs' stomachs with these American novelties and for wasting butter, he nevertheless ate the potatoes with pleasure, and thereupon made Appeles his chef, especially to entertain visitors to his estate. Foreign guests never tired of praising the new cook, who delighted them with culinary masterpieces from the cuisines of different overseas lands. The Boyar Struisky, however, had little interest in this genius of foreign potages: despite his refinement, Struisky preferred to eat buckwheat *kasha* and sour-cabbage soup, or sometimes simply a glass of vodka and a pickled gherkin, a diet that he would maintain for weeks on end if there were no guests – and visitors were not frequent. Thus at the first opportunity Boyar Struisky traded his chef to the British ambassador in exchange for an antique hubble-bubble, with a pound of Turkish tobacco for good measure, and thought that he had got the better of the bargain.

The British ambassador took the serf Zyablov to London, where he was destined to enjoy a brilliant career. The ambassador's lunches became famous all over London, the fame of the splendid Russian cook Appeles spread throughout Albion, every aristocratic household copied his recipes, and it reached the point where he was finally granted the honour of becoming the chef for one evening at Buckingham Palace. By royal decree he was created a British subject and given a house on the banks of the Thames; newspapers wrote about him, and he won the hand of the widow of one of the richest merchants in England. What more could a man have needed, who in Russia had been regarded not as a man but a dead soul? Appeles, however, began to be seen ever more frequently in the taverns of London, where, according to rumour, he would eat raw potato-leaves as he drank his ale spiked with Cuban rum. A year later *The Times* reported that '. . . the former Russian serf, now a subject of the British crown, Appeles Zyabloff, was taken to the Royal Hospital with fatal convulsions of the stomach, in a state of nakedness, directly from the Turkish baths, where, by report of eye-witnesses, having climbed into a tub of water and chastised himself with a switch of fresh birch-branches until he drew blood, he thereupon drank down the dirty water in the tub in one gulp – mixed though it was with soap-suds and blood, having first eaten of the birch switch, soaked in the same tub-water, before swallowing the boiling concoction.' The conscientious newspaper correspondent had also made his way to Zyablov's hospital bed, where the latter explained his action as the result of homesickness, and uttered an aphorism that was long afterwards repeated by the *beau monde* of London, although no one, of course, understood the true meaning of the remark: 'There are fish here and fish over there. But one should not confuse a saucepanful of fish-soup with an aquarium.'

Only Konstantin's hero, the Soviet history professor who was studying the life of Zyablov in the archives of the British Museum's reading room, understood what Appeles was hinting at in his *obiter dictum*: a Russian, used to stewing in the fish-soup of Russian life, could not survive in the company of cold-blooded fish from the aquarium of Western civilisation.

So this former serf, having become a chef and a freeman in England, had abandoned both his Thames-side house and his rich widow and fled back to Russia, back to serfdom, back to his tyrannical, sadistic master; thereafter nothing but home-distilled vodka and pickled gherkins had passed his lips. He had committed suicide after the Boyar Struisky ordered him to prepare a dish of fish according to a French recipe, in honour of a visit to the estate by the new British ambassador. Instead of this, Appeles had prepared a quantity of Russian fish-soup in a huge sixty-gallon copper, and had then dived head-first into the boiling liquid. One can imagine the shock felt by the British diplomat when his fork speared the head of Appeles, staring at the guest with dumb reproach from the empty eye-sockets of the boiled skull. This luncheon marked a sharp deterioration in relations between the British Crown and the Throne of all the Russias.

'Having passed from a purely cerebral admiration for the West, I have arrived through my stomach at a gut Slavophilism,' said Konstantin, commenting on his epoch-making work with an ironic expression. In paraphrasing the macabre adventures of his pseudo-historical characters, I have also digressed slightly on a note of parody – not so much because of the absurd bombast and artificiality of the story about Appeles, the serf who was a culinary genius, as because of Konstantin's over-emphasis on the significance of the behaviour of the book's hero – the professor of history who is, as it were, the author's *alter ego*.

The longer I listened to Konstantin's monologues during our meeting in prison, the more complex grew the figure of the Soviet professor in his treatise. For just as rust will show through a coating of shiny oil-paint, so there emerged a sub-text of some kind of ultimate loneliness, separateness, alienation – and not only in relation to the West, where the professor-hero found himself as an emissary of Russian history, but a physiological alienation from Russia itself – Soviet Russia, of course. That eponymous 'homesickness' was a disease, a cancer, a plague, a leprosy, a pathological condition

– not only because that same nostalgia swallowed up and superseded all his other emotions, thoughts and acts, but because it was not clear that he had a homeland at all. In that sense his homesickness, his nostalgia was a mania – schizophrenia, an obsession with something that did not exist but which was simultaneously the object of all his thoughts. And so being deprived of a centre of gravity, deprived of an authentic way of life on which to model his everyday existence, he starts to blame those around him for lacking that which he himself lacks at the core of his being. This professor, with his parodic surname of 'Pokhlobkin' made up from the Russian word for 'broth', who researches the biography of a serf-cook, has, unlike his hero, no master; he is a serf without a master, without a tsar inside his head, without a master in his servile soul. At least his Appeles had something to long for – his primitive hut with its chimneyless stove that smoked directly into the room; the whips that flogged him; an established, fixed, if slavish existence. Pokhlobkin the Soviet citizen, however, who had nowhere to go back to, suffers in consequence not so much from nostalgia, not so much from homesickness as from the lack of it, the lack of that wholeness, the sense of belonging which, morbid though it may have been, was yet possessed by the serf Appeles. Full of self-disgust, he invents pretexts for disgust that are outside himself. With grim, contemptuous sarcasm he holds forth on the vulgar materialism and philistinism of Western civilisation, yet at the same time he is irritated by the slightest defect in the well-adjusted machinery of his everyday comfort; he is infuriated by the exaggerated politeness and restraint displayed by the English in their relations with each other, while at the same time being infuriated when his mistress, an interpreter at the UN, tries to have things out with him: in his eyes she becomes a virtual nymphomaniac, whose psychological importunity is disturbing his private, brittle, inner world.

In short this Professor Pokhlobkin, one felt, was almost Konstantin's analysis of himself, and the whole thing had all the makings of a tolerable novel, had it not been interspersed with interminable philosophical digressions and the heavy-handed symbolism of various recipes that the hero studied in the course of researching his biography of the serf Appeles. This insistent culinary symbolism supposed to underline the fundamental divergence of *Weltanschauung* in the gastric sense – i.e. according to the professor, the gut-religious sense – that separates East from West. Konstantin's hero was naturally a pessimist, that is to say he considered the fatal gulf in this concept to be unbridgeable and that Western man would never be able to understand the charm of the malodorous dried roach, just as the Russian would never be persuaded to eat frogs; in other words, he implied, Pushkin would always remain as incomprehensible to foreigners as Dante would always be an entrancing enigma to the Russians. A convergence of the two cultures, in fact, was a completely lost cause. The only thing that I could not understand was what this Professor Pokhlobkin was doing in fog-bound Albion. It appears that he was cultivating in himself a love of his native country; not a superficial love of the 'Slavophile' or 'Westernising' kind, but that ineradicable love which the more hopeless it is the stronger it becomes, and the stronger it is the more fanatical it becomes. 'There is nothing left for us but to love our hopeless destiny' – thus he muses during one of his solitary walks over a potato-field – his favourite geographical location; on the edge of the potato-field, where he squats down to answer the call of nature, he has a vision of the outskirts of a Russian village, a sparse wood on the horizon in the hazy evening twilight and the sodden roofs of a line of rickety, wooden, Russian peasants' cottages. It is at this moment that he thinks up the parable of the potato: a farm labourer was puffing and panting for a long time as he tugged at the stalks of a potato plant, until finally he pulled up a single potato. The tuber spoke and asked the man: 'Why did you pull me up into the light?' The labourer replied: 'So that I can eat you!' And the potato said to him: 'And I thought you were pulling me up into the daylight because I was lonely down there in the dark and rotting from the damp.'

Obviously the author of the treatise intended this parable as a warning to those who complain of the loneliness, the dark and the rotten existence in their native soil and who try to crawl out of it by emigrating to the light of the West, which, as might be expected, will simply devour a Russian along with the potato leaves which, out of homesickness, the serf Appeles had eaten as he drank his rum and ale in the taverns of London.

What annoyed me about Konstantin's hero was his tendentiousness: the author had invented him with intentions that obviously extended beyond the framework of the narrative. Given that all dubious and ambiguous points (for instance – how had this Soviet professor been allowed to live and hold forth so freely on both sides of the Iron Curtain, with an English wife and a mistress as well?) had been simply brushed aside, the authorial tone was remarkable for its inconsistency, its ingratiating attitude towards the reader, its reliance on his understanding, as though the author possessed limitless credit: I promise to make ends meet, he seemed to be saying, so meanwhile be patient! Because of this, the narrative was littered with corrections, inconsistencies, slips of the pen and stylistic lapses; everything about this hero was imprecise and fuzzy – it was all 'as if', 'suddenly . . .' 'by curious coincidence'; everything in the story happened by chance, yet was at the same time subordinate to an ultimate aim and therefore lacked internal consistency. It was the monologue of a double agent (between East and West) who was flung alternatively into the heat and the cold, both spurious, who tried to convince you, the reader, of the ultimately honourable intentions of his double-dealing: the hero and, I suspected, Konstantin were both secretly inclined towards a certain primitive form of anarchism, a rejection of any social structure, a back-to-the-soil urge, an inclination to opt out and simply grow potatoes on the outskirts of life. It was anarchism as a non-acceptance of any kind of spiritual order, hierarchy, way of life.

Significantly, the only person with whom this professor had any rapport in England was a loner among the inhabitants of the Western world – a home-grown anarchist. This anarchist had kept his wife in the equivalent of prison for four years: when he found out that his wife had fallen out of love with him and wanted to leave home, he had fastened an explosive charge to his body and tied himself and his wife together in such a way that if either of them were to go more than ten metres away from the other, the wire would tauten, the bomb would explode and both of them would have been blown to pieces. It was moral blackmail. Amazingly, the wife had tolerated this moral blackmail, and had ended up by loving her jailer-husband. She had somehow come to terms with him, had got to know him better over the years spent side by side with him in their prison. That was a love that Konstantin's hero could comprehend, and Konstantin was giving us to understand that this was just the kind of love that a Soviet person feels for his prison-like homeland. The crafty Konstantin, however, went much further than this.

The fact was that after living side by side with his wife in this prison regime for four years, the jailer, because of it, fell out of love with his wife. He began to despise her, as every jailer despises his prisoner – but at the same time he pitied her, and while pitying his wife the jailer-husband decided not to disconnect the explosive – otherwise he himself would be able to leave home. They ordered food from the grocery by telephone, and it was delivered to them. (In Russia the plot of this story would have been impossible; both would have died of hunger before they had had time to fall in or out of love with each other.) And so they continued to live thus, wired together, until the wife died. Konstantin's hero had met this anarchist when the latter was already a widower. His neighbours regarded him as the village idiot, but when the Russian history professor heard this Englishman's story, he had made friends with the widower and together they used to spend long evenings in the pub, discussing the universe and international politics. In an obvious reference to Clea and her pacifist friends, Konstantin put the following statement into the mouth of the elderly anarchist:

'The atomic bomb is a weapon of mass destruction that ties our two worlds together – the worlds of socialism and capitalism. East and West. The fact of being tied together forces us to love one another!' And the old anarchist, grinning behind his moustache, would propose a toast to a long life for the atomic bomb.

'You're naive,' Professor Pokhlobkin, Konstantin's hero, retorted. 'We are joined together by a weapon more powerful than the atomic bomb, a weapon of mass destruction that binds our two worlds inseparably: double-think!' And Professor Pokhlobin launched into the following sequence of what I would call poetic syllogisms: the West, which is obsessed by materialism, has finally discovered the concept of the fission of matter – it has split the atomic nucleus and thereby created the most terrible weapon, the nuclear bomb; however, in its obsession with the material aspect of the universe, the West has overlooked the spiritual, emotional and intellectual side of existence, over which the Russians, deprived of material prosperity, have racked their brains for so long; the Russians, inclined towards a communal form of life, towards the idea of sharing and of spiritual equality, have finally achieved the impossible, the unthinkable – the fission of thought and spirit at the level of the community, the state. The Soviet regime, declared the professor, is the materialised, incarnate concept of double-think – on earth, here and now – whose embryonic form we find, for instance in the double standards of Victorianism; but only the Soviet regime, it would seem, has achieved the improbable: when double-think, the split conscience and divided loyalty as a spiritual and emotional ideal, have become the everyday way of life – the ontology of Soviet existence, so to speak – then disbelief in the principles of Marxist-Leninist-Stalinism (like, for instance, disbelief in resurrection in the Judaeo-Christian culture), combined with loyalty to the Party (the church) and its Marxist-Leninist slogans becomes the necessary and sufficient condition of adherence to the Soviet religion. This institutionalised dualism, tempered during the years of purges, cannibalism, and internal and external wars, has turned every Soviet person into the most powerful weapon on earth – a split nucleus, a sort of equivalent of a nuclear bomb that can conquer not the world of matter but the world of the spirit. So all those nuclear bombs and missiles – borrowed, of course, from the West – and draped around the frontiers of the USSR, are regarded by the Soviet regime as no more than the rattles that shamans use to frighten people – ritual scarecrows, which the naive West perceives as totem-like symbols of fear and destruction; and the Soviet regime shakes these intimidating rattles purely to scare the West and make it listen – listen to the Soviet regime; for all it needs is that other people should listen to it, that they should start talking frankly to it, bare their soul, reveal the seeds of their own dualism – after all, there is plenty of that mental dichotomy and infantile double-think here too. Anywhere where there is, even in embryonic form, a false sense of guilt, a feeling of one's own sinfulness, a crack in the loyalty towards one's own government or political system or one's own country (with or without justification, it doesn't matter), the Soviet regime is in there like a shot, establishing itself like a radioactive cloud in people's hearts and minds, splitting them and taking them over, trying to turn the whole globe into one super-bomb. And then peace will come – perpetual and inviolable, the peace of universal double-think, that dispenses with thought as such and with it – war. 'The combination of the atomic bomb and Soviet rule,' the professor concluded, 'is the only possible way to achieve harmony between anti-matter and anti-spirit. And who can hold out against harmony on such a scale?'

'But to achieve such a mass fission of human minds (to use your nuclear terminology) you need a chain-reaction, and a critical mass, for which there must be cohesion. In other words, you're going to need heavy chains, handcuffs,' I said, trying to pun my way out of the chain-reaction of Konstantin's reasoning. 'But in the Soviet Union there is a shortage not only of food but of chains as well. The West may export barbed wire, but it doesn't produce sufficient handcuffs to export a chain-reaction.'

'I suppose you're relying on the dissidents to prevent people from cohering into a critical mass, are you?' Konstantin gave a crooked grin. 'You're putting your hopes on heterodoxy, on those who think differently. When double-think reigns all around, your dissident, as a sign of protest, tends towards integrity of thought, towards a single, unified truth. He starts, like Solzhenitsyn, by turning his house into a fortress and raising his altars behind barbed wire amid the hills of Vermont; or like Anthony he stuffs his own and other people's heads with the idea of pacifism; or like my stupid Nuclea, who set off to bow down to Moscow as if it were a new Mecca. But at bottom none of them give a damn about any of that – whether it is Russian Orthodoxy, or the atomic bomb; even for queers like Anthony the arsehole is not their ultimate objective. Because dissidents on either side of the divide are fundamentally as much monks as they are thinkers – in other words, their real aim, as it is with monks and hermits, is not to soil themselves by participation. Not to soil themselves with evil deeds, to keep their *own* lily-white hands clean. And this is where Soviet ideology steps forward, offering a ready-made rationalisation: "We will take all evil upon ourselves!"'

'In exchange for what?'

'In exchange, you are to sit tight, shut up and not rock the boat. That's all that is asked of you. We will take all evil upon ourselves, and your dissidents can talk dissidence but not publicly; you can do it among yourselves, in your separate niches in the spiritual Pantheon. You can discuss the "holy fool" phenomenon in medieval Russia and the use of syncope in Mandelstam's poetry, Byzantine ikons and Siberian shamans, Vysotsky's hoarseness and Okudzhava's sadness – only keep your ideas out of the machinery of government. Keep away from power; power is evil, leave it to us. You will remain innocent, unsullied, and at the same time you will grow spiritually – like potatoes in rich soil, with a nice clean, pink skin. And be assured, we won't touch you: just stay down there in total darkness, maturing in your own inner light. The compromise has been found. And I assure you that no chains will be required to achieve cohesion. Stalin wanted faith and devotion, he needed everyone to think alike. Even Khrushchev believed in the standards set by Lenin, just as the intelligentsia of that time believed in socialism with a human face. With each thought they were proving to the other that they were right. Now, though, we all know what's what. Nobody demands fidelity and devotion any more. Complete division of labour. No need, even, to put people away; all the potatoes are long since safely underground, and anyone who couldn't get on in his native soil has emigrated long ago – they too were defending the ideals of liberalism by refusing to participate. But I'm telling you: all this emigration is just another attempt to cock a snook at the Soviet regime, nothing more, an effort to prove that the Politburo is not all-powerful, that we, too, still have some power – the power to slam the door. Well, you've slammed it. And so what? Even here, it turns out, you haven't got much scope: here, too, you're a participant in crimes – admittedly, different ones – and here too, incidentally, there's the local brand of double-think. In other words, once again there is a Soviet regime on an embryonic scale. And the scale, by the way, is increasing. There was absolutely no need to emigrate to find that out. Sensible people, who sat at home ensconced in their own culture, are still sitting there and not rocking the boat. Because they know that the fight against Soviet double-think is a lost battle, and so far no one has invented a more powerful weapon than splitting the mental nucleus.'

'You talk as if you were not an *émigré* yourself but a representative of the Soviets at negotiations on stopping the arms race,' I said in an attempt at irony.

'Me? An *émigré*? How can I be an *émigré* when I still have a valid Soviet passport in my pocket? I'm in a state of divorce from the West, and if I ever was married, then it was a fictitious marriage. Whereas you are married to it for ever.'

Until that moment the conversation between us had been

conducted on equal terms. Or rather, I had perceived it as yet another idiotic *émigré* argument on the eternal subjects: 'What is to be Done?' and 'Who is to Blame'? At first I had considered Konstantin's ideas about the nuclear bomb and thought-fission as the usual hot air – the age-old fruit of Russian philosophising, which can never manage without a theory of a world-wide plot, a universal conspiracy and so on and so forth. In the remand cells of a London police station, where they keep drunks and obstreperous tramps, there was a moment when this garrulous prophet of total double-think struck me as a straightforward schizophrenic, a graphomaniac who had finally gone round the bend from lack of recognition. The possession of a British passport and my long experience of life in the West had created in me the illusion of my own normality, stability, even a certain sense of psychological ease, of sitting in the comfortable armchair of the dispassionate judge; in leaning back in this chair I was leaning back on a creditable past, and I was quite ready to launch out upon something I had forgotten: a cloud of endless Russian hot air that had no relation to anything whatsoever – or rather, which had no relation to the daily struggle to survive, to the attempt to retain some human dignity, which, in this country, is the starting-point for both sublime philosophy and cheap inferior art. And suddenly, with one sentence, Konstantin drew a magic line between us: the line represented by the Soviet passport. At that moment the whole ordeal, the muddled lunacy of emigration, that dizzying leap over the Iron Curtain suddenly came back to me like an unwanted guest that I thought I had got rid of. However persuasively this fictitious husband of Western civilisation might talk about the inevitable victory of the most powerful nuclear weapon in the world – communism – that victory had not yet come about, thank God, and until it did and we were all merged into the unity of double-think, whatever Konstantin might say was neither a joke nor mere hot air: he was defending his allegiance to a world from which I had been scandalously divorced and whose death I longed for with all my soul.

'How long have you thought of yourself as a "fictitious husband", as you put it, in the West?' I enquired drily, trying to change the direction of this protracted conversation.

'How long?!' Konstantin was genuinely astonished. 'Ever since I got together with Clea. It was never mentioned in court – just try and prove it! – but as far as I'm concerned it was obvious to any fool: our marriage was a fictitious one. What else could it be? You don't really imagine I could seriously fall in love with that horse-faced Englishwoman, do you? Do you know what they used to call her in Moscow? The drowned rat! With her thin, straggly hair and that kiss-curl, always buzzing around the room at parties or, quite the opposite, skulking in a corner and waiting for something to happen. But whenever she did open her mouth, everyone had to cover theirs with their hand – to hide their smiles. She learned by heart all those meaningless conversational remarks like "You know" and "I mean" and simply sprinkled them everywhere without rhyme or reason. Among our circle, if someone has a Ryazan accent he will be accepted – but only just; but whenever Clea spoke, what came out of her mouth was like a lump of frozen vomit. People stopped coming to see me. And she didn't give a damn. I told her she'd do better to speak English – it might be incomprehensible, but at least it wouldn't sound so offensive. All she could say in reply was her favourite word – "stupid"! She would purse her lips and drawl it out: "Styoo-oo-pid". Ugh!'

'How on earth did you contrive to get together with her when you felt like that about each other?' – I was aghast at the unfeigned fury and revulsion in Konstantin's voice: there was no longer a trace in it of the cool perspicacity that had marked him in his role as arbiter of Russian and world history.

'How did I contrive it? Ask Margot. Who brought Nuclea to Moscow? Who pushed her at me? Who persuaded me that Clea was the ideal candidate for a fictitious marriage? Margot! Get yourself hitched to Clea by a fictitious marriage, come over to England and then we'll think about a double divorce.

She fooled me by saying that she couldn't get a divorce immediately because at that particular moment she didn't want to damage her queer husband's career.'

'Who fooled you? What queer husband?' But Konstantin appeared not to hear my question.

'None of this would have happened if it hadn't been for that idiot Anthony and his ideas about socialism with a human face. What he wants is an areshole with a human face, dirty little bugger! And I, gullible Russian fool that I am, took all Margot's arguments at face value: Anthony, she said, was constantly going to Moscow to tie up some Anglo-Soviet trade deals in which very big money was involved, and she had promised him not to sue for divorce until the contracts were signed – divorce, it seems, would have greatly harmed Anthony's reputation, stories would get out about his carrying-on with little boys – oh, God knows what else she said. Finally, she made out that it was in our interests – that is, hers and mine – to wait until she could divorce Anthony, because when the property was divided we would be a great deal better off. So altogether, she claimed, a bogus marriage to Clea was the ideal solution, until we could both go to court and she and I could then get together. But how did it all end? I went to court all right – but on a charge of manslaughter.' – He nervously gulped yoghurt, frowned, spat on the floor and, without looking, threw the plastic tub in the direction of the garbage bucket in the corner of the cell.

'I take it that you forgot to inform Clea of the plans that you and Margot were making?' I enquired in the ensuing pause.

'Don't give me that sly, reproachful look. If you'd have been in my skin in Moscow and had eaten potato leaves you'd have grasped at any chance. As I told you: the idea was Margot's. I was only carrying out orders so to speak. What was Clea? Just another of those Englishwomen who go slumming among the natives, put on a turban or something to make believe she's one of them, and then imagine that by doing this she's saving humanity. She saw herself as one of those do-gooding Russian Populists of the last century, who went to live among the peasants and tried to teach them to read. She didn't realise, the little fool, that no one in Moscow thinks about money because they haven't got any, and they cuddle because it's cold outside and there's nowhere to go. At first I even felt sorry for her. Who'd have thought she was such a fool that she didn't know I was sleeping with Margot? Hasn't she got eyes? I thought she was perfectly well aware that our marriage was fictitious, and she was simply keeping quiet about it for two reasons – so as not to arouse any suspicions at the Foreign Office and, in general, because there's no point in spoiling a friendly affair by raising awkward questions. How could anyone have imagined that the whole business could go so wildly wrong – and in a foreign country, too? I tried, incidentally, to make her understand by every possible means that I would never make a husband for her. I tried to turn her off me as best I could, by playing the bully, playing the fool and acting like a crank, so hence the stinking dried fish, the shoulder of mutton boiled in onions – well, you know all about it! But she clung on to me for all she was worth. And then, if you please, comes this "incident" with that young half-wit. Why did he have to impale himself on my knife?' Konstantin paused slightly. 'By the way, did you hear that Clea tried to poison herself with fly agaric because of that little tyke's death? There was some kind of mysterious relationship between those two; she was almost prepared to adopt him. All these illegitimate children – typically English phenomenon. Every English person, as I see it, has either a little secret passion or some other fateful secret, but at the same time they impose on us, the outsiders, what is almost a duty to treat these mysteries and secrets with respect, as though we had been told all about them in advance. In short, Clea now won't talk to me except through her lawyer. She is suing for divorce. So at last I've got what I wanted. Anthony isn't going to Moscow any longer: Britain has declared a trade boycott. What more does Margot need, you might think? Not a bit of it! She couldn't even be bothered to come forward as a surety so that I can be let out on bail. Couldn't spare the money? She's got money coming out of her ears. No – that's not it: she's frightened for her reputation!' – And with a gesture of hopeless scepticism Konstantin waved towards the iron door of the cell, where the rights and duties of prisoners were displayed under glass.

'The amazing thing is the way these free-thinkers can so easily turn and kick you when you're down. Margot used to think nothing of dashing off to China for a week to study Maoist slogans, and then a week later to spend the night in a Palestinian's tent in Beirut – all of it, of course, accompanied by sexual escapades under artillery bombardment, to the sound of cymbals clashed by Chinese *apparatchiks* or the roll of drums on parade in Red Square. A fearless woman, you might say. But that dim little social misfit only had to impale himself on my knife, imagining that I was a murderer, and immediately her class instincts came into play. She decided that involvement in this affair might harm her reputation. A gang-bang with dissidents on the filthy staircase of a block of flats in Moscow: that's all right, because it's studying communism, or fighting the paper tiger of imperialism, or the struggle against bourgeois prejudices – call it what you like. But as soon as it's a question of her reputation among mutual friends, then she instantly starts acting all virginal. Oh how vulgar . . . a trial, some silly murder, the jury, legal costs – it's all so boring, she would say, so trivial, so banal. In fact, she simply didn't want to get involved when it became clear that I wasn't an object, a *thing* that she could wave about among her circle like a banner heralding a new set of ideas, and which she could then cut up and make into a skirt to wear at a few parties. In short, as soon as this trial got under way I lost the attraction of novelty for her and became a squalid bore. I've long since worked out how these people tick: that famous freedom and Western democracy is all very well, but only so long as there is someone to show off to. All these people on the lunatic left are, broady speaking, repeating the philosopher Chaadayev's dictum: "The truth is dearer to me than my country." He is right, of course; only to act out this piece of Chaadayevism one must first of all *have* a country.'

This Samson, shamelessly deceived by women and shaved by the prison barber's electric clippers, once more recalled God, the motherland and the chosen, messianic role of Russia. Then he went on:

'I don't know how you've managed to make out here, but personally I've long since realised that a Russian abroad is never seen as anything but a half-wit. And for perfectly understandable reasons: how else can they perceive a foreigner who comes here, when everything about him, from his face to his clothes, is equally absurd? To say nothing – and here's the rub – to say nothing of the language: all this maa-ing and baa-ing, this animal mooing as they scratch their heads and wink at you, imagining it will produce mutual understanding. I must admit when I was in Moscow, I too used to think: nobody here understands me because they all grew up in a prison, but people abroad, in freedom, *will* understand me. But what sort of free, mutual understanding can there be here, when what you say sounds to them like the stuttering and burbling of a three-year-old mental defective, and when you can't express any thoughts beyond the gibbering of a savage escaped from an undiscovered island – which is exactly how people here think of Russia? Anyhow, what's the use of trying to utter any thoughts in this double-dutch of theirs, when even Clea, who spent quite a time in Russia, thought I was nothing but a half-wit obsessed with cookery? She still thinks that because of a famine in Russia I have gone crazy about exotic recipes. What an irony of fate: you try to solve the dilemmas that trouble the whole world and they take you for a plain psychopath. And they even try to cure you. They have classified me: a fungophile! Clea was incapable of realising that I was writing a philosophical novel, a treatise – not a cookery book! Do you see? So go and sweat yourself silly in the kitchen while the people in the sitting-room drone on about the division of the world between capitalism and socialism, totalitarianism and democracy.'

'Whereas you, I believe, perfer to divide the world into coffee-zones and tea-zones?'

'And you, I believe, prefer to pretend that Soviet rule came down from Mars, and, with the help of a few Bolsheviks, enslaved the freedom-loving Russian people, do you? Of course I overdid it slightly with all that stuff about the samovar and tea-zones and coffee-zones, but it's equally stupid to make out that the great prison-camp zone stops at the Soviet frontier. There are plenty of home-grown bolsheviks here, too – under different names. The difference is that with us it's all honest and above-board: a single-party system; communist absolutism; keep your head down and don't rock the boat, and if you don't like it you can go and peg out in a labour camp. Here, though, they talk about freedom of speech and freedom of movement but most of them stay at home and keep their thoughts to themselves – just as Soviet people do, because it's the same people up at the top who dictate how to live, except that here they call it democracy instead of totalitarianism. In any case, there's basically no difference between East and West: I even agree with the local lefties, except that they're struggling for a brighter future, while I think one should be fighting to speed up the sovietisation of the whole world – which, incidentally, is historically inevitable. And I must say that Soviet rule is no worse than any other. Of course there were excesses; of course a few little people are being harassed there – but where are people *not* being harassed? In principle, though, how do the elected soviets differ from the British parliament? I've been reading all sorts of articles written by what you might call the *émigré* Politburo, Solzhenitsyn, Maximov, etc., firing off their bursts of verbal machine-gunfire in all directions – and I'm telling you that all they are doing is settling a few scores with the Soviet leadership; their disagreements with the Soviet regime are purely personal. If they were in power, they'd be jailing exactly the same people who are in clink now. The members of the real Politburo are even inclined to look favourably on the renaissance of the Russian Orthodox Church, provided, of course, that it occurs in the framework of a coalition with the Party autocracy. The church only has to take one more small step: to agree that the

Soviet regime is not the offspring of the devil but is lawful and sanctified – and the whole thing's in the bag! Solzhenitsyn will be greeted on a white horse in the middle of Red Square; the Politburo will wave from the top of Lenin's tomb; Maximov will be put in charge of the saluting-battery; and Sinyavsky, as the black sheep, will be put on show in a cage for the crowd to jeer at. The freedom-loving Russian people accepted Soviet rule whole-heartedly, and if you're for the people, then you must accept Soviet rule too. In any case, there's no need to make too much of an effort: Soviet rule is well and truly in our bloodstream by now. We were born with it, just as we were born with an image of Stalin in our brain, and it can never be blotted out of our memory: memory is amoral, and what you love with all your heart is what you *remember.*'

'So you, too, feel the urge to go back there: back to the fusty cupboard full of spiders, back to Svidrigailov's paradise?'

'So you've heard of that idea, too, have you? Now don't you be sarcastic. What does everyone dream of? What are we all striving for? Carefree idleness. Here they spend all their lives busting their guts and making other people bust their guts, just so that they can finally retire on the pension they've earned and can tell the rest of mankind to go to hell. With us, though, you get used to saying that almost from childhood. Total irresponsibility – that is the eternal ideal. That is freedom. We over there are deprived of the right to vote, so how can I possibly consider myself responsible? Of course, we are still a long way from the ideal: they force you to attend meetings, they make you hold your arms up in "unanimous" shows of hands, and you have to race each other from one queue to another. But how can that be compared with the way you're hassled here? Here you're responsible for every single step you take, you have to be making decisions the whole time – where to live, where to work, who to vote for – and you have to be constantly protesting and hustling otherwise you'll die of starvation or die in a doss-house, not to mention the fact that you may easily be murdered. Why did we leave Russia? In order not to soil ourselves by participation, so that "they" will keep their dirty paws off our souls. But here, it turns out, you'll be treated even more like mud if you don't opt out soon enough. When I use Dostoyevsky's image of the cupboard full of spiders, what I mean is that paradise of irresponsibility: to lock yourself away, sit in the dark and think of absolutely nothing at all. And I must say that in the Soviet Union there are more chances of finding that cupboard – the cupboard tradition in Russia goes back farther, and what's more you get it rent-free.'

'Why not just go straight into the grave?' I muttered. Obviously having noticed that I had turned pale, he moved his chair closer, patted me on the knee and said:

'Come now – why go to such extremes? It's your Russian-Jewish strain coming out, even though you regard yourself as a representative of the West – but with a Russian soul, of course. But I don't regard myself as anyone in particular, I'm not one of the live wires of this world, and I cherish the dream of the Soviet cupboard purely because I don't know or like any other. And as to who is going to run the Soviet regime outside the door of my cupboard – Solzhenitsyn or someone else – I really couldn't care a damn. And I assure you that the better part of the Soviet intelligentsia thinks exactly as I do, not to mention the popular masses in both East and West. You see, you and I are birds of a feather, or rather we're potatoes from the same field, even though we are rotting in the ground on different sides of the fence, which in any case has been full of holes for a long time now. And it's no use kidding ourselves that we're responsible for anything over here.'

'But look here – Clea has, after all, gone insane and that boy Colin was killed. And now there's this trial . . .' I mumbled in embarrassment, trying to avoid his glowering, insolent, intransigent look. I somehow felt guilty – I, and not he. He crossed one leg over the other and began to rock gently backwards and forwards on his chair.

'She went mad and he's dead – so what? What is it to do with me? As we used to say in Moscow: if a girl has bandy legs, of course it's not her fault – but it's not my fault either, is it? Clea, you see, was one of those who were dying of boredom here and thought they'd like to go prancing all round the world. Well, she wanted her fun and she had it in Moscow. Now I'm the one who has to wriggle out of this spot of trouble. But let *them* go in for self-flagellation if they want to. I advise you not to get involved in all these pseudo-subtleties – you'll simply go off your head. You, I know, have this tendency to compare pigs with oranges and draw parallels. I've read all your esssays in the magazine *Syntaxis*. Talented, lively, but too much beginner's ardour – in the sense that you're a born-again *émigré* who has discovered a new spiritual homeland. Hence your endless comparisons: there and here, here and there, the Iron Curtain and the tragedy on the other side of the footlights, the convergence of distant points *à la Lomonosov*, and, of course, the inevitable bow towards the Poseidon of all three waves of emigration – Nabokov. You talk of some literary circles in Moscow; to be honest, there is now nothing left of them but ripples in water. And there is always a sub-text in your work, the need to read between the lines – yet what's the point of a sub-text? No one in the Soviet Union bothers about a sub-text nowadays. Everyone knows, anyway, what they can say and what they can't, so there's no need for a sub-text. There have been no secret thoughts for a long time, because, as I said, there is just one rule: don't stick your neck out and then you can say what you like. But you here, in emigration, are always looking for some mysterious significance in the spiritual impoverishment of Russian literature – you're always searching for sinister censors who are suppressing free expression, hoping for a revival of underground thought. How can you talk about "underground thought", when *everyone* around has long since gone underground? And if there is still a handful, as Dostoyevsky would have said, of "our people" left over from the sixties, they're all staying at home like good boys and keeping their thoughts to themselves. But you make heroes of them, and in doing so, by the way, you're deceiving Western public opinion with rose-tinted hopes of the alleged inevitable demise of the Soviet regime!' He spoke the last few sentences standing up – or rather he didn't speak them but shouted them into my face. I wanted to object, but the only sound that would come out of my half-opened mouth was an incoherent, helpless 'uh-uh-uh'.

When I left the police station I walked around for a long time at random, trying to stop the trembling in my hands, my lips, my whole body. I was not trembling with fury but with a feeling of ultimate humiliation – humiliation from an awareness of the catastrophic difference in myself before and after my visit to Konstantin's cell. I had gone to meet him as a famous (in certain narrow, select circles, of course) writer, condescending to respond to the request of a compatriot of dubious reputation. I had gone to that prison-cell encounter as a citizen of the free world, exactly aware of my modest but honourable place in the hierarchy of Western culture, unashamed of my past and with no fear of looking into the future, cherishing my position as one of an élite who, although writing in a language other than that used by my brothers of the pen in my new spiritual homeland, was nevertheless accepted by them with literary hospitality. The word 'exile' was the spice in the cake that fate had carefully baked out of the second half of my life. And now someone had spat on the cake. My God – what if that impudent but eloquent scoundrel were right? And I knew that he *was* right. Right, at least, where I personally was concerned. Right, because I, like all of us 'ex-people' here, had surreptitiously retouched and reshaped my past so that it wouldn't cramp my style too much, wouldn't hinder my forward movement. I knew that I had fudged things, rubbing out one inconvenient stain, brightening the colours in another place, altering the perspective so that my present, as seen from my past, looked like a bright future; so that those who had not been able to make up their minds to emigrate, those who had stayed behind, would look like fools whose troubles were all of their own making, while I would look like the principal victim who, by my brave feat, had earned for myself the status of a priestly oracle. When setting off for that meeting in the remand cells, I had been absolutely convinced that no one could ever catch me *in flagrante*, that no one could ever tear off my mask. Those who had stayed behind and therefore still inhabited the past, would never be witnesses of my present, whilst the witnesses of my present would never discover the convoluted, seamy aspects of my past life. I was protected not only by geography, I was not only clad in the armour of the Iron Curtain – I was guarded by the distance in time that allowed me to rewrite the mistakes of the past so as to make them into a pledge of future successes; and no one was going to catch me red-handed, because the witnesses to those victories and defeats were separated by time and space and would never be able to sort out the historical fakery in my life-story in order to frame a single, logical, coherent charge against me.

Suddenly there had appeared, from God knows where, this cocky, insolent Russian – with dubious political antecedents – who jabbed his finger at me and shouted: 'But the emperor has no clothes!' Armed to the teeth, thanks to his familiarity with the life of his country, which my pliant memory had long since transformed into a fiction, he announced that this country of his existed in its own right independently of my personal attitude to it and my cunning manipulation of the past, and that it existed in a form which was not the form that I required for my spiritual comfort. I had emerged as a hanger-on, a fellow-traveller of Russian history engaged in doing business on the side. With nauseating clarity I had descried within myself, as on an X-ray photograph, the malignant tumour of *his* Russia – a sarcoma that was hindering me from breathing and had spread its metastases into my brain. Everything that this reptile had said about Russia, about the Soviet Union, was the irrefutable truth. The reptile was right. The reptile was historically right. If you can divine the nature of all historical evil and trace that evil for a dozen or so years ahead, you will never be mistaken. History is always on the side of the reptiles.

The reptiles are always on the side of history. The only salvation is to jump overboard from the ship of history, without a lifebelt, straight into the stormy sea of extra-historicity, extra-temporality. But then this chaos that lies out there, overboard, like every eternity that knows no end, no death – that is, pity – differs from historical evil only in that this chaos is devoid of the logicality that history acquires *ex post factum*; good is only a rare moment, a brief interval when time chances to stop, an instant of illogicality in the malignant chain of cause and effect, a double agent operating between two sinister variants of eternity. Perhaps, too, a leap overboard into the deep will grant one that suspended moment, a moment of good between the evil chaos of birth and the historic evil of death. I was a double agent. But I preferred that duplicity, the protracted flight of a suicide trying to gather his thoughts in the short interval between birth and death. At that moment I was knocked down by a motorcycle.

As I remember, I was crossing Shaftesbury Avenue. It is one of those wide London streets in which a narrow strip of concrete has been laid down the middle, something like a false pavement that divides the traffic into two halves. Before crossing the street, as one should in a country where they drive on the left, I naturally turned my head to the right; I reached that concrete strip in the middle and stopped there, pondering on the next metaphysical turn in the train of thought described above. Having mentally arrived at the appropriate deduction, I decided to resume my progress and, before crossing the second half of the roadway, I again turned my head to the right. It is hard to know why, after ten years in this country, I looked in the wrong direction. It may have been that as I stood on the central strip in the middle of the street, I imagined that I was standing on the pavement behind me and was only just starting to cross the street – with its English, left-handed, traffic – and that this was why I turned my head to the right again. It is also possible, however, that while standing on that false pavement and rehearsing in my memory the recent conversation about Russia, I forgot which country I was in and, imagining that I was standing in the middle of a Moscow street, I looked to the right, Soviet-fashion. I even remember my astonishment at seeing the street empty, just my luck – the centre of the city, the middle of the day, and not a single car! And I stepped off. Immediately I was hit – from the left – by a motorbike. 'This is the end,' I thought as I fell.

I was lucky: the motor-cyclist managed to jam on his brakes at the last moment and only knocked me down. I remember that what I felt was not so much the pain of falling as shame at the absurdity of the scene. Still not feeling anything I immediately jumped to my feet and began to assure the motor-cyclist, whose face had gone pale with horror under his helmet, that I was entirely to blame, and I asked him to forgive me for causing such trouble. A crowd had gathered by then, someone shouted that he was going to call an ambulance and a policeman was approaching the motor-cyclist, but I was already walking away, with exaggeratedly confident, long strides, in the direction of Piccadilly Circus. It was only in the Underground, waiting on the platform for a train, that I realised I could not walk on my left foot. By the time I reached home, I was unable to pull the swollen limb out of my trouser-leg. There was no fracture, but I could not even move around my flat without crutches. During this unexpected spell of house-arrest, every morning for two weeks I watched my swollen, bruised leg changing colour from a heavenly dark blue to corpse-green.

Remembering the barrister's request, I tried to cobble together something like a witness's deposition on the subject of Konstantin's treatise, trying honestly to overcome my personal distaste for the whole affair and to be as objective as possible. Nothing came of it. One morning I was sitting at my English typewriter, intending to compose a letter to the lawyer politely declining to appear in court because of the severe pain in my left leg, when the morning's copy of *The Times* was pushed through my letter-box.

On the front page, with a continuation on the central spread, under the headline:

Soviet Money in British Court Case

there was a report on the unprecedented developments in the case of the Soviet citizen accused of manslaughter. It appeared that Konstantin had finally been released on bail. The reporter was able to explain (obviously with the help of someone inside the Metropolitan Police) who had put up the bail: on receiving a photocopy of the cheque he had recognised without difficulty that the money had been paid by the London branch of a Soviet bank.

Without finishing my perusal of *The Times* I rushed (on crutches) to telephone Konstantin's lawyer. The number was engaged for about an hour; I was clearly not the only person trying to call. When I finally heard in the earpiece his exquisite Oxford-Jewish accent, I began by apologising for being unable to keep to my undertaking, due to the business with the motorbike, but he broke off my mumblings with another staggering piece of news: Konstantin had disappeared. His car had been found abandoned, not far from the Soviet embassy.

Russian *émigrés* – and the press too – waited for weeks, expecting a statement from TASS about a press conference in Moscow, at which Konstantin, his face pale from torture and interrogation, would denounce the machinations of British Intelligence and the evils of capitalism. There was, however, no statement from TASS and no press conference. Konstantin had quietly disappeared without trace – and without facing his new trial. *Emigré* circles were full of rumours: some saw Konstantin as an *agent provocateur* and a double agent, who had originally been sent over to discredit the campaign to allow freedom of emigration; others thought he had become a double agent, as it were, under duress, being frightened by the prospect of a prison sentence; a third body of opinion obstinately insisted that he had been kidnapped, and in proof of their theory they adduced the fact that Konstantin had not appeared to make any denunciations of the 'bourgeois West'.

For lack of hot news, the journalists descended on me. Neither my visit to the remand cells nor my accident with the motorcycle had passed unnoticed. I said nothing and decided to leave London for a while. When the pen of some imaginative hack produced the suggestion that the business with the motorcycle in Shaftesbury Avenue was an attempt by the KGB to eliminate a witness, namely myself, after I had wormed some state secret out of Konstantin, I decided not to refute the story. Perhaps it was true? How could I know? Soviet history, after all, is so full of phantasmagorias that one more road accident ascribed to the KGB would not do them any harm, while it might lend a little much-needed spice to the lives of *émigrés* bored with living in freedom.

London, 1984